The Unquiet Stairs

L. J. Hutton

Wylfheort Books
Magical Mystery
Fantasy ~ History

ISBN: 978-1-7396943-6-4

Published by Wylfheort Books 2024

Introduction

A brief word before we start: even nowadays, it is still traditional for Scottish women to retain their maiden name once married, while any children take their father's name. So one of our heroines is Elspeth Allen, with her father being Johnne Allen, but in the historical records her mother would be Jonet Clark – confusing to us, but your family history was in your name.

It is also traditional for women to take their mother's maiden name as their second name, so for example you might get, Janet McGregor Fraser, McGregor being her mother's surname. But her husband and children's surname could be something totally different, which adds to the puzzle when chasing people through time!

I have retained the seventeenth-century spellings of first names, if only to separate characters out. So, by separating Jannet from Jonet or Janet, rather than using the modern spelling of Janet for all of them, it at least allows readers to have some idea of who is who. And many of the people in the past in this book are real and taken from the records of the time, so I've kept them as they are in case anyone wants to go and look them up. Unfortunately, that does mean that there are two sets of sisters called Margaret and Agnes, for which I apologise for any confusion.

Chapter 1

The white bridal gown hung like some haunting vengeful ghost on the wardrobe door. Behind her on the four-poster bed, her bridegroom snuffled and snorted in his sleep, drunk as a lord and thankfully comatose. Anna didn't know quite what she'd have done if she'd had to face him tonight. She had already fled the wedding reception hours before when it was still in full swing, and now the hotel was silent, the guests all gone, and the confetti long since swept up. Then Jensen had arrived in the room swaying on his feet, hiccupping, and giggling at nothing and everything, and had just made it to the bed before keeling over like a felled oak.

He hadn't even got undressed, for which Anna was glad. If someone came to wake him, they would see that theirs had hardly been a night of passion, and that this, at least, couldn't be laid wholly at her feet – not that she had any intention of being here by then. Feeling dreadful remorse for what she was about to do despite her own panic, Anna pulled and pushed Jensen until she'd got him rolled over and into the recovery position. Sharing even one more day with him might feel like more than she could stand, but she didn't want him choking to death in his drunken stupor either. Pulling off the expensive rings, she put them on the bedside table on her side, where he wouldn't brush them off onto the floor and lose them. He could have those. She didn't want to ever see them again. But then Jensen had never really seen her, she thought, not as a person, and tonight he'd clearly been having far too much fun to notice she'd deserted her post as the supposed blushing bride. And when he had finally come to bed, he'd been even more oblivious of her sitting shivering in the corner with only a bedside light on, and of the dark tear streaks on her face from where her mascara had run. No, Jensen didn't see her at all.

Within the hour Anna fled the glass and chrome horror of the huge leisure complex without a single backwards glance, running to the taxi which had pulled up outside and tumbling in to collapse on the seat in relief.

"Where to, love?" the driver asked, and Anna rattled off her address and then huddled in the corner.

This should have been the start of the rest of her life.

What was now yesterday should have been the best day of her life.

Instead, it had turned into a living nightmare.

As the months of build-up to the wedding had gone on, the worse she had felt. All control had been ripped out of her hands, and every time she had tried to scale the wedding back to something simpler and more manageable – something she could actually face – she had been overridden by her mother, and worse, by Jensen's mother. And it had been all the worse because she'd kept saying to herself, *For God's sake Anna, stop being a drama queen. It's the twenty-twenties not the nineteen-fifties. Nobody's marriage gets totally organised by parents anymore without consulting the bride.* Except it turns out hers did.

Her inner doubts had begun springing up like weeds in a perfect flowerbed, each one multiplying like baby monsters hatching out by the dozen, and although friends had assured her that it was just normal wedding nerves, by the time the week of the wedding had come around, Anna had known it was far more than that. It was far worse than that. Jensen the easy going, ridiculously handsome man she thought she had been beyond lucky to have show even *some* interest in her, let alone wanting to marry her, had gradually been revealed as someone else entirely.

Not that he'd changed. No, Jensen was still exactly as he was – and that was half of the trouble. Jensen would *never* change. He would never change no matter what happened, whatever crises they endured; Jensen would just drift through life with his gorgeous smile and his money to dig him out. Or rather his parents would dig him out, and it had finally dawned on Anna that she was going to have no say in her married life on any level until the day that his parents died, at which point she would be expected to pick up the reins of organising Jensen's life for him. He wouldn't look after her, she would become his second mother!

Shivering in her fleece despite the taxi's heaters being on to combat the winter chill, Anna knew that most of that was a delayed reaction to yesterday and the weeks before. And when she was dropped off at her flat, she was just grateful that, despite assurances that she wouldn't need her bank card, that she'd taken it with her anyway, along with her keys. Her mother had wanted Anna to give her the keys, but mercifully the one thing Anna had managed to hold out on down the years was not giving her mother access to the flat.

Stumbling inside, she put just the table lamp on in the lounge, and then went through into the kitchen, grabbed her largest mug, and filled it with hot chocolate. Then taking it through to her bedroom, she pulled down what she still thought of as *her* case from off the top of the wardrobe.

"I've got to get away," she said to the much-hugged teddy bear sitting on her bedroom chair. "I can't do this anymore. I can't pretend, and they'll never forgive me."

Staying here wasn't an option, it was the first place that they would come looking for her. Worse, she had been bullied by both sets of parents into thinking that giving up her job was a good idea because of a move for Jensen's career, but now that gave her freedom she hadn't expected. Nobody was waiting for her to return in a fortnight's time, brimming with excitement and tanned from the exotic honeymoon which had been planned for her. She had no obligations to anyone. The flat she could decide what to do with once she'd got her head straight, and luckily, she'd been sensible enough that once Jensen had started throwing his money around, she'd shoved most of her wages into her savings account. So there was probably four or five months' worth of mortgage in there at least, and all she needed to do was to transfer the money across each month, and hopefully after a couple of months she would be settled somewhere else, with a new job, and could make a sensible decision.

She began throwing winter clothes into the suitcase, realising that she'd probably need her big bag, too, and her overnight case. At the same time, she contrasted it with the huge suitcase which she'd left behind in the bridal suite. Not a single item of clothing in that had truly been hers. Everything had been new, and virtually none of it even chosen by her.

She had come to dread her mother turning up on the doorstep with shopping bags exclaiming, "Look what I found for you!"

Had it been genuine excitement for her on her mother's part, it might have been different, but Anna knew that ninety percent of it was her mother trying to keep up with Jensen's mother, who had developed a nasty habit of doing the same – or had it been Jensen's mother who had started revamping her wardrobe? At this distance Anna neither remembered nor cared.

"This is what you get for being your mum's 'accident' baby," she had often told friends, and there was much truth in that. She had been neither planned nor wanted, her parents being very much a couple who happened to have children, rather than them ever being a close family. And her brother and sister had been twelve and fourteen when she'd been born, so they had never been companions for her. Her mother's often repeated mantra of, "We did it for your brother and sister, so we'll do it for you," had become the source of much pain, because it never mattered whether Anna wanted or needed whatever 'it' was. If Heather and Nigel had had it, then Anna was having it, and that was the end of that. But Anna would have given everything to have had less money thrown at her and more love, or at least consideration.

And that had been why Jensen had seemed such a catch, despite his connections to her parents. Having lived in a household filled with eternal rows, he had seemed calm and content. Her parents' passionate arguments, and the inevitable passionate make-ups (even though they were now of an age where people might not have expected there to be much fire left), had been a wonderful rollercoaster of a life for them, but rough on the rest of the family, who never knew what was coming next. So being around Jensen, who never seemed to get worked up about anything, had at first been a balm to her shattered soul, even though she had long ago fled the family home if not their manipulations.

But they'd barely been going out for six months before he'd started talking about getting married, and back then Anna had thought this was his desire for her – which was a heady experience for a young woman who'd not had much success on the dating scene. Only in the last preparations for the wedding had it come out that Jensen had been acting under instruction.

"I told him, you need to get a ring on this girl's finger," his mother had tactlessly come out with as they'd stood in the bridal shop for the second fitting. And if Anna had been anticipating some comment about what a catch she was, she was soon disabused. "It's time you settled down, I told him," his mother had rattled on. "Companies like married men with families, it keeps them stable, that's what his father keeps saying. John worries that Jensen will start to look like a flighty bachelor and miss his opportunities at work to rise through the ranks."

"Oh yes, it's so important for men to give the right impression at work," her mother had chipped in. "Marrying the wrong sort can really do damage to their prospects. I was always so careful to present the right image at Gordon's work functions."

And the two of them had prattled on on the same tack, but the dressmaker had seen Anna's stunned expression and given her covert pitying glances. So that was what it had come down to, was it, this haste to get married? It wasn't Jensen's desire for her at all, it was him doing what he was told. And it had been at that point that all of the niggling doubts had come crashing in on Anna. Little things that she had thought were a bit off for months now all suddenly added up, and instead of little things, they became one great big ball of worry that began to snowball and kept going.

Suddenly she could see Jensen clearly. He too had been a late child for his parents – who contrastingly had been trying for a child since their early twenties and only had him a decade later – meaning that in his case, he was the adored and much longed-for only one. Every bump in the road had been smoothed out for him by either his father's force of personality, or with a hefty lubrication of money. And if he'd inherited his father's rugged good looks, he was also his mother's son in personality, willing to go along with whatever gave him the easy life.

But the final straw for Anna had been the day after that dress fitting, when it had been equally callously let slip that their engagement had been the key to Jensen being offered a promotion to the London office. Jensen himself had never thought to mention to her that, once they came back from honeymoon, they'd be moving immediately to a flat that his parents had already paid the rental deposit on for him. That had come as a bolt from the blue when her mother had demanded her flat key, saying, "You won't have time to pack your flat up yourself. You leave it to me, I'll throw out all the rubbish you don't need and send the rest on to you."

Suddenly the push for her to ditch her own job had made sense. And as it had all come out, Anna had gripped her keys so tightly that they left imprints in her hand for days. Her mother going through her flat and throwing everything out that she loved was an unbearable movie running on a continuous loop in her head. She'd only just been in time to save most of it when she moved in here, her mother thinking that the supposed trips to the recycling centre were getting rid of things, when in fact Anna had temporarily taken over a colleague's garage for a couple of months.

Now she looked around the flat and had a gut-churning panic attack. What if they got someone to break in for them? And with that in mind she went around making sure that all of the window bolts were securely on, thanking her lucky stars that she had the attic flat in a big old house. Being up on what was effectively the fourth floor, nobody could just break a window and climb in. The fire escape came out of her kitchen via a small French door, and in the summer, she enjoyed sitting out there on that tiny iron square with a cup of coffee, enjoying watching the birds and squirrels in the big old chestnut tree she could look straight into from up here.

Now, though, she went out onto the fire escape landing and pulled up the ladder section she would have to use to get down to the main iron fire escape in the event of a fire. Coming back in she bolted that French window as well as locking it, then dragged her kitchen table across and wedged it firmly against the door, piling her two chairs on top of it for extra weight. No way was she having anyone gaining access that way!

It was a complete overreaction she knew, but right now she was in panic-stricken flight mode. And in that whirl of frantic activity, she wrote notes to the other flat owners, assuring them that she was fine and was going away for a while, and to please not be coerced into calling the police to break into the flat by her parents or Jensen's. Because that was another nightmare scenario which wouldn't leave her alone.

It had been four in the morning when she had called the all-night taxi service and fled the leisure centre's hotel, and it wasn't quite eight when she lugged her cases down to her battered old Ford, then ran back up the stairs for other treasures she couldn't bear to leave behind, stuffing them into the large carrier bags she normally used for her grocery shopping or trips to the laundrette. When she realised that she must leave now, or be trapped again, she set the burglar alarm, dead-bolted the door from the outside, and ran down the stairs, stuffing the notes under the other front doors as she went. The beloved Ford started first time, and she headed out of Worcester on the back roads.

Already she knew where she was going.

Aunty Rita.

She was the only one who would understand, and who would shield her from the coming storm. Rita was her father's younger half-sister, the black sheep of the family in her parents' eyes, and the one person whom Anna adored. Rita hadn't even been invited to the wedding, despite Anna saying over and over that she wanted her there. Her father made the excuse that it was too far to expect Rita to travel, but Anna had known that wasn't the reason at all. At first, she'd thought it was because Rita would challenge him over making the wedding more about him than Anna.

Now she knew he didn't want Rita there because she would have seen straight through this god-awful farce, and would have demanded to know what on earth was going on. Feisty, fiery Rita would have had no qualms about speaking her mind, and Anna knew that, even had she not realised what a dreadful mistake she was making, Rita would have soon told her. But Rita lived in the far north of Scotland up near Inverness, and Anna needed to get there without getting caught.

She had avoided the motorway network in the Midlands for years when she travelled up to see Rita, and once she had been living alone, those trips had been three or four times a year, so she knew the route like the back of her hand. With the motorways around Birmingham being the busiest in the country, Anna always found it unnerving to be blocked in by heavy goods vehicles, and so she had soon resorted to a different route, which took her up through the lovely countryside and Wolverhampton to Stafford.

Normally she would re-join the M6 at that point, but now she had a dread of the motorway cameras being trained on her. Instead, she would take the A-roads and cross the Mersey at the Runcorn Bridge, and then skirt Liverpool to pick up the A6 all the way to Carlisle. By then, she hoped, she would be safe to get onto the last stretch of the M6 and pick up its extensions, the A74(M) and M74, into Scotland.

She'd never driven the whole five hundred miles in one go before, but sheer terror was lending her energy. She stopped at a remote service station and filled up the car's tank, also adding in plenty of high calorie chocolate bars and cans of Coke. There'd be no stopping now except for toilet breaks.

By the time she'd almost reached Glasgow and was now safely over the border, Anna had to pull over at one of the services and take a nap – she just couldn't go on any longer. But an hour later she was awake and blessing the fact that the Scottish road network was never as busy as down south, and also that she didn't need to get through the centre of any cities but could bypass them. As she finally turned off the arterial A9, and left behind all of the traffic heading into Inverness itself and beyond, a sudden sob welled up. She was free. She was home.

Not far to go now.

Only a few more miles.

The turn off for Grantown-on-Spey came up, and with it the tears she had barely been holding back began to flow. She could just about see where she was going if she kept wiping her eyes one at a time, and she knew she was being stupid to carry on driving like this, but somehow, she couldn't stop. The unsigned turn-off came up, and she gratefully swung the car onto the single-tracked road. Only Rita, a couple of farmers, and her three closest neighbours ever used this road because it was a dead end, and Rita's cottage was right at the far end.

As she pulled up outside of it in the winter darkness, she was surprised to see the yard gate was unlocked and open, and even more surprised to see Rita herself coming out before she'd so much as had the chance to knock on the door. Opening the car door, Anna almost fell out and into Rita's embrace.

"My poor wee girl," Rita's familiar Glaswegian growl came in her ear as she hung on to her. "What have the bastards done to you, eh? I knew you'd come here. Knew it as soon as that idiot brother of mine rang me up demanding to know if I knew where you were."

And Anna could instantly imagine what that conversation would have been like – her father throwing accusations, and Rita telling the truth that she didn't know where Anna was, but also giving him a piece of her mind, and in no uncertain terms. Rita was possibly the only person who ever did that with her father, Gordon, and while he hated her for it, he also never stood up to her, let alone crossed her. She was too like their flame-haired mother for that. A mother who'd had enough of her pompous husband, but who'd been dragged through the courts and had lost Gordon on the back of a parcel of lies which had been told about her. That was something which Grandmother Marcia (who Anna had never known), had never forgiven her ex-husband for, having nearly lost custody of Rita to his malicious scheming in a second legal battle, even though Rita was Marcia's by her considerably better second husband. If Marcia had been like Rita, then Anna knew she'd have adored her, but she had died before Anna had escaped her father's clutches and could make her own decisions about who she visited.

"Leave everything in the car for now," Rita was saying. "Come on into the warm and let me get some food into you."

And once she was sitting by the inglenook fireplace, with the log burner glowing brightly, Anna sudden found that she was ravenously hungry. Yet it was only as Rita bustled in with a huge bowl of soup on a tray, along with a chunk of her homemade soda bread, that Anna realised that something was different.

"Why have you got oil lamps on, Aunty?" she asked.

"Oh, the electricity went off in that storm last night," Rita said with a dismissive wave of her hand. "Happens all the time up here, especially in the winter, like now. It's just that you've never been up here when it's gone before. Like I've said before, that's why I have the Aga. Don't you worry, there's plenty of hot water for you to have a good warm bath, and we'll be snug as bugs even if the forecast snow comes."

And that night, as she snuggled under the thick duvet in Rita's spare room, Anna prayed, *Oh please let it snow. Please let us be cut off from the world, if only for a few days.*

Chapter 2

When Anna finally surfaced from her exhausted sleep, through the curtains the world seemed to be very bright, and when she drew them back, it was to see a deep, crisp carpeting of white across the hillside which rose behind Rita's house. The snow had come. And quite irrationally, Anna felt a surge of happiness and relief. The world had been swept clean, it felt to her, or at least her world had. Just like the pristine white surface outside, there was the great white sheet of life ahead of her, and she could take her time choosing what to do with it.

Pulling on comfortable jogging pants, thick socks, and an even thicker sweater – much-loved clothes which she had progressively been bullied out of wearing, she realized – Anna padded down the small, tight staircase to the living room, and was horrified to see by the clock on the wall that it was beyond midday.

"Oh my god, you should have woken me!" she protested to Rita, who looked up at her and smiled from where she was sitting reading.

"Nonsense, girl! You were exhausted. The state of you last night had me fair worried." She got up and came and drew Anna through to the kitchen, steering her towards a seat by the well-scrubbed table in its centre. "Now then, I've already got the kettle on the hob for a cuppa, and you can decide what you want to eat. I've got a pie cooking in the oven for our meal tonight and a pantry full of fresh veg, so save some room for that later."

She gave Anna a wink, knowing that Anna knew how filling that pie was going to be.

With several rounds of the same soda bread toasted and inside her, and on her second mug of tea, Anna finally felt more human and must have looked it.

"That's better, you've got some colour in your cheeks again," Rita said with approval. "I still don't like those dark circles under your eyes, though. That's not just one tiring day. You've been running on empty for a while now, so come on, tell me…what the hell happened?"

"In short? I woke up and found that my dream had become a nightmare."

"Ah, I feared it might have been something like that."

And there it was, that wonderful acceptance of what she'd said. No, 'Don't be stupid', or 'Why didn't you realise it sooner, then?' Just her word being good enough, and knowing that, the words came flooding out of her.

"I can't believe I didn't wake up sooner, Aunty, I really can't. You know that one of the ways to keep Mum and Dad off my back was to turn up at his Christmas party, where he schmoozes all of his contacts. So there I was, this time last year, standing in the corner of their kitchen and wondering how soon I could make my escape, when the dishiest young man at the party walks in and starts talking to me. I mean, that sort of thing never happens to me!" She shook her head and said bitterly, "My own common sense should have warned me it was too good to be true."

"Ah," Rita said sagely, "but that's precisely why you were so swept away, wasn't it?"

Anna nodded. “Yes, it was. And to be honest, by the time I got home that night I thought he’d probably had a bit too much to drink, and that was why. But then the next morning he rang me up. I mean in the *morning*? I’ve never had a boyfriend *that* keen! And it just went on from there. Flowers delivered to me at work, and all the other girls saying I was so lucky, and then them seeing him when he came to meet me from work a few times, and all of a sudden I was the girl who’d hit pure gold. He talked to everyone I worked with without being all snobby, in fact came across as the all-round nice guy.”

A couple of big fat tears slid down her cheeks. “And it was so insidious, Aunty. Everyone saying what a catch I’d got. How lucky I was. If it had just been Mum and Dad, I’d have been much more alert, but when other people were all saying the same, it was hard to find where the flaw was, or if there even was a flaw.”

She had to resort to tissues before carrying on. “His mother and father welcomed me with open arms, and if they knew my parents, as far as I knew then, it wasn’t that they were so close as for me to suspect it was some kind of setup. Of course, it *was*, I belatedly realised. They wanted Jensen married and my parents had me going spare. Nice pliable Anna, who’d be so bloody grateful for any man taking notice of her. Because God knows my mum had been going on at me for long enough about my lack of dating.”

Rita reached over the table and took Anna’s hand. “Your trouble, hen, is that you’ve never moved in the right circles to meet the kind of man who would value you. Working in the office of a supermarket, however posh a one, was never going to introduce you to someone with a bit of backbone and some fire in his belly. But it's worried me for some time that you've set such little store in yourself. I'm so bloody angry that my idiot half-brother played such a dirty trick on you, instead of building up your self-confidence."

"Aunty, he was never going to do that. I've never been considered worth that much attention. Don't forget, I was just the mid-life mistake. They'd had what they wanted in Heather and Nigel, there was no space in their lives for me to fill."

"*Hmphf!* They should have been grateful for what they got!" Anna knew that Rita's disgust came in good measure from never being able to have the children she and her late husband had so desperately wanted. "So when did you start to smell a rat?"

"Too damned late! I was startled, I'll admit, when he proposed after just six months, but I thought that we'd have a long engagement, you see. I mean who gets married within the year? All of the girls I've ever known who've got married had to book venues more than a year in advance – every last one! …And in most cases closer to two years to get the places they wanted. And of course, I stupidly thought that it would be Jensen and I who went around looking at churches and reception places. I was totally knocked sideways when a month afterwards, he turned around to me and said that the wedding was all planned! I mean, I hadn't even heard him mention anything about it yet beyond the proposal."

"Ah! So that's why I got your letter rather than a call telling me about the wedding," Rita said knowingly.

"Well, I didn't know what to *say* to people!" was Anna's blurted confession. "I mean, what *do* you say under those circumstances? I'd hoped for a nice summer wedding where we could have photographs outside and things, and then all of a sudden, I'm confronted with an early December wedding, and worse, at the hotel of one of the poshest leisure complexes in the area. And you know I'm not religious, but even so, I always thought I'd be walking down the aisle of one of the lovely old churches near us, not strolling in in between rows of chairs in the big room where we were going to be sitting down to eat."

She shuddered at the memory of what had come next. "So there I was, already having had second and third thoughts about this wedding, and then finally my father is walking me in, but he's pausing to nod and smile at all of his old cronies and Jensen's fathers', too. He wasn't even bothered that I was there. My wedding was a bloody corporate event!" And though she didn't want to start blubbering again, a heartfelt sob escaped nonetheless.

Rita gave another one of her growls, muttering darkly, "I'll bloody strangle Gordon if I ever see him again, I swear I will. Selfish bloody bastard! …But I think you've skipped forwards a bit. That was the wedding day. What happened in between you suddenly realising that the wedding was all planned and it actually happening?"

Anna gave another shiver. "That was the problem for most of the time. I was either at work, or with Jensen, or with my mother and his, arranging things like flowers and the dress and menus. For about three months I never had a moment to myself to stop and catch my breath. We met in the December, he proposed in the June – as I now know because he'd had the tipoff that the promotion opportunity was coming up, and he'd told his parents about it. They then booted him into proposing, and it was the end of July when he told me it was all set for this December!

So August, September, and October just vanished in a whirl. But it was in October that I started trying to put the brakes on a bit – well, no actually, I tried to put them on a lot. I felt like I was in some runaway car, careering down the road with no control of where I was going.

"I started to ask both mothers to cut the number of guests down. I asked for some more of my friends to be invited. I wanted to know when the evening bit would start so that I could invite people from work. And it was the last one that really shook me, because I was told in no uncertain terms that I was not having 'people like that' at *Jensen's* wedding."

Another rebellious sob broke out of her despite her trying to hold things together. "Jensen's wedding! Like I was nothing but an add-on! And when I protested to my mum, all she said was to stop being silly, and that I ought to be grateful that they'd *found* me such a worthy husband." Another hiccupping sob. "That was the first time I realised what a bloody setup it had been. That Jensen had been shoved my way. What a bloody fool I'd been.

"But worse, it made me stand back and take a good hard look at Jensen, and for the first time I think I saw him for what he was. Oh, he's not a bad person, Aunty. He's just…he's just a nobody. Once I knew there was a pattern there, it didn't take me long to see it. If Jensen's mother or father said he ought to do something, he'd do it. He'd do it because Jensen's life is all about taking the easy option, the easy road.

"And the really sad thing is, he's got enough intelligence to be able to do his job competently enough that the cracks don't show at work. He's bright, really bright, but he's lazy. On his own he wouldn't have given a damn about that bloody promotion, you know. But he's been so conditioned to do what makes his parents happy, he does it without even thinking of what the consequences might be. He's come to rely on them to steer him through life, and they wanted a daughter-in-law who wouldn't rock the boat. Well I've bloody rocked it now, I've sunk the sodding thing!"

Rita's hoot of laughter at that lifted Anna's spirits in a way she hadn't expected, and she felt able to say, "Jensen is one of life's grey men, Aunty. He hasn't a malicious bone in his body. And that's one of the other things that blurred it all for me, you see, because that affable nature of his isn't a front, it's genuine. That was why, right up to the last, I thought I'd be able to go through with it all. He won't argue with anyone. But it's to an extent that he wouldn't stand up for me, not ever. His parents are the dominant ones in his life, and as long as they're happy with him, he's happy.

"So when I started going against them in October, he got really upset. Not angry – never that – but upset as if I'd done something like put his favourite pet down behind his back. Both upset for his loss, and with this weird kind of disappointment in *me*. Can you see what I mean? I was made to feel like I was the bad guy, and because it wasn't fake emotion like I'm used to from my mum and dad, it really threw me.

"Even so, it took until a couple of weeks before the wedding before I began to see the light for real. Our whole lives would be lived dancing to somebody else's tune. One night I had this horrific nightmare where I was holding a baby and the hand of a toddler, and Jensen was telling me what the new baby would be called…and whatever the name was, I hated it, and he said that his parents had picked it and that he'd already registered the baby with that name…and then he took the children away from me, and he said that I was too distraught to look after them, and he was taking them to his mother."

That last had come out in one huge long, tongue-tripping stream, her voice rising in panic even just recounting it, and Rita came around the table to pull Anna into a hug.

"That wasn't a dream, hen, that was a premonition if ever I heard one. They can be awful powerful. I know, I've had a couple in my time. Your grandmother had the Sight, you know. There are wise women in our line going back centuries, and I think you were right to be frightened silly by that foreboding, because it was sent to do precisely that and to get you out before things got that bad."

"Do you think so?"

"Convinced of it, hen! I believed you'd done the right thing from the moment I saw the state of you when you arrived, but I'm ten times more so now you've told me that. …So, you obviously couldn't get out of the wedding, but why didn't you run sooner?"

Anna shook her head and shrugged. "I had some daft idea that I would be able to get Jensen away from his parents, and then we would have time to see whether we really were compatible… because I don't hate him, Aunty, I truly don't …it's the life that comes with him which terrifies me. It was in the days immediately before the wedding, when I was told that his parents had arranged a flat for us in London, and that my mum was planning to come and do my packing up for me while we were on honeymoon, that the overwhelming panic really set it. It was like being run over by a juggernaut. It finally sunk in that there was no stopping this monstrous thing once it was going."

And she told Rita about her mother and Jensen's mother even buying her the complete case-full of clothes to take away on honeymoon, and presenting it to her two days before the wedding, when they'd gone to see the hotel arrangements for the Nth time.

"I was so shocked, Aunty! I knew we were going somewhere hot and sunny, though not where, and I'd got what I thought I'd need all washed and ready, but of course I hadn't actually put it into the suitcase yet in case it got all creased and crushed. And yes, they'd bought me stuff for what they called 'afterwards', but I thought they meant once we were back and me having to do some fitting into the corporate world – not our own honeymoon! They'd kept turning up with clothes that they then took away to keep 'safe', but I still thought that *I'd* be the one packing my own case!

"But that specific night, Jensen was off on his stag do, and for the first time I was home alone. Every other night we'd either been at his flat or he'd come to me, you see. I had the worst panic attack I've ever had in my entire life, and about three in the morning I knew that this marriage wasn't going to last. It couldn't last…or at least not with anything being left of me…not even after the first year.

"I managed to find out which estate agent my parents had put my flat on the market with without my consent – because that was something else that my mother let slip that I hadn't known was coming – and told them in no uncertain terms that the flat was not for sale, and that I own it, not them. They were pretty shocked I have to say, especially as I think the area manager knows Dad. It may be mortgaged to the hilt, but it's mine, and the bank records show that, thank

God. Bless Mum's aunty for leaving me the deposit in her will, or I might never have got away from home, but it does mean that they can't sell the place from under me, not even if they paint me as the biggest lunatic walking."

"Speaking of lunatics," Rita said firmly, "while I've still got some charge in my phone, I'm going to ring the police both here and down south, and let them know that you're safe and here of your own free will. We don't want those fools of parents of yours, *and* his, orchestrating some manhunt, and wasting police time because they've painted you as some mentally fragile waif who's likely to jump off the nearest bridge!"

"I suppose I should have thought of that," Anna said weakly. "Do you want me to do it?"

"Oh no." Rita said sternly. "I know the superintendent for this part of Police Scotland from the work I've done with traumatised service men and women. He'll take my word for it. And if I then tell whoever is in charge down in your area that *he's* fine with it, they're not likely to doubt it, are they?"

Up until a couple of years ago, Rita had worked in one of the Scottish centres which catered for service personnel with PTSD, her late husband having been based at Fort George down on the coast closer to Inverness. And having been a Colour Sergeant's wife, Rita had amassed a huge number of contacts in the area, so it didn't surprise Anna that the local superintendent would be one of them. She'd not thought of her parents painting her in quite that fragile a state just to get the police to set up a hunt for her, but now that Rita had said it, it made worrying sense.

Half an hour later, everything was sorted. West Mercia Police were grateful for the call, and it was their battle now to convince her parents that she was where she was of her own volition, and that they couldn't just drive on blue lights all the way up to the Highlands and drag her back. She'd had to speak to the police herself after Rita had explained the situation, but the person on the other end of the phone had been sympathetic, not critical, and had assured Anna that she was not in trouble.

"I'm switching my phone off now," Rita declared. "I don't think either of us needs your father ranting down the phone at us. He can calm down before he starts slinging insults at us. Is your phone off?"

Anna nodded. "It has been since I walked out of the flat. In fact, I took the SIM card out of it in case they somehow tried to track me by my phone."

"Only the police can do that," Rita reassured her, "and then only if they think your life is actively in danger. But I do understand why you'd have been frightened of that happening. Two prominent businessmen standing shoulder to shoulder demanding action could be very persuasive."

"Oh, I don't think they'll be shoulder to shoulder," Anna said morosely. "In fact, I think it's fair to say that Jensen's parents will cut all contact with mine as soon as they can, now this has happened. They were always a step higher up the corporate scale than Dad. They were his step up, they aren't equals, and they'll want to avoid 'contamination' by association with him now."

"Then ever serve him right!" Rita declared. "For once, your father's scheming has come back to bite him on the arse, and it couldn't have happened to a more deserving man!"

Chapter 3

The snow brought them a day's grace, but the following morning the expected storm arrived by phone. Anna and Rita had barely got their first mugs of coffee before the phone rang, and since Rita was taking the recycling out and Anna recognised the number appearing on the phone's screen, she sighed and answered it, feeling that the least she could do was take her fair share of the abuse.

"What the hell do you think you are doing up there?" her father's voice all but screamed at her before she'd even got a second word out of her mouth. "Do you know the trouble you've caused me?"

And there it was, the way her father turned everything around so that it became about him. No, 'Are you all right?' Not a hint of, 'I was worried sick about you driving all that way in this weather.' None of the things most normal parents would say, even if they were hacked off about having paid so much for a wedding which had come to nothing so fast.

"You ungrateful little wretch," he was thundering on. "We find you the catch of the century – since on your own you seemed to be incapable of finding a decent man to keep you – we pay a fortune for you to have a wedding that would be the envy of any decent girl, and what to you do? You bugger off on your wedding night! Did you even think of what it would do to Jensen's reputation?"

There it was again. Not *her* reputation. Not *her* happiness. And she knew that it wasn't even about the young man he'd barely known a year before, either. What lay behind his thinking was the tirade he had undoubtedly had fired at him from Jensen's father, who himself was worried about what would rebound on him, having done so much to shove Jensen forward into the view of men he did business with in the guise of soon-to-be happily married family man.

And now that she was out of that toxic maelstrom, Anna felt an icy calmness come over her. Cutting in as her father had to take a breath, she told him, "I would feel a good deal more remorse over Jensen if he hadn't come to the bridal suite so drunk he could barely stand. Do you know what he was muttering over and over? 'What have I done? What have I done?' What woman wants to hear that from the man who is supposed to be so in love with her?

"And what's this rubbish about you finding me a man to look after me?" She could hear her own voice rising in fury now. "*Look after* me? I've been looking after myself for several years quite successfully, thank you very much! I pay my own mortgage. I pay my own bills. Have I *ever* come running to you or Mum for so much as a penny? No, I bloody well have not! I'm not like Heather, who can't seem to make-do no matter how much her poor sod of whichever current husband brings in, and who is forever begging Mum to go on shopping expeditions because she can't live without the next fancy whatever-it-is."

"Well at least your sister is a proper woman who knows how to behave!" her father threw back at her. "And she knows how to dress and to look nice for Jacob. *He* doesn't have to come home to some slob, wandering around in jeans and baggy sweaters!"

"No! He comes home half the time to an empty house, because Heather is off down the gym trying to work off an extra ounce, and chatting up the men there in the process, always hoping that someone better will come along. Christ, Dad! How have you never seen that about her? She's forty-three years old this year and on husband number three already!"

"Don't you make this about Heather!" her father shouted down the line at her. "*I* want…"

"…Oh yes, *you* want! That's all we ever heard while I was at home. Never mind about the rest of us. The whole bloody house revolved around what you wanted! Even our damned kids' parties were all about inviting the children of your contacts who you wanted to schmooze, never about our school friends. The only time I ever got invited to other kids' houses was out of pity on their mums' part, because they knew that their kid would never get the invite back to ours! God forbid that the child of an ordinary couple, who could do nothing for *you,* would ever cross our threshold! Unthinkable!"

"Don't you dare take that attitude with me, young lady," came back at her. "But if that's the way you're going to be, then that's *it.* I wash my hands of you. Don't come crawling back to me to sort your troubles out. I'm done with you. It's going to take me all my time to repair the damage you've done to my and your mother's reputations by behaving like this. Jensen's father could ruin my good name thanks to you, you selfish wench!" And with that he put the phone down on her.

With a huff of relief, Anna cut the call at her end and put the phone back into its recharging cradle. That hadn't been as bad as she'd feared. Her father making it all about himself was so normal that she could handle that. Had he gone on about how upset Jensen was, she wasn't sure how well she would have handled it, because in truth she was still feeling horribly guilty over that.

"Does Gordon know he doesn't need to shout all the way to Grantown?" Rita's voice came from behind her. "That's what phones are for." Anna turned around to see the sparks of anger in her aunt's eyes. "Jings! I bet every time his contacts see his name come up on their phones, they must put them on speaker half a desk away for fear of going deaf!"

The mental image made Anna giggle, not least because she knew that her father's long-suffering secretary always picked him up on the speaker for precisely that reason.

"*Hmph*," intoned Rita in that way that only the Scots could do, investing it with a weight that no English person Anna knew could manage. "You're taking that better than I feared."

"You mean I'm not sobbing in a crumpled heap? Oh Aunty, if he'd said much at all about Jensen, I might have. But that was just Dad being Dad. I've had so much of his rants about himself down the years, they've lost the ability to hurt anymore. Or rather, I shed all the tears I'm ever going to shed over his lack of caring about me a long time ago. He's never going to change. And as long as Mum keeps taking his part, there's no possibility of me trying to make my relationship with her any better, either. Nigel did the right thing emigrating to Australia when he got married. He's too far away for Dad to manipulate him, and he gets to drip feed them only the things that they want to hear. His kids are hopefully having a much more normal life out there, especially as his Grace's parents went out there with them, and from the little I saw of them, they seemed like a perfectly normal family. I just wish my brother thought of me once in a while."

"Do you never hear from Nigel?" Rita asked, her brow now furrowed with concern. "Not even about the wedding?"

Anna shook her head. "I know that Mum told him all about it. She writes him these incredibly long emails and gets about two lines back. And I'm sure that she invited them all to come over for it, but there was never any question in my mind of him coming. He's never come back for anything else, so why would he come back for that? I was just a kid of ten when he left – his youngest is older than that now by a year or two, and I've never even spoken to them on the phone."

Rita shook her head in dismay. "*Tsk*! But that's just what I was getting to. Now that he's got kids of his own, does Nigel not realise what your life was like?"

"Aunty, I think he was so glad to leave, I don't think any of us register on his radar much anymore. I doubt he gives me a second thought unless I crop up in one of Mum's email rants, and then only briefly. He just doesn't *want* to know, you see, so if he even reads the damned things, it's only a cursory glance. I'll never see him again, and I doubt anyone else will either."

"What? Not even Heather?"

Anna gave a snort of disgust. "Especially Heather! Have you forgotten? Her first husband was Nigel's friend from school."

"Oh Lord," Rita remembered with dismay. "Yes. I'd forgotten how they met."

"And that Heather got pregnant by him at eighteen, and they forced them to get married. Poor Charlie got led a dog's life for those five years they were together, and then Heather upped and left with god-awful Adam, leaving Charlie with two kids who were still pre-school age. Heather got the bloody accountant she thought she wanted so badly, much good it did her, but Charlie got put through the mill by Mum and Dad, trying to get the kids off him – though God knows what they would have done with them if they had. Probably hired a nanny, because heaven forbid that Mum should start over again with sticky fingers and broken nights!

"That was when Nigel invited Charlie to come over and join him in Australia and they all went. I believe that Charlie remarried to some nice Australian lass, and they too have a little one now. But Heather's never shown any concern over those two children of hers. The only time she plays on it is when she meets some new man, and wants to come across as the hard-done-by one …you know, 'He took my kids away from me, sniff, sniff.' Not that that works for long, because the moment the nice ones start asking about these children, she can't tell them much because she doesn't know – and I can't imagine that it's because Charlie has never let her know, he's too decent a bloke for that."

"What a bloody family," Rita said disgustedly, pulling Anna into a hug. "Hen, you're the only sane one of the bloody lot!"

"And that's probably because they've never bothered much with me. Up until Jensen, I've never had that many expectations pinned on me. Both Mum and Dad put all of what little energy that had for their children into Heather and Nigel. By the time I came along, that had long since run out, and they were focusing on their own lives, not mine."

"Pair of bloody narcissists," Rita growled, making Anna laugh.

But Rita was serious. "Oh, I'm no' joking, hen. After all these years being around psychiatrists and psychologists, I've picked up a fair bit, and your father is a classic narcissist. My pal Dr McCreary up at the clinic would have a field day with Gordon! I've talked a bit to him about my bloody brother, you know, and how he's just like his own father. I got a bit of help myself, you see, after my Archie died. Grief does funny things to you, and all of a sudden, all of the crap my poor mother took off her first husband reared its ugly head, especially the way the damned man tried to make out that my own lovely dad was some kind of bloody deviant just to get back at her for leaving him.

"Well Gordon's a chip off that block alright. That's why they had such dreadful fights once Gordon was grownup, and why you never knew your Grandfather Dennis on that side. They both wanted *their* way all of the time, and narcissists can't abide someone else stealing their thunder, not even if it's their own father or son."

"Or daughter," Anna added, surprised at the bitterness in her own voice.

"Or daughter," Rita agreed. "Your two half-aunts by Dennis' second wife were poor wee shadows of things as kids."

"What happened to them?" it occurred to Anna to ask. "I know this may sound daft, but I knew they existed – of course I did – but I can't remember ever meeting them, or Dad even speaking about his half-sisters. It was only some photos in an old album that made Mum tell me that I had an Aunt Louise and an Aunt Lucy, and even then, she said best not to mention them to Dad. I was only about ten at the time and already I knew not to set Dad off. You develop good survival instincts when you grow up around volatile parents like mine."

"Hmm, about ten, you say?"

"Yes. Why? …Oh! Mum was looking at the photos around the time that Nigel left! Good grief, Aunty, why did I never see that connection before?"

Rita's expression became wry. "Probably because you were too busy being in survival mode to worry about *them*," she said knowingly. "But your bloody grandfather, Dennis Gracie, badgered his daughter Louise so much he made her life a living hell, and she committed suicide when he cut her off from the lad she loved, and would probably have married given the chance. Mum finally told me all about it when I was old enough – because of course, with me being by *her* second marriage too, I was born between Louise and Lucy, so she didn't want to traumatise me while I was still in my teens. I've been eternally grateful that I arrived after Mum's divorce, and that that damned Dennis is no blood relation of mine!"

Anna was aghast. "No! Oh my God. That's awful. I've never heard about that."

Rita gave a snort of disgust. "Well, no, you wouldn't, would you? Gordon was never going to bandy it about that his own father was such a monster that his daughter killed herself to get away from him. But after that, Ellen – that's Louise's mum and your Grandfather Dennis' second wife – took Lucy, and they emigrated to Canada. Lucy was sixteen by then you see, and the courts were on Ellen's side after the inquest into Louise's death when her diaries were read by the court, and all the mental abuse came out. Bloody Dennis hadn't actually broken any laws, so there was no question of being able to prosecute him, especially not in those days when child protection was less of a thing. But he and Gordon were terrified of stuff becoming public knowledge, and that was Ellen's hold over them. She threatened to take Louise's diaries to one of the red-top newspapers."

"Bloody hell! Dad would have kittens over that!"

"And so did his father! So Ellen and Lucy got away. I'm in contact with them, you know. Only a letter with a Christmas card, I'll admit, but Ellen finally realised what my mum must have gone through before her, in her own divorce from that damned man, and asked her to testify if their god-awful ex-husband tried to drag her through the courts over Lucy as well. One ex-wife might not be believed, but…"

"…two standing side by side telling the same story!" Anna caught on, and getting an approving nod from Rita, continued, "Blimey, Aunty! No wonder my dad hated his and your mother so much – she was the vital link, wasn't she! The means to drag them down with her if they pushed too hard. And gosh, no wonder my dad didn't want to kick up too much of a fuss about Charlie taking Heather's kids out of the country. I always wondered why, out of the blue, he let them go so easily once Charlie went to court to get them put onto his passport, but it all makes sense now. He didn't want the pasts of his father's and his own half-sisters' raked over in public – there's always some hack journalist lurking around the courts, isn't there!"

Rita nodded. "And that's why he'll let you go, hen. If you're not there singing from his bloody warped hymn sheet, he'd rather let you go than fight to keep you and risk bad publicity. No child should have to hear this, especially as you're not to blame, but I suspect that's the last you'll hear from either of your parents for a long time."

Anna shrugged. "That's nothing worse than I was expecting. I know Dad too well by now. No, it's Jensen's dad, Mr Coleborn, who bothers me more. If Dad's all fire and fury, that will burn itself out fairly soon – because even he doesn't have *that* much energy to expend on *me* – whereas Mr Coleborn is all ice. He'll plot his revenge on me, because unlike me, Jensen is genuinely the apple of his parents' eyes, and they won't forgive or forget what they think I've done to him. That man will drag me through the divorce courts if he gets his chance, not for the money like my dad would care about, but for the pleasure of seeing me wrecked by his high-powered lawyer."

Rita pursed her lips and shook her head in disapproval. "For heaven's sake, Jensen is a man of what…thirty? He's no' a kid of eighteen needing his mammy's protection! …And by the way, what was that I heard you saying about Jensen muttering something when he came to bed?"

Anna blushed, but Rita was persistent. "Come on now, hen, let's have it all out in the open. Don't hang on to that stuff, it'll only sit inside you and fester. Tell me."

With a sigh Anna began, "He came upstairs…well I presume he actually took the lift, because he was more sliding along the wall when he came in than walking upright, that's how drunk he was. So drunk that I don't think he realised it was me who was there, if that makes sense. He barely registered that there *was* someone in the room, much less who. I could hear him mumbling, and when I got to him turned over to make sure he didn't choke, I could hear him saying,

'What have I done? What have I *done*?' and he sounded so horrified!

"I think that was the point when it sank in for me that *he'd* been railroaded into this marriage as much as me. He'd never been overly passionate, but to be honest, I'd held back from jumping into bed with him at first because I just don't…not with anybody until I really know them, even someone as handsome as him. I've heard first-hand too many horror stories from girls who got some very nasty diseases that way. And then when we did commit to one another, that of course was when the whole lunacy started, and we were both falling into bed at night absolutely shattered from trying to balance going to work, and then all of our parents' expectations in the evenings. In those early days of our engagement, I think I thought that things would heat up once all the pressure was off us, because to be frank, I was too tired myself to want to spend a night in wild passion, so I certainly wasn't going to push Jensen. But then once all my doubts started to bubble up, I began to wonder…"

"You think he was having an affair? Or was he like Prince Charles back in the day – in love with someone totally unsuitable from his family's point of view?"

Anna had no hesitation in saying, "An affair? Oh no! Good grief, Aunty, the poor man hardly had a second when he wasn't at work, or with me, or them. I can't imagine where he would have found the time, let alone the energy, for an affair." She paused and thought. "As for him being in love with someone he couldn't have, I suppose it is possible. In truth, though, I don't know who that would be …*could* be. I never heard him talking about anyone at all in what I would call overly affectionate terms, not even old girlfriends. He seemed to be on reasonably good terms with the ones he'd had longer relationships with, though there were only two of those and neither was that long, but I got no sense that he was pining for any of them."

"No obliging secretary at work, maybe?"

"No, Aunty. Don't forget the days of the typing pool are long gone. Everyone in Jensen's office, aside from the top boss, who had a PA, did all their work onscreen, they didn't need a secretary. And the few women who were in his team were all having to work twice as hard as the men to prove that they were worthy of being there. God knows, my job wasn't great, but at least I wasn't treated like some interloper by men with egos the size of Everest."

"What do you think Jensen meant, then?"

Anna sighed miserably. "I think that it finally dawned on him what he'd committed to. I don't think he thought I was awful – though he probably does now, if he's had to withstand his father's wrath alone, because *someone* must have found him in that drunken stupor and asked him what the hell he was playing at, getting in that state when he should have been all over his blushing bride. It was simply that he belatedly realised that he wasn't 'in love' with me. He got on well enough with me as a friend, even a friend with occasional 'benefits'. It was when it finally sank in that he was supposed to carry on the dynasty with me, that he got a rude awakening."

She blushed again. "I overheard them, you see. Jensen and his dad. I'd gone to the ladies when we'd gone to take stuff like those bloody cupcakes to the hotel two days before, and I was about to come out when I realised that they were talking right outside the door. They must have thought I was somewhere else, and I let them move away before I left, so he doesn't know I heard them. Jensen was saying to his dad about how I wasn't happy about the sudden move to London, which I genuinely wasn't in any way, having had that dropped on me out of the blue. And then Mr C said, 'Oh, just knock a couple of kids out with her. That usually calms the women folk down. It did with your mother, especially once you came along.' And all I could think then was, 'Poor Mrs C,' because she had several miscarriages before she had Jensen, so no wonder all the spark had gone out of her!"

"Bloody hell!" Rita growled. "Charming man! To say that about his poor wife. No wonder she dotes on Jensen after that."

"Exactly! I never blamed her for being like that once I knew. But when I heard him saying that, I think I immediately thought, 'I know I've passed thirty, but I'm not that far gone that I can't wait a year or three before having kids.' I mean, there are mums who have their first at forty these days, aren't there? Not that I want to wait that long if I have any option, but you know…"

Rita patted her hand. "Aye, I do. Was that by any chance the night when you had that premonition about the children?"

"Oddly enough, no. I'd had that one weeks beforehand, so that rather confirmed all my fears rather than starting them. But for Jensen, I think it was the point when it all came crashing in on him. No more nice, single life-style for him – which is what *he's* happiest with. And if I was going to be up to my ears in nappies and toddlers, either he was going to have to climb the tree enough to be able to afford a nanny, so that I could go out to work as well; or he was still going to have to pull his finger out, because he would be the only wage earner. God forbid that we should live a life more ordinary! His parents would insist that certain standards were maintained, for public view at least. And lovely though Jensen can be, I came to realise that he doesn't handle responsibility well, so I bet he's still freaking out about that as much as losing me."

"And if Jensen is freaking out, then his mum will be all over her darling boy being upset?" guessed Rita.

"And Mr C will take it as a massive insult to his beloved son," Anna added, "which is why he's not going to let me just leave in peace."

"Then in that case," Rita said firmly, "we're going to have to get you to somewhere where he can't easily find you."

January 1650

Elspeth

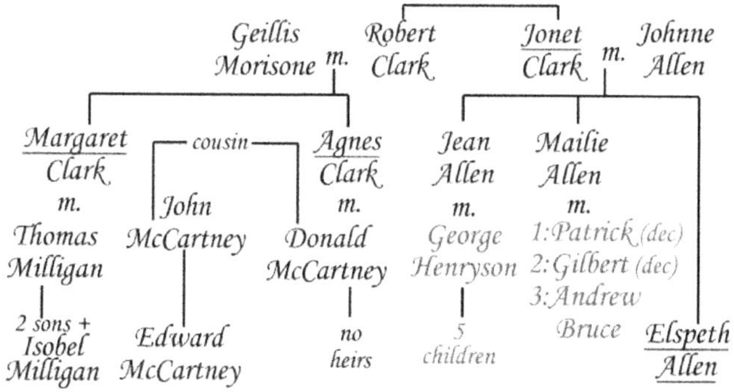

Elspeth was running for her life.

Never in all her eighteen years had she been so absolutely terrified. She could hear the dogs and the cries of the drunken young men behind her, and knew that if they caught her, her life was as good as over. The very fact that they were the sons of the local bailies, and she was just a crofter's daughter, meant that in any official hearing they would automatically be believed over her, even if they were lying through their teeth whilst having their hands on the Holy Bible.

"A witch! A witch! Burn her for a witch!" she heard the raucous voices echoing across the night-time fields.

She wasn't a witch any more than Marione Corsan was, who right now was being held prisoner in the cellars of Irongray Manse. Presbyter Veitch, the minister of Irongray, was infamous far and wide as being a hard and unforgiving man, and in these months since the King of England had been beheaded and the Commonwealth had taken over, it seemed as if the fiercest of the Covenanters here in Scotland had finally got the government they desired. So much so that it was more than anyone's life was worth to say a word against ministers like Presbyter Veitch. And that meant that if he decided that Marione – or God forbid, Elspeth – needed to be put to the question, nobody was going to tell him he couldn't.

Yet to Elspeth, Marione was the intelligent and caring woman who had a wonderful knowledge of herbs and tinctures, who had sometimes conferred with her own mother on the best way to heal someone. If you didn't have a wise-woman for a mother as Elspeth did, you would want Marione by your side in childbirth and in sickness, for although nobody could cheat death if their time had come, she could surely ease the pain of your passing if nothing else. And if it was curable, then the chances of that cure being found were far higher with Marione than with many of the other women in the area with some vague knowledge of herbs. But that had gone against her when she had failed to cure old Mother Rammage of what was surely mere old age. James Rammage, her son, no doubt egged on by his sharp-tongued and eternally dissatisfied wife, had complained to Presbyter Veitch, and before the dawn had broken on the following day, Marione had been dragged from her home by the bailies' men, and shoved into the cellars at Irongray Manse.

It felt worse for Elspeth and her family, for her own mother, Jonet Clark, had been detained and questioned there as a witch all the way back in 1630, when Elspeth hadn't even been born, leaving her father – Johnne Allen – fearing he would have to bring Elspeth's two older sisters up by himself. It had been a close thing, but Jonet had been released, yet thereafter had never been quite the woman she'd been before. Elspeth had never known the carefree, happy mother her sisters had.

Such brutal 'questioning' had broken stronger women than Jonet, and the nightmares of that time had haunted her for decades. Then only six years ago in 1644, Jonet's niece and therefore Elspeth's cousin, Margaret Clark, had been similarly hauled in for questioning, even though she had only been Elspeth's current age at the time – a fact that was doing nothing to quell Elspeth's fears right now. Just because Margaret had been questioned down in Kirkcudbright where her family lived, didn't mean that the association between her and Elspeth wouldn't count against her in a county court if these drunks caught her.

Moreover, Alexander and William McBurney, the brothers who were the local bailies, had envied her father's smallholding for years, and now Alexander's third oldest son was of an age to want a place of his own. Given that Alexander's poor wife had given him five sons – four of whom had grown to near manhood by now – he could hardly leave his farm to all of them. And so he was ever on the hunt for potential homesteads he could bully the occupants out of in favour of one of these sons. The oldest would eventually inherit the main house, while the next two he had already settled with crofts closer to Annan, but the youngest two were still to be provided for.

However, it was not Alexander's sons but William's pair who were now hunting Elspeth! Should they connive to prove her a witch like they'd tried with her mother and cousin, it would be all her father could do to keep the roof over their heads, let alone save her, for with the minister against them, few of their neighbours would dare to speak up in their defence. And she knew that others so accused had had their homes ransacked, anything of worth seized never to be returned, and all of their herbs and potions either burned or thrown away; meaning she had a dread of running for home in case she brought that fate down on her parents. Only her father's good standing in the neighbourhood had saved them when her mother had been investigated, and Elspeth feared that wouldn't stand up to a second bout of accusations if she got caught.

...But where to go?

...Where to go?

Elspeth paused to rub the painful stitch in her side, and tried to think which way she should run. There weren't that many places that these lads didn't know or wouldn't fear to enter, including lesser cottars' homes – and anyway, Elspeth wouldn't dream of leading them to some other poor soul's house. That would be beyond cruel, for nobody would believe that she'd ended up there by accident, and then they, too, would stand accused of harbouring a witch.

No, it would have to be someplace else.

...Somewhere not a home.

...But where?

Running in heavy, woollen, homespun skirts wasn't easy or quiet, either. Not when they snagged on twigs and bushes, making her dread being heard. She had little enough of a lead on them as it was, but right now moving silently would be better than trying to be fast. Anyway, while she could walk all day if necessary, running full tilt wasn't something she could do for much longer. So it would have to be somewhere not too far away.

The Apostles' Stones?

Would they dare to chase her if she got within the stone circle?

Rumour had it that the fairy folk could be seen dancing along the two circles of ditches, and in and out between the stones themselves. Elspeth had never seen the like herself, but then she'd never risked going there on a new moon or on the nights of the year's old quarter days which Aunt Geillis, along with her daughters Margaret and Agnes, observed, albeit careful to do it out of sight of the Presbyter and kirk elders. Midwinter had already passed, and the moon was barely waxing towards full right now, so she ought to be safe from the fae, but would the lads know that too, and risk hunting her into the circle?

No, the Apostles' Stones might be full of ancient power, but if she was caught running to there, that could also count against her. A potent pagan place was not the clever place to seek sanctuary when hunted by the likes of the McBurneys. But that suddenly prodded her exhausted mind the right way.

Sanctuary! The refuge offered to the accused in the old days by the Kirk. Get within a kirk's doorway and nobody could summarily drag you away! That had been in the days when the Catholic Church, or more recently the Scottish bishops of the Episcopalian Kirk, had held sway over all of Scotland, though. Moreover, she was far from any kirk except Irongray's, and these days she wasn't sure if the concept of sanctuary even held with the currently largely Presbyterian-controlled Kirk of Scotland. But there was the old nunnery!

In truth, heading into the roofless chapel of the abandoned nunnery felt almost as bad as being caught. Too many local people had said they had seen the shades of the last nuns walking there at night – and many of them who'd seen things were amongst those she would not have thought gullible, or given to flights of fancy. But right now, she hadn't got much choice. It was the sanctified ruins or the cellars of Irongray Manse, and if Elspeth didn't know what the ghosts of the nuns would do, she surely did with the Presbyter.

She had walked over to the Manse with her mother, to see if they could maybe slip some food and comfort through the cellar's iron barred window, the last time Presbyter Veitch had had a poor woman held captive. And they'd heard the screams and her begging for mercy, and for the pain to stop.

"Dear God! The Minister fancies himself a witch pricker!" her mother had said, after she'd had to hide in a hawthorn coppice to be sick with shock.

A witch pricker's needles were not some dainty dressmaker's pin, but six-inch shanks of thin steel, with which the pricker would jab any wart or blemish to determine whether there was any feeling or not. If there wasn't, then it was deemed to be the Devil's mark, and the person condemned as a witch. The fact that, after being jabbed multiple times with these instruments of torture, it would be amazing if the suspect could tell one spot of pain from another, never seemed to occur to the zealots who did it.

Therefore, for Elspeth the ghosts were the lesser of two evils, and she trotted as silently as she could towards the nunnery's ruins. As she panted up the gentle incline, the land rising away from the river valley of the Cluden Water, she saw in the distance the clouds parting, and the moonlight illuminating the stone circle for a moment. Just as they began to cover it again, she saw the first of the hunting dogs streaming into the central space.

Dear God, they had jumped to the wrong conclusion!

Or the right one for her, at least.

They thought her a witch, and that a witch would go to the circle. But she wasn't and she hadn't.

Then she saw it in the final shaft of winter's early moonlight – a fox, vanishing into the undergrowth just beyond the circle.

It and the dogs were little more than blurs in the distance, but she could hear the pack picking up the fox's trail, and baying at their quarry. The young men hunting her had assumed she would head that way, and pulled their dogs towards it, only letting them go when they were close enough to make no difference. And of course, with the dogs being more used to hunting foxes which raided hen houses and young lambs, the dogs had then done what they were trained to do.

"God bless you, mister fox," Elspeth prayed from the heart, her tears now coming for the innocent beast which might yet get torn to shreds in her place. She didn't think she would ever look on a fox in the same light again after tonight. But she didn't dare slow down. Soon enough those men would realise that she hadn't been there at all, and then they would back-track until they could pick up her trail again.

In a gasping and ungainly, hobbling trot, she managed the last of the close on a mile to the ruins, which lay near the river on its next loop northwards. Built high enough so that the medieval buildings would stay dry when the Cluden Water was in flood, it had also allowed for the nunnery to have an under-croft and crypt, albeit very modest ones compared to some of the great monastic houses hereabout, such as the abbey down nearer the coast. Elspeth wasn't planning on going into either under-croft or crypt if she could avoid it, hoping instead to find some partly ruined dormitory stair, which she could climb up away from the dogs, and remain hidden on.

With a sob of relief, she saw the fingers of ruined stone that had been the chapel's east end sticking up against the half-lit scudding clouds.

Not far now.

Then she heard the baying of the hounds again.

God curse those men's miserable souls! They'd had the advantage of being on their shaggy hill ponies, while she was on foot. So, of course, they had covered the ground between the circle and here far faster than she had.

She stumbled her way inside over a tumbled bit of side wall, forced to move more slowly now or risk twisting an ankle, or worse, on the chunks of fallen sandstone which littered what had once been the nave of the nunnery's chapel. The altar was where she was making for, desperately hoping that the great stone table which had been consecrated by the nuns' priest might still be there. Surely being found clinging to the most sanctified part of the whole place, and not being struck down from above, ought to count for something?

Yet as she got almost to the east end, her worst nightmare surfaced. From out of nowhere a spectral figure appeared, and it was all Elspeth could do not to scream in terror.

Which was worse now, the ghost or her hunters?

However, far from flying at her, the ghost swam more clearly into view, and revealed herself to be a kindly-faced nun. A nun who was frantically beckoning her to follow her.

Swallowing her panic – quite literally in that Elspeth had been on the verge of throwing up in her terror – she followed the white wisps of the ghost, only to find that she was leading her towards the crypt. At that point Elspeth froze. The very thought of going down those stone steps into the dark was enough to paralyse her.

Yet the ghost's beckoning only became more urgent. And out of nowhere, a voice in her head was saying, 'Come with me! …You must come now! You will be safe with us! We will not let them harm you.'

Frightened almost out of her wits, Elspeth knew that she had little choice but to trust the ghost, not least because it dawned on her that out here where nobody would hear, the men could beat and rape her, and never be questioned later as to why she was in such a state. They could, and would, say that she had tempted them with lewd words and gestures, and only her family, and those who knew and cared for her, would know that she would never do such a thing. Instead, these sons of righteous men would sit back and smirk while she was dragged through the dirt, and possibly through a trial which she had no chance of winning.

With one last gasp of courage, Elspeth crossed herself, and then began a careful descent of the worn and moss-slippery steps into darkness.

Utterly blind in the complete blackness of the crypt, all she could do was grope her way along the damp, mouldy wall, following the faint outline of the ghost. When she was as far as she could get, she collapsed onto a table-tomb and hugged her aching sides. If she was caught now, she was doomed.

Yet up above, when she finally heard the men's voices and the baying of their hounds, nobody came down. The hunting dogs came as far as the steps, and then went away, and she heard the whining from them as something frightened them more than their brutal masters. For one horrible moment, she thought that at least one of the men was going to be bold enough to risk the dark. Probably one of William McBurney's sons, she suspected, for they wore their piety like a badge of honour, but it was well known in the parish that they merely went through the correct motions, rather than with any great faith. Young men like those were not easily frightened by the fear of what was to come in the afterlife, being devoid of anything close to sufficient imagination to be able to visualise what Hell might be like.

Then to her stunned amazement, she suddenly heard one of them let out a scream.

"Get way!" he yelped, sounding more like a scared girl than the all-powerful man he pretended to be. "*Aagh*! …No! …Leave me alone!"

"Patrik! Run!" she heard another voice calling to the first, then another of the men shouting,

"John, lad! Behind you! …Watch out! She's coming for you!"

In a clatter of heavy boots, Elspeth heard the men running from the chapel, and then the distant pounding of hooves as they rode their ponies as fast as they would go away from the old nunnery, their dogs panting to keep up as they too fled.

For a while Elspeth was too relieved to move, but when she did, she was surprised to see that her ghostly guide had been joined by others. Twelve others by her count – which made them an arcanely potent thirteen in all, if Aunt Geillis was to be believed. And their ghostly shades gave off enough light for her to make her way out of the crypt without falling over any of the rubble on its floor.

"Thank you," she managed to gasp, when she'd made it out and up onto the nave floor once more. "I fear I would have died here if not for you."

And there it was again. A voice. Not heard so much as inside her head, and coming from a different one of the ghosts this time. Later on, she would wonder if that ghost might have been the prioress.

'Evil men came for our last three sisters,' the voice within her head said. 'They came dressed as priests, but their desires were anything but pure. They raped and battered our sisters to death, then had the nerve to claim that these godly women had fallen by the wayside, and left their vows behind them. Their blood fell on this floor, and while this place lasts, we are connected to it and we shall not allow that to happen to any other woman.'

"I'm no nun," Elspeth said weakly, fearing that they had somehow thought her a latter-day sister.

'We know this,' the ghost voice said kindly. 'But you are a young girl, barely of an age to be wed. It is wrong in every way that you should be so treated for nothing more than being a woman.' A smile could just be seen on this leading ghost's face. 'Have you lain with many men?'

"Dear God, no!" spluttered Elspeth. "Not one!"

'Have you given yourself over to evil spirits?'

"N…no*oo*!" That shocked Elspeth even more, yet it seemed to be nothing more than the ghostly nun expected.

'Then you do not deserve to be treated as one of the Devil's own,' the nun said firmly. 'Those men have no right to judge you when they fall so far from the path of righteousness themselves. If you fear being hunted by them again, come back here. We will guard you, never fear. Now rest for the night, and when the dawn comes up, make your way back home across the fields. I do not think those men will be back for a long time to come.'

Chapter 4

Anna wasn't sure how she felt about Rita's pronouncement. In her mind she had thought she would stay with Rita for a while and then probably go back south. Yet talking it over with Rita now, she could already see that going back to the Midlands was not going to be one of her better ideas. Being back there and effectively all alone would make her a ripe target for the Coleborns' wrath, and alone she would be, because the casual friends she did have would never understand why she had run out on Jensen. That was another of the wretched hangovers from her dysfunctional childhood – making close friends was something she'd struggled to get the hang of, not having had the chance to mingle with kids out of school like normal families did. It meant that she had a lot of general friends who, once upon a time and before Jensen, she had enjoyed a girls' night out with, but nobody whom she could turn to in this kind of crisis.

"How far away were you thinking of, Aunty?" she asked, wishing that her voice hadn't suddenly developed a noticeable wobble. "Only I don't think I can face doing a Nigel and starting over in a different country."

Rita rolled her eyes, but with a smile too. "I'm not talking about leaving the country, hen – or at least not the UK. No, I was thinking of you simply being somewhere where people won't expect you to be. Such as here in Scotland, but not with me. All of those contacts of mine have to be good for something, and while I'm not like your father, hoarding up favours against the time when they might serve me, nonetheless I do have folk who owe me one and who would be glad to help."

She picked the phone up and headed for the little ground-floor room, which she used as her office. "Bear with me. I can't imagine this will take long. Go and put the kettle on, and I'll give you a shout when something turns up."

To Anna's astonishment, she'd hardly had chance to put the coffee in the cups and pour the water onto it before Rita was calling her through.

Holding the phone in her hand, she asked, "In that job of yours, you did use a computer, didn't you…? For customers, I mean. I know I've heard some of the ladies in Tesco saying how they hate computers, but you were in the office."

Anna blinked in surprise. "Heavens, yes. Pretty much everything I did involved putting something into one, or printing something out."

"You could handle being a hotel receptionist, then? You wouldn't be fazed by having to deal with customers face to face?"

"Customers? Oh no, they're no problem. I used to have to do my stint up on the Customer Service Desk at peak times like Christmas and Easter, so I've had my share of stroppy ones and dealt with them."

Rita beamed, saying into the phone, "Did you hear that, Gary? …Great! You'll give me a call when you've spoken to the manager about when she can start? …That's brilliant! Thanks again."

"Gary?" Anna asked faintly, and could have sworn she saw a hint of a blush on Rita's face.

"Aye, well Gary's known me a long time. We're good friends."

"Just good friends?" teased Anna.

Rita sighed. "That's the thing. For me he's a lovely friend. For him it was becoming something more."

"But Aunty, you've been widowed for how long? It must be fifteen years or so? I know you loved Archie dearly, but you can't tell me that he would have wanted for you to spend the rest of your life alone?"

"I'm not alone! I have loads of friends and an active social life."

"That's not what I meant and you know it. And I wasn't implying that you should be out picking up random blokes, either. That's no more you than it is me. But someone who you admit is a really good friend is surely a different matter? You know him, and given that you're about to ship me off to him, and he had to have been your first call going by how fast you called through to me, you must trust him implicitly. So what was the problem?"

Rita sighed. "I don't know. I think I just got cold feet over the idea of starting over with someone new at my age. I'm not as flexible as I was when I was younger. I think I was frightened that once we were on top of one another twenty-four hours a day, stuck in a small house together, that that's when the rows would start, and it would be the end of a lovely friendship. A friendship I've come to count on."

"But something happened. If you're sending me *away* to him, then he's not on the doorstep anymore, is he?"

"No, he's the night porter at a hotel down in Dumfries & Galloway. He's been down there for a couple of years now. Said he needed to have some breathing space and a fresh start."

"And you didn't try to talk him out of it?"

"Didn't really get the chance. He applied. They practically bit his hand off to have a military man like him around the place. All I got was the call to say he'd applied, got the job, and was starting immediately. Since then, I've discovered that he's got a nice little cottage that's part of the converted stable block where he and some of the other staff, like the chefs, live. He's got a river with fishing rights virtually at the end of the grounds, so he gets to take some of the newer fishermen out, which is right up his street, and he's got acres of land to go walking in with proper hills not far away. He says it's not the Highlands, but it's a heck of a lot better than where he grew up in Clydebank near the remains of the old, bombed-out docks."

Anna was bothered by the way that Rita had become so downcast while she was telling her this. Clearly Rita had underestimated her own feelings for Gary, and suddenly Anna realised that if she was going to be working with this man, then she might be able to do something towards mending bridges between him and her beloved aunt. Then she wouldn't be merely sitting here expecting Rita to sort her life out for her without trying to pay her back in some way, and that made a big difference to how she felt about accepting the job – presuming she got it, of course.

By the end of the day, she was packing her bags again, because either the hotel was absolutely desperate, or Gary's recommendation held a lot of sway there, since he'd called back to summon her south.

"It's called *Nuns' Kirk Haugh Hotel*," Rita told her, pulling up the hotel's website to show her. "Isn't that lovely?"

The screen showed an old and gorgeous sandstone building, complete with a square tower on one side, and a lower, round-turreted tower on the opposite side. A porticoed entrance dominated the centre of the frontage, with huge mullioned windows on both sides; the upstairs windows in the main building also had imposing windows looking out over an immaculate lawn. The square tower to the left had a proper third floor of rooms, while the turret at the other end of the building on a lower, squatter wing, wasn't as high but clearly had attic rooms up under its conical eaves.

"Wow! That's so romantic," Anna gasped, already in love with the place. "It looks really old!"

Rita waggled a hand. "Yes and no. The building as you see it is pure Victorian Gothic, built in the wave of enthusiasm started by Queen Victoria, and helped along the way by Sir Walter Scott's great Romantic novels. That said, it *is* on the site of a previous house, and that was built out of the remains of an even older tower house and its tiny chapel, which had a handful of nuns living in the tiniest of nunneries beside it, praying for the laird and his family's souls in return for their living. So a lot of the stone has been repurposed down the generations, as have some of the features. Wait 'til you see the fireplace in the main hall – it's a cracker! Huge great inglenook of a thing. You could just see some kilted Jacobite laird warming his arse in front of it with his deerhounds sprawled at his feet!"

Anna's eyes were getting wider by the moment. "And do they have proper fires in it? I do love a real fire."

"Oh yes, proper logs, not some daft fake thing." Rita gave her a wink. "You'll have a proper Scottish

Christmas and Hogmanay this year. No having to stand in your mum's bloody kitchen like the Boxing Day leftovers, you'll be in the thick of it there, because Gary says they're booked solid through the festive period." And Rita thought, *This will be so good for you, Anna. You won't have chance to mope or fret. You'll finally be able to enjoy yourself, and start living the life you should have had years ago.*

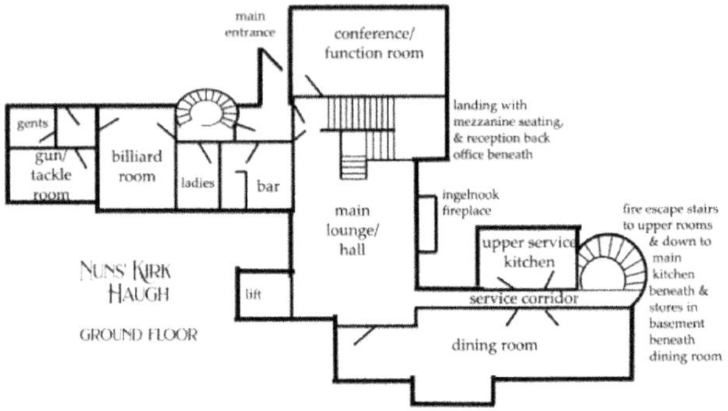

A week to the day after her dreadful wedding, Anna found herself walking in through the imposing entrance of *Nuns' Kirk Haugh Country House Hotel*, and contrasting the glamorous entrance those lucky enough to have a Highland wedding here would have against her own wretched affair. Under the portico was a huge, arched and very solid, oak door, complete with iron studs and a hefty, roped-iron, round handle to turn its latch – though she did notice the very modern security lock on the door as well.

"I believe the door is older than the building," Rita said, giving it a loving pat. "Beautiful old thing, isn't it."

"Don't go going all fey on me, Aunty," Anna teased. "I don't want to have to prise you off the door on my first day."

Rita laughed. "It does have a vibe to it, I can tell you that. But then a lot of this place does."

"Oh!" Anna gasped in surprise. "You've actually been here before, then?"

"I came down here for last Christmas and I'm coming again this year," Rita confessed, hurriedly adding, "as a *paying* guest."

She didn't fool Anna, though. Rita had come here to see Gary, even if she hadn't stayed in his cottage with him, so she could protest all she liked that she didn't have feelings for him. Anna could see that she did.

Once beyond the imposing main door, she found herself in a short lobby of a hall which turned right at ninety degrees only a short way ahead. In that right-angle, on the left were glass double doors through which Rita now ushered her. In front of them was a desk at which sat a tall, well-built man who was probably in his late fifties, and who was staring ferociously at the computer screen through his half-moon reading glasses and swearing,

"C'mon you wee bastard! Stop feckin' around wi' me!" And a large index finger clicked maniacally at the mouse. "Stop with the wee whirly blue light, will you! …Ach Jeez! You're doin' this on purpose now, you wee bugger!"

"Having problems, Gary?" Rita asked, Anna hearing the suppressed giggle in her voice.

Gary looked up at her over the top of his specs. "This bastard thing is no' playing fair wi' me!" he growled.

Anna took a breath then dared to say, "It might help if you took your finger off the mouse. You're giving it so many commands it can't process them."

A pair of piercing blue eyes turned on her. "Do you know how to make this wee shite work? Because if so, for the love of God will you come and sort it out?"

Anna laughed. "I'll give it a go." And leaving her bag with Rita, she went around the big desk and slid onto the seat Gary had just vacated.

"Why, by all that's holy, have they let you loose on the computer?" Rita asked him, her suppressed laughter barely hidden. "Surely that's the receptionist's job?"

Leaning back and letting the computer recover from Gary's assault, Anna looked up at him as he gave a very Scottish growl and told them, "The bloody manager walked out this morning! Not that she was any use. One of those smart-arse late-twenty-somethings, who can bullshit their way in, but then can't do the job. Margaret, the old manager, was a true professional, but she retired in the summer and is now somewhere in the Med' with her husband, enjoying a well-earned rest. So the owners hired this jumped-up little know-it-all, and she's done nothing but cause trouble since she got here five months ago.

"That's why we're in the shite over receptionists! She altered the rotas for the three women who come in from the nearby villages, telling them that they *had* to do their share of evening shifts. Well, two out of three have got kids who're at school. They can't be out until eleven at night on week nights, make a half- to three-quarters of an hour drive home, and then get everyone up for the school run.

"Polly only lasted a week before quitting, and Gemma managed during the school holidays but then quit after a dust-up with Herself. We've had three useless kids via agencies, but they didn't know hay from a bull's foot about dealing wi' customers, so the complaints started rolling in. Cora's been signed off wi' stress for three weeks, this being the end of the second one, and she told the owners straight that if yon Perdita was staying in charge, then she wouldn'a be coming back at all!"

He gave the mouse another couple of exasperated pokes.

"So this very morning someone from the owners rang up and demanded to speak to miss high-and-mighty Perdita, and told her to pull her socks up and stop bullying the staff. She got in high dudgeon, had a screaming fit back at them – which didn'a go down any too well wi' the guests trying to pay and leave, by the way – and then stormed off saying she was done wi' the place, and if we didn'a recognise her talents, then that was our loss."

"Gosh!" Anna gasped. "She had a high opinion of herself, didn't she!"

"Oh aye," Gary said with a wry smile. "Probably because nobody else did," and gave Rita and Anna a knowing wink.

Anna decided that she liked Gary…a lot! Frustrations with the computer aside, he was probably very good at keeping the peace with any raucous guests, and soothing ruffled feathers with that dry humour of his. This man would be so much easier to work with than some of the arrogant boy-managers she'd suffered in the past.

"But why are *you* on the reception desk?" Rita persisted. "Surely if you've been on call all night, you shouldn't be here now? It's what…three in the afternoon? Your shift should have finished hours ago."

Gary sniffed. "Aye, well I would've gone, but there was nobody to take over. Ceri, the agency lass Anna's taking over from, was rota-ed in for today until four, but she quit four days ago. We're still one lass down from the other agency one who left, and Miss Fancy-Pants-Perdita was supposed to be covering until Brenda comes in at four."

He smiled at Anna. "You'll like Bren'. Knows the job like the back of her hand. Been here for years, and now Herself has buggered off, hopefully will be here for a good few more." Turning to Rita he explained, "Brenda did all day yesterday to help out, so she was shattered by last night. I got her hubby to come and collect her, 'cause I wasn'a happy about her driving half-an-hour home down the narrow lanes when that tired, and told her not to come back until later on. …So there you go, that's why it's just me here right now."

By now the computer had finished having a nervous breakdown, and Anna could see what Gary had been trying to do.

"Okay…you're going to email these receipts on to these four customers, right?" she checked.

"Aye. If the bloody printer would speak to this thing, I would'a given it to them when they left, but it all went base up at that point."

Anna covered her grin at Gary's black looks at the computer by ducking her head down and, with a few swift clicks, sent the receipts on their way. She was just about to log out when a thought occurred to her.

"Gary, are you logged into this thing as you, or is this someone else's login?"

He looked at her with blank incomprehension, forcing her to clarify,

"Did you just sit down and start typing? And if so, who was on here before?"

"I've no idea why it matters," he said in confusion, "but I just sat down and got stuck in. Those screeny things were already there. I didn'a do a thing."

"So who got the 'screeny things' up? Because they're surely not here all the time. That would be breaking all sorts of confidentiality rules for the customers if anyone could waltz in here, and start looking folks up."

Beginning to understand, Gary told her, "That would be bloody Perdita. She was sitting here when she got that phone call and all the shouting started."

"Great, so the 'manager' is still logged in?"

"Aye. …Why?"

"Well wouldn't it be an idea to get into the system and make sure that she can't access it remotely?"

"Christ!" Garry gasped, horrified. "She couldn'a steal money through that thing, could she? I know she went out screaming that we'd be sorry, but I didn'a think of anything like that!"

"Take money? No, she couldn't do that because all the actual transactions go through the card machine," Anna reassured him. "But if she thinks her login is still active, she could be waiting for you to logout and then log back in remotely, at which point she could do something like wiping all the booking records. That's the sort of thing that could cause you untold chaos, because you wouldn't be able to take any more in case you double-booked with someone already coming."

"Gawd help us," Gary said in awed tones. "That would really screw things up over Christmas! Can you sort it out?"

"I'll do my best," Anna said. It took a bit of careful digging around in the files, but Anna found the screen with all of the staff on it, and their respective logins.

"Okay, there are a lot of names on here," she said. "How many of these are still here?"

Gary leaned over her shoulder, and as Anna clicked on each one, told her which ones had left. In the end they had purged nearly twenty names out of the files, which as Anna pointed out, should have been done long ago in some cases.

"It's a security risk," she explained to Gary. "It would only take them telling someone they know what their login staff number was, and what their password was, and that person could come in and access your system. Like I said, they couldn't get money, but you would be open to prosecution if someone got hold of a person's address and then robbed them, for instance."

"She's good," Gary said approvingly to Rita, who had taken up residence in one of the pair of customer chairs on the other side and was watching Anna work with pride. "She's going to be worth her weight in gold."

"And I'm about to make you the manager," Anna said, which got her a cough and a splutter from Gary. "It's okay, I just mean that temporarily I'm going to put you in as the manager on this machine. Someone has to be able to get into this bit where you add and take off staff, and it shouldn't be me when I've literally been here five minutes. I've put myself on the system so that I can do the standard reception stuff, but when a new manager gets here, someone needs to be able to get into this bit for them to put themselves in. It'll be no good if *everyone* is locked out of this, and this isn't a screen we should be leaving open. …So here you go, Gary, that's your staff number, so now you put a password in that you'll remember."

Taking her place at the keyboard, Gary looked more as if he was about to wrestle a wild beast, but with some ferocious jabbing of index fingers, put in a string of letters and numbers. Anna didn't like to tell him that she was watching his fingers as he did it, and memorising them too – just in case he forgot what he'd input. He needed to trust her right now.

When he was done, a few quick clicks and the dreadful Perdita was consigned to electronic history.

"There you go," Anna said, sitting back. "All safe and secure."

As she did so an older female voice said from the doorway, "Oh hello, Rita, is this your niece?"

Chapter 5

To Anna's relief, Brenda thoroughly approved of what she had done in securing the booking system and other files, and she was a good deal blunter about the dreadful Perdita, saying,

"I wouldn'a trust that wee flighty bit o' skirt further than I could spit! And she was always flirting with the male customers, even if their wives were with them. Any halfway decent looking chap and she was there, fluttering her bloody false eyelashes and her pumped-up lips at them. That's not the way we do things here. We've got a lot of regular customers and she upset a fair few of them. Hopefully they'll come back after Gary and I apologised for her, but there's no doubt we've lost a few too, and in this day and age no hotel can afford for that to happen."

Brenda obviously thought that Anna was made of better stuff, though, and within minutes was showing her the different parts of the booking-in systems, and as Anna found it all very straightforward, she was put into the rota for manning the desk first thing in the morning alongside Gary to check out the guests leaving on Sunday.

"I don't suppose you've ever worked a bar before?" Brenda asked hopefully, "because we're absolutely rammed tonight, and although we've got four waitresses in in the dining room, only Jessie the head waitress is old enough to serve at the bar, and she really needs to be supervising the youngsters."

"Oh, I can show Anna how to do that," Rita said confidently. "I helped in the bars on bases when

Archie was posted overseas. Things can't have changed that much. As long as Jessie can deal with the questions over fancy wines, I can handle the beers and spirits. I might even remember a cocktail or two!"

"Thank God!" Brenda said with relief. "Otherwise, I have to keep dotting about between reception and the bar, and tonight we have folks arriving late who I'll need to see to."

Then as if to prove her point on how busy they were going to be, four different couples all turned up around the same time, and Rita took Anna's bags upstairs to their room while Brenda showed her the ropes. By the end of the night, Anna was already being left to get on with the reception desk, and Brenda was merely supervising her and Rita at the bar.

When Anna and Rita headed upstairs to bed, both worn out, some semblance of order had been restored to the hotel. The chef was no longer talking about quitting, the waitresses were happy because nobody was screeching at them at every turn, and all the new guests were booked in in the right rooms, while the existing ones were in blissful ignorance of any crisis having taken place.

"Job well done, ladies," Gary had said with a grin, as he settled in behind the reception desk to wait for the small party which had gone into Dumfries after dinner, and who would be coming back late on.

What surprised Anna was that both she and Rita were up in one of the turret rooms.

"Like Gary said, they're fully booked tonight," Rita explained, as Anna headed for the tiny shower room. "No room for me at the inn itself, so I'm bunking up here with you. This is going to be your room."

"Could you not have stopped with Gary?" Anna asked innocently, then seeing Rita's expression shift towards dismay, added, "Not that I don't want you here, Aunty! I just thought that you'd have been less cramped in his cottage."

"I believe he only has one bedroom," Rita said very pointedly, making Anna smother a smile as she closed the shower room door. Rita really was fighting this all the way, and yet Anna couldn't see why. Gary reminded her of what she'd heard of Archie in his ways, so it wasn't as though Rita wouldn't be compatible with him. But then that similarity might be the very sticking point, she belatedly realised.

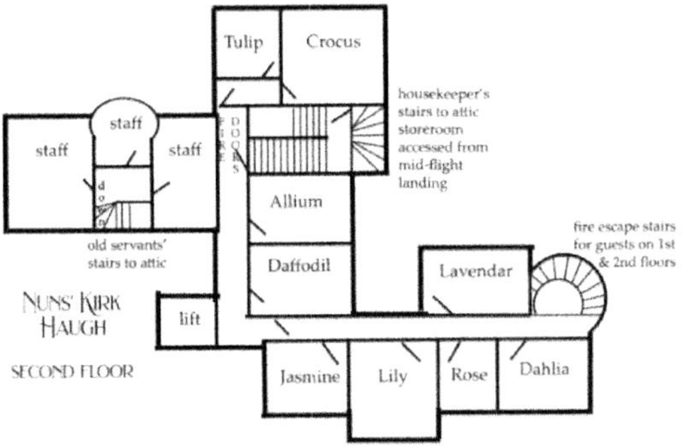

In the morning, Rita made her excuses and scurried off rather hurriedly, leaving Anna to get to grips with her new surroundings, and for the next two weeks in the run up to Christmas she was kept so busy she didn't have time to fret. The job itself was something she could practically do with her eyes closed, and so because she was living on site, she gladly took on the awkward shifts. With no manager to mess things around, everyone chipped in, and if one person couldn't do a shift, they got around it by swopping shifts between themselves. Cora came back from her sick leave in time for the main rush, as did Polly, and they and Anna found that they could get on. Even Gemma was enticed to come back and work at the hotel by Brenda and Gary, now that she could have her old shifts back.

Consequently, despite being still a bit short-handed, the festive season went by without any crises apart from the usual handful of awkward guests that any place could anticipate getting. One businessman complained vociferously upon checking out over not having been able to have his 'usual' room, and that the one he'd been given was too noisy. Luckily Gary was at the desk with Anna when he appeared, and cut him short by looming over him after the man had started thumping the desk with his fist.

"Look, you booked too late, that's all there is to it," Gary said firmly. "You know what Christmas is like! We get bookings coming in right from back in the summer, and if you don't tell us that you're coming until the week right before Christmas, then we canna hold a room on the off-chance. You only come for one night, man, but the couple who had 'your' room booked in for five all the way back in August. Book up earlier next year!"

"But I don't know my schedule back then," the man protested, and went away grumbling about never coming back.

"Ach, don't mind him," Gary said with a wink. "He just has to have his wee tantrum to let us know how important he is. He does it every few stays anyway, like he thinks we need to be kept on our toes." And he rolled his eyes before adding, "He'll be ringing up in a couple of weeks to book in for the start of February, you mark my words."

That was pretty much the kind of complaints Anna dealt with – the room was too hot, the room was too cold, there weren't enough towels despite the proper number having been put in by housekeeping – none of which amounted to much of anything. However, one really was out of the ordinary.

"That man upstairs gave me no peace last night!" a distressed lady came to the desk saying. "Up and down the bloody stairs in those damned heavy boots! Why do you allow reenactors in?"

"Reenactors?" Anna repeated, completely taken aback. "Madam, I can assure you, we have no reenactors booked in at all." She checked on the screen. "You were in Crocus, right?"

"Yes!"

Anna was puzzled. "Well, there is no 'upstairs' from your room. There was just Mr and Mrs Covington in the room next to you in that bit of the house, and they're a lovely older couple in their late seventies. I can't imagine that they would have been causing much noise. And there truly isn't a room up above yours, only the attic space. Was it the fire doors at the top of the main staircase that were banging? …I mean, they shouldn't…they have dampers on the closers precisely to make sure that doesn't happen, but I can have them checked."

"No, no, you silly girl!" Mrs Whittard snapped. "It was a man. I saw him! Saw him when I went out to look, though I wasn't going to show myself when I was in my nightie. All got up in his gear he was. Kilt, plaid, and bonnet – though all of it looked like it was second-hand and needed a damned good wash – *and* carrying one of those long gun things. You shouldn't allow those in a hotel!"

Being one of those hotels which catered for shooting parties in season, Anna knew that they did allow guns, but also that they were strictly locked away in the gun cabinet which only Gary and the manager (when they had one) had the keys to. More to the point, right now they had no shooting groups in, so the gun cabinet was empty. She was just about to point out that the chances of anyone getting past Gary during the night were nil, especially given that the main door had been locked all night, when Brenda came out of the back office – which was really more of an under-stair cupboard, but at least somewhere out of sight where the safe and other important things could be kept.

"Oh, that's one of our ghosts," she said blithely with a smile to Mrs Whittard.

"Ghost?" Mrs Whittard puffed herself up. "Well he was bloody noisy for a ghost!"

"Oh, he is," Brenda agreed, giving the customer her most winning smile. "We've tried to get rid of him, but he just won't go. Here, let me give you a discount on your stay for the disturbed night."

Anna let Brenda sit at the keyboard and saw her enter the discount in, but was puzzled when in the reason box, which only they ever saw, she saw Brenda type in BGAIA.

After Mrs Whittard and her husband had huffed and puffed their way out, Anna asked, "Bren', what's BGAIA?"

Brenda laughed. "Bloody Ghost At It Again."

Anna giggled at that but had to know, "Does it happen often, then?"

Brenda handed her the coffee she'd been making for them both and took a sip of her own. "Not enough that we're handing out those discounts all the time, thank heavens. But these two are strange ones."

"Two?"

"Oh yes. That's how we came to know your aunt, you see. When Gary came and found out about the ghosts, he knew Rita had a bit of a way with her with all things spooky. So he asked her to come down and see if she could put them to rest."

Anna thought that he might also have hoped that seeing him settling in somewhere so far from Grantown might have pushed Rita into making more of a commitment to him, but said nothing. That was between Gary and Rita, and Brenda didn't need to know that.

Instead, she asked, "And did she manage to quiet them down a bit? Clearly, they aren't fully gone."

Brenda shook her head. "Rita said that they have some really powerful connection to this place, but also to each other. She thinks one won't go until the other one does, and since we have no idea why they're haunting the place, that could be difficult to do. What a shame she's already been and gone before this one appeared again – she might have had another idea about what to do." Rita had indeed appeared for the main Christmas days, choosing to share with Anna again to allow the hotel to use the room she'd booked, but had fled north once more before Hogmanay and any risk of celebrations with Gary.

"Are both ghosts men?" Anna wondered.

"Yes, so no lost loves going on there. In fact, on rare occasions, you can actually hear them fighting…with swords! Doesn't happen very often, thank heavens, but I've heard it twice in the years I've been here. The thing which surprised Rita is that they seem to get more 'active', for want of a better word, if there's a lot of tension in the hotel. You know, if we have couples in who are obviously at odds with one another, or we have, say, a business group in mid-week for a conference, and you just know that two or three of them can't stand the sight of one another."

"Can you tell them apart? Do they haunt different parts of the hotel?"

"Sort of. We've never heard a peep out of either of them in the rooms in the back range – the ones above the dining room and kitchen – nor the ones over that end of the main hall. It's always focused on the front of the building. I've wondered where they would appear if the frontage was wider, you know…if we had a twin to the turreted tower on the other side at the front, I mean, not just the square one which lies further back. They've never been seen or heard out in the gardens there, but then they don't appear much on the ground floor either."

That made Anna ask, "Is it because the ground floor has been messed about with more, do you think? Do we know whether the hall and around here has changed much down the centuries?" Then she remembered what Rita had said about this building being Victorian, although over an older building, and before Brenda could answer, thought aloud, "Hang on, though. If this current place is Victorian, that doesn't sound as if it matches with the soldier, does it? …I mean if this 'house' in its current form was built in the 1880s, then by that time, even the Scottish regiments weren't fighting in plaids. Kilts or tartan trousers with jackets, maybe, but not full plaids."

Brenda agreed. "And you have to remember that the army was very slow to allow the kilt back as uniform. When this place was built, they were only a bit over a century away from the Jacobite rebellion in 1745, and the English were still wary of grassroots rebellions rising up. Personally, I've always been curious about who these two might be, but Margaret was very superstitious for such an otherwise sensible woman, and she wouldn't entertain the idea of what she called 'meddling with the dead'."

"What era do *you* think they're from?"

Delighted to have someone to talk to about this, Brenda grinned. "Oh, I think they might be Covenanters! Or at least one of them could be."

"What in heaven's name is a Covenanter?" Anna asked. "I've never heard of that…them…is it a 'them'?"

"Oh, it's definitely a 'them'! It goes back to Cromwell's time, you see. The people of Scotland – lairds and commoners alike – were right cheesed off with the way King Charles thought he could impose the English prayer book, and heavily leaning towards the Catholic forms of service, onto them. Across the country, people signed up to a document still known as the Solemn League and Covenant, which basically told King Charles where he could shove his prayer book and services. They were Protestants, you see – though that was still in in its relatively early days up here – and they dreaded there being a time when Scottish Protestants might suffer persecution the way English ones had under Henry the Eighth's daughter Queen Mary, before Elizabeth the First came to the throne. Not that either was ever our queen up here, because the thrones only merged after Queen Bess' death when James Stuart got the English throne."

"Wow! Full Tudor scandal, then." Anna gasped.

"Not Tudor but Stuart," Brenda corrected her. "That's when the Stuarts get the English throne, but the hoo-ha over the Covenant goes on for decades after James' succession. If you go up the road to Thornhill, there's a monument in Dalgarnock Kirkyard to the Nithsdale Martyrs, and there are dozens of names on that. And in Dumfries itself, in St Michael's Kirkyard there are memorials to the Pentland Martyrs and the Dumfries Martyrs.

"When I was at school we did a project on them, you see. Never forgot about that because our teacher at the time was really passionate about the subject. I can't remember all the ins and outs of the history, but I do remember that he said that, in his opinion, you can't understand the Jacobite rebellions until you know what came before, and what the divisions in Scotland already were by the time that Bonnie Prince Charlie put in an appearance."

"Ooh! The hero prince. He's very romantic," Anna gasped, making Brenda laugh.

"Aye, well I think the reality was more political history than your Walter Scott version. 'Dry as dust' is how I've heard a few folks describe the period, and a chap who used to stop here regularly at one time said it was as complicated as the Wars of the Roses down in England, although later on."

At that point they got busy again, and Anna had no further chance to talk to Brenda about it.

However, when the mayhem of Christmas had died down and they were in the brief interlude before the wildness of Hogmanay, Anna found herself sitting with Gary by the log fire in his cottage one afternoon. She had come to realise that the one and only downside of this job was that once she came off shift, she was faced with sitting on her own upstairs in her room for long periods of time. If one of the others was on an evening shift – and in fairness to the others, Brenda did do most Saturday nights as the senior receptionist, while Gemma and Cora were willing enough to do one late shift a week, just not all the ones they'd had forced upon them – then at least she could pop down for a chat and a coffee if it was quiet. Mornings off were easier, because she'd brought her old car down with her, and so she had begun exploring the area when the weather allowed. But at this time of year, it got dark so early that there wasn't time to do much if she was checking people out first thing, and then was handing over to one of the others until things got busy around dinner time. And so she had taken to wandering down the drive to Gary's, finding it more homely to sit in his tiny lounge and read, even if he was catching up on his sleep, than being alone up in the attic.

He'd made it clear that she was welcome any time, and so although she tried not to abuse the invitation, she was very glad of his generosity. More than that, Gary turned out to be a fascinating conversationalist. He could talk knowledgeably on a wide range of subjects without lecturing, and Anna loved hearing about some of the foreign places he'd been to, but also some of the things he'd found out in a lifetime of reading. So it was inevitable that one day they should get around to the subject of the ghosts.

"I think Brenda's right," Gary said. "The Covenanters would be the best fit for our lost soldier, but the thing is, there weren't any major battles around here. Over around Edinburgh it got very bloody, and another famous fight was at Killiecrankie up in Perthshire, which is kind of the point when history shifts to being about the Jacobites as a political entity rather than the Covenanters, who were all about religion."

"Killiecrankie? What a glorious name!"

Gary laughed. "Aye, that's a proper Scottish name for you. And it's a glorious spot right enough, right on the gorge of the River Garry. The autumn colours in the trees are something to see, but then that goes for the whole area up there around Loch Tay and Loch Tummel."

"I know those names. Aren't they in a song or something?"

"That they are," Gary said with a grin. "There was a time when you couldn'a get away from it around this time o' year." Then he grimaced. "Andy Stewart…every bloody Christmas on the telly, murdering every popular Scottish song, and reducing them to a god-awful mockery of Scottish culture fit only for the English – no offence to your presence there, Anna."

"None taken."

"But I've marched into some tough spots wi' pipers playing those tunes, and they fair stir the blood under those circumstances. The one you're thinking of is called *The Road to the Isles*, and I think it's harking back to the escape of Bonnie Prince Charlie to Skye after The Forty-Five all went wrong. I'm told it was first used to pipe troops into battle in World War Two, mind, because it was only composed early in the twentieth century, so the song itself isn'a that old. The bit you're thinking of is," and he sang,

"Sure by Tummel and Loch Rannoch and Lochaber I will go,
By heather tracks wi' heaven in their wiles.
If it's thinkin' in your inner heart, the

braggart's in my step,
You've never smelled the tangle o' the Isles."

"That's the one!" Anna exclaimed. "So those are real places, are they?"

"Oh, very much so. Going directly west from up around Culloden, you soon get into a huge mountain range, though I don't think geography could've been the composer's strong point, because there are other ways to get to Skye without coming all the way down to Loch Tummel. But once you *are* at Loch Tummel, you pretty much follow your nose on to Loch Rannoch, which even these days is pretty cut off, and then you're into the wild country of Lochaber, which is a region over in the west that these days is partly in the modern Highlands region, with a bit of north Argyll. Mind you, I'm no' that sure which way the prince himself went, partly because I always thought him a bit of a useless tit, myself," Gary confessed, making Anna giggle,

"That's no way to talk about a national hero."

"Hero, my arse! The wee shite buggered off back to Italy and left a lot of good men behind to die. And if he'd listened to the men who knew the country and the terrain well, he might even have won. Instead, he pithered and farted around, trying to play pretty politics, wasting valuable time, so that it all came to nought."

Then Gary gave a huff and dismissed the prince with a wave of his hand. "But that useless wee ninny himself wasn'a what I was coming to. A lot of the reasons why Scots fought on both sides by then goes back into the previous century to the Covenanters. And just like the English Civil War and the American one, families were split in two by this, and all the worse for it being a religious division. God knows, no war is good, but there's a damned good reason why, even before the famous Jacobite rebellions, that period in Scottish seventeenth century history is called The Killing Times."

1650

In Dumfries

A day later, Thomas and Robert (Rab) McBurney stood before their father and uncle with Presbyter Veitch.

"I demand this wench be brought to me and be put to question!" Veitch hissed almost manically.

Yet Alexander McBurney silenced him with an irritated wave of his hand.

"For the love of God, man! What do we charge her with? This has to stand up in a court of law. Not just before the Kirk. Do you want a repeat of the last time you dragged a member of that family in? The Kirk Session didn't back you, did it? They told you to let her go. So we cannot drag a young woman into the court on nothing but these accusations by my nephews and you. What if it backfires? What if the person who sits in judgement questions *their* morality?"

"They are sons of godly men!" Veitch spluttered. "Who would say such a thing?"

"A man who does not know them," Alexander said pointedly. "You know that the sheriffdom is about to change…or you should if you have paid any notice at all to worldly matters these last few years. King Charles is gone, and who knows what Cromwell might do? He now has the authority to appoint or dismiss any sheriff in any shire which was formerly under King Charles' rule."

Veitch blustered. "Scotland has always been separate from England. Cromwell has no authority north of the border."

"Oh, don't be a naive fool!" William McBurney interrupted him impatiently. "And how long do you think that will last in the face of Cromwell's army who have so resoundingly defeated the King's men? About as long as my hens when the fox gets in, that's how!"

As William and Presbyter Veitch ranted back and forth, Alexander McBurney sighed and thought back to their father. An astute survivor, Archibald McBurney had had the wit to flow with the political tides. If it was in favour of bending his knee to the bishop, then he would smile and invite him into his home. If it was more in favour of a man deciding his own path to God, then he would demur and regretfully decline a visit from a senior churchman, and conveniently be away from home at the relevant time. It was a skill which Alexander had made sure he had studied and learned, but it was one which his younger brother by eight years had singularly failed to master.

Another lesson learned was the advantage of sowing his wild oats far from home, where they would not rebound upon him. Right now, his own two younger sons were in St Andrews, admittedly doing who knew what, but with no danger of their indiscretions following them across the width of Scotland from the east coast into the west. Whereas William's sons were barely literate and with no chance of lasting even a month in some place of learning – especially when the family coffers were not extensive enough to be able to pay handsomely to keep them there despite their ignorance. It was something which he was developing a definite sympathy with their late father over, for he had complained to Alexander of the same dullness of mind in William, on the occasions when he had returned home from his studies for a break.

"What I shall do with your brother when he is of an age to start chasing skirts, I do not know," Alexander recalled his father saying to him in private. "I truly fear that he might drag us all through the dirt with his thoughtlessness."

It hadn't happened with William in the end, praise be! But it was looking perilously as if his sons might do the job for him. Presbyter Veitch might be a curmudgeon with no friends to speak of, but that didn't mean that the Presbyterian Kirk – governed by *The Solemn League and Covenant* of a few years ago – would disregard his complaints if he chose to make them. And against powerful men close to the government in Edinburgh, a local man of influence like Alexander wouldn't stand a chance. No, wild accusations of witchcraft thriving in this area must not get that far.

"Presbyter Veitch!" Alexander cut across his diatribe in an icy tone. "It is bad enough that a local woman died in your cellars without ever having the benefit of coming to trial. Do you really want me to have to report that another woman from your parish has died at your hands and in similar fashion?"

He saw Veitch gulp, before taking a deep breath, undoubtedly about to bluster and protest.

Holding up his hand almost in Veitch's face to halt him, Alexander ploughed on relentlessly, "Your piety and willingness to sully your hands in God's service does you great credit." That shut Veitch up. "But you must appreciate how it will appear to those who do not know a backwater such as this."

Dumfriesshire was hardly a backwater, but it was certainly a long and difficult journey across the width of the country from Edinburgh. Enough that Veitch had never been to the capital, nor attended any Presbyterian meetings there in the beating heart of Scottish politics – whereas Alexander had, and Veitch knew it, and that others did too.

"Therefore while your commitment to seek out any deviance within your flock is commendable," Alexander hurried on with, determined not to let Veitch get a word in as yet, "we have to bear in mind always how our actions will be seen by our superiors, do we not? The Kirk may lean towards every man determining his own fate with God, but that does not include flouting the laws of the land. So, while I do not doubt that this young woman may not be the most pious of your congregation, I cannot countenance you doing something which amounts to you taking the *law* into your own hands. And rightly or wrongly, the *law* does not allow you to subject women to questioning to the extent that they lose their lives. …Am I making myself clear?"

Veitch knew he had been outmanoeuvred, and William knew his older brother well enough to guess that things weren't going to go the way he had hoped, but Thomas and Robert had not caught up.

"She taunted us!" Thomas protested, his words slightly slurred by the quantity of wine he had drunk, even at this early hour, to brace himself to face his uncle.

"Presbyter, please leave us. I will handle this," Alexander said firmly. And with a face which could have curdled milk, Veitch stormed out, irate at having walked into a trap he hadn't foreseen, but unable to think his way out of right now.

As the door slammed behind him, Alexander turned on his nephews in fury.

"You lack-witted pair of empty scrotums." he fumed. "Taunted you? You mean she was possessed of a pair of breasts and a cunny, and she didn't fall flat on her back the moment you looked at her? I know who this girl is, and she is no whore. I do not doubt that some in her family have been suspect in their practices for many years, but *she* has not! Anyway, why you would want *her* when there are many girls better favoured in the neighbourhood, and more willing to subject themselves to your less than gentle attentions, I do not know. But you *will* stop this persecution of her this instance, do you hear me?"

As Robert and Thomas made to protest, he gave a curt chop of his hand to halt them. "No! You listen to me! We have no way of knowing how things will go in the next few years. If you've never paid attention to parliament and the king before now, then make sure you start.

"King Charles may be dead, but his son became King Charles the Second the moment the axe severed his father's life. And how many Catholic lairds are there in the Highlands, eh? Enough that, even if King Charles never regains the English throne, he could take back the *Scottish* one with the aid of a Catholic force from across the sea. And he's more Scotland's king by heritage than he ever was England's. Well, the border lies *south* of here and that means that Cromwell may yet lose to the king's supporters up here." And he thumped the wooden arm of his chair repeated with his fist for emphasis as he went on.

"Up *here*, it's been far less clear who might win. Montrose has had his victories for the Royalists, and Argyll has been every bit as successful for the

Covenant, but history hasn't decided the winner yet. Moreover, while every man and his dog signed up to the Covenant back when it was first drawn up, there are many whom nowadays – and decades on from when their forebears signed – find the strictures of such a censorious Kirk hard to live with, and would welcome a more …shall we say *practical*, way of life. And that includes many far more powerful than either your father or me.

"Therefore if we, over here in Dumfriesshire, are seen to be a hotbed of radical Presbyterianism, there is no guarantee that our actions will be looked upon kindly even by the *current* heads of the Kirk. Do I make myself understood? So you *will* attend kirk like good Christian men, and you may *verbally* condemn all who practice witchcraft. But you will *not* hunt them down like the fox that just raided the hen house! Am I clear?"

With sullen nods Robert and Thomas signalled their understanding, but Thomas couldn't refrain from snapping at his father as they turned to leave, "I thought I was getting Johnne Allen's croft?"

"Johnne Allen's croft?" his Uncle Alexander bellowed at the pair's backs, forcing them to turn and face his wrath once more. "You couldn't run a croft if your lives depended on it! Either of you. God and all his saints have mercy. You pair haven't a grain of sense between you! Johnne Allen is better left where he is and *paying* us handsomely for the privilege of being left alone. You leave the thinking to me, do you hear? Now get out!"

But outside, Thomas turned to Robert and said, "I won't forget this witch humiliating us like this. One day I'll get her and her witch of a mother, I swear I will!"

Chapter 6

Anna gave a shiver. "The Killing Times? That sounds grim."

Gary gave a terse nod. "Aye, it was. I don't know nearly enough about it to tell you anything in detail, just that it happened, and a lot of it around here. So when it comes to our ghosts, it wouldn't surprise me in the least if they weren't related in some way to back then."

As a result, Anna found herself with a new project to while away the spare hours with. A trip to Dumfries to register at the library had her coming back with a couple of books to get started with, but she soon realised that she was going to have to get a whole lot more information to make sense of it all. A glossy booklet gave her a brief introduction to the great houses of Dumfries and Galloway, including the great castle of Drumlanrig, owned by the Duke of Buccleuch and Queensbury and containing an incredible art collection, but that wasn't the kind of information Anna was looking for.

Resigning herself to the fact that she was going to have to buy the books she needed via Amazon, she feared that because of that, her research was going to be slow going. And in truth, her feelings of urgency had faded. With the dull months of late winter now here, the hotel was quieter, especially at the weekends given that the weather was less inviting for those wanting weekend breaks away, and presumably as a result neither ghost had reappeared. The business customers were still arriving, but in general, the hotel was emptier and they didn't need to use as many rooms, sticking to the ones at the rear of the hotel where possible.

More personally pressing, all of the staff were getting a touch anxious over the rather more important fact that a new manager still hadn't yet appeared. Between them, Brenda, Gary, and Anna were doing a good job of holding the fort, but as Brenda pointed out, they were coming into the season when people would want to start booking weddings for next year, and neither she nor Gary was happy about taking bookings of that size and value off their own initiative.

"We're talking thousands of pounds," Brenda said worriedly. "I mean, I can talk to Emilio," who was the head chef, "and ask him what he can cope with, but bloody Perdita harassed the sous chef so much that he left a couple of weeks before you came. Emilio coped over Christmas by us taking on a couple of kids from the local college who were doing catering, and wanted the experience during the Christmas holidays. And you know I've been covering breakfasts on Emilio's day off.

"But we can't carry on like that through the whole of the summer, not least because of the weddings we've got booked for *this* year! We *have* to have someone here who can hire people. The weddings start in late April when the two kids we used at Christmas are doing exams and so can't help much, and it's unfair to ask Emilio to cater for a huge wedding party alone, even if they have taken over the whole hotel, meaning he hasn't got to try and cater for other guests as well. And if we get it wrong, then the bookings will soon dry up for next year, because you wouldn't believe how fast the word gets around that somewhere's standards have started to slip."

"Oh, I would," Anna sympathised. "Social media is a nightmare for that! One complaint and you can lose dozens of customers. That was dinned into us at the supermarket. You do whatever you can to keep the sods happy, because it's more cost effective to take the hit of one person's unrealistic expectations, than lose the trade for months from multiples of others after they've told every man and his dog how hacked off they are – rightly or wrongly."

Brenda reached over and squeezed her hand affectionately. "Thank God we got you, because you get it. I'm not so bloody sure our owners do!"

"Who does own us?" Anna asked. "I don't think Gary has ever said."

Brenda rolled her eyes in exasperation. "Well, that's another of life's little mysteries, isn't it!"

"How do you mean?"

With a huff of exasperation Brenda explained, "Up to Christmas 2019 we were owned by one of those pension investment funds, and had been for about ten years. But of course, with the whole Covid thing, we obviously didn't look like such a secure prospect anymore. Oh, they paid us furlough out of the government scheme, so we kept our jobs, but they put the business up for sale pretty much as soon as the first lockdown ended.

"It took a while, but then we were bought by the current owners. We all had a letter saying that our jobs were safe for now, and that they weren't planning on making any major changes – which to be frank, at the time we were relieved by. I think we'd all been dreading that someone would want the building and the grounds to make into luxury flats or something, you see. Well, they wouldn't need any of us for that, would they?"

"Oh gosh, no!" Anna sympathised. "Heavens, you must have all been worried sick that you would lose your jobs. And to be frank, there's not much around here besides tourism and farming, is there? Not unless you go into Dumfries itself. I mean, there's probably work at the hospital and in retail, but with so many people coming out of hospitality right now, jobs like those – or at least the ones worth having – would be as rare as hen's teeth."

"That was exactly it," Brenda said, with an approving smile for Anna's instant grasp of the situation. "So it all seemed good for a while. But then Margaret retired. I can't blame her. Her William was retiring, and their kids don't live locally anymore, so the chance to go and see the grandchildren more often, plus being able to do the stuff they'd always promised themselves they would when they retired, was too much to pass over. And that's when we started to get a bit worried. It began to feel as if there was no hand on the rudder, if you get my meaning. No sense of urgency that we needed a manager."

"Oh dear."

"Oh dear, indeed," Brenda said witheringly. "And look what we got! Miss flighty-pants Perdita! Who the heck interviewed her and thought she'd be a good idea I do not know, but they surely don't know hospitality! Nobody with an atom of experience would have hired her!"

Things suddenly became clearer for Anna. "So that's why Polly and Gemma walked out! It wasn't just Perdita, it was everything that had led up to her coming. They must have wondered what on earth was going to happen next, because even if she went, if the owners are that clueless, then you could get another one just like her. Oh dear. That's not good. Not good at all."

"I've sent emails to the head office email address that I've got," Brenda said, glowering at the computer screen, as if daring it to suddenly ping back into life and announce that an email had just arrived. "But all I've had so far is a bloody stony silence! If they're professionals, surely *somebody* would have sent a reply, even if it was only an acknowledgement of the fact that I've contacted them?"

It was something which niggled away at Anna for the rest of the day and the next, until finally she managed to get Gary alone, and away from where they might be overheard. Explaining what Brenda had said, she tentatively asked him, "Do you think that I should apply for the manager's job? I mean Brenda is effectively the assistant manager, even if she's called the head receptionist. So I don't think she'd be too appalled at working with me, would she? ...Unless she's said something to you when I wasn't there?"

Whatever response she was expecting, it wasn't Gary's huff of relief and, "Oh, thank God! I was wondering how to try and push you to get you to apply."

"Really?"

He nodded vigorously. "Yes! Heavens, lass, you've been picking up the reins without even realising you're doing it. You're a bloody natural. But better still, everyone likes you, and even Gemma is talking to Sarah – another old hand who quit – about the possibility of coming back if you were to take over."

"But Gary, I don't have a clue about organising

weddings. I could cost the company a fortune if I get it wrong!"

"Lass, Brenda can do weddings in her sleep as long as she doesn't have to try and do everything else as well. She can teach you everything you need to know. And anyway, the kind of more-money-than-sense couples who want the fancy 'Highland wedding' experience usually bring in their own wedding organiser. All *we* have to do is liaise with *them,* and tell them whether or not what they want is possible, and *that* you'll have no issue dealing with."

Anna was stunned. She hadn't really thought about making this her permanent home. In her mind she'd be here for a year, maybe, while she got her life sorted out. Though what she was actually going to do was something she hadn't got around to deciding as yet, primarily because it had been such a relief to get here and then have nothing more than the job to focus on. Jensen, and all the complications connected to him, were blissfully absent, and when she wasn't on shift, she'd tried to work on getting back to her old self. Life pre-Jensen might not have been exciting, but she hadn't gone through it feeling as if she was permanently treading on eggshells, and moreover eggshells which contained hidden bombs which then unexpectedly blew up in her face, as happened whenever her mother and Jensen's got together.

Yet sitting here with Gary, she realised that she had enjoyed these last few weeks more than anything she'd done in the way of a job in a very long time. The little room up in the turret had begun to feel like home rather than an isolated eyrie, and as she'd got to know everyone better, all the staff were people she could get on with, and some were rapidly becoming friends. Nobody was clawing for promotion, or to make themselves seem better in the eyes of senior management, and if Emilio was rather volatile, that was only to be expected given that more than any of them, he was run ragged. With the icing on the cake being the glorious location of *Nuns' Kirk Haugh* itself, she wondered now how she would feel if she was told that she would have to leave?

And there was Gary himself. If he was a bit young to be the dad she'd always wanted, he was certainly fitting into the role of a trustworthy uncle she could talk to about just about anything, and that was something which she'd never had before. It was such a novel, but lovely, experience to discover a man she could talk to as freely as she did with Aunt Rita. Not necessarily about the same things, of course – if only out of respect for not embarrassing him, there were certain subjects she would steer clear of – but he was someone she certainly felt comfortable discussing practical matters with, and whose advice she would accept without fear of him having the kind of agendas her parents had always had.

"Are you going to apply, then?" Gary's voice broke her reverie. "Only if you are, for the love of God, would you do it soon? We don't want another bloody Perdita landing on our doorstep before you've even sent anything."

There was an affectionate twinkle in his eye, and she found herself responding with a grin. "I'd better shift myself and go and find the application form, then, hadn't I."

Together they walked down the short track from the old stable block and into reception, yet when they got there and told Brenda what Anna wanted to do, to their collective surprise they could find no current application form. Until now, Anna had let Brenda do any contacting of their owners, thinking that that was more appropriate, but as she now tried to help Brenda hunt down any form, Anna was shocked at how little information there was.

"Who the hell are these people?" she muttered in frustration. "Who doesn't have a website these days? It's like *Ferguson Investments* as a company doesn't really exist!"

They tried searching Companies House but drew a blank there too.

"This is getting worse by the minute," Brenda said worriedly. "If our wages hadn't been paid on time every month, I'd be downright panicking!"

"Maybe it's not a 'them' but a 'who'?" Gary suggested. "Some rich multi-millionaire?"

Anna worriedly glanced up at him. "I'm not sure that that's not worse. Rich playboys aren't known for their stability, are they? They move from one new thing to another, making money all the way, but leaving trails of devastation for ordinary people in their wake. *Nuns' Kirk Haugh* might have been owned by 'him' for over a year now, but does that mean that the reason why we've had no contact is because 'he' – whoever he might be – is now running out of interest in us? We could be in a shockingly precarious position if that's the case."

"Now dinna fret, ladies," Gary said soothingly, catching Anna's eye and then looking at Brenda, whom Anna belatedly realised was rather pale and looking very worried indeed. It made Anna realise that in many ways she was the one with the least to lose here. If the worst came to the worst, she still had her flat back down in Worcester, and with no particular ties, she could move to wherever there was work. As an older lady with family to consider, Brenda was in nothing like as good a position, and neither were most of the rest of the staff. Even Gary could end up sofa-surfing at friends' houses if *Nuns' Kirk Haugh* folded, because Rita had told her that a messy divorce many years ago when he was still in the army, meant that Gary had retired from army life with no house to call his own.

"I'll send an email," she said firmly. "Surely they must have at least read your emails to them, Brenda? So that seems like the way to get someone's attention when we don't seem to have a postal address, and you said the phone doesn't always get answered. And I'd been planning on moving jobs even before Jensen came on the scene, even if I hadn't found anything yet, so I know my CV off almost by heart. It won't take me long to type it in."

That evening Brenda broke the news to the others who'd come in on duty that Anna was applying, and immediately Emilio and Gemma insisted on sending emails of their own to whoever *Ferguson Investments* might be, begging them to please approve Anna's appointment, Emilio in particular pointing out that he needed someone he could work with and who would get him the staff he so desperately needed. He even threatened to leave if they didn't – which startled Anna as she helped him write it out, written English not being his forte – because as he pointed out, there were a lot of hotels clamouring for head chefs of his calibre post-pandemic, and the only reason he'd stayed so far was because he liked the people he was with.

"I like it here," he told Anna as they walked through to the kitchen – she to get a much-needed cup of tea, and he to start preparing the evening food now that he knew how many guests they had in tonight. "It remind me of home." He waved a hand at the window. "I grow up in hills like this. Not quite so green, especially in summer, but better than London where I first come to England." He pulled a face. "I don't like the concrete jungle."

Anna laughed. "I don't like concrete jungles either, Emilio. And like you, I would be very sad to leave this place. I don't know why, but I feel like I belong here in a way I've never felt anywhere else."

She didn't add that she also had a quiet nagging feeling that she was supposed to do or accomplish something while she was here, and whatever it was, she hadn't done it yet. Time and again she would turn a corner when she was in the main building, and feel as if she had just missed seeing something or someone. More often than not it was when she was on one of the upper floors, but even down here on the ground floor, there were times when she was on the reception desk and she'd get the sensation of someone watching her.

Even odder, that ought to have creeped her out, yet didn't. There had been one Christmas at the supermarket when they'd been hideously understaffed due to an outbreak of flu, and Anna had had to do several shifts up on the checkouts. And it had been there that she'd witnessed one of their local oddities just standing and staring at one of the younger checkout girls through the large plate glass windows at the front of the store.

He'd clearly got something of a crush on the very pretty teenage girl, and had done nothing more than stare, until the store manager had told him in no uncertain terms that it had to stop, not least because of the distress it was causing the object of his attentions. And even though Anna had done nothing but be a bystander, the experience then had deeply unsettled her. The fact that a stranger could develop such an interest in you without you having done anything more than speaking to them in passing was not a comfortable thought, and she had been quite jumpy on her way home for several weeks. So getting the sensation that her ghostly watcher was no threat was not how she would have expected to feel.

The following day Jessie, the head waitress, was on duty, as was Polly, and both of them insisted that they too would like to send an email pushing for Anna to stay. It was very flattering, if a bit overwhelming, and Anna began to have a touch of nerves, hoping that she wouldn't let them all down. Yet to everyone's astonishment, late in the afternoon an email came through from someone signing themselves as Helen Wiseheart, saying that she was pleased to confirm Anna as the new manager, and that a letter to her personally would follow.

"I thought most people sent things like that by email, these days," a rather shell-shocked Anna said, as there was an outbreak of universal joy around her. "But then given that they've never asked for a personal email address off me, I suppose it's better that they don't send something like that in an open email to the hotel's address."

"I don't care how they bloody do it!" exclaimed Brenda. "I'm just so relieved that we all know where we stand once more. I'll ring Sarah and tell her that she's safe to come back, and that will get our front of house team back up to full-strength, because with Sarah taking the remaining shifts, I can get back to running the bar only part-time at the weekends and without being on my knees."

"How many kitchen staff do we need?" Anna asked Brenda, realising that two glasses of celebratory prosecco had gone down rather fast, and that she was feeling a touch lightheaded over everything that she now needed to get done.

Gary wrapped a comforting arm around her shoulders. "One who knows one end of the kitchen from the other, for definite. We need to give Emilio a fortnight's leave as soon as possible – or at least the weekdays off – so that the poor man can go into the Easter weddings not totally exhausted. So an assistant chef for him and another new full chef would be a good idea." He drew Anna over to the huge inglenook fireplace, away from the excited conversation going on over the phone between Brenda and Sarah. "Up until Herself turned up and mucked things up spectacularly, we had one young waitress on the dining room duty on Monday through to Thursday, and another with her who was old enough to serve drinks. Weekday lunchtimes we don't do full food service, as you know, but Polly, Sarah, or Gemma would serve drinks from the bar to those who wanted, and make the odd sandwich or salad if asked."

Getting her head around the idea of rotas, Anna breathed a sigh of relief as she realised that actually it wasn't even going to be as complicated as sorting the rotas in the supermarket. There, they'd needed at least one or two people continuously around on all sections from eight in the morning until nine at night, with no gaps in the middle, and more at peak times. Here, once breakfast was over, she could forget about the dining room until the evening. The three ladies who did housekeeping – Kim, Laura, and head housekeeper Sally – plus Madge and Colette the cleaners for the public areas, hadn't been disrupted during Perdita's toxic time, and so had ticked along on their set rotas, and therefore now didn't need to be worried about. So her real priority was getting the catering sorted, not least because *Nuns' Kirk Haugh* had built a reputation for high-quality Scottish cuisine.

"Right!" she said with more authority than she actually felt. "Who got in touch with the lads we had at Christmas?"

Gary grinned rather ruefully. "Ah, that would be me. …Well, I couldn'a let Emilio walk out, could I? Jings, lass! He makes the best tattie scones I've ever tasted. And his haggis, neeps, and tatties could win awards."

Anna inhaled the last of the prosecco she'd just been drinking. "Gary! You crafty sod, you!" she spluttered, hurriedly grabbing a tissue to mop up and hoping that nobody had seen it coming out of her nose. "What about his truffle sauce and his pigeon en croûte?"

"Bugger the pigeon en croûte!" Gary said in horror. "A man could starve to death on what's on those wee things! I need something that sticks to my ribs a bit more than that to keep me going, and so do those lads who keep coming back here when they're working in the area."

Anna had to laugh with him, but then said firmly, "Right then, if you made contact with them the first time, you're going to do it again. If we've got no chance of recruiting all those staff we need in the normal way, we're going to give the youngsters a chance. We're going to approach the local college, and offer to take on some of those leaving this summer with part-time contracts so that they can carry on studying. That way, we can have help in the kitchen every night, and at the end of it we can pick the best of them and keep them on, while the others will have a reference from us to help them in their next job."

"Now that is what I call a plan," Gary said approvingly. "See I told you you were a natural."

"Well don't get too carried away yet. I've got to find an experienced chef yet, and for that I'm going to have to advertise further afield."

"Oh, that won't be a problem," Gary said airily, words which would come back to bite him in a way he couldn't have anticipated.

Chapter 7

As a result of Anna and Gary's conversation, two days later they were sitting in the local college in Dumfries, chatting to the head of department having already had a conversation with the principal over the phone. Anna could quite legitimately say that she was the new manager at *Nuns' Kirk Haugh*, and with a bit of nifty footwork, they managed to get around saying what Gary's precise role was, Anna covering all bases by saying, "Mr McAllister has been the stabilising factor during my predecessor's rather chaotic few months."

It was emphasised by Gary's characteristic Scottish sniff of disdain and his terse comment of, "Aye, she upset everyone. Customers. Staff. Even the delivery men who only came a couple of times a month. It takes a rare talent to be able to do that much damage in such a short space of time, but she had it!"

Anna then moving swiftly on with, "I'm not going to pretend, Mr Morris, that we're anything other than a little short of desperate for staff at this stage. We've got a calendar full of weddings coming up over the summer, a brilliant head chef, but nobody to help him. We were very impressed with Callum and Richie at Christmas, and so I'm really hoping that we can offer some more of your students the chance to get hands-on experience.

"I'm not expecting miracles. I know these young people are still learning their trade, and I'm not trying to cherry-pick your brightest and best either. I'd rather have students who aren't at the top of their classes, but who genuinely want a career in catering. It matters less to me that they're headed for a slot on *Master Chef* than the fact that they turn up every day. Someone willing we can bring on. The student who has an absolute flair, but who is at college only to mark time until they turn eighteen and can leave, is of far less interest to me. The ones with a genuine desire to become chefs we can bring on at their own pace, but we don't have a big enough operation to cope with those who get bored after the first week and don't turn up for shifts."

The result was that by the time they left, they had the names of two more late teens that would be joining Callum and Richie in the kitchens as Emilio's apprentices, both of them more than delighted to accept the offer of one evening shift during the week, and another at the weekend. Two shifts a week, they had agreed with the tutors, was unlikely to interfere with their studies, and if they couldn't cope with weekend work then they were never going to get very far in the hospitality industry anyway. Anna thought it was a shame that none of them were girls, but they had four girls who were almost desperate to come and learn the front of house stuff, and who would be happy enough to do things like preparing desserts and cold starters if necessary.

"I think we got away with that," Anna said, as she sank gratefully into the passenger seat of Gary's battered old Toyota pick-up. Taking off the jacket of the suit she had acquired only that morning, she pulled on her warmer quilted jacket against the January chill. They had got into Dumfries in time to be at the local Marks & Spencer when it opened to get Anna a couple of suits, and then had nipped into a nearby coffee shop so that she could get changed in the loo in order to present a professional appearance. Gary had double-checked her for stray price labels which might have given the game away, and so now, like a couple of giggling teenagers themselves, they headed back to the hotel to break the good news to Emilio.

Rather more difficult was the acquisition of at least one more experienced chef, and Anna decided that rather than waste time advertising locally, she would put an advert into one of the trade magazines. With rather nice accommodation potentially on hand in one of the cottages next to Gary, there was at least the incentive of someone not having to drive miles to and fro after a hard shift.

"What we need," Anna confided to Gary as they drove home, "is some poor chef who's absolutely skint after a divorce, experienced, and who will grab a job with accommodation with both hands, and stick with us because of it. We don't need Jamie Oliver or Gordon Ramsey. We need someone who will follow Emilio's lead and not upset the apple cart. Dear God, with the hours most chefs have to work, there must be more than a few failed marriages out there!"

It was the opening Gary had been waiting for. "And what about your marriage?" he asked as he negotiated his way out of Dumfries. "What are you going to do about that?"

"Do?" Anna was surprised. "I wasn't thinking about 'doing' anything much about it as yet. I was waiting for everyone to calm down before I even picked up the phone."

"So what name are you going to sign your contract as?" Gary said pointedly.

Breathing a sigh of relief, Anna told him, "It will be Anna Gracie, the same as it's always been. That way, if they do decide to ask for references, that's the name everybody knows me as. What possible point would there be in using the name Anna Coleborn? The sad fact is that I was her only for a matter of hours. I didn't even sign the register as that, did I? Because you do that for the last time in your maiden name. There isn't a single document where I've signed my married name, so why would I use it now?"

She saw the truth of that sink in, and then Gary said, "Aye, well put like that, I suppose you're right. But what if yon Jensen's father comes hunting you? Would he no' be looking for Anna Gracie? It's no' exactly a common surname, is it?"

Anna shook her head. "Not south of the border, no. But we're not south of the border, are we? Up here, though, it's less rare even though you're right, and it's not common. And I'm hardly where he's going to be looking for me."

Gary mulled that over and then agreed, "I suppose you're right. And the only alternative would be to change your name by deed poll to something totally unexpected …and that would take time. I don't suppose Jensen's father is a patient man when it comes to things like that, so whichever name you use, there's a chance he'll find you."

"To be honest," Anna said with a sigh, "I'm far more concerned with getting everything ready for Valentine's Day than my unloved in-laws turning up. We've got just two weeks, once the apprentices start, to get them halfway up to speed before the hotel gets rammed full again. That's definite. My in-laws aren't."

To Anna's intense relief, all of the young people they'd engaged via the college turned out to be enthusiastic and willing to learn.

"That's a major feather in your cap to start off with," Brenda told her happily, as they waited at the desk for the first of the Valentine's Special Break guests to arrive. "Nobody Perdita took on stayed even as long as they have so far."

With Valentine's Day this year falling on a Monday, Margaret had set up the Valentine's Special Break offer even before she left, aware that many couples would want to make a long weekend of it. Even better, Perdita had been so busy wrecking what was in front of her that she hadn't bothered about something which she had seen as far away in the calendar. It had resulted in Gemma and Brenda quietly taking the bookings in the autumn, and keeping everything crossed that the dreadful woman wouldn't still be with them when it happened.

"And she isn't!" Gemma declared with delight when she spoke to Anna about it. "How great is that? All twenty-one rooms fully booked, and the self-catering cottages as well."

It was certainly going to be a good workout to test things before the weddings fully began, Anna thought, because some couples were arriving on the Friday but would only stay until the Sunday – merely making the token nod towards the day itself – at which point those rooms were booked for the special three-day/two-night break with people arriving then, who would stay until the Tuesday. Brenda had had the excellent idea of offering a late checkout for those leaving on Sunday, allowing them to vacate their rooms as normal by eleven, but with their baggage stored and a special Sunday lunch (or special Tuesday lunch for the others) laid on for them included in the price, to allow for a leisurely end to the break. That one-off weekday lunch was unlikely to be the breaking point for the chefs.

"Thank God it's half-term at the college and the students are up for all the shifts they can get," Anna had confided in Gary regarding that. "Poor Emilio would be on his knees by Tuesday if he hadn't got any help. As it is, Callum and that new lad Roger are good enough to cope with the limited lunch menu on Tuesday by themselves, so if Brenda can do Tuesday breakfast, Emilio can collapse after Monday night's evening meal."

There hadn't been sufficient time between Anna placing the adverts for anyone to start yet as Emilio's right-hand chef, and Anna had hoped to have had a couple of instant responses by now, yet none had been forthcoming.

"The only thing that could have been better is if we could have had a trial run of a new chef," she sighed to Brenda, as they heard the crunch of tyres on the gravel outside, speaking of guests arriving and about to unload bags.

Yet when the problems came, they weren't in the kitchen. Down on the ground and lower-ground floors, everything ran like clockwork. The students in the kitchen followed Emilio's lead, and the girls doing front of house happily mucked in with preparing the cold starters and desserts in a way that the other waitresses didn't. Even better, their example and enthusiasm seemed to be the shot in the arm that the existing waitresses needed to up their standards. So it was a shock to Anna when Sally came tearing downstairs on the Saturday morning looking very worried and saying, “Anna, I don’t suppose you could come and lend us a hand, could you?”

Anna looked at the booking screen to double-check. No, she was right, nobody was due to check out today, so there shouldn’t have been any need for any more work than making beds and providing clean towels for those that wanted them.

“Whatever’s wrong?” she asked, getting to her feet and feeling safe to abandon the reception desk for now.

Sally visibly cringed. “It’s the couple in Rosemary. It looks like a bomb’s gone off in there! I’ve no idea where they are, but the room’s absolutely upside down! Heaven knows what they were getting up to, but even on a Valentine’s weekend this is a bit extreme.”

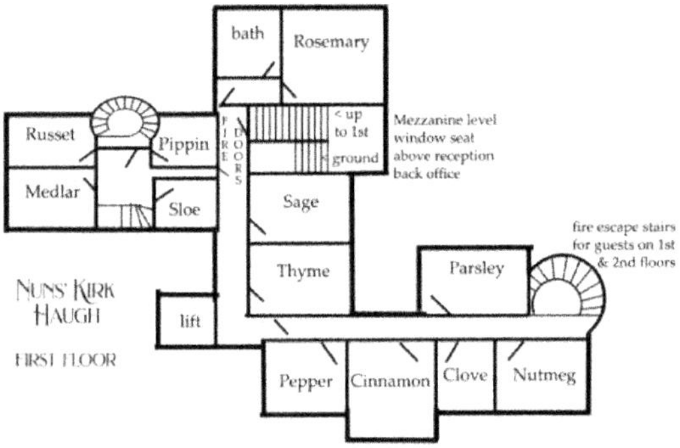

Her heart sinking into the smart black ballet shoes she’d taken to wearing while on duty, Anna followed Sally up the main staircase to the first floor, and through the fire doors to where Rosemary formed almost a suite by itself. It was the largest of the rooms facing onto the front and the most prestigious, which meant that damage to it could cost the hotel dearly if they couldn’t accommodate the guests who were next in should repairs need to be done. What on earth she could hope to do if the generous en-suite bathroom was damaged she couldn't imagine, because even an emergency plumber over the weekend was going to be hard to get.

As she walked in through the door behind Sally, she couldn't help but gasp, "Oh my God!"

The bed's mattress was tipped up on one side and off the bed, the bedclothes were strewn across the floor, and there was even a towel hanging from the light fitting! Lipstick was scrawled across the mirror of the lovely antique dressing table – though what the 'words' said was anyone's guess – and the curtains on the side window of the room had been ripped off their pole. Mercifully the main curtains were still attached, and as best Anna could see in one glance, undamaged. Dashing into the bathroom as best she could without getting her feet entangled in the sheet and duvet, she breathed a ragged sigh of relief when she took in that all the taps and shower were still attached, and the loo looked like it was still functional.

"Phew!" she gulped, and Sally, realising why Anna had prioritised that, gave a shaky smile in agreement.

"I've got Kim doing the other rooms," she said, "but I can't shift that king-sized mattress on my own."

"No problem," Anna assured her, "but I'm going to get Gary first, and ask him if he can bring the steps up to put the curtains back up and check that the pole isn't about to come off after the way they've been yanked around. Whatever possessed them to make this mess?"

It was only as she was going back downstairs that it dawned on her that she hadn't seen Gary that morning. It wasn't automatic that he would be there every day, not least because he got two nights off mid-week, but when the hotel was full like this, it was unusual for him to not be around when she came on duty at seven in the morning to make sure everything was in order for those wanting early breakfasts. At reception she picked up the phone and dialled over to his cottage, then got more worried when he didn't answer after three attempts. By that time, she'd gone back upstairs and helped Sally lug the heavy mattress back onto the bed, and had fetched cleaning stuff to get the lipstick off the mirror.

Only when Gary came and stuck his head around the bedroom door, as she was buffing the mirror to a gleaming finish, did she find out why.

"That bloody ghost's been at it again," he said grimly. "There I was, just thinking that I could go and get my head down for a bit on the camp bed in the back office when the young couple from in here came batting down the stairs, scared out of their wits. The young lass, Sandy, was in tears, and I don't think Josh was far off."

"Where the hell are they?" Anna asked worriedly, having visions of Gary having to help them pack and them now about to sue the pants off the hotel.

"Over in the sous chef's cottage," Gary said with more calm than Anna was feeling. "It's not quite what they booked, but I've told them we'll sort something out with the bill, and that they can stay for an extra night on us if they want. It's not as though we've got a chef in there at the moment."

"Ah, so just for once Perdita did something right in getting that decorated so that it could be used as an overspill, even if she failed with the furnishings," Anna recalled with relief. "Granted it was a daft idea to think that we wouldn't need it for a chef, but a blessing today."

"Aye," Gary said with a sniff. "I suppose I have to give her that. And once I'd got the log burner going over there, and poured them both a large glass of wine, they did calm down a bit. I came back over and got all of their things from out of here for them, because nothing would persuade them to come back."

"I did wonder where all their things had gone to," Anna admitted. "Was anything damaged?"

"Apart from being thrown around? No," Gary reassured her, looking a bit puzzled.

"The lipstick," Anna said pointedly. "Was there more?"

"Lipstick? What lipstick?"

She took her phone out of her pocket and showed him the photographs she had taken before she and Sally had started to clear up. "I took these thinking that the guests had done this," she explained, "and wanted proof in case they balked at paying for the extra cleaning." Then she took in Gary's shock as he took the phone off her and scrolled back to the mirror and what had been revealed on one of the windows too. "Did you not see this?"

"That was definitely *not* here at three a.m.!" he said firmly. "I came in and the bed was all in a mess, and their clothes were all out of the wardrobe. But the mattress all tipped up like that? No! Nothing that bad. That has to have happened after I grabbed their things. I must have missed one of Sandy's lipsticks for the ghost to have used it."

Anna winced. "Then I'd better brace myself for complaints from the people upstairs too. They're bound to have heard the bumps and bangs."

Gary grimaced and sucked air in through his teeth. "Aye… Well I may have pre-empted you a wee bit there. I was trying to be as quiet as I could, but I think they must have heard something. …Ach, well clearly, they *did* hear something, albeit afterwards!"

"Gary?"

He looked uncomfortable. "You know I carry the phone around with me, so when they called down to the front desk I was able to pick it up. They'd heard Sandy scream, and at first they thought it was all a bit passionate…you know, Valentine's and all that. Well, they're a loved-up young couple themselves."

"Oh yes. They're the young couple in their twenties who've just got engaged." Anna remembered.

"Michael and William, aye. I might not have gone up to their room if there had been a lady there – wouldn't want to embarrass anyone in their nightie, you understand. But two lads… Didn'a think I'd be seeing anything I hadn't encountered in the army."

"Emm…quite. So you went and knocked on their door?"

"Aye. Told them that the hotel's resident ghost was a bit frisky tonight. They seemed to take it as an added bonus rather than wanting to complain. Said they couldn'a wait to get back to Edinburgh and tell their friends."

"Well I hope they still feel that way this morning," Anna said, crossing her fingers, "because it looks like it got a lot rowdier in here after you left."

When she got downstairs again, she managed to track down Michael and William, who'd been out enjoying a post-breakfast walk in the wider grounds and had just come back in to warm up with a coffee in the hall.

"I do hope you weren't too upset by the noise," she apologised straight away. "Since I've been here our ghost has only put in an appearance once, and that was to walk up and down the stairs."

"Ooh! There were *two* of them!" Michael told her, his eyes shining with excitement. "We heard them, didn't we, William? The one shouted at the other that he was the servant of the Whore of Babylon! And then the other one shouted back that he was a faithless cur. Didn't get much of the rest of it, did we, William? Their accents were a bit strong, and they kept fading in and out."

William was nodding vigorously with everything Michael was saying, adding, "We did a ghost walk in Edinburgh for our two-year anniversary last year. It was nothing like as good as this, though."

"I'm afraid we can't guarantee the ghosts will come to order," Anna said faintly, "so I wouldn't raise your friends' expectations that they'll get the same experience if they come here."

They positively simpered at that.

"Then it's our special treat." Michael said with relish, and all Anna could do was thank them, and be very grateful that they weren't demanding a full refund.

If there was also a benevolent spirit watching over them, then he or she must have been working overtime that night, because the couple in the nearest other room on the first floor, Sage, had gone to bed absolutely blotto, and wouldn't have noticed if the building had collapsed around their ears. The most they bothered Anna with was pleas for Alka-Seltzers and aspirins, plus some very strong coffee, to be sent up to their room around mid-morning. Meanwhile those above Rosemary, and next to William and Michael in Tulip, were an older couple in a second-chance romance. The lady having already taken sleeping pills to ward off her lover's raucous snoring, and he admitted that once asleep, nothing woke him up.

"Dear God, I think we've got away with it." Anna declared to Gemma, collapsing into the receptionist's chair, as Gemma made them both teas. "Please tell me this doesn't happen every Valentine's? I don't think my nerves will stand it."

Gemma shook her head. "Brenda and I were on last year, and although the one ghost did tramp about a bit, it was the one who walks about more up around where you are, and where Brenda sleeps if she's stopping overnight. Did you hear nothing?"

And belatedly Anna realised that she vaguely had, it was just that she'd thought that one of the guests in the room beneath was being inconsiderate playing the TV that loud so late in the night.

"Bloody hell! I thought it was some costume drama repeat, stuck on to fill the schedule in the dead hours."

Gemma gave her a look. "It was the dead hours, all right! And let's hope it doesn't repeat tonight."

1650

Elspeth

By the time Elspeth got home, her parents were frantic.

"Where have you been?" her father demanded, thinking that it would almost be a relief if she'd been out late with one of the local boys who'd shown an interest in her – however great the risk to her reputation – rather than what Jonet had been fearing after hearing Presbyter Veitch's goings on at the Manse. Yet as Elspeth shakily explained, he found himself wrapping his arms around her and Jonet, who had instantly pulled her daughter to her and held her as if her very life depended on it.

By the time she'd got to the part about the men chasing the fox in the stone circle and then her hiding in the crypt, Johnne was feeling sick. It wasn't just because Elspeth was the youngest of their three daughters that made him more protective of her. There had always been a special bond between them. He would have cared if it had been either one of the others, of course he would – he wasn't that unnatural a father – but losing Elspeth would crush him entirely, for she was the one he could depend upon without question.

After Jonet had been questioned for a witch, her two older daughters had come in for taunting from other children, and they had noticeably distanced themselves from their mother, marrying and leaving home as soon as they could. But Elspeth had always been protective of her mother, even as a little girl somehow understanding far beyond her years how damaged Jonet had been by the experience which had happened before she'd been born. Even as a toddler she'd offered consoling hugs on those days when Jonet did little else but sob.

By the time she was eight, Johnne had been able to say to her, 'Look after your mother' while he went out into the fields, and get a calm nod of understanding off Elspeth, whereas he would have got sulky arguments from the other two about how it should be their mother looking after them. The fact that on all but her worst days, Jonet was a wonderful mother never seemed to count with the older ones. With Elspeth it meant everything, and on this dreadful night, Johnne's heart broke all over again at the way that Elspeth was pulling herself together to comfort Jonet, who was on the verge of collapse.

When they had managed to help Jonet into the box-bed on the one side of the room, and Elspeth had made them all a calming hot drink with every useful herb she could think of in it, Johnne came and drew Elspeth over to the other side of the room to sit on what was now just her bed. Once upon a time the two oldest had shared it, with little Elspeth on a pull-out truckle beneath, but now it gave Johnne and Elspeth a place to sit and speak without disturbing Jonet, who had the thick, woven drapes pulled across the other bed's front. In the winter the pair of double thickness wool curtains kept the bed warm, but tonight it was muffling their voices.

"You're sure it was McBurney's boys?" Johnne asked first.

Elspeth nodded, finally releasing more of her tears now that she wouldn't upset her mother even more. "They came upon me while I was picking the last of the rushes to patch that hole in the henhouse roof. Thank God I was up to my knees in the freezing cold water, because they wouldn't damage their fancy boots by following me in. And thank God, also, I had tied my own boots around my neck by their laces, or I'd have been running bare foot. I managed to get into that clump of willows and haul myself up enough to get my boots on. They got wet again when I had to get down to struggle across to the bank, but I hugged the trees as far as I could get, and that hampered them following me on their ponies. I was so cold from the river, but I soon got warm running!"

"You said they had dogs with them?"

"Yes. I think they might genuinely have been out trying to hunt down that male fox that's been such a pest just lately." Her voice suddenly cracked as she told her father, "If it was him who they hunted across the Apostles' Stones, then I hope he got away. …He saved my life, Pa. …He drew the dogs away. Without him I'd never have had time to make it to the nunnery."

She didn't add that she knew what Aunt Geillis, and cousins Margaret and Agnes, would say, which was that the fox must be one of the fae in the guise of a familiar. Up until now she'd always been careful to be very neutral on such matters when her aunt and cousins had come to visit, or when she and her parents had gone to Jonet's brother Robert's house. Her father had been much relieved when first Margaret and then Agnes had married, for without their daughters there, it was easier to steer Geillis onto safer subjects. And Robert Clark was only too grateful to have guests who both understood how dangerous his wife's talk of spells and rituals could be, and at the same time could be trusted never to repeat what they'd heard. But on this night, Elspeth was finding it hard not to believe that there had been something very knowing about that fox.

Jonet's anxiety was not helped two days later when they went to market in Dumfries, and heard the news from Geillis that the poor woman in Irongray Manse, Marione Corsan, was not the only member of her family to be so detained. Marione's mother, a woman by the name of Grissell McCartney, was being held prisoner in the tolbooth in Kirkcudbright on the charge of being a witch. Margaret Clark, Geillis' younger daughter, was married to man called Thomas Milligan who had a fine house in that small coastal town, and so Geillis was always the first to hear news from Kirkcudbright.

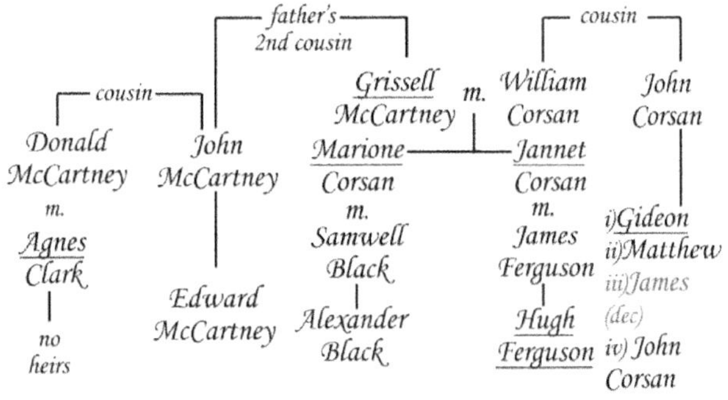

"That poor soul," Geillis said furiously. "She's about the same age as me. A respectable matron. She shouldn't be thrown into a jail with rough men!"

Johnne Allen gave Elspeth a covert roll of his eyes at that, which said that 'respectable matron' probably wasn't the most accurate description of Grissell McCartney if she'd ended up on the wrong side of the provosts, but he wisely said nothing in

Geillis' presence. However, he took Geillis' next news rather more seriously.

"Their case is going before the Presbytery Session," she said with dread in her voice. "If they're all like damned Patrik Veitch, that's the last we'll see of either of them until they're dragged into the market square here to die."

Managing to keep his voice steady, Johnne protested, "Not every member of the Kirk is a fanatic like Veitch, Geillis. Look at George Campbell here in Dumfries, or Johnne MacMurdo over at Tinwald – they're not like Veitch. They're reasonable, godly men who can be relied upon to behave with some common sense."

"If you say so," Geillis said darkly, clearly thinking all Kirk-men to be suspect.

Then only a couple of days later, with Johnne Allen out in the fields once more, Jonet suggested that she and Elspeth go out one afternoon and harvest what they could of the remaining hips, haws, and crab-apples, which had finally fallen to within their reach from the top layer of hedgerows. None would be good for eating, but they would help the first of the softer fruits to set into preserves if they were bottled properly now. Yet very soon Elspeth realised that this was not the primary purpose of them going out together, which after the news in the market place she shouldn't have been so surprised over. For a start, Jonet had a bundle which she was holding onto very tightly, not just cloths which their gatherings could be bundled into to carry. And then Elspeth saw the Apostles' Stones coming into view.

"Ma!" she hissed urgently. "We shouldn't be here. What if we're seen?"

"Better to be seen then risk the fae's wrath by not giving proper thanks for your rescue," was Jonet's emphatic response, and she wouldn't be deterred.

Only when they got to the stones did Elspeth realise that her Aunt Geillis and cousin Agnes were there waiting for them, Aunt Geillis' old pony happily cropping what was left of the winter grass well outside of the circle, while still harnessed to the small dog cart they'd come in.

"The moon will be full tonight," Geillis said approvingly, squinting up at the building clouds. "We'll be hidden from its light by all that up there, but the fae will know. They'll know it's full."

Elspeth was rather more relieved that the heavy clouds, which threatened to soak them before they were done, were dark enough that unless someone was passing right by the circle, they wouldn't be seen. She looked to Agnes and saw her give a faint, worried smile, as if she understood the foolish risk of what they were doing, making Elspeth remember that it was Agnes' sister, Margaret, who had always been the more ardent follower of Aunt Geillis' ways. That was a bit of a relief, because Elspeth realised that Agnes would hustle Geillis away as fast as Elspeth would her own mother if something went awry, whereas Margaret would be more likely to refuse to leave until the whole ritual was done.

Right now, Jonet and Geillis were lighting small rush candles at each of the stones. Real candles made from tallow were too precious to use outdoors, whereas the soaked rush-heads would burn for long enough – indeed Elspeth was hoping that they would burn through fast in the rising breeze so that they'd have gone out before they left, leaving nothing but bits of ash that the coming rain would wash away.

When all were lit, Elspeth was pulled into the centre of the stones and the three others linked hands around her. *Oh Lord*, Elspeth found herself thinking, *three witches in a circle! If anyone sees us, we're done for!*

When Geillis and Jonet began chanting in Gaelic, Elspeth's hair on the back of her neck stood on end, and from behind her she was sure she heard Agnes gasp in shock too. Neither of them had learned the ancient language, both of their fathers insistent that it was too dangerous, but Geillis was a Highlander who, many years ago, had come to Dumfriesshire to act as a nanny to one of the Grierson children down the road at Lagg, and was a native speaker. With Jonet working in the same big tower-house before she married, that was how Geillis had met Jonet's brother, but it had also been where she had taught Jonet that the spells she had known from her mother were all the more potent in Gaelic.

"You're calling on the spirits in their own language," Geillis told her, and subsequently Elspeth on many occasions, but this was the first time that Elspeth had actually been part of anything even vaguely as powerful as this. She'd assisted at the odd difficult birth, and heard her mother praying in Gaelic in a barely audible whisper over the mother to bring the child safely into the world, but this was different. Geillis and Jonet weren't holding back here, their voices ringing out loud and clear, and if Agnes was stumbling over the words her mother had obviously been making her repeat on the way here to learn, it didn't lessen the effect.

Then Geillis, Agnes, and Jonet began to step around Elspeth, rotating clockwise gently in time to the rhythm of their words, and Elspeth realised that they'd scattered herbs on the ground around her, which were now releasing a pungent smell as the women's feet crushed them. It was quite heady, with the sharper scents of mint and rosemary blending with other deeper notes, and somewhere in the back of her mind Elspeth realised how seriously her mother was taking this, because rosemary didn't grow well over here in the damp west of Scotland, and had to be bought at fairs on the rare times it was available. There was something else in the rush-candles as well, which she thought by its scent might be the sticky resin of frankincense, which was something else her mother had in the tiniest quantities and brought out for only the direst of emergency treatments.

Losing track of time, Elspeth was suddenly conscious of something or someone else with them, but it wasn't the worrying presence of a neighbour. Out of the corner of her eye, she was sure she saw the fox once more, this time sitting in between two stones and watching them intently, and then as she drew in a deep breath to try and steady herself, was sure that instead of the fox she saw a woman all in white. Whether it was the ghost of one of the nuns again or something else, she couldn't say, but it looked her straight in the eye and nodded.

The moment Elspeth blinked it was gone, but at the same time Geillis and Jonet were slowing their pace until they were all once more stood still.

"It is done," Geillis said with satisfaction. "Proper thanks have been given and accepted for Elspeth's safe return."

Although Elspeth was well brought-up enough to thank her aunt and cousin for their care and time, a day later she managed to get away from her mother and go up to the nunnery. If the fae had been thanked, she herself hadn't thanked the nuns, and she didn't want them to be offended by the pagan ritual when they'd played their part too. She'd woven a small wreath out of ivy and holly, though the last of its berries had long gone. Instead, she'd placed the first snowdrops of spring in it, and against the dark foliage they looked like tiny white stars. A sign of purity for the pure souls of the nuns was how Elspeth thought of it.

At the altar she knelt and said a prayer, then carefully placed the wreath onto the old stone slab. Standing in front of it, she looked around and said, "I don't know if you can hear me, but I wanted to thank you for your help. I don't know what you did to those men who were chasing me, but I'm grateful you did it. My mother couldn't stand seeing me in Irongray Manse's cellars like that other poor woman – she'd die of a broken heart before I even got to trial. How a man of God can do that to another human being, I don't know. It can't be right, surely?" Then thought that that wasn't the most sensible of things to say out loud when she didn't know if anyone was lurking and listening behind one of the walls, because back there she'd never spot them.

Yet in the dim light of the winter afternoon, once again she felt something shift, and to her amazement she saw the fox again, though this time it was a ghostly version, and standing on either side of it were two of the nuns. And without the flickering of the rush lights to distort her vision this time, she saw the fox dissolve into a female figure which was both taller and more slender than the nuns on either side of it, its white hair flowing freely and moving in a breeze which was only felt in whatever world it was in. Was it one of the elven kind? Suddenly Elspeth realised she had no idea of what one of the fae was supposed to look like, but this ethereal, stern, and yet beautiful female certainly fulfilled every preconception she had.

'We are all sisters under the moon,' the fae's voice said in her head with just a hint of an strange accent, and two other voices said,

'Amen to that.'

Chapter 8

Gemma's words about her hearing something stuck with Anna, and when she came off duty at noon and went up to her room to change into more casual clothes, she found herself sitting on her bed and pondering on it. When stood outside of the hotel and looking at the front, it all seemed to have been built as one, but once inside it was clear that the porticoed entrance and the block of the tower to the right of it were a separate addition. On the ground floor you would never have noticed, because the joins came at the glass doors into reception, and around the corner at the door through into the hotel's small bar. But up on the first floor, there was only the narrowest of corridors and doors to the right of the main landing linking the four bedrooms beneath the round turret. And up on the second floor there was no way through at all.

Anna's was the bedroom butting up to the main building under the eaves of the conical turret, and all three were accessed by the narrow little flight of twisting stairs at the rear of the turret's first-floor space, not any continuation of the beautiful oval sweep of stairs which came up from the tower's ground floor to the first. These top ones had been servants' rooms, and if they had to go back down to the first floor to get through to the other side, then nobody had been bothered about their inconvenience.

Consequently, she had been too busy thinking about other things for it to sink in that if, all those weeks ago when she first came, the lady in Crocus had been complaining about that much noise on the main stairs, then Anna had been barely a wall's thickness away from it too. Granted, that wall was a great chunk of sandstone blocks, and so it was hardly any wonder that it had muffled noise a good deal. But nevertheless, it made Anna wonder now whether this was in part why Polly and Gemma were so reluctant to do the back-to-back shifts which necessitated an overnight stay. And also, why they had seemed strangely pleased when Anna had accepted the room tucked under the conical eaves in the accessible bit up above parts of first-floor rooms Pippin and Sloe. Because of course, if she was in that one, then they would occasionally be using the one which sat above the oval stairs, the third bedroom being reserved for use by a duty chef, once they could get back to being able to run such a rota.

Having a sudden burning desire to go exploring, for the first time she was glad of Gary's advice to make it clear by her clothes whether she was on duty or not.

"It's different for Brenda, Gemma, Cora, Sarah, and Polly," he'd told her. "They go home more often than not, and on the odd nights when Bren' stops over, she's only getting nabbed by the customers for the one night. But like me, you're going to be here all of the time, and you have to make sure you send the right signals out. If not, you'll never get any peace, because the guests will never stop to think that they're the fourth one in a row that's disturbed your day off. Make sure your civvies are very clearly your off-duty clothes."

And she'd noticed that when he was on duty, he always wore a smart tweed jacket with coordinating moleskin trousers, looking very much the military man with his neatly cropped silver beard and moustache, and perfectly buffed black shoes. But off-duty he wore jeans and well-worn army-style khaki sweaters and tough boots – often with a flat tweed cap, because as he said, "My natural covering receded a long time ago," – making it very clear that he was on his own time. It didn't stop him answering questions from the fly fishermen who came, but that was because it was also his personal passion, not because he was obliged to.

It had been this advice which had prompted the purchase of the suits for Anna, and she'd made sure to keep her smartest blouses to wear with them, and her comfy tops for time off. So now she was in jeans and trainers, and a baggy Snoopy sweatshirt, hair scraped back in a short ponytail, and feeling confident of being able to move about freely, especially as in the early afternoon the hotel was usually quiet, even on a busy weekend like this.

Going out of her room, for the first time she went and had a look in the room above the stairs. Tonight, Brenda was stopping over, but she was in the more comfortable 'chef's room', meaning that Anna was invading nobody's private space. It was a quaint room, with its walls echoing the oval of the stairs below, and its tiny dormer window. And it was also a room which had a definite atmosphere to it, she now thought. More than her own room actually, and that surprised her. She would have expected Cora in particular to really have nerves about spending a night in here. But clearly it took the ghost to actually be making his presence felt before any of the others reacted.

It made her remember what Aunty Rita had said, when she'd first got to her house, about their family having a long line of wise women and 'sensitives' in their past. Was she more tuned in to the old house than the others? But if so, why hadn't she reacted more to the ghosts?

Going out onto the tiny landing, she paused at the top of the tight-turning stairs. They were narrow and cramped – the servants' comfort being of lesser consideration than the cost of a better staircase, back when the place was built.

"Well, none of you could have been portly ladies," Anna said softly. "A big person would have a tight squeeze getting up these!" But then, given that those working here would probably have been the children of the poor farmers, crofters, and labourers from the vicinity, the chances of any of them being fat was non-existent. Most of them would probably have been well on the way to being malnourished when they first came here, Anna realised, and if she'd had to put an extra throw on the bed as well as the electric blanket to fend off the cold, for most of them, it would probably have been both warmer and drier than what they'd grown up with.

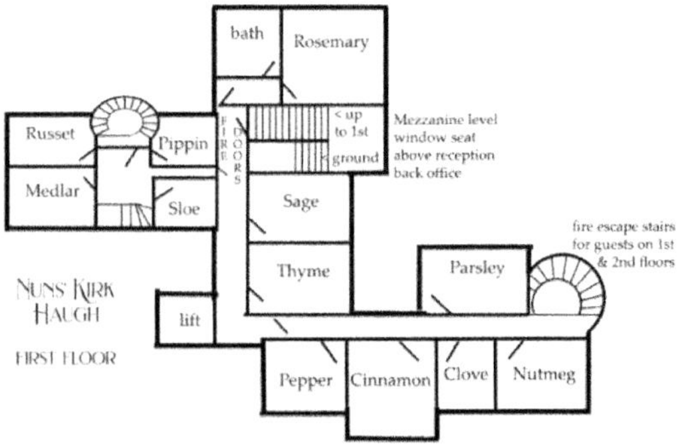

Going down to the first floor, she passed the point just on the last turn of the stairs where she always found herself giving a little shiver. Something had happened there in the past, of that she was sure, but whether it related to the ghosts was something else altogether, and right now she didn't know. And that sensation always passed the moment her foot hit the last step, and she came down onto the first-floor square landing to bedrooms Medlar, Russet, Pippin, and Sloe.

Medlar was a good-sized room looking out over the back of the hotel to the fields beyond, whereas the other three were among the hotel's smaller rooms. That said, they were still generous by modern standards, and these four rooms were where they preferably accommodated guests who brought dogs with them, especially if they were gundogs, likely to get muddy. And the very fact that no guests ever complained about their dogs being spooked, convinced Anna that these lovely late-Georgian rooms must have been built later on, and avoided whatever it was that had triggered the ghosts.

On the ground floor of this wing lay the bar, the public toilets for guests, and a rather splendid billiard room, which once upon a time must have been the pride and joy of the gentlemen of the house. Nowadays the billiard room was popular with the younger guests, and she could hear the good-natured banter going on between William and Michael and another young couple, whom they seemed to have struck up a friendship with. Beyond it lay the gunroom and fishing tackle store, but that was so clearly an even later addition that Anna didn't feel any need to go and check it out, even though she now had one of the sets of keys to it.

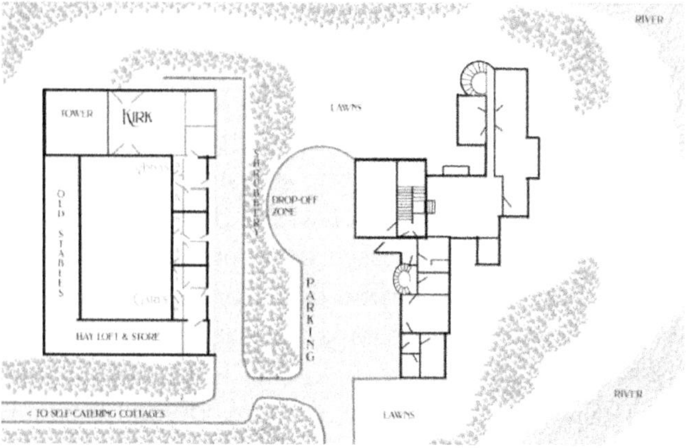

Pushing through the swing doors to reception, she could hear Gemma tapping away on the keyboard and chose not to disturb her. Instead, she went into the big room right at the front of the hotel, which these days they used as a conference and function room. For smaller or winter wedding parties taking over the hall, this was where they set up the tables for food, rather than using the marquee in the garden, but right now there were just some tables set up to take advantage of the lovely view across the lawn to the river beyond. Some guests liked to eat in here if they had pets with them, and others found it a comfortable work space if they were here on business.

Standing in the patch of weak late-winter's afternoon sunshine at one of the windows, Anna closed her eyes and tried to 'feel' the room. This had to be one of the oldest parts of the building, and yet right here she wasn't picking up a thing. With a sigh, she went back out and decided that it might be an idea to walk around the outside to see if she could pick up any clues. She'd grabbed her thick fleece jacket, just in case, and now shrugged it on. Every day she tried to get outside for a breath of fresh air, finding that it cleared her head if she did. Most of the time she either walked up and around what had once been the gardeners' two pairs of semi-detached cottages (which got let out as self-catered accommodation), and the stable block – which housed Gary's cottage and two others, and still had storage space to spare for things like the ride-on mower. Otherwise, she went on the river walk, or the walk over the fields if it wasn't too muddy. Now though, she stayed close to the walls for the first time, trying to figure out the different phases of the house.

It surprised her that she hadn't noticed how massive the foundation stones to the central frontage of the building were until now. They were huge blocks of sandstone of the sort she normally expected to see in a castle or a church. Following them around, she had to temporarily break off to go through the gate in a fence which kept the guests away from the working part of the hotel. In part it was because it was unfair for the chefs to have to work with someone gawping in at them from the vantage point of the higher lawn, but also it was for safety, because the land dropped away sharply at this point and the wet grass was treacherous.

What she hadn't expected to see was that the great inglenook fireplace in the hall was actually built on more of the huge slabs of stone, as if there had once been a massive pier of stone propping up more of the original building. Taking it carefully, because the last thing she wanted to do was to slide on the damp grass and have to go back in covered in mud and twigs, she managed to edge down to the foundations.

"Yes!" she exclaimed softly, as she saw that the massive foundations appeared to turn at the end of the fireplace, and return to go under what was now the rear-facing part of the hall.

She didn't go down into the dank corner where the main kitchen and its store (as the lower part of the square tower) joined the back of the hotel, but she could see that though its foundations were solid, they were nothing on the scale of the frontage. If they had all been built together, then surely the heavier foundations should have been down here too, where they had to take the weight of a four-storey building on a slope?

Keeping back to where her footing was sound, she walked past the ground-floor service kitchen (used for things like the desserts and anything that didn't need actual cooking) which was currently quiet, and the small circular stair tower which was tacked onto the main square tower. These days the upper reaches of it were the designated fire escape for some of the bedrooms at this end. But given that it meant guests walking past the kitchen and service area to get out to the hall, bar, and front door – and with the risk of collisions with staff rushing around with hot plates and dishes – guests were discouraged from using it except in an emergency. These stairs actually ran right down to the basement, and down at that level was the outside door where all of the deliveries came in. Given that the ghosts had never been seen down here by either the staff or anyone dropping off goods, Anna felt fairly sure that there was no connection here.

Yet the lines of the stone blocks from by the main hall stayed true all the way around here and on to the back. In perfectly overlapping courses, they rose from the basement up to the rear-facing dining room's huge windows, which let in so much light in the mornings, and on up to the two floors of bedrooms.

"Now isn't that a puzzle?" Anna mused, craning her neck to make sure she wasn't missing anything. "So those big foundations just at the front have to be for an earlier building that doesn't exist anymore. I wonder..."

She had picked up one of the leaflets which they had on hand for guests who were curious about the history of the building, and now she fished it out of her pocket and began reading it, as she strolled on around the rest of the back of the hotel. The nuns who had had their home on this spot had apparently been around from the Middle Ages to after when Henry VIII had dissolved the monasteries in England; but of course at that time Scotland had had its own king, and Henry's writ had never run north of the border, meaning the nunnery had continued on for a while after its English counterparts had been crushed.

> Scotland became Protestant in 1560 after a rebellion against the regency of Mary of Guise, the mother of Mary Queen of Scots, the pamphlet said. At the time the young queen was married to François, the Crown Prince of France, making Scots want to move closer to an alliance with Protestant England under Queen Elizabeth I. The nunnery here is poorly recorded, and it is thought that it was dissolved at some point in the next twenty years after the Reformation in 1560.

"Hmm... So neither of our ghosts is likely to be a priest who got on the wrong side of some avaricious supporter of King Henry," she mused aloud, aware that in those days even nuns had had to have a male priest to do things like officiate at mass and take confession. "Doesn't mean that the nuns or their priest didn't fall foul of some knight at a different point in time, of course, but I don't think these are my guys." And remembering Mrs Whittard's description of a ghost in plaid and carrying a gun, that really didn't sound like any kind of medieval person.

However, the leaflet did give her a more likely clue.

The stone from the nunnery's kirk was used to build a fortified tower house on the site. The leaflet continued. The living quarters of the nuns are thought to have been attached via a cloister, going on some early foundations found in the grounds during repair work to the driveway and forecourt in the 1950s. It was called Blackpark after the original Benedictine foundation – the Benedictines being known as the Black Monks or Nuns in reference to the colour of their habits.

There was a pencil drawing of a square tower, which looked to be at least three storeys high, and possibly four.

> The tower house of what was known as *Blackpark House* was built in 1605 by Robert Grierson, a distant cousin of the Douglas family which went on to own Drumlanrig and become Dukes of Queensberry by the time of the first Jacobite Rising. From then on, the Douglases would be the Marquises and Dukes of Queensberry. Here however, by the 1689 Rising, the house had changed hands more than once, with the final heiress being a Jean Corsan who married Captain Hector Fergusson who was involved in the Jacobite uprisings. However, this line also ended without heirs, and upon the death of Captain Fergusson in 1715 it was acquired by the McCartney family. When the house was demolished for rebuilding in 1787 by new

> owners, the old refectory walls were found to be eight-feet thick and the fireplace twelve-feet wide.

"I reckon that's not far off what the current inglenook is," mused Anna, reading on.

> The almost ruinous house of *Blackpark House* was sold to Major Thomas Grant in 1877, who built the house as it currently stands in an attempt to match the splendour of several other country houses in the area. The tower was remodelled to make it more commodious, and the great hall with its restored inglenook fireplace was extended along with the rear wings, and was renamed *Nuns' Kirk Haugh*.

The leaflet then went on to talk about how the house had served as a hospital for wounded soldiers in both the First and Second World Wars. But again, although Anna didn't doubt that having men suffering the after effects of horrific wars wouldn't have done much for its atmosphere back then, she didn't think that the ghosts were that modern.

I reckon I need to find out more about what was going on around here from about 1600 to 1745 and Culloden, Anna thought. *If it was close to being a ruin by the middle of the Victorian era, I doubt if much was going on here after the end of the Georgian one. And anyway, weren't the Jacobites pretty much done for after the '45 and Bonnie Prince Charlie? Hmm, must ask Gary.*

By this time, she was back around at the front of the building, and with time still to spare before the light went, but with it being already too late to go into Dumfries in time to catch the library open, she decided to take a walk down to the river and along the path. For the first time since she'd been here, they'd had a fully dry week, and so the one path which had been inaccessible now looked dry enough to tackle without wellies – which was another thing on Anna's shopping list for the next time she got a weekday off.

The trout fishing season was still a few weeks off, and salmon didn't start until much later on, though the Cluden Water was a bit small for salmon Anna suspected, but she wasn't surprised to see Gary out in the river's shallows in his waders. Apparently the Cluden Water – quite a respectable river if not as big as the Nith which it drained into – also had a type of fish called a grayling in it which made for good fly fishing, though Anna hadn't got a clue what they were like or whether you could eat them. She also knew enough to know that she shouldn't disturb Gary by calling out to him, and so she walked on past, not even waving given that his back was to the bank and her.

Instead, she concentrated on not wandering into the remaining mud puddles, but because she was going slower, for the first time she spotted a long, low, slab of stone lying just up in the tree-line. The trees themselves were a relatively modern plantation, and Anna guessed that at some point they would be cut for their timber in the way she'd seen huge swathes of Forestry-Commission-owned hillsides being cleared. So the trees had almost certainly not been there when the stone had been placed.

Clambering up the steep bit of bank, it was only when she stood up properly that she realised that she wasn't just looking at some commemorative stone – it was an actual tombstone!

"Bloody hell!" she gulped in astonishment.

In her experience you only got those in churchyards, not stuck out here in somebody's garden, no matter how extensive. It was more than a bit creepy, here under the lowering winter darkness of the pine trees, but her curiosity got the better of her, and she went closer. Somebody had recently been tending to the grave, and her money would have been on Gary for that. He had a soldier's sensibilities about respecting the fallen, of whatever persuasion. As he'd told her one night on a rare occasion when he'd had enough single malt whisky to be less guarded, "When you've seen men you know dying by the side of the road, and wondered whether you'd ever be able to give them a decent burial, you have a different perspective on honouring the dead."

She brushed a hand over the top, but there was no writing on that. However, when she squatted down to look at the sides, she discovered a chiselled epitaph which read,

Erected in 1785
In memory of
Hugh Ferguson,
Whose body lay near here.
Murdered by Col James Douglas
And his party for his adherence
To the Word of God and
Scotland's Covenanted
Work of Reformation, 1685

"Good grief. Murdered?" gasped Anna, stepping back in shock and almost cannoning into Gary, who had walked up unheard behind her.

"Steady, lass," he said with a faint smile. "I see you've discovered our resident martyr."

"Martyr? Really? As in properly martyred?"

"Oh, aye. The Covenanters were killed for their faith, often brutally."

"So was he a member of the family here?" Anna wondered.

"I'm no' sure," Gary admitted. "I think if there was a family connection, then he was very much the poor relative. Come and have a look at the other side." He led her around the slab-topped tomb to the even darker side.

Pulling a torch out of one of the many pockets in the quilted gilet he was wearing, he shone it onto the stonework. "See here… '*Faithful to God and his master to the very end*,' it reads. That doesn'a sound as if he was part of the main family, does it?"

"What's that bit below it? I can't make it out."

"Ah, that's the bit that shows the sentiments of the person who made this monument. It says, '*Crushed unto dust to satisfy Rome's inexecrable lust, cut off e'en from prayer at his last.*' Colonel Douglas was notorious for being a bit of a zealot, y'see. This isn't the only tomb where he's accused of not even allowing the men he had shot to death time to pray for their souls beforehand."

"Good grief! That's chilling."

"It is. Colonel James Douglas' name is dirt here about. As far as I can gather, he went more than a bit above and beyond the call of duty to round up the Covenanters in these counties. The Douglases are hereditary lords around here, and there were tribes of the buggers of different levels of importance. By this time, their star was waning a bit. Certainly, they weren't the king-makers they were in medieval times. But not all of the Douglases were fanatics like this James, and some families called Douglas had the surname simply because they were part of the clan, not blood relatives."

"He sounds a thoroughly unpleasant sort if he wouldn't even let a man pray before being shot – I presume we are talking about a firing squad, not just someone in the heat of battle?"

"Oh, there were no battles to speak of around here. A few bloody skirmishes, yes, but you're right, these accusations come from times when he and his men had taken prisoners and then executed them in cold blood. This was no killing in the frenzy of a battle, to be repented of later on when sanity returns," and Anna had the strangest feeling that Gary was talking about himself there for a second.

Had he killed someone in the heat of battle that he'd regretted ever since? Now wasn't the time to ask, though, but she did make a mental note to keep an eye open for when the time would be right to ask, remembering what Rita had said about not letting old wounds fester, not even – or maybe especially not – mental ones. Gary had been such a good friend to her, she was determined to be a good one to him if she could.

For now, though, she linked her arm through his, leaving him the other free to pick up his rod. Clearly the fish hadn't been biting today, because there was no catch to take back, but she was beginning to understand that Gary needed those precious hours standing out in the freezing cold water to get some mental equilibrium back. So she kept the conversation on the Covenanter whose memorial they had just found.

"Do you think we can find out some more about him? Only I think there's a fair chance that he's one of our restless spirits up at the house if he was murdered around here."

Gary looked down quizzically at her from his full six-feet-two. "You think that's important?"

Anna gave a little shrug. "I don't know. But do you think that if we could get someone from whatever the surviving version of his church is up here, and said those prayers over him that he never got to say himself, that maybe he at least would be a bit more at rest? I know Aunty Rita told you and Brenda that he and the other ghost are interlinked, but we don't have that Colonel Douglas bloke buried somewhere on site, do we?"

"*Och*, heavens, no!" Gary said with a wry laugh. "*He* was the brother of the Duke of Queensbury, that much I do know. No, he wouldn'a have been buried in some unmarked grave in the woods, not even if he'd fallen there. The likes of him got taken back for proper burial in the family crypt or mausoleum. Only the poor buggers who followed him to their deaths suffered this fate. And in truth, yon Hugh Ferguson probably isn't actually buried back there. That's a memorial erected later on in the Victorian era."

"Really? How do you know?"

"Well, the lettering on the tomb for a start off. One of these days I'll take you around some of the old kirkyards and show you the gravestones that are from his era. They're definitely more of the upright-slab type, not a big tomb like that. And if Hugh was just an ordinary bloke, his family could never have afforded that much stone – his actual remains are probably in an unmarked grave somewhere not too far away. But there was a real embracing of the Covenanters about a century on from when they were active, and when the politics had been forgotten and they could be looked back on with all of the Victorians' romantic notions. So I doubt he's haunting us from his actual grave out here."

"Then can we find out more about what happened here, please?" Anna begged him. "I had a shot at reading up on stuff when I first came here, but after that ghost trashing the bedroom, I think it's got a bit more urgent that we try and put them to rest."

They strolled back up the gentle slope of the lawn, mulling over ideas, and so it was only as they got up level with the forecourt of the hotel that Anna saw it.

"What's the matter?" Gary asked as she stopped in her tracks, pulling him back at which point he saw how pale she'd gone.

"The Jag'," she managed to croak out.

"Aye, what about it? Nice car, not the basic model either. What's so special about it?"

"I'd know that number plate anywhere. That's Jensen's! What's my husband doing here?"

Chapter 9

The shock of seeing that car invading her sanctuary was almost enough to buckle Anna's knees. It wasn't that she was frightened of Jensen. She didn't remotely expect him to be violent. It was just that she wasn't prepared for what she might say to him, or him to her. If he got upset and started crying, as she feared he might, she knew she could feel so bad she might agree to try again, and the sensible side of her knew that that would take her into her own version of hell. Then a blessed thought occurred to her.

"Oh, thank God! He can't stay here. We're fully booked!"

Gary was already steering her towards the tackle room, and added, "And now is not the time to be telling him that we've got a spare cottage, even with that couple from the haunted room in the other one."

"No! God, no!" She spun around to face Gary. "He'll never understand. He won't get it. He sees nothing wrong at all with his parents ruling his life from sun up to sun down." And she could feel the tears welling up already.

"This way," Gary said firmly, taking her into the tackle room, and when he'd hauled his waders off and hung them to dry, took her through the back way into the billiard room, and then into the small lobby at the bottom of the oval stairs. "Go on…*shoo*! I haven't seen you if I'm asked. I'll go and find out what he's doing here."

As Anna fled sobbing up the stairs, Gary gave her until he heard the fire door at the first floor close behind her, and then, knowing that she couldn't be heard anymore, pushed the door open into the corridor and sauntered down to reception as if he hadn't a care in the world. Pushing one of the doors open, he wandered in, casually asking Cora, "Everything alright? Didn't think we were expecting any new guests until tomorrow."

He rather implied that Jensen might be trying to push his way in, even though they were fully booked, and when the younger man turned around, had time to size him up as Cora said excitedly, "This is Anna's *husband*! He wants to make it up with her and take her back! Isn't that romantic on Valentine's Day?"

Putting on his best sergeant's glower, Gary pulled himself up to his full height and was amused to see Jensen realise that here was someone who topped his own height by an inch or so, and him blinking before taking a step backwards.

"She's no' some stray puppy to come and be collected from the pound," Gary said sternly. "I think it's rather up to Anna whether she wants to be taken back or not, don't you?"

"But Gary," Cora pleaded, looking rather doe-eyed at the handsome young man before her, "he doesn't know why she left."

"Then he'd better open his lugs and listen properly when she tells him this time, shouldn't he?" was Gary's unrelenting riposte. "Sensible young ladies don't do a runner on their wedding night for no reason. For some flight o' fancy. And Anna is *verra* sensible. We've all seen *proof* o' that in the last few weeks." By now the glint in Gary's blue eyes had become positively icy, and his accent even broader than normal.

"But I *don't*!" blurted Jensen. "I woke up and there she was, gone, and only a note to explain which I couldn't make sense of. I don't understand why she didn't say something earlier if going to London was that much of a problem."

"Did you give her chance?" Gary asked, leaning back against the newel post of the staircase, which perversely seemed far more threatening than if he had stepped into Jensen's personal space. That absolute assurance that he could handle himself in any circumstance was deeply intimidating all by itself.

"Wha… What do you mean?" Jensen spluttered.

Gary kept him pinned with his glare. "Did you give her chance?" he repeated, as if to a particularly dense child. "It's no' a hard question, is it?" And then seeing Jensen's continued blank expression, he spelled it out, "From Anna's point of view, you were dating and then you proposed. Now that's all fine and dandy. But what she wasn'a expecting was for you to turn up a couple o' weeks later and tell her that your mammy had got the bit between her teeth and organised everything without even a word to her."

"But… But I thought she would be fine with that." Jensen protested. "She didn't have any of the stress."

"Any o' the stress?" Gary threw back at him. "For the love o' God, man, what bride doesn'a want to be consulted about her own wedding? Even an old army horse like me knows better than that, and I thought you younger lads were supposed to be modern men, and all that bollocks! Going with all that 'understanding' of the women in your lives, and 'respectful of their wishes', stuff." He gave a snort of disgust, which came out rather like a bull about to charge, worrying Jensen even more. "Christ! Even daft old buggers o' my generation didn'a fuck things up quite like that."

"But her mum was involved as well," Jensen tried to justify himself with.

Gary feigned a look of surprise. "Oh! *Her* mammy was involved. And that's supposed to make everything right, is it? And how did Anna talk about her mammy to you when you were alone, eh? They've no' exactly the loving relationship, have they? At what point did you forget what sort o' childhood Anna had wi' that pair o' narcissists, and turn a blind eye to everything you knew, 'cause it gave *you* less grief from your own mammy to go along with it all?"

Jensen looked genuinely shocked that Anna should have put such a slant on things, and Gary realised that Anna was right, it would take a lot to get Jensen to fully understand. All he now said was, "But I want her back!"

And as Gary came upright from his leaning, about to give this idiot the bawling out of a lifetime, Cora chose to interrupt, "Well we could fit you in," she said with even more chirpy brightness than normal. "We've got a room we don't normally use up on the…"

"…Guests moved out this morning!" Gary thundered, drowning her out. "You can have it for one night and one night only, on account of us having someone else booked in from Sunday night. Go get your bags and I'll show you up."

Luckily Gary's expectation of being obeyed, and Jensen's weak will, meant that he got flustered but promptly headed out of the door towards his car.

Gary rounded on Cora. "What the fuck were you thinking, lass?" he snapped. "Please dinna tell me you were proposing to set him up in the staff room *next door* to Anna?"

Cora's expression fell. She wasn't used to seeing this side of Gary. "But he's so lovely," she protested. "I'm sure it's all a mistake and Anna overreacted."

"Really?" Gary bent to lean on his fists on the desk to fix her with his stare. "And would you say the same if it was one o' *your* two ex-husbands who turned up here, and it was Anna who was offered to let them stay?"

"But they weren't like him." Cora protested.

"So you married them *knowing* they were violent arseholes, did you?"

"*Nooo*! They were lovely when I met…" The implications finally suck in for her.

"Aye," Gary growled, rolling his eyes in despair. "You have a knack of falling for the sweet-talkers, Cora, and no' seeing the real men, so you're no' the best judge o' character, are you? And just for the record, that overgrown man-boy you're dating at the moment is another such – take it from me, I've seen enough of their likes to spot one a mile off. Do yourself a favour and cut him loose before he thinks he's got his feet under the table and starts wiping the rug with you like the last two did. And keep out o' Anna's business. He goes tomorrow, end of story!"

At that point Jensen came back into the outer hall and hovered until Gary came out with the key to the Rosemary room.

"This way," Gary said, holding open one of the double doors into the main hall for him, and then leading him up the imposing main staircase. He was damned if he was going to carry Jensen's bags, despite the idiot having a matching suitcase, overnight bag, and some strange kind of man-bag that made Gary wince just at the sight of it. They weren't even in decent black, but some strange kind of chestnut coloured leather that was veering far too close to a pinkish-red for Gary's liking.

"Here you go," he said when they'd gone through the fire doors at the top of the first flight, opening the outer door from the landing. "Bathroom's through there, here's your bedroom. Like I say, this was fully booked, but the guests had a wee issue they needed to sort out and they left this morning. But we have a couple coming in for the Valentine's Special tomorrow, so you'll have to find other accommodation after that. …We can fit you in for dinner at six." And at that he closed the door and went back out onto the landing.

Lingering just long enough for Jensen to have the chance to sneak out and be turned smartly back, when he didn't appear, Gary went through the narrow access corridor to the landing of the oval stairs, and then up the back servants' stairs to Anna's room. He knocked the door and when she answered and let him in, pulled her into a hug.

"Bloody, Cora!" he growled. "Reads too many o' they daft romances for her own good. I'm sorry, lass, but she was one step away from giving him the room next door."

"*What?*" squeaked Anna, pulling away from him and staring up at him in horror with tear-reddened eyes.

Gary gave her a wink. "Ach, dinna fret. I knocked that daft idea on the head. I've put him in Rosemary."

"Rose…?" Anna snorted with unexpected mirth and had to grab a tissue quickly before she covered Gary with snot. After her wild sobbing fit, she was still sniffly, but realised that Gary probably wouldn't be shoving her away with disgust the way her father would have done. "Oh, bloody hell, Gary! What if the ghosts get…"

"I sincerely hope the ghosts do 'get'!" Gary said with a wicked chuckle. "I hope the bloody pair conduct battle royal in that room tonight, and scare some sense into the daft bugger. *Sheesh*, Anna! When you said he doesn'a get why you left, I never imagined he was *quite* that clueless."

"Oh yes," Anna sighed. "And that's what makes this so bloody hard. If I went back with him now, it would be straight back to square one. Nothing would change, because he genuinely doesn't grasp on any level why it should. There would be cringingly embarrassing Sunday lunches at his parents, where nobody actually *says* anything, but with all those knowing looks telling me not to dare do something like that again to their darling boy. And it won't matter what he promises me here, because the moment he gets back into his parents' company, he'll return to his default behaviour, which is total compliance."

She sighed. "It's so easy for him. He's been loved to the point of wrapping him in cotton-wool all his life. There's no bump in the road that hasn't been smoothed out for him by money or influence. And that means that he just can't find a way to grasp what my childhood was like – what it was like to be completely ignored as a person. All he sees is that my mum and dad threw money at my well-being, in the sense that I had a comfortable room in a nice house, and was fed and educated. He can't seem to see that I was treated as a mini-Heather. That regardless of my own personality, what had been right for her was automatically applied to me." She shook her head in despair. "I think at some stage I'm going to need some serious therapy to get over that, because Aunty Rita is right, I was virtually groomed to become an ideal target for the bloody Coleborns and their damned aspirations!"

Gary took her firmly by the shoulders and held her back from him so that he could look her fully in the eyes. "Then we make sure that he gets the message here and now. He needs to leave here fully acknowledging that you are never, nor ever were, going to be what he thinks you are. You're going to have to talk to him, but if you want me to sit in for moral support, then I will."

She managed a watery smile. "Thank you, Gary, that's really kind of you. And I might yet need that support, but I think to start off with I need to speak to him alone. The last thing I want is him going back to his parents, and telling them that he never got the chance to talk to me because this great big Scotsman kept butting in. That's just asking for his father to come storming up the motorway and causing even more trouble here – and this early on into my job, I really can't afford for someone to be sneaking behind my back to head office, saying I've got family members coming here and making huge scenes."

He gave a huff of disgust. "And you don't need to name names for me. Cora's never been your greatest fan, and with her going all dewy-eyed over Jensen she's no' thinking straight…well in truth, thinking at all is a bit of a strain for Cora. She looks grand sat behind the desk, but she's no' the sharpest knife in the drawer, is she?"

Anna giggled. "That's very naughty, Gary, but I know what you mean. She doesn't think things through, does she?" Then she frowned, asking, "Was she really that taken with him? I thought from everything she's said that she like the rougher types."

Gary grimaced. "I don't think it's his *type* so much as his Jag' and his designer luggage that's the pull! Cora's got a bit of a reputation, shall we say. Well, the whole bloody family has. Her mum got around a bit in her youth, and her aunty is what you might politely call a lady of negotiable affections."

"She's a street worker?"

"Is that what they're called these days? Aye, well she was a lady o' the night at times, though not recently. Others she didn'a make pay in money, but they paid in favours, you understand. Cora may pretend that her mammy's husband of the time was her dad, but I doubt it would stand up to a gene test."

"Blimey!"

"Aye. So you see, no respectable lad from around here would take much notice of her, especially as she was no' a shrinking violet herself in her school days and just after."

"So the rough lads were the only ones who took any notice of her? And presumably for all the wrong reasons? That's very sad. Nobody should be judged like that."

"You're very charitable towards a lass who just tried to stick your ex in the room next door."

"Oh, Gary, can't you see that she and I aren't much different? I was condemned by, or at the very least saddled with, the expectation that I was going to identical to my older sister, and that's not so far from Cora being damned because of her mother's reputation. I'm not saying what she did was right. Just that I can see how she's ended up where she is."

"Well it does you credit, lass," Gary said affectionately, and gave her another hug. "So, when are you going to talk to him?"

Squaring her shoulders, Anna sighed, "No time like the present, I suppose. The sooner I start, the more time I've got to work on him if he just won't see sense."

She went down to Jensen's room, but Gary let her knock and go in before stationing himself in the small corridor within earshot. Jensen might have backed down in front of himself, but he was still a big man and Anna at least six inches shorter and lighter built. If this big booby threw a temper tantrum, then he could easily hurt Anna without meaning to, and Gary wasn't going to stand for that. Men of Jensen's age should have grown up by now, in his opinion, not still be going around tied to their mammy's apron strings.

Inside the bedroom you could have cut the atmosphere with a knife.

"Why did you leave?" Jensen demanded, obviously upset, but now that he had Anna in front of him, also finally getting angry. What he wasn't expecting was Anna's riposte of, "If you hadn't come to bed so drunk you could scarcely walk, you would have known!"

"I wasn't that drunk!" Although seconds later he blushed furiously, making Anna think that he was only now remembering the terrible hangover he must have had.

She took advantage of that to plough on with, "You came into the room saying over and over, 'What have I done?' …Not exactly what any bride wants to hear at that point. No romantic snuggles under the duvet for me. Oh no! My bridegroom didn't even notice that I'd left the celebrations *hours* beforehand.

"And did you come to find me, Jensen? No, you didn't. You were having far too much fun being congratulated by your mates. Whereas my friends weren't deemed posh enough to invite to our fathers' joint corporate event. And that's what our wedding was – a bloody exercise in networking and pressing the right palms!"

"But why didn't you say so?"

"I did, Jensen! Over and over again! But every time I said I wanted to slow things down …every time I asked if we could wait until the summer, at least…all you said – in fact the *only* thing you said – was that your *mother* would be so upset after she'd put so much work into it. Not once, Jensen, not bloody once, did you take in how much it was upsetting me. For all the input either of us had in our wedding, we could have been a couple of shop-floor mannequins. Dummies that were moved around as required to the correct positions!"

"That's ungrateful. My mum tried to tell you what she was doing but you took no interest!"

"Is that what she's saying now? …Is it, Jensen? …Because if it is, it's a bloody lie! And can you not hear what's coming out of your mouth? Your mum tried to *tell* me? How about her *asking* me once in a while? Would that have been so hard?"

"About what?"

"Christ! You really are unbelievable!" And for the first time Anna was well and truly angry, not just upset. "How about the cake for a start?

"The cakes? But they were lovely cupcakes."

"No, they weren't! They were smothered in butter-cream icing, and in what world did you think that someone of my age would want them decorated with boy and girl blue and pink unicorns? What I *wanted*, Jensen, was a traditional fruit cake, which could have been made months in advance – saving all that angst only days before over whether the bloody things would be ready or not – and for it to be covered with a thin layer of royal icing with a few tasteful decorations on it.

"I tried to persuade your mum and mine that that would have been far better, and a lot easier for all concerned. But no. Your mum's best friend had had blue and pink wizards and fairies on her daughter's wedding cupcakes, and that wedding was deemed in her eyes to be the epitome of what a modern wedding should be like. At the very least, it was what we were supposed to keep up with.

"Well, I didn't want to keep up with anyone, Jensen. I wanted us to be our own selves. I wanted us to pick our own first house together. Decide how we wanted it furnished. But your mother went ahead and picked out the flat in London – which by the way, I learned of long after it was a done deal – and my stupid mother was so desperate to keep up with her, she was about to throw out everything from my flat that ever meant something to me, so that she could finally be done with me, and she and my father could go back to being a couple once more. Why the hell she thought that I do not know, because as you know full well, I had been living independently of them for years. But in that warped social circle both our parents mix in, having an unmarried daughter or son is tantamount to having a prostitute in the family – someone who *can't* be married because there's something wrong with them."

She had to pause for breath, and saw the shock and horror on Jensen's face.

"You've changed," he said miserably. "You never used to talk like that."

"No, I haven't!" Anna fumed. "I *haven't* changed. It's just that this is the first time you've had to really listen to me without your parents being on hand to erase it, and put back in what they wanted you to hear." She scrubbed her hands through her hair, one step short of grabbing hold of handfuls and trying to pull it out in her frustration. "Jensen, if you would just stop and *look* at your life for a second, and ask yourself, 'Is this what *I* really want?' you might begin to understand. But you *don't.* You've been so conditioned into doing what you're told, you never as much as pause.

"Yet on our wedding night I think it finally sank in with you that you, too, were not happy with the way things were going. Or at least once you were drunk enough to stop thinking about what *they* wanted for a second. When you turned up at my parents' house last Christmas, having been told to chat me up, I don't think for a moment you yourself thought that by this Christmas just gone that we'd be married, did you?" She saw him about to bluster. "*Did* you? Come on, Jensen! For once in your bloody life, be honest with yourself even if you can't be with me."

For one instant there was stunned silence, then Jensen screamed, "Stop! Just stop! I don't want to hear this! You're not supposed to be like this."

And that was when the temperature plummeted, the duvet was suddenly flung from off the bed to crash into the dressing table, and an unseen hand picked up Jensen's man-bag and threw it at him.

Chapter 10

Anna was subconsciously half prepared for something to happen, Jensen wasn't, and even so, Anna was shocked by the violence. As Jensen went white and fainted, his overnight bag followed the man-bag in being hurled at him, only missing his head by inches because he was already on his way down to the floor.

An eerie disembodied and furious voice shouted, "Don't you touch my women folk!" and the mattress was once again up-ended, this time coming off so that it shoved Anna back against the bedroom door, and prevented her from opening it enough to get out. As she stood rooted to the spot, she realised that on the other side of the bed frame she could see the outlines of a man. Not a very tall man, and quite gaunt, yet as an arm lifted and the plaid over his shoulder fell back, she got the fleeting impression of a sinewy arm, not with the massive muscles of someone who bench-pressed at the gym, but of someone who'd worked at a tough job all of his life.

"I'll bluidy kill ye, Corsan, and McCartney too!" was the ghost's hoarse cry, and he reached over temporarily out of sight and picked up what Anna could only assume was a musket. He brought it up to his shoulder and took aim, though not at Jensen down on the floor, but at some unseen foe beyond him who was presumably still standing.

In that other time, the musket went off, a cloud of ethereal white smoke masked the ghost, and then when it cleared, he was gone. All that was left in Anna's time was a strong smell of gunpowder.

"Anna! Anna!" Gary was calling frantically from behind the door. "Are you all right?"

"Yes, I'm fine," she managed to call back shakily. "That was the ghost!"

"I heard gunfire!"

"Yes, in his time he fired his musket, but it's done nothing to me or the room."

"What about Jensen?"

Anna looked down at the man still flat on his back. "Oh, my hero passed out. One whiff of the ghost and he was out for the count."

Something very uncomplimentary drifted through the closed door, and if Anna didn't get all of the words Gary was using, she could make a good guess that Jensen's parentage and sexual practices were being called seriously into disrepute.

"You're going to have to shove the door while I pull it," she called to Gary. "The mattress is too far this way for the door to open, though it's not actually leaning on it. But this morning, Sally and I only just managed to move it together. These super-king mattresses are a hefty weight."

Between them they got the door open enough for Gary to wriggle in, but then they both had to scramble over the bed's base to get around to the other side of it to get to Jensen. He was lying flaked out almost under the one corner of the mattress, which was poised to topple his way at any moment.

"Come on." Gary said brusquely, giving Jensen's cheek a none-too-gentle slap. "Man up, princess!" However, all that happened was Jensen coming around enough to stare up into Gary's face and the looming mattress, and for him to faint again. With a disgusted sneer, Gary got his hands under Jensen's armpits and tugged him across the floor to where he was in less danger of getting squashed.

"You can do so much better than this big jessie," he told Anna. "Christ, he'd never have managed out in Iraq or Afghanistan! One flash of the Taliban's skirts and he'd have been wetting his panties and calling for his mammy!"

Anna looked down on Jensen with disappointment. "I don't think I realised until today what a mummy's boy he is. I thought he went along with her for a quiet life. I'm starting to wonder now whether it wasn't so much going along with, as having no bloody idea what to do if she *wasn't* at his back all the time telling him."

As she and Gary heaved the mattress back onto the bed, and sorted out the sheets, pillows, and duvets once more, she said, "Up until now I at least felt sorry for him. I'm not sure I even feel that anymore."

"Grab his feet," Gary told her, once more getting hold of Jensen under his arms, and between them they hauled him up onto the bed. With him propped up on the pillows, they finally managed to get him to come around.

"What was that?" he whimpered weakly. "I don't want to stay here anymore! I want to go home!"

Gary regarded him with disgust. "What in the name of all that's holy do you do for a living, lad? Because it canna be much that requires any backbone."

"Hedge funds and securities," Jensen managed to choke out, trying to hang onto the last shreds of his dignity. "I manage pension funds and people's investments."

"God help us," was Gary's world-weary response. "No wonder the country's going to hell in a hand cart if the likes o' you are running the economy." He looked around and saw that the only things that Jensen had seemed to unpack were a smart pair of silk pyjamas and his Louis Vuitton wash-bag. Shoving both rather unceremoniously back into the overnight bag and zipping it up, Gary picked it and the man-bag up in one hand, and grabbed the suitcase with the other, saying, "When you can stand up wi'out pissing yourself, come downstairs and I'll drive you into Dumfries. One o' the hotels there is bound to have a free room, even if it's no' as grand as this." And turning on his heels, he walked out of the room.

"Who the hell is that?" Jensen asked weakly. "Has he been your sugar-daddy all this time?"

The very idea of Gary as anyone's sugar-daddy was so ridiculous that it released all of Anna's pent-up emotions in a burst of near hysterical laughter. When she'd calmed down a bit, she managed to say, "He's the man who's in love with my Aunty Rita."

"Who the heck is Aunty Rita?" was Jensen's immediate response, then it seemed to dawn on him that this was another thing he was supposed to know if only he'd been paying attention.

"Aunty Rita," Anna replied scathingly. "You know…the one I kept saying I wanted at the wedding, and the one my father kept saying 'no' to. She's his younger half-sister. Same mum, different dad. My grandfather treated their mother like dirt, but she wasn't standing for that, so he dragged her through the courts in a divorce so acrimonious it left her damned near destitute. Then he went south of the border taking my dad with him, never letting him stay with his mother again and only having short, supervised visits. Grandfather got remarried to another unfortunate woman and had my two half-aunts, one of whom killed herself thanks to his bullying. Long story, none of it good. Then my grandmother also remarried and had Rita.

"The thing is, Rita is like her mother – a down-to-earth, no-nonsense kind of lady, who never has bought into my father's bullshit about me. She's the one who I ran to after you went comatose on me on our wedding night, and she's the one who found me this job. But that's something else, isn't it, Jensen. Time and again over the year we were together, I asked you to come up and meet Aunty Rita. I told you over and over how special she was to me, *and* why. But instead, you went running to my father like the classroom snitch, and asked *him* if you ought to go.

"If you'd really loved me, you shouldn't have needed his permission. The fact that I love Aunty Rita dearly should have been enough. I never asked you to lie to him. I just wanted you to back *me* up. To come and meet the one member of my family who I really care about."

Jensen blushed, finally beginning to realise that he had thoroughly messed things up. He couldn't seem to find the right words, though, and regretfully Anna realised that this was the way things were always going to be. Even when it dawned on him that he was in the wrong, he couldn't make the decision as to what to do about it without checking back with his parents first.

"Gary looks after me because *he's* listened to Rita, and knows how much I mean to her," said Anna, making one last effort to din it into Jensen what was so wrong with their relationship. "I wish he had been my dad – and no, I definitely do not mean a sugar-daddy, but a proper, normal, dad. He's shown more concern over my well-being in the weeks I've been here than my actual father has done in the whole of the rest of my life. So don't you dare go back south and start slandering Gary, and trying to drag his good name through the mud, because I won't stand for it, and neither will Rita!" She put a hand under his arm and tugged at him. "Come on. You're leaving."

She got him out onto the main landing of the first floor, but one look at the stairs and the way he was wobbling, and she marched him further onwards to the end and the lift. Jensen going head first down the stairs was the last thing she needed, not that the stairs were a straight flight, and there was a large mezzanine landing with some window seats at the return flight, so he wouldn't have fallen the whole way. But all in all, the lift was a safer bet.

Gary must have been on the same wavelength, because he was perched on the edge of one of the chesterfield sofas in the hall, waiting for them.

"Do you want me to come with you?" Anna asked.

Gary gave Jensen an up and down look which ought to have had him shrivelling up in shame on the spot, but which went unnoticed. "No, lass, I think I can manage this flabby wee baw-bag by myself."

Following them out to the forecourt, Anna realised that the time it had taken to get Jensen moving had been enough for Gary to sprint up to his cottage, and bring his truck down. As he chucked the cases rather unceremoniously onto the back seat, Jensen managed to turn to Anna.

"Baw-bag?"

"I think he just called you an empty scrotum," said Anna, trying to smother her mirth at Jensen's shocked expression as that sank in. Nobody said things like that to Jensen. It just didn't happen in his world. But maybe he'd have been more the man she'd believed him to be if it had happened a bit more often, Anna thought regretfully.

Feeling utterly drained, she wandered back inside and saw Cora looking at her balefully.

"You don't know what you've got there, Anna," she said bitterly.

Realising that she had to put this straight with Cora, if only so that they could carry on working together, Anna sank into the customer's chair in front of the reception desk, and said, "I'll grant you that he's not like the men that you regularly meet. But Cora, he's too much the other way! You think he's a nice man, and he is. But his parents absolutely rule his life, and you'd soon find that it's not much fun when everything you say gets disregarded. They don't so much love Jensen as *own* him! His sole function in life, as far as they are concerned, is to do whatever it takes to make *them* happy.

"That was what the final straw was for me. Sitting there on my wedding night and hearing a very drunk Jensen blurt out that he didn't love me and was dreading our life together." That wasn't quite the truth. Jensen had never said the actual words that he dreaded living with her, but it had only been him passing out too drunk to say another word that had prevented that sentiment being said aloud, of that she was sure.

"He's a personality vacuum, Cora." She saw the younger woman pout as if to say, 'I'd have made him take notice'. "It's not that I couldn't out-shout his mother. It's that he'd had thirty years of indoctrination before I even came along. You don't undo that with a few tantrums and chucking the crockery around.

"…If you want to make a pass at him, be my guest, but be warned, you won't like it once you find out what life with him is really like. Your ex-husbands may have used their fists, but words can cut just as deeply, and the wounds linger longer. Jensen's worst weapon is his indifference. He'll smile and nod along with you to your face, and then the moment you're out of sight he'll carry on as if you'd never been there."

"*My* men never forget *me*," Cora bit back with, and suddenly too tired to argue, Anna got up and went back upstairs.

Without really thinking about where she was going, suddenly she found herself back in Rosemary. Flopping down in the small armchair by the side window, she looked across the room, not quite knowing what she was looking for, but certain that she was missing something. What was the trigger for the ghost showing itself?

With her and Jensen it was clearly a result of the acrimony between them. Especially with what the ghost had cried out. But which women folk were they, and who were Corsan and McCartney? Was the Colonel Douglas of the dreadful reputation involved as well? Was he haunting here too, given that he was mentioned on the tomb out in the grounds? Probably not, because would an ordinary soldier have dared to take a pot-shot at the Earl of Queensbury's kid brother? No. Even in his grief, he might well have thought twice or thrice about doing that. So were Corsan and/or McCartney someone serving under Douglas? One of the colonel's retinue, perhaps?

Rather more concerning was why had a ghost appeared to the young couple who'd been in here last night? As far as Gary had been concerned, they had just been a normal young couple, out on a Valentine's Day special break – and she thought Gary was a shrewd enough assessor of people to not be taken in by some mask of romance. So had it been the same ghost which she'd seen who had appeared to them? Could it have been the other ghost? And did he have something against young love? Had he in his life on earth been jilted by a woman who had then gone on to marry the other ghost?

There was one thing she was sure of: she was going to have to get to the bottom of this, because the hotel could not afford to keep having guests frightened out of their wits. It would have been bad enough in one of the lesser rooms, but Rosemary was the premier bedroom, and the only one to have one of the original house's smaller bedrooms made into its bathroom, making it into almost a suite. Up on the next floor, Crocus bedroom sat with its own en-suite shower cubicle above Rosemary, but the equivalent space up above Rosemary's bathroom on the next floor was Tulip bedroom, also with its own shower cubicle, and large enough to contain a generous king-sized bed as well – that's how big those spaces were. So having the best room in the hotel out of action was not a long-term option.

When Gary got back it was to tell her that he'd left Jensen at the *Premier Inn* out on the Annan road out of Dumfries.

"I canna think that there'll be anything in that place to scare what's left of his wits out of him," Gary added dryly. "And while they're well busy during the week with business travellers, they don't do

Valentine's Specials like we do. He'll be comfortable enough there for as long as he cares to stay."

Neither of them saw that Cora was lurking in the back office doorway and heard his words.

With Anna not due on duty that night, Gary invited her over to his cottage with the promise of food. "I'm no' Emilio," he confessed, "but I make a mean spag bol, if that floats your boat?"

"Spaghetti Bolognese sounds divine," Anna told him gratefully, and was glad to just sink into one of the squashy old sofas in his lounge and let him do the cooking. She was exhausted.

However, with an ample portion of Gary's speciality inside her, and well on the way through her second large glass of red wine, she felt able to tell him of her fears.

"In a way we were lucky, you know," she confessed. "Lucky in that it was me and Jensen who had the marital falling out in that room. Another of our guests might not be as fortunate. Heaven forbid, but it could be some older couple who can't stand the sight of one another most of the time who have a row, and we can't risk one of them having a heart attack when our ghost fires that musket off!"

Gary immediately took a large swig of the red. "God, I hadn'a thought of it like that. But you're right!"

"There wasn't anything off about the young couple who are now in the cottage next door, was there? Didn't look like they'd been interrupted mid-fight, or anything? No sign of the woman being red-eyed from crying, for instance?"

But Gary shook his head. "No. Nothing off at all. In fact, young Josh was genuinely concerned for

Sandy as best I could tell. I mean, I'm no psychologist or anything…"

Anna was already waving his objections aside. "No, fair enough, Gary. I hear what you're saying, but I think you're a pretty shrewd judge of character, even in the middle of a night shift. It would have to be a pretty practiced charmer to put one over on you to that extent."

Gary smiled. "Thanks for the vote of confidence, but I'm no' infallible."

"No, you're not, but I still think that being scared half to death in the middle of the night would put most scoundrels enough off their stride for you to spot them."

Gary nodded and thought for a moment, then asked, "So you're thinking that both ghosts appeared up in Rosemary, but not at the same time?"

"I think it's the only way it makes sense. I think strong emotions set both of the ghosts off. The one I saw becomes defensive of women, because somewhere in his time somebody – whether it was one man or a troop of men – harmed the women he loved. I can therefore only guess that the other one is inflamed by its sensing of people being very loving in that space. Jealousy? Betrayal? I'm not sure what the trigger is, but I tell you this, Gary, we're going to have to find out."

1658

Elspeth

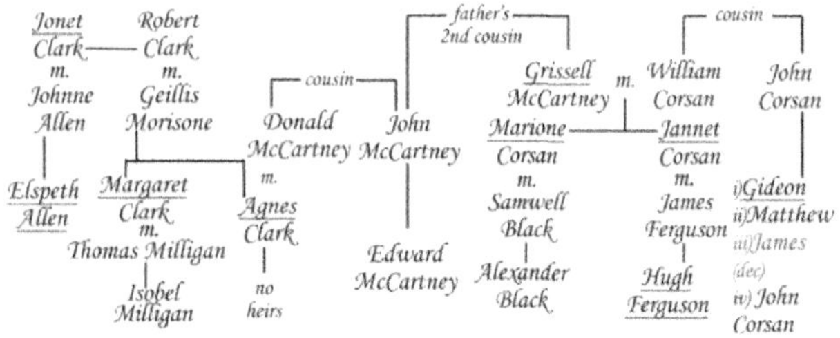

It would take some time for word to reach Elspeth and her family, but the Presbytery Session in 1650 in the end determined that there was insufficient evidence to condemn either Marione Corsan, or her mother Grissell McCartney, and they were released. Yet the effect of their imprisonments, alongside the investigating of six women only two days' ride away away at Old Luce – though none of them went to full trial – had the worst kind of effect on Elspeth's mother. Now, Jonet could not bear to be even in the same place as Presbyter Veitch. Every time she saw him across a street or the market place, she made signs to ward off the Devil, even to the extent of permanently carrying a small purse of salt with her to fling a pinch in his direction if unexpectedly encountered.

After Jonet's sister-in-law Geillis died of a dreadful hacking cough a couple of winters later, Geillis' Agnes continued to stay in touch with her sister Margaret in Kirkcudbright, and then brought news from there the handful of miles up the road to the Allens. Bizarrely, Grissell McCartney had fared better in the jail at Kirkcudbright Tolbooth than her daughter had in Irongray Manse. Poor Marione's hands would never be the same again after all the stabbing with Veitch's 'witch pricker' – the shaft of razor-sharp iron with which he prodded every blemish, wart, or mole, to see if it was a Devil's mark. Given that Marione had been a gifted dyer of wool and other cloth, her hands had been speckled with all sorts of marks at the time she had been taken by Veitch, but once he'd finished, she would never be able to wring a length of cloth out ever again. It therefore made little difference in that respect that the charges had been dropped by the end of such a dreadful year, because she had to give up her dyeing, thereby depriving her of an income aside from what she could manage on the croft, where she and her husband now existed as best they could.

Marione's husband, Samwell Black, was a good man who stood by her through thick and thin, as did their son, Alexander. Yet they'd hardly been well-off to start with, and with Samwell being a weaver who in the winter months worked in the shed beside the croft, it had been Marione's skilful dyeing which had raised the price of his cloth. Like them, Johnne Allen relied on seasonal work, such as weaving during the winter, to bring in extra money beyond his crops and sheep, and if nobody would buy off him, then the family would soon feel the pinch. Therefore the Blacks' fate was one which Jonet feared could be theirs at any moment should they cross the irascible Veitch, and if Elspeth and her father prayed she might be more circumspect, they also understood how her nightmares were driving her nowadays.

Everyone could tell by Presbyter Veitch's expression after he'd been thwarted over Marione, that any time he passed by a woman he was assessing her guilt. And while Agnes might have been able to breathe a little easier once her mother had passed beyond earthly torments, but also from fearlessly inciting his fury, she and Elspeth continued to share their worries. For Agnes' sister Margaret had reacted as badly to the increased suspicion as Jonet had – not helped by Margaret being a friend of Marione's.

Both suspected women now held their heads high and refused to adopt the kind of cowed deference to presbyters that some, like Veitch, expected, with Agnes and Elspeth agreeing that it was a good thing that with Margaret being in Kirkcudbright and the rest of the family closer to Dumfries, at least Jonet and Margaret weren't nearby enough to egg one another on. And it was a strange blessing when Jonet's aching joints got the better of her, and Elspeth did the trips into the market in Dumfries for her. Not that Elspeth had forgotten what it was like to be hunted, but she could master her feelings enough to dissemble and remain unnoticed.

Yet if her mother's actions had one personal impact, it was the drying up of any suitors for Elspeth. She'd never had men queuing up for her affections, but she'd had her share of attention, and always thought that there was a strong chance that she would marry one of the young men she'd grown up around. But the more Jonet made her distaste for the Kirk apparent, the less the local lads spoke to Elspeth. Once upon a time it was nothing for Rychard Graham or Jon Dougleish to come to their croft on some pretext or another, and others of her age group would chat openly to her at the markets, some even flirting, though none bar Rychard and Jon ever made any further advances. Yet although she guessed what was happening, it was only Rychard who did her the kindness of telling her to her face.

"Elspeth, you know if it was just us, I would be properly courting you by now," he told her the second summer after her being hunted, and the pain in his eyes told her that his affections were still true. "But my folk depend on the McBurneys for their croft, and Veitch is forever at one or the other of that pair's houses, calling some woman names.

"I can't risk bringing their wrath down on everyone else, especially with three younger sisters to think of. If I marry you, their chances of getting a good man to look after them once our parents are gone get tainted too, because nobody wants to be tarred by contact with a witch." He'd seen Elspeth's eyes fill up and hurriedly added. "Not that I think your ma *is* a witch! But she's…well she's suspected, isn't she?" And Elspeth had had to agree.

She never told her mother that, though. Jonet's nightmares, which had subsided in the twenty years following her own incarceration, had come back with a vengeance after what had happened to Elspeth, and sometimes Elspeth knew that she didn't sleep for days. And because of that it was probably no bad thing that Elspeth remained at home, because by the end of a run of sleepless nights, Jonet didn't know what day of the week it was, often forgetting to do even simple tasks like tending to the cooking fire, but also talking wildly of seeing fae creatures and witches flying.

It was hard on Elspeth's father, Johnne, too. Jonet was no longer much of a wife to him, someone he could look to to help him with the croft, let alone the friend and confident she had once been. Yet to his credit he remained steadfastly loyal and understanding of her, and if he said any words of condemnation, it was on those nights when he sat by the fire with Elspeth after Jonet fell into an exhausted sleep. At which point he would roundly curse the souls of the men who had tormented Jonet way back in 1630, and almost broken her, after which she had never quite been the same bright and cheerful girl he had married.

By the time 1658 came around there was a general tension in the shire that no woman could ignore. The word they had from farther afield hinted that in many places, folk had tired of the harsh limitations of ministers like Veitch, and there was an unspoken but general consensus to allow things to relax back to the way things had been before the wars. Part of that was due to the arrival of Cromwell's right-hand man, General Monck, in 1655 as Command-in-Chief of Cromwell's army in Scotland. A man of moderate beliefs, Monck had condemned the fanatical witch hunting and what he saw as more excessive religious observances, to the quiet relief of many.

If the Kirk was now sending ministers into kirks in Edinburgh and Glasgow who had no objections to having bishops within the Kirk once more, it was by and large accepted. Not in Dumfriesshire, though. If a congregation didn't like the minister who had been sent to take over a parish, he was likely to find his kirk half empty on a Sunday, and hear of conventicle prayer meetings taking place out on the hillsides, with radical speakers firing up his flock with inflammatory words.

And none of it was helped in the current year by

concerns over Oliver Cromwell's health, and what would happen once he died.

"They're saying that he's going to make his son Protector," Elspeth told her father, as they unloaded the panniers off their pony after her trip to the last market to be held before Easter. She leaned in closer, almost afraid to speak in their own yard of the other thing she'd heard. "Isn't that making him a hereditary leader like the King was? Some are whispering that the English Parliament is even in discussion with the old king's son. The one in exile. A *king* might even come back!"

Johnne Allen groaned and leaned his head on the pony's shaggy neck. "Dear God! That will cause bloodshed."

Elspeth clasped her hand over his. "Yes and no, Pa. Again, the news from much farther away is that people just want peace. There's no appetite to fight anymore. But you're right, there were men in Dumfries who were openly saying that the Solemn League and Covenant must be upheld by whoever follows Cromwell, and that they will fight for the right to determine how they pray."

She sighed, remembering how she had hidden in a doorway as Thomas McBurney had strutted through the market place, crowing about how he would stand up for Presbyter Veitch and the Covenant, accompanied by young Gideon Corsan, hanging on his every word and trying to strut like Thomas, despite only being fourteen. Elspeth was almost more scared of Gideon than Thomas, for all that he was barely more than a boy, while Thomas was a married man of coming up twenty-five. The fact that Gideon's father, John Corsan, had not only failed to help Marione – his own cousin's daughter – in her time of need, but had actively been heard to condemn her, made that branch of the family very dangerous men.

"Poor old William Corsan must be revolving in his grave," Agnes had said the last time she had come to see them. "Our Margaret tells me that his Grissell is penniless. She's holding on to hers and William's croft by the skin of her teeth, and it's only because it's down on the coast and not up here that John Corsan hasn't been able to spend sufficient time to get his hands on it. He's greedy, that man. He covets his own cousin's land as much as he does other people's. You watch yourself around him, Elspeth. You live too close to him for safety."

"And you be careful, too," Elspeth remembered urging her cousin. "I know your husband is only distantly related to Grissell's branch of the McCartneys, but the word in Dumfries is that your Donald's cousin, John McCartney, is trying to ingratiate himself with the provosts, the mayor, and even the sheriff. You've always said how Donald defers to John – just be very careful he doesn't unwittingly give John the means to harm Margaret because his cousin has wheedled around him to give up information."

"Donald wouldn't!" Agnes had protested at the time, but since then Elspeth and Johnne had heard some worrying whispers about the amount of time Donald and John McCartney had been spending together.

"I'm worried about Agnes as well as Margaret," Elspeth now confided to her father. "Margaret could end up in trouble because, like Ma, she won't back down. But Agnes could be as much in danger!"

Johnne Allen looked at his daughter with worried eyes. "How so?"

"John McCartney…you know, Agnes' Donald's cousin who lives on the other side of Dumfries."

"What about him?"

"He's been named as a 'chancellor' – whatever that might be – for any future witch trials. It sounds as if he's going to be in charge of whatever proceedings there are."

"But Agnes has never done anything even faintly suspicious," Johnne protested.

Thinking back to that evening at the Apostles' Stones, Elspeth wasn't sure she could protest too hard over that, but since her father knew nothing of that, she said instead, "Maybe not, but Donald's not been the healthiest of men of late, has he? And it's not as if Agnes has a handful of strapping sons to defend her. All she ever had were two sickly daughters – now gone too young, bless them – and two stillborn sons. If Donald dies, she's got nobody to stand up for her, Pa. And that croft of his is worth the having.

"It's well known that John McCartney has had his eye on Grissell McCartney and her late husband's house down in Kirkcudbright for years – if not for himself then for one of his sons – because she might not have *money*, but it's in a good situation and McCartney does have a family claim through her, albeit distantly. In truth, that conniving younger cousin of old William Corsan's, John Corsan, is in a better place to get his hands on that, but it's the very fact that John McCartney is so grasping that everyone knows it that worries me.

"A man who doesn't care what his neighbours think of him as long as his superiors have a good opinion is someone you don't want to cross. And both times I've been to Dumfries of late, those two John's have seemed to be conducting more business than just selling sheep to one another. There's something going on between those two, and it gives me the shivers every time I think of them with their heads together at the ale house."

Her father nodded, glad all over again that his daughter had her head on firmly. "I was going to take your mother over to see Agnes this Sunday," he said sadly. "It's a good thing I hadn't mentioned it to her yet, because I don't think we'll be going now."

"No, Pa, I think that's sensible. Ma doesn't think about what she's saying anymore, and one wrong word while Donald is listening and it could end very badly for all of us."

Chapter 11

With the second lot of Valentine's Day Special bookings arriving the next day, Anna was kept too busy to do much about researching until the middle of the week. That didn't mean it was any more peaceful, though. Cora wasn't due on again until the Tuesday, but when she did return it was with a very self-satisfied, smug expression. She practically looked down her nose at Anna on the times when their paths crossed, and finally Anna could stand it no more.

Getting Brenda on one side, she begged her, "Will you please find out what Cora has been up to? She's obviously itching for me to ask her, and to have something out with me, but I'm not going to give her that satisfaction. We can't have a situation where she and I can't work on the desk together, and if she flies off the handle at me, I'll have little choice but to pull rank on her. I don't want to do that, not least because if she then moans to Polly, Sarah, and Gemma, I don't want to put them in the position of picking sides between a girl who they've known for a long time against the new manageress they have to work with."

Brenda understood without any need for further pleading. "Leave it with me. I'll winkle it out of her. It never takes long with Cora anyway, and she's obviously bursting to tell someone."

And so Anna made herself scarce, going into the kitchen to talk over some applicants with Emilio. What she wasn't expecting was for Brenda to come storming in with a face like thunder. For one dreadful moment, Anna feared that she had done something without realising it, and that Brenda's anger was aimed at her. It wasn't.

"That bloody stupid little girl!" Brenda fumed, going over to the kettle and making herself a very strong mug of coffee. "My God, nothing in trousers is safe from her."

Anna felt her heart already sinking. Jensen. It had to be about Jensen.

However, it was Emilio who asked, "What's she done?"

Brenda leaned back against the deep Belfast sink and rolled her eyes in despair. "Oh, she only heard where Gary had taken your ex, Anna. And what did she do? The next day, being her day off, she goes into Dumfries and according to her, gave him a shoulder to cry on." Brenda's eyes narrowed. "Well, she gave him a good deal more comforting than just her bloody shoulder, didn't she. Absolutely full of herself, she is. Silly little minx! And would you believe it, she's going to ask you to give her the rest of the week off!"

Oddly, Anna felt nothing but relief, and it dawned on her that this was proof, had she needed it, that Jensen was hardly heartbroken over her. No man who'd lost the love of his life would be jumping into bed with his wife's colleague, especially knowing that it couldn't fail to get back to her. This smacked of him wanting to punish her, a touch of 'See! I can have any woman I want,' – not wanting to make up.

To Brenda she said, "If Cora wants the rest of the week off, she can have it. We're quiet enough to not need her. I'll do her shifts."

"But Anna! She's trying to poach your husband!" Brenda protested.

Anna went and gave Brenda a hug. "I don't think he was ever *my* husband, Bren'. For my part, once the wool had fallen from over my eyes about what kind of life I'd lead with him, there was never any question of me going back to him. I may not have had the kind of battering that Cora's had off her exes, but my God, I took some mental punishment. And the longer I'm away from him and both sets of parents, the more I can see how I was manipulated by them. Not least, because between them they ensured that I never had a moment to myself where I might have been able to think straight.

"I'm not walking back into that. Not for anyone. And certainly not for a man who thinks as little of me as Jensen does. …No, if Cora wants to tumble in the hay with Jensen while he's here, she's welcome to him – he's not the most ardent of lovers she'll find out."

"He's not staying." Brenda blurted out. "She's planning on going south with him!"

To her and Emilio's astonishment, Anna burst out laughing.

"Anna?" Brenda asked worriedly. "Did you understand what I said?"

"Oh. I understood," Anna replied with a happy giggle. "Oh, poor Cora. She's in for a rude awakening!" Then she took in the genuine worry on Brenda's face and explained. "Cora's not going to be going anywhere with Jensen. For a start off, he'd never take home someone his parents haven't vetted first. And I can assure you that Cora would be about as welcome as a rabid dog in their world!

"She has no connections she can pull for them, no business talents or associations they can use. If she thinks that a couple of quick fumbles with him is going to get her into the passenger seat of the Jag, and off south for a social whirl of cocktails, parties, and a lifestyle that's probably come straight off the TV, then she's in for a nasty shock. Don't worry Bren', she'll come creeping back into work next week praying that nobody asks her how her time off went. Please, go and tell her that she can go."

Brenda departed, still nursing the coffee, and giving Anna strange looks.

"She don't understand," Emilio sympathised, "but I do. He never really love you, did he? Because you were right, if he come up here truly wanting to make things right with you, he would never be easily distracted by some woman coming and throwing herself at him."

"That's exactly it," Anna said with relief, glad that Emilio could see the truth, and knowing that Gary would too.

When she went out to the reception desk, Cora was gone, and Brenda was telling Gary all about it.

"I thought she'd be delighted when I told her Anna said she could have the time off," she was saying. "But she seemed really put out instead. I don't understand."

"She wanted to have her chance to brag to me and make me jealous of her," Anna said sadly. "We robbed her of the chance to crow, but next week she'll be glad we did."

"You're really certain that's what he'll do, aren't you," Brenda said, perplexed, her frown only deepening when Gary added,

"And I am too. …Ach, Bren', he's never going to fall for whatever limited charms Cora has! Anna's right. No girl is going to cross his threshold without a full inspection by his mammy, and she's no' here is she? So the chances of him taking Cora down south on the off-chance are nil."

"Oh dear, poor Cora," Brenda murmured, looking worried. "And she rang up her boyfriend and broke it off with him this morning, too."

"Ach, he's no loss," Gary said cheerfully. "And if she's given him the heave-ho, she's saved herself getting another black eye – that one's got a nasty reputation from all I hear. No, Cora's better off with neither of them."

As if to prove him right, only an hour later a phone call came through for Anna.

"This is your last chance," Jensen told her, sounding more aggrieved than upset. "I can't take any more time off work chasing around after you."

Anna had put the call on speaker, guessing that there wouldn't be anything in it that Gary and Brenda shouldn't hear, and Brenda's face was a picture. This clearly wasn't the broken-hearted lover she'd imagined him to be.

Finding it oddly difficult to keep giggles of relief out of her voice, Anna told him, "I never *asked* you to come chasing after me. Honestly, Jensen, I'll sign any divorce papers you like on the grounds of desertion – I'll own up to running out on you, even though non-consummation would be a better reason." That raised Brenda's eyebrows even higher, though Anna had confided in her that nothing had happened between her and Jensen on their wedding night.

"How very magnanimous of you." And Anna could hear the worry in Jensen's voice even before he added, "And what am I supposed to tell the parents, eh?"

"That really is your biggest worry, isn't it?" Anna said with regret. "Not how you're going to carry on your life without me, but what your parents will say when you come home from Scotland empty-handed. What were you supposed to do, Jensen? Bring me back, kicking and screaming, so that I could have a good telling off from both sets of parents, and then go down to that flat in London and behave myself?"

There was a stunned silence on the other end of the line.

"I thought so," Anna sighed. "Jensen, you need to decide what *you* want in your life. As long as you keep dancing to their tune, you'll never be happy."

"I'm fine." Jensen said defensively.

"Are you? Are you really? Because I don't think so. Not deep down in your heart of hearts. I'm not going to pretend that I know what it *is* that you want, but I do know that it wasn't you and me living the corporate couple's life down in London. Take care of yourself, Jensen, because you can't keep on putting your parents first. You won't see me again, but I wish you well, I truly do, because I think you're going to need all the good will you can get." And with that she cut the call.

"I didn't expect that," Brenda said sadly. "Dear me, it sounded as though he was *sent* here to come and find you."

"I have absolutely no doubt that he was," Anna agreed, "and if I feel sorry for him, it's because for the first time he's bearing the brunt of his parents' out-and-out disapproval and disappointment. Jensen is used to being the blue-eyed boy. He can't cope with being blamed. But somebody must have gone up and found him in a right state on the morning after, and my guess would be his father. And there's a man who would never understand why a son of his hadn't started trying to knock out heirs the moment the bedroom door was shut. I reckon Jensen is dreading going home empty-handed, and with good cause!"

She was proven right again when the next week came around and Cora slunk in for her next shift, visibly subdued and trying not to meet Anna's eye. For the morning, Anna let her stew – she wasn't that much of a saint that she couldn't enjoy being proven right – but before Cora left, she made sure that she took the chance to say, "I'm sorry you got burned, Cora. I did try to warn you what he was like. Jensen is bad news for any girl who crosses his path, not because he's that nasty, but because he'll never be his own man. So let's forget about it, shall we? I don't want to talk about him, and I'm sure you don't either."

Cora didn't reply, but when Anna glanced back as she walked away, she could see that Cora was an embarrassed shade of red, yet still had her head ducked down. There would be no answering back this time.

Of more significance – though they wouldn't realise it until later – was the arrival of a new guest the week after. Anna was sitting at the reception desk when, out of the corner of her eye, she thought she saw a wolf. Blinking, and then swivelling in her seat, she turned to find herself eye to eye with a huge shaggy deerhound. It gave a gentle huff as Anna gasped, and then stepped forward to lean its noble forehead against her shoulder in a mute supplication to be fussed.

Her surprise evaporated in a laugh, and as she reached up and silked the soft ears, got a little grunt of happiness from the dog.

"Harris! Harris!" a male voice came from out of sight through the main doors. "Come here, you bloody rogue!"

"I think your boss wants you," Anna told the hound, but he only leaned into her harder. As he almost pushed her off her chair, Anna called, "If you're looking for your dog, he's in here."

Moments later, a tall, well-built man, with a shock of floppy chestnut coloured hair, was towed in through the door by another huge dog of more mixed lineage.

"Oh God, I'm so sorry," the man said, fixing her with eyes as brown as his dog's, but with twinkling amusement in them. "Harris is just such a big sook, but he's a terrible ladies' man. I might have known he'd make straight for the reception desk."

"It's better than the kitchen, I suppose," Anna agreed with a laugh. "We had three Jack Russells do that last week."

"Don't!" he said with a grimace of despair and a nod to the dog he was still attached to. "This one's been known to do that too."

By now the other dog had come around the desk and was demanding his share of the fuss.

"And what's your name?" Anna asked her new friend, finding herself with a hand ruffling each of them.

"This is Lewis. Not a full deerhound as you can see. Harris was supposed to be going to breed with a lady deerhound, but he managed to sneak out and have a night of passion with a lady standard poodle as well. No chance of denying it – he was still there in her kennel with her in the morning!"

"Oops!"

Their owner grinned ruefully. "Aye, that's not what her owner said, though. I got Harris through the deerhound rescue, and he's got all his pedigree papers, so the woman was really keen to breed from him when she saw him. I didn't intend to have any of the pups – was quite determined not to feed the breeding money-machine if I'm honest, quite aside from the question of having the room for another big dog in my apartment. It was just her persistence which ground me down, so I thought just once wouldn't hurt.

"Well the deerhound pups were absolute beauties, but within the day the poodle had her litter too, and it was quite clear, even if Harris hadn't been caught *in flagrante* with her, that the male poodle who arrived a couple of days later had been beaten to the winning post." He winced but with a half-laugh.

Gary's chuckle came from the door into the front conference room, and immediately Lewis went to him.

"See what I mean?" his owner said with good-tempered exasperation. "Harris is a ladies' man all the way. Lewis? He's just a tart with everyone! …I'm Cameron Wiseheart, by the way," although he pronounced his surname 'Wish-ert', and it was only looking at the guest register later that clarified it for Anna.

"Gary, night porter," Gary introduced himself, shaking hands with Cameron, "and this is Anna, our manageress."

"Great to meet you both," said Cameron, attaching a lead to Harris and in vain trying to tug him back to the guest's side of the desk, made harder by Lewis' refusal to leave his new best friend in the form of Gary.

As Gary ruffled Lewis' fur, he said, "So going I what I heard coming in, I guess Harris had to own up to his responsibilities, and you take one of the pups?"

Cameron nodded. "Couldn't very well refuse, could I?"

Anna had come around the desk as the only way to get Harris to move, and said, "But I thought people paid insane amounts of money for poodle crosses? Don't cockerpoos fetch something crazy like a grand each?"

There was another roll of Cameron's eyes, and Anna noticed when he spoke in Gary's company that his accent became more broadly Scottish. "Oh, aye! But that's for wee cute, fluffy things you can put in a tartan collar and dicky bow, no' a big hairy teuchter like this great lug."

Gary nodded sagely. "And there's no cute name that trips off the tongue for the likes o' him, is there? I suppose if you can have a labradoodle, you could have a deerdoodle, but it's no' great."

Without realising that she was thinking aloud, Anna added, "And definitely not a poohound!"

Instantly Cameron hooted with laughter. "Oh, he's that, all right! If you saw how much I have to clear up…! A forty-four kilo dog can produce an awful lot! I spend a fortune on wee black bags dedicated to the goddess Cloaca."

They all chuckled at that, Anna in particular over the idea of there being a goddess of poo, let alone one receiving dog poo offerings.

"What happened to the rest of the litter?" Anna then asked worriedly. One of her parents' so-called friends had bred pedigree gun-dogs, and Anna mentally shuddered at the memory of how callous they had been over pups that didn't meet their standards.

"Well Lewis was the biggest by far," Cameron told her to her great relief. "The rest were more their mum's size, and she only had six, two of whom didn'a survive – turns out that despite a pedigree as long as your arm, she wasn'a a great breeding bitch. So she and the other three pups went to family homes, thank God. I took Lewis precisely because I knew he'd be the hardest to home. Even at a few weeks, he was half as big again as his sisters, you see."

Already liking this guest, his last statement endeared him even more to Anna. No picking the best pup, or the prettiest. He'd gone for the one with the greatest need of a good home.

"I think they're both gorgeous," Anna said truthfully. "And Lewis' lovely wheaten cream fur is a stunning colour." Then looked down at her smart black trousers which were rapidly changing to the same colour.

"Ach, sorry about that," Cameron said with a wince, "nobody told him that as a poodle-cross he wasn'a supposed to shed."

Gary chuckled. "Missed the memo, did y' lad?" as he too brushed himself off.

"Are you here on holiday, Mr Wiseheart?" Anna asked politely. "Only we've got a few leaflets of good dog walks if you're interested."

"Actually, I'm here on business," Cameron told them. "I'm just lucky that I can bring Harris and Lewis with me."

"What sort of work do you do?" Anna queried, hurriedly adding in case he thought she was being too nosey, "Only we've got the ability to set you up for conference calls in the front room if you want."

Luckily, he didn't take exception to her asking, saying, "Investments, mainly. But not for a company as such. My brother is one of those tech geniuses who is brilliant at coming up with ideas, but has no idea how to handle the vast sums of money he earns. So although I'm actually the younger brother, I look after his interests while he does the inventing."

Remembering Gary's disgust at what Jensen did, Anna was quite surprised to see him giving a nod of approval. "Looking after family should always come first," he agreed, yet Anna was surprised to see the faint flash of hurt on Cameron's face. Was he his brother's reluctant keeper?

"Austin is quite high on the autistic spectrum, you see," Cameron was continuing to Gary. "Or at least that's the nearest we've ever got to a diagnosis – he does rather defy pigeonholing to one condition. Dealing with people stresses him out. He has his own apartment in Aberdeen, but our mum goes in most days to make sure he's got things like food in and the washing done."

"That has to be a strain," Gary agreed sympathetically. "And what about your dad? Presumably someone has to be taking care of the essentials for your parents' lives – can't be easy having an adult child to care for taking up one parent's life? If you're the younger brother, then he must be an adult physically at least?"

Cameron grimaced. "Dad is only my dad. Mum was with someone else when she had Austin, and he was already a boy of seven when she met Dad. Oddly, it was easier to deal with him then, because they sent him to a special residential school, which did wonders for bringing out his talents. It's as he's got older that it's got harder to cope with him.

"After he'd had one of his spectacular meltdowns at Mum, because something wasn't just so in his rigid world, Dad had just had enough. He pretty much gave Mum an ultimatum. Said that they'd never had the chance to have a proper married life together. He'd taken her on with Austin knowing what he was like, but never dreamed that Austin would still be taking over their lives decades later, and that he wanted to live a bit before he got too old. So the compromise was that I took over keeping Austin financially independent, we took on cleaners and other people to help with Austin's care, and Mum just keeps an eye on them. Not that that's worked out as planned."

He suddenly gave a bitter laugh. "God, you must wonder what the hell kind of person I am, washing all our family dirty laundry in public when you've hardly met me."

"I think sometimes you need to talk to people who don't have a stake in the game," Anna sympathised. "Gary must sometimes think he's a priest with his own confessional the number of times I've chewed his ear over my family."

Cameron grinned at Gary. "So you're the guardian of people's secrets as well as the door to the hotel, are you?"

"Aye, something like that," replied Gary affably, but tactfully changing the subject by asking, "Are you comfortable up in Medlar? I know Brenda said you'd asked for a largish room because of these two big lads," Lewis was still nuzzling his hand every time he stopped silking his ears.

"Oh very!" Cameron instantly responded. "In fact, if I'd known just how big the rooms are, I wouldn't have made that request, because one of me and two of them would have fitted easily into the smaller rooms, going on what I saw of them when housekeeping was in this morning."

He waved a hand at the grand staircase and hall. "It's a fabulous old building, isn't it. Do you know much of the history of it?"

Anna fished out one of the leaflets. "This is the potted guide. However, we're really trying to fill in some of the details, especially around the seventeenth century."

"Oh really? Why then in particular?" Cameron wanted to know.

"The small matter of some noisy wee ghosts," Gary told him with a wink, not wanting to make too much of it in case this guest was a sceptic.

Cameron's face lit up. "Ghosts? Oh, how fabulous. That's just perfect for an old place like this. Let's face it, a lot of people would really hope that somewhere like this *would* have a ghost or two. Do you know who they're supposed to be? Some jilted former lady of the house? Or a Jacobite laird, hunted from the field at Culloden?"

"Ah," Anna said apologetically, "not quite that romantic, I'm afraid. And we're not entirely sure who they are beyond roughly the century in which they lived. As for the noise, one of them will insist on firing his musket. It can't hurt anyone, of course, but it is a bit disconcerting to hear."

For a moment Cameron looked at her in astonishment, then with enthusiasm said, "Time for a ghost hunt, then!"

1658

Elspeth ~ May onwards

It was mere weeks after Elspeth had brought the warning of trouble on the horizon that the Allens heard that once again, Marione Corsan and her mother, Grissell McCartney, had been taken to the Tolbooth at Kirkcudbright for investigation for being witches. Who exactly had brought the accusations, at that stage wasn't known, but the very fact that two women, whom the higher authority of the Kirk had ordered to be set free just eight years previously, could now be imprisoned again, came as a dire warning. Nobody was safe.

And then only a week or so later, the thing that John and Elspeth had feared for so long happened. Out of the blue, Presbyter Veitch, accompanied by a smirking Thomas McBurney and a couple of rough-looking men, came to the Allens' croft.

"We are here to take Jonet Clark in for questioning on the grounds that she is a notorious witch," Veitch said pompously, though Elspeth noted that he didn't get down off the hill pony he was riding, no doubt scared of the punch he might get off Johnne Allen for dragging his wife away. He left the rough stuff to McBurney's men, one of whom punched Johnne so hard he was laid out cold on the rough pebbled yard.

As Elspeth held onto her mother, looking in dismay at the way her father was lying unmoving,

Thomas McBurney sneered "Want to be brought in too, little witch? It can be arranged!"

At which, Jonet shrugged her arm free from Elspeth and gave her a hard shove away. "Look to your father," she wept, clearly feeling that having Elspeth brought in alongside her would be more than she could bear.

"Good choice, witch," McBurney said, looking down his nose at her from the advantage of being up on his horse. "Right, let's get her to Irongray. You're going to have your hands full with this one, Presbyter."

"The Lord will give me strength," Veitch replied sanctimoniously, and rode out at the head of the party alongside McBurney, with the two roughs following behind them, Jonet slung across one of their saddles as if no more than a sack of grain.

Sobbing in distress, Elspeth ran to the well and got the bucket of cold water, taking it to where her father lay and liberally dousing him with it in the hope that the cold would shock him into waking. It did, but far more slowly than Elspeth liked. And when he could sit up, he was promptly sick and felt dizzy, meaning it was all Elspeth could do to get him inside in slow stages.

It took nearly a week for Johnne Allen to recover, and in that time Elspeth was beside herself with worry. She didn't dare leave him, yet she was frantic with fear over what was happening with her mother. In the end it was an elderly neighbour, Christian, who brought them news.

"I'm too old to be scared of the likes of Patrik Veitch," the old lady declared stoutly. "My time can't be far off, so if I go a bit sooner than expected, I won't be afeared. I've been a God-fearing woman all my life, and I don't believe the Lord will hold it against me that yon pompous wee man has it in for me at this late stage."

Elspeth offered the old lady a hot beaker of herb tea, May being a rather chilly month this year. "I'm just so grateful that you've come," she said, feeling herself welling up all over again, as she'd done so often in these last days. "I didn't dare leave Pa, you see. He's getting better, but he still keeps getting giddy turns, and I'm scared of him falling over onto the cooking fire if I'm not here."

Christian nodded sympathetically. "Knocks on the head can be funny things. You're being a good daughter to your pa, and you can't be in two places at once. And in truth, I don't know as there's much anyone can do for your ma. But I came because my oldest, Alester, works for the sheriff in his stables, and he overheard the sheriff saying something about your family possibly raising a bond.

"I don't know quite what that means, and neither did Alester, but he said that it sounded very much that if your pa made a formal appeal, and promised to pay up against your ma behaving proper towards the Kirk, then they'd have to let her go. Something about there being no witnesses against her, you see. Those women down in Kirkcudbright have practically got folks lining up to swear against them, even if it's out o' fear o' their accusers, no' them, but your ma hasn't.

"And I tell you something else: Alester said that that conniving swine, John Corsan had a face that would curdle milk when he heard the sheriff saying that. He and Bailie McBurney's sons have been thick as thieves – not Alexander McBurney's, no, he's got more sense, and anyway, his sons are far away. No, it's William's boys you need to watch out for, because they fear you thwarting them and Veitch, and the law being on your side…which wouldn't look good for them."

It wasn't much, but it was more hope than Elspeth could ever have believed they might have, and so as soon as Johnne was clear-headed enough to think straight, the two of them started working out what they could sell to start raising money.

"I don't care if we lose the croft," Johnne told Elspeth. "I'd rather live as a vagrant with your mother beside me, than keep this place and watch her be strangled and burned. May God help us, we might have to go on the road and look for somewhere totally new to live, but we can only do that if your ma lives too."

"How much do you think we'd need?" Elspeth asked worriedly, knowing that they might be selling everything they possessed.

"I doubt we'll get away with less than thirty merks," Johnne replied, his expression grim.

"Oh, Pa! That's a lot of money."

In reply, Johnne got up and went to the house's doorway where a large slab of stone formed the threshold, but rather than lifting the huge slab itself, he worked one of the stones to the side of it free. Most of their house's walls were packed pebbles held together with mortar, and lime-washed against the weather, protected from the frequent Scottish rain by a considerable overhang of the turf roof, the same as all of their neighbours' crofts, but around the door Johnne had strengthened them with large stones to give more support to the doorframe. What he pulled out now was one low down on the door's hinge side, down in the shadows where nobody would see that it hadn't been as secure as the rest. And once it was out, he put his hand into what had to be a cavity and drew out a small box.

"I always meant to tell you about this in case of emergencies," he told Elspeth. "I never dared tell your ma for fear of her using it to save someone like Geillis. I knew, you see, that I'd only ever be able to get this much once. This is everything I've saved from right back when I first married your ma. At first it was in the hope that we'd be able to get a croft rather than me just working for old man Parton. And then when my pa died and I was able to take this one over, it was in case I needed to have someone come and live here to help look after my ma, because back in those days Jonet was having your sisters and helping me in the fields."

He shook his head in despair. "I've always managed without touching this right up until now. I just worked harder and longer to get us through the tough times, and put aside what I could in the good ones. But this isn't something I can cure with the strength in my arms."

"Oh, Pa!" Elspeth gulped again, coming to wrap her own arms around him as she fought back the tears. There was part of her that right now thought, much as she loved her mother dearly, that Jonet hadn't appreciated just how much her husband had looked ahead and tried to provide for what troubles might be on the horizon. It made Elspeth wish that her mother had chosen to stay away from people if she knew she couldn't mask her feelings better. That was all it would have taken to avoid this. She knew that Jonet hadn't deserved to be dragged in for investigation by Presbyter Veitch's father all those years ago in 1630, of course she understood that, but once it had happened and then times had become more dangerous again, her ma could have behaved differently.

Brushing the tears away, she looked up at her father and squared her shoulders. "I'm not as good with the dyes as Ma, but I'll do my best. And if we both work the fields, and then I spin and dye while you work the loom, I reckon we can have those fleeces we've got from this spring's shearing ready for market by early autumn. We'll have nothing to sell over the winter, mind you, but we'll worry about that when we've got Ma home safely." And Johnne wrapped his daughter into a tight hug and blessed the day she'd been born, for without her he would have been lost right now.

It was another blessing that they were coming into the lighter nights, because while Johnne worked the fields, Elspeth tended the vegetable plots and chickens, and then spun yarn until her hands were thick with the lanolin from the wool. Then when she had sufficient yarn, in the mornings when the light was best in the little shed where Johnne had his loom, she had him show her how to use it. She was never going to be as good as Jonet at getting the slubs out of the yarn. Her mother was far more talented at that – so much so that it was another of those things where jealous neighbours hinted at otherworldly help – so it was no bad thing that Elspeth's looked just like the fabric that other crofters produced. Where she did have an advantage was in having learned her mother's recipes for dyes. There would be precious little left of the dried plants by the end of the summer, because Elspeth had no time to go out picking and then drying them, as she'd done last year for her mother to restock her stores, but again, that was a worry for afterwards, not now.

By the time Lammas came around, Elspeth had lost weight and was dark under her eyes, but the pile of woven cloth had built up enough to hope that they would get a fair price if they went to market early enough to avoid all those who hadn't been as fast with their production.

"We might yet do it, Pa!" she said one night, as they carefully folded another length of cloth which had been dyed and dried. She'd managed to create some pretty patterns in blues, yellows, and mauves with her dyes, even if the richer colours weren't as dense as she'd like, and she was sure these would sell. A couple of weeks' more work and there'd be enough to go to market.

Yet before then, out of the blue they had a midnight caller. When the knocking came at the door, Elspeth and Johnne feared the worst, but realised that whoever was there was tapping as if fearing to be heard, rather than demanding entry. When they opened the door, it was to find Elspeth's oldest sister, Jean, looking worriedly over her shoulder into the darkness.

"Jean! What's happened?" Johnne asked, fearing that someone – most likely Jonet – had died.

"I've brought you this," Jean said, thrusting a soft leather pouch into his hand. "It's not much. It's all I can spare. George didn't want me to give it, but I told him I couldn't go before God having seen my own mother burned, and without trying to help the rest of my family."

None of the family had taken to Jean's husband George, so his response wasn't unexpected.

"Don't expect the like from our Mailie," Jean hurried on with, referring to the middle of the sisters. "I don't know where she is anymore."

"What?" Johnne and Elspeth gasped, both wondering if Mailie had come to harm in the way Elspeth had so nearly done.

Yet Jean gave an exasperated wave of her hand. "You know her Patrick died?"

"No," was Elspeth's shocked answer. "We've heard nothing of her since they moved away to Berwick." That had been all the way back in 1645, shortly after Mailie had married against her parents' wishes at the tender age of seventeen, and since then war had rolled over Berwick and the family had feared her dead, but prayed she wasn't.

Jean gave a prim sniff. "Hmph! Well Patrick was fool enough to get involved in the fighting in Berwick ten years ago. He was taken prisoner and died not long after."

"Why didn't you tell us?" Elspeth cried in dismay. "Heavens, Jean. She's our sister at the end of the day. Just because she moved away doesn't mean we don't care. What if she'd needed help?"

Jean pursed her lips and pronounced sanctimoniously, "Mailie has ungodly appetites when it comes to men," making Elspeth swallow reflexively as she realised that this sister was probably one of those holding hard to the Covenant, which was why they'd seen nothing of her in years. Her mother being suspected as a witch nearly thirty years ago alone would be enough to keep Jean at a distance if that was so. Neither Elspeth nor their father dared to ask exactly what Jean thought ungodly, for fear of how that might be taken. As far as they knew, Mailie had simply been as she always had, a little too free with her smiles at any good-looking lad, rather than being an outright whore.

Mercifully, Jean adopted a pious attitude and, looking as if the very words might choke her, told them without them having to ask further, "Mailie took up with a soldier after that. She sent word to me that she was following him and the army into England." There was a disdainful sniff. "That was nearly ten years ago. I've heard nothing since."

Elspeth looked in horror from her father to her sister and back again. She and her parents had presumed that Mailie hadn't come to see them because she didn't *want* to, not because she might be lost or dead. They'd always hoped that one day, when the world stopped spinning out of control, she would at some point reappear, healthy and happy, and with Patrick and the children she'd been assumed to have had alongside her, to everyone's rejoicing.

Moreover, Jonet had always said that she thought Jean and Mailie would stay in touch with one another, and had trusted Jean to let them know of any crisis. And if Jean lived way over in Newton Stewart, which was far enough to make casual visits difficult, again, there had been the assumption that if she'd needed them to know something, then she would have come before this, or at least sent a message. Clearly they had been horribly wrong to presume this.

"You won't see me again," Jean declared, already turning and walking away without so much as a hug. "I've done my Christian duty towards my mother – not that she deserves it – and to you both." She made it sound more as if she was handing out charity to a poor servant than helping her own father and sister. "I won't risk my own husband and children by further contact."

And with that she disappeared into the night, the

sound of a horse plodding off westwards coming a moment later.

Johnne and Elspeth stood staring into the darkness in shock, unable to fully comprehend what had just happened.

Then Johnne slowly disintegrated, falling to his knees to sob uncontrollably. "My poor Mailie," he sobbed. "My poor Jonet."

"Why has this happened to us?" Elspeth found herself saying over and over, as she coaxed her father inside enough to close the door against the night chill.

Johnne Allen had never been a drinking man, but there was a stoneware bottle in the cupboard filled with *uisge*, brewed out in a hidden still in the hills by one of the Highlanders who, in the past, had served as a bodyguard to the lordly Grierson family at nearby Lagg. And right now, Elspeth felt they both needed a dram. She poured a tot into a mug for each of them and added some water, knowing full well how potent it was. When her father knocked it back in one go, she didn't hesitate to fill it back up, and the second one seemed to steady him a bit.

Taking her hand in one of his work-calloused ones, Johnne told her, "You ought to know this now. God knows, I never wanted to make the distinction, and I never did when you were children, but Elspeth…Jean is only yours and Mailie's half-sister."

"What?" Elspeth was aghast.

"It goes back a long way," Johnne sighed. "Your mother was a bonnie lass who caught the eye of many a local lad." He smiled at the memory. "There was even a bit of danger about courting her, because your grandmother was a wise-woman of some repute." He saw Elspeth start, and nodded. "Oh yes, your grandmother was what they would now condemn as a witch. – Strange how back then she was more revered for her healing skills. But times change, and in this case not for the better."

He held the mug out for another dram, and Elspeth obliged, now on the edge of her seat.

"It was in 1624 that things turned for the worse," Johnne recalled. "That was the year that Patrik Veitch's father came as the minister to Irongray and brought Patrik with him. God alone knows what happened to Minister Veitch's wife. She certainly wasn't with them when they came, and I've never heard either father or son speak of her."

He paused and shook his head at the memory of what he was about to tell Elspeth. "Young Patrik, as he was then, was a headstrong boy. His father was so full of the Bible, God, and reforming his parish, that he had no time for his son, and as a result Patrik ran wild through the district.

"Well, it wasn't long before your mother caught his eye. He'd have had to be blind not to notice her. But she wasn't interested. Can you imagine your ma as a minister's wife?" and they both laughed weakly at the very thought. "And I can tell you that the whole district knew that her mother had sent him packing the one time he dared to arrive in their croft's yard *demanding* to see her. It probably wasn't wise of the old lady, but she cursed him up hill and down glen. I've no doubt that she saw the fanatical gleam in his eye even at that early stage, and didn't like what she saw.

"But young Veitch didn't take being repulsed well. One late autumn evening, as your ma was making her way home from market, young Veitch waylaid her and raped her."

"Oh, God, no!" Elspeth cried. Already fearing

what was coming. "She got with child by him? Jean is Veitch's bastard?"

Johnne nodded. "I don't know what Patrik expected, but when his father saw your mother's belly starting to swell, and heard the accusations of her mother, he forbade Patrik to even go near her."

"So you married Ma to save her reputation?" Elspeth guessed, loving her father even more for doing this, and then was moved to more tears as he said, "I married her because I *loved* her! …Still love her. I'd have taken her sooner if she hadn't been so spoiled for choice from all the young men of the district. I never thought I'd be in with a chance. But when old Minister Veitch started dragging her name through the muck, and people started seeing just what a dangerous man he could be to cross, it was frightening how fast some of those keen young men found other girls to catch their eye. That and their parents warning them of the dangers of crossing a witch like her ma.

"Your grandmother was a good mother, Elspeth, never doubt that. Her fury was that of any loving ma at her daughter being brutalised by a young man who couldn't be forced to face what he'd done. I was received with open arms, and to the day she died, your grandma told me she couldn't have wished for a better husband for her Jonet. I'm not bragging at that. I just wanted you to know that your grandma saw that I really loved her daughter. …But when your mother got taken in for questioning as a witch by old man Veitch only five years later – and strangely only months after her ma died, as if the old man didn't quite dare cross her while she lived – everyone hereabouts knew that it was more to take his revenge on Jonet over the way she'd accused his son, than anything she'd actually done."

He reached over and squeezed her hand. "I know it's been hard on you. The way that your young men have stopped calling. But can you understand that our older neighbours are seeing history repeating itself? That with Patrik Veitch now Presbyter in his own right, that they're fearing that he's settling old debts? That's why they aren't helping us. It's not that they don't care. It's because they're scared."

Elspeth found herself needing another *uisge* to stop herself from shaking.

"Does Jean know?" she finally managed to ask, and was heartbroken to see her father nod.

"Veitch himself told her when she was about twelve. I don't know why. Spite, I think. He couldn't stand to see us happy, even after what his father had done to your ma in the Manse."

Suddenly it all made sense to Elspeth. The way her sister had turned so cold around the time she herself had been about five. The way she had repeatedly dragged Mailie – only a couple of years younger – away to play or do chores. Anything rather than be around their mother and herself. And also, she realised a moment after with a start, it was possibly the reason why Jean had embraced the Covenant so strongly. Did she feel the need to impress her natural father in case he turned vicious towards her?

"And Mailie?" Elspeth wasn't sure if she could bear to hear that Veitch had forced himself on her mother again, but had to know.

"Oh, Mailie is mine," her father said with a watery smile. "Not that Jean didn't lay down the poison just like her natural father and grandfather did – God forgive me, but she's so very much like them in that. I tried to talk to Mailie, but in the end, she chose to run from all of us rather than try and sort the truth from the lies."

"Oh Pa, I'm so sorry," Elspeth said, coming to sit at her father's feet and wrap her arms around his waist.

"Not as sorry as I am if we've lost Mailie forever," Johnne Allen said, and broke down again.

Chapter 12

The following day was Anna's day off, and had it been anything like decent weather, she would have gone on the hunt for more Covenanters' graves. Brenda, being very much a local, had assured her that there were plenty around, both in Dumfries and in nearby Thornhill, Moniavie, and Caitloch – and those were just the really local ones. It seemed you didn't have to go very far in this south-west corner of Scotland to find evidence of the Covenanters.

But today, with rain blustering in, coming up from the south-west and drenching everything in sight, it was not the day to be traipsing around graveyards. Gary had been off last night and was off tonight as well, but had vanished, declaring that he intended to wreak havoc on the local fish population at some isolated loch. Having spoken to Rita a few times about him since getting here, Anna now knew enough to know that it was probably the anniversary of some grim event, too small to register upon the national consciousness, but which Gary needed to respect in his own way. And so with Rita's assurances that he was 'nowhere near as bad as he was when he came out of the army,' and that 'he'll be okay,' she determined not to fuss and flap over him.

But a whole day spent up in her room didn't appeal, and she didn't want to use Gary's cottage – even though she had the open invite to do so – in case he decided to pack up on account of the heavy rain, and wanted some peace and quiet in his own lounge. With the heating on in the front conference room, that seemed like a good place to sit and start working on the pile of books she was steadily accumulating. She picked a table that was close enough to one of the huge windows to take advantage of what little light there was, but was even closer to one of the big old cast-iron radiators. Sitting huddled over one of those reminded her of her school days in a monstrosity of a building from the 1950s, which was all metal frames and glass windows, and which was as cold as charity in the winter. Back then it had been a race every time they had a class in one of the rooms at the front of the building to grab a desk by a radiator, whereas today she could take her pick.

She was already engrossed in her work when Cameron came in with Harris and Lewis and his laptop under his arm.

"I'm afraid I'm going to have to make a couple of conference calls via Zoom," he forewarned her. "I hope I won't disturb you."

"Heavens, no," Anna assured him. "Anyway, I'm on a day off. You're working. That takes priority."

That didn't stop Harris from ambling over and plonking himself down by Anna's feet, but promptly falling asleep. The next time Anna looked down, he was on his back, all four paws in the air, and propping himself up in that position by a fore and back paw on the radiator – clearly, he was a dog who had his creature comforts prioritised.

Her giggle made Cameron look up and then shake his head in mock despair, then pointed to Lewis, who had adopted a similar position at the radiator closer to Cameron. He'd been considerate enough to use headphones, so Anna had only heard his responses, and now he pulled an earpiece out and muted his mic momentarily.

"No shame," he said. "Neither of them! Flat on their backs, showing everything they've got – or not, in their cases." Anna realised now that both dogs had been neutered. Clearly Cameron had no wish to be presented with another illegitimate offspring!

Harris half opened an eye at his master's voice, then, realising that nothing was happening, gave a contented huff and went back to sleep. It was actually quite soporific, Anna realised, listening to the steady, relaxed breathing of the two huge hounds, so much so that on one occasion she almost found herself nodding off with them until Harris began dreaming, and the big paws began running in his sleep as he yipped with excitement. Knowing that she had to move or fall asleep for real, Anna got up to go and make a coffee, and seeing that he'd finished his call, offered Cameron one as she passed him.

"Oh, yes please," he said gratefully. "How much do I owe you?"

Anna laughed. "It's a mug of instant, not a latte with a double shot of real coffee, whisky, and cream. I think we can stand you that one."

"I'll take coffee in any form," Cameron said, stretching so hard Anna could hear his joints creak. "Good lord, my brother is a magpie. He's invested in anything that took his eye, but the trouble is, it's all in bits and pieces."

"Can you sort it out?"

"I hope so. I've already sold several ventures which I wondered why on earth he got involved in them in the first place. Like a coffee shop! My brother doesn't know one kind of coffee from another. For heaven's sake, I don't think he knows a cappuccino from a mocha or an espresso. It was horrible having to tell the woman who runs it that we're pulling out, but in truth it's been losing money from day one. It's in totally the wrong place and it's got no captive market."

"Could you not just scale back your investment?" Anna wondered, feeling very sorry for this woman, who had no doubt poured her heart and soul into her dream venture.

However, Cameron shook his head. "Austin, or possibly my mum acting for him, fell for her sob story when the other investor pulled out and only sunk himself deeper into the mire in the process." Then scrubbed his hands across his face.

"God, that sounds cold! What I meant was, the owner's grief is totally understandable, but she's a terrible businesswoman. She was undoubtedly a brilliant assistant manager at her old job, especially with the customers, but she hasn't a clue about stock ordering and staff levels. And now that she's had to let all the other staff go, she's trying to stay open seven days a week by herself. It's just not viable anymore, but she won't have it."

"Ouch, that sounds tough if you're having to be the bad guy all of the time," Anna sympathised.

"It is. But until I've plugged all of the leaky holes, I can't start pushing money into the viable investments. The ones which are really going to show a return for just a bit more cash thrown at them. I know which ones they are now." He smiled. "That's what this trip was all about. I was seeing the last one on my list. …The good news is that it's the best of the lot!"

"Oh, that's nice," Anna said with genuine warmth. He seemed so relieved that he'd got no more businesses he'd need to pull the plug on that she decided that he wasn't really cut out for this kind of work. She'd known her father be utterly ruthless over investments that weren't bringing in the money. Never once had she heard him fret over the human cost of what he was about to do.

When she returned with the coffee, Cameron was deep in conversation with someone else via Zoom, and so she put his mug down quietly and left him to it. Only at that point did she realise that it hadn't been such a good idea to bring him some shortbread from the kitchen too. Both Harris and Lewis went from deep sleep to high alert in a heartbeat, both of them lumbering to their feet and wandering over to her, tongues already licking lips.

"Good grief, you two are incorrigible," she told them softly, slipping them a corner each, which vanished at the speed of light. As she moved her own plate to the side of the table which Harris couldn't get to, Lewis padded over to Cameron's table and Anna saw his black nose getting ever closer to his plate.

"No, you thief!" she remonstrated with him, dashing over and moving Cameron's plate closer to him, mouthing 'sorry!' as she did so.

It didn't stop Lewis, though. He just stood with his noble head resting on the table, willing the shortbread to move his way.

As he finished his call, Cameron whisked the shortbreads closer to himself, saying very firmly, "No! You'll get fat."

The mournful deep sigh from Lewis was so comical it reduced Anna to giggles, and even more so as Cameron tried to out-stare Lewis, and instead ended up breaking a corner off a shortbread for each of his dogs.

"I know, I'm a sucker," he confessed. "This pair of rogues know they've got me where they want me."

"There's no shame in that," Anna said warmly. "Why have dogs if you don't love them?"

"My thoughts exactly," Cameron agreed, getting up and stretching mightily before ambling over to her table. "So is this the ongoing ghost hunt you're working on?"

Anna nodded. "It's not going very well, though. It might help if I'd been through the Scottish education system rather than the English one, because I didn't know a thing about the Covenanters beyond their name up until now, and that they were to do with something religious."

"I can't say that going to a Scottish school would have helped you any," Cameron confessed. "It wasn't something I can ever recall being taught us much. In fact, I'm pretty much clueless about them."

"Oh!" Anna was surprised. "Gary seemed to know a bit."

Cameron smiled. "Then I'd say that like a lot of guys who've been in the military, with not a lot to do with their off-duty hours when stuck in some random place in the back of beyond, he's probably read a lot in his own time. …So come on then, tell me, who were the Covenanters, and why do you think they matter here?"

Anna leaned back in her seat as Cameron plonked himself down in the chair across the table from her.

"I can tell you a bit more about the general period than the Covenanters themselves," she began, "and that's because of where I lived. In one of those weird tricks of fate, both the first battle of the English Civil War, and what turned out to be the last one, were fought at Worcester. Where I went for a walk in the summer, down by where the River Severn meets the

River Teme, there's a memorial to the Scots who fought there."

"The Scots? In *Worcestershire*?" Cameron was amazed. "What the heck were they doing there? Down in the middle of England?"

"Ah, it's the final battle of the Civil War that's significant for them, not the first, and it's because by then all English support for Charles the First had evaporated. And the poor Scots took an absolute hammering at the Battle of Powick Bridge – these days that's on the southern edge of Worcester, but then it was a separate village mile or two away. They were hundreds of miles from home, supply routes cut off, and facing local militia who were rested and knew the lanes and fields like the backs of their hands.

"So that's when I first came across the Scots specifically. But I did the period of the English Civil War back in school for my A-level History, and religion plays a huge part in that war. You see, King Charles was married to Henrietta Maria, daughter of Marie de Medici and Henri the fourth of France, and sister to Louis the Thirteenth of France, and it was felt by many that he was being lured back to the Catholic Faith by her.

"If you're struggling to place the era, by the way, this is the time when *The Three Musketeers* is set! Lots of spies going back and forth between England and France as in the book. And don't forget, Charles' father, James the First of England and the Sixth of Scotland, was the heir to Elizabeth the First, and there had been terrible persecution of Protestants during her sister Mary's reign. That's not Mary Queen of Scots, of course, but Catherine of Aragon's and Henry the Eighth's daughter, making another connection with another Catholic country just across the Channel in the form of Spain.

"Those Catholics around Queen Mary tried to push back against the rise of Protestantism that had been fostered by Henry the Eighth's only male heir – so that's hers and the future Queen Elizabeth's younger brother, Edward the Sixth. Under Edward there had been dreadful persecution of the Catholics, and then a violent backlash against the Protestants under Mary, and in the time we're talking about that wasn't so very long ago, as family memories went. So when the son of Good Queen Bess' heir started looking like he was trying to be the most Protestant king of all, even to the extent of burning so-called witches at the stake, you can understand why, in some quarters, there was a real sense of panic. And that they might be heading back to a time when martyrs would once against be burned at the stake just for being Catholic. After all, Queen Mary and Queen Elizabeth's half-brother, Edward, had committed atrocities against them when he inherited as the first of Henry Eighth's children. It's only two years after James the First takes the throne that you get the Gunpowder Plot in 1605 – Guy Fawkes and Bonfire night, and all that – and that was basically Catholics panicking over what they saw as extreme Protestantism, given that it had been made a crime to be a Catholic in England."

"Good grief!"

"Indeed. So it wasn't as if after 1625 King Charles didn't give them reason to be worried that things could potentially swing the other way, given that Charles had been engaged to the Infanta of Spain at one point, even though that never came to anything. His number one influencer over things religious was a guy called Archbishop Laud – his name is embedded on my memory forever after swotting up for my exams! And even down in England, we were taught that Laud came unstuck when he tried to force his new prayer book onto the Scots. …I mean in a modern secular society like ours, it sounds nuts that people would get *that* upset over the wording in a prayer book, and the way a church service was conducted. But you only have to look at the Troubles in Northern Ireland to see how toxic such religious divisions can get."

Cameron nodded sagely. "I met a cousin of Dad's who served in the Army in Northern Ireland. He found it worse than any other posting, not least because as a Scot he was expected by various people on both sides to be on *their* side."

"That must have been grim," Anna sympathised, "but if you know that, then you can start to understand how bad things got back in the Civil War days of the mid-seventeenth century. Charles the First was beheaded by Oliver Cromwell and others at the beginning of 1649, because he was far more inclined to lean towards Catholicism than his father had been. And by then, there had already been fighting in Scotland over religion, as well as the Scots coming south to support the King. It sounds as if this covenant thing had been signed and there was a rift between the people and their leaders over religion, but that's something else I'm really fuzzy over.

"I've already found out now that there were far more openly Catholic families still up in the Highlands. What's harder to unravel, I'm discovering, is when any fighting would have taken place down around here. Was it during the Civil War? Was it before then in what are called the Bishops' Wars which only affected Scotland? Or was it later during the Commonwealth of Oliver Crowell?"

"And it makes a difference?" Cameron asked.

"Well, yes it does, because Cromwell – who, if I've read this right, was himself what you might call a bit left-wing as Protestants go – was initially sympathetic to the Scottish Presbyterians, who had objected so strongly to being drawn towards a Roman Catholic form of service in their kirks, though even he had to eventually admit that they'd gone a bit too extreme in their reforming. Part of the problem, you see, was that James the First was born and brought up in Scotland, so he knew how things worked up here. It meant that he knew when to butter up his nobility, and when to turn a blind eye to things. And whatever he personally believed, he knew which side his bread was buttered on, and had done what he needed to get his hands on the, by then, very Protestant English throne. Whereas Charles was born in England, had been influenced by Catholic courts in Europe and their overarching power over people, and thought that he could lay down the law to his Scottish barons and subjects the way he had to his English ones."

"Knowing the Scots," Cameron said with a grin, "he came unstuck with that."

"Very much so. But what's got me bogged down at this point is the divisions between the Scots themselves. And boy, are they significant! Even before war broke out in England, fighting had taken place between the different Scottish factions, and worse, many men and clans seem to have changed sides over the course of the wars."

Cameron was surprised. "So a man could start off fighting for one side and end up fighting men he'd been allies with earlier?"

"Exactly."

"Well, well, that would explain the hatred between your two ghosts, wouldn't it? It'd be one thing if your house got burned down and your family killed by someone who had always been on the other side. It'd be a whole other thing if it was someone who had once fought shoulder to shoulder with you. That would feel like the ultimate betrayal."

"And my other issue," Anna said with some embarrassment, "is that these writers talk as if you automatically know where everything is. Every time a place name comes up, I have to stop and find out where it is."

Now Cameron couldn't help but grin. "Scotland a wee bit bigger than you thought it was?" he teased. "I had to point out just now to a guy south of the border that I couldn'a just nip across to Aberdeen – that I'm two hundred miles and the thick end of a five-hour drive away, and I'm no' even across the border."

Yet Anna laughed with him. "Oh, I get that! My Aunty Rita, who is the one who found me this job on account of knowing Gary, lives in Grantown-on-Spey. So I've driven up from Worcester to Grantown on many occasions. When the folks I worked with asked why it took me so long to get there, I often had to point out that I was driving only a whisker under five hundred miles, despite it being a pretty straight run north. Personally, I blame all those years of the weather maps on TV being canted over, putting the emphasis on the south and London area. They made Scotland look unnaturally small."

"Aye, they don't know that Scotland forms a whole third of the main British land mass. It's no' just a wee bit tacked on at the top."

Anna nodded. "And if you show a lot of folks a map of the UK, they honestly don't know where the border lies. A frightening number of my colleagues thought it lies where the ancient Roman Antonine Wall ran, across from Glasgow to Edinburgh at that narrowest point. Once I'd pointed out just which cities those blobs were, and that obviously they aren't right on the border, they got really confused. Show them the actual border and most were shocked."

She sighed. "That's why I thought I'd never get tracked down by my ex-husband here. *I* knew I was about two hundred and seventy miles away from Aunty Rita, yet still on the Scottish side of the border, and I thought that would be enough."

"Sounds like you had reason to not be found?" Cameron was clearly trying to keep his voice neutral, but Anna guessed that he was suddenly wondering if some violent man was about to appear on the hotel's doorstep.

"Oh, I do. But only because I made a terrible, terrible mistake in allowing myself to get pushed into a marriage before I'd got to grips with what I was letting myself in for. Very pushy in-laws! A husband who just did what they said. And my parents wanting to keep in with his lot to advance my father's businesses," and she shuddered.

Cameron blinked in shock. "Oh! That all sounds rather …controlling?"

Anna nodded. "It's a long story I won't bore you with now, but cut short, I never got a chance to draw breath in the months running up to the wedding, and it was only when I got a cold sharp wake-up call at the last minute that I realised just what my life was going to be like if I didn't get away fast. Down there I had no back up. Nobody I could turn to to help me. So I ran up here to where I do," she winced, "on the morning after my wedding." She winced again. "Not something I'm proud of. But then he was too drunk to notice, so he's hardly covered in glory either."

"He was too drunk on his wedding night to notice that his wife had done a runner?" Cameron was aghast. "What kind of man was this? I know I'm no' married myself, but Jeez, every one of my friends who's got wed couldn't have been prised away from their wives with a crowbar at that stage!"

That comparison made Anna feel suddenly very sad for what she'd lost out on, and clearly her expression must have made that clear to Cameron, who hurriedly changed the subject, asking, "So which are these places you're struggling to find?"

"Auldearn? Apparently, the Marquis of Montrose won a battle there in 1645, and there's a book on it, but I don't know if it's relevant or not. I can't keep on buying books, not least because my room here isn't that big for me to store them in."

"Ah, well if you're looking for local connections to here, then no. Auldearn is right up on the Morayshire coast, roughly speaking between Elgin and Inverness."

Anna groaned. "Oh, of course! That's why the name was familiar. I've driven past it with Aunty Rita when we've gone into Nairn to shop. I knew I'd seen it in that kind of context, but thought it might have been down here."

Cameron was impressed. "So you know more of Scotland than I thought."

"I *love* Scotland," Anna confessed. "In fact, I can't think why I didn't have the sense to move jobs and come up here years ago. …Damn! That's what Aunty Rita kept hinting at me to do. She could see that I needed to get away from my parents, but then I went and bought my flat, and I think she must have thought I was happy down there once that happened."

"And were you?" Cameron found himself wanting to know more about Anna, and strangely it bothered him that she might have a secret desire to return to where she'd grown up once the dust of this odd breakup settled.

To his great relief she had no hesitation in answering. "I don't think I was happy so much as just ticking along. It was such a relief when I finally managed to move out of that dreadful house of Mum and Dad's, that I think I *thought* I was happy with just that. But compared to how I've felt since coming here, no, I wasn't. Looking back, I can see that really there were still too many things dragging me down. I'd go shopping and run into Mum, who'd start grilling me in the frozen aisle about my dating prospects."

"Bloody hell!"

"Or I'd meet up with old school friends, and all they'd talk about was times when their mums and dads felt sorry for me and invited me for sleepovers to let me have a bit more of a normal childhood. …Oh, don't get me wrong, I was very, very grateful for those weekends away! But in recent years it began to feel as though those so-called friends had been told to *stay* friends with me by *their* parents, and it was *them* who were worried about me, not my supposed mates. Because it was clear with at least one group that they met up as a threesome without me a lot more often than the times when I was included. I started to get embarrassed about it, because I'd gradually come to realise what was behind those once every six months invites."

And with that confession, although Anna wasn't behaving in any way as if she was feeling sorry for herself, but rather just telling it how it was, Cameron felt unbearably sorry for her. If he had spent his childhood in the shadow of an older brother whose needs had always had to come before his, at least there was a genuine medical reason for it. And his dad had always made a point of making sure that even if his mum had to give more time to Austin, that he gave Cameron a life something closer to normal. It had never been about either parent's disinterest in his well-being. What it must have felt like to be so unloved he struggled to imagine, but he thought a lot more highly of Anna for her determination not to be crushed by it. The only thing that really worried him now was, what would she think of him when she found out who he really was?

1658

Elspeth ~ September onwards

As if the news that Jean had brought to her family wasn't enough, Elspeth and her father heard more bad news as September rolled around. Samwell Black, the husband of Marione Corsan who had been accused, held, and questioned in Irongray Manse eight years ago – just as Jonet was again suffering – was now himself hauled summarily in for questioning by a session of the Kirk. Not in Kirkcudbright, as might have been expected, but by the main court in Dumfries. If his wife's accusers felt safe to throw aspersions at him as well, then Elspeth and Johnne felt they had little chance of getting Jonet free.

Yet all did not go as feared. By Christmas, Samwell was a free man once more, though Marione remained imprisoned. Her accusers were too many for her to go free without a trial, but it was faintly reassuring that even being as closely connected to her as he was, Samwell had had as near to a fair hearing from the sheriff and provost as could be hoped for. And by the time the Christmas markets came, Johnne and Elspeth had amassed their thirty merks. Much as they'd wanted to go to the sheriff as soon as they had a decent amount, they had reasoned that it was better to go once with an amount that would be likely to be accepted, than go several times, each time adding on a merk or two and looking increasingly desperate.

Moreover, as the autumn had approached, they'd had help of a different kind from an unexpected quarter. Johnne and Elspeth were in Dumfries market, him with a couple of healthy male lambs – which in spite of being castrated, had become pests around the older ram and were therefore not even worth holding onto for their fleeces, but were now big enough to be worth selling for their meat – and her with some preserves she had made up from hedgerow fruits. She was waiting for her father when Robert McBurney – or Rab, as he was now known as by everyone except his father – spotted her standing alone. Never quite as cunning as his older brother Thomas, nonetheless Rab had a vicious streak, and he too had not forgotten that Elspeth had eluded them on that fateful night over eight years previously. And if Elspeth was no longer assumed to be quite the desirable virgin she'd been back then – or so they presumed, despite Elspeth having had no lover in truth – sheer spite drove Rab to try to make her life a misery.

"Well look what the cat dragged in," Rab sneered, coming to stand uncomfortably close to her.

He stank of stale wine and cheap tobacco, not being wealthy enough to afford something to smoke that hadn't been cut with herbs to make it last longer. It meant that he stank like an old, damp bonfire, but to see him puffing on his clay pipe all the time, you would have thought he owned a whole plantation in the Americas.

Coughing on the smell, despite trying to ignore him, Elspeth found that retreating only made him lean in closer, and she backed up until she was pressed against the timber wall of the nearest inn's stables. Just when she thought that this was the day when he finally dragged her out of sight and raped her, a dangerously calm voice from someone masked from her view by Rab said, "Aren't you the big man, then.

Is this the only way you can get a lassie to look at ye', eh?"

Rab spun around, fist at the ready, and then stopped so fast he nearly overbalanced as he saw a dagger coming up to point at his throat.

"I wouldn'a do that, laddie, if I were you," the slender, dark stranger said, the glint in his eyes saying that he would take great pleasure in showing Rab what a mistake he'd made if he was daft enough to take him on.

"Who the hell are you?" Rab blustered.

"Bodyguard to Grierson of Lagg," the other replied in an accent that was pure Highlands, not Dumfriesshire, and she saw Rab swallow hard. Grierson outranked William McBurney in both station and family wealth, and it wouldn't do for his bodyguard to complain of being drawn into a brawl by a mere bailie's younger son. Moreover, Grierson was known to favour real hard men from the Highlands as his chosen bodyguards, and though they came and went with the seasons, he was vocal in his trust of all of them, and none were men you would want to get on the wrong side of. The fact that this man was the best part of a hand's breadth shorter than Rab was more than made up for by the fact that he was clearly fighting fit, and all muscle and sinews, whereas Rab was too fond of food – good or otherwise – and could best be described as flabby.

As Rab sidled away from her, desperate to put distance between himself and that vicious looking dirk – that seemed to be getting bigger every time he looked at it and the way it never wavered from his throat – Elspeth saw that the Highlander had the clearest grey eyes she had ever seen. Like a winter sea, they seemed to reflect the hues of the sky, rather than having any colour of their own, but there was no mistaking the fiery gleam in them.

"Go on. On your way, laddie," the Highlander said, as Rab finally edged around enough to be able to step back. It was said calmly and quietly, but there was no mistaking the menace in it either, and Rab turned and scurried off, diving down the nearest vennel between buildings as soon as he could.

For an instant Elspeth wondered what was going to happen now, but the moment Rab was gone, the Highlander's expression softened.

"Are ye' all right, lass?" he asked, seeming genuinely concerned.

"Er, yes …thank you," Elspeth managed to splutter out. "Thank you, Master…"

He smiled. "I'm no' 'master' anybody. I'm just Sorley McAllister. At your service, mistress."

Now it was Elspeth's turn to demur. "Oh, I'm not married. I'm just Elspeth Allen, here to the market with my pa."

McAllister's eyes twinkled as he said in mock amazement, "Is there something wrong wi' the lads hereabouts that a bonny lass like you isn'a spoken for?"

Elspeth sighed, her initial amusement draining away like rain down the drain-gullies as she told him, "It's not the lads, it's me that there something wrong with. You might not want to be seen near me once you know that the local Presbyter has my ma in his cellar being questioned as a witch."

She saw McAllister's expression harden, but his response wasn't what she expected. "I canna abide those sanctimonious men," he said with feeling. "How many poor folk depend on women like your ma for healing and comfort, eh? And can he do any better for them? Will all his praying and thou-shalt-nots cure a baby's croup, or an old man's painful joints? No. You have to have a bit more earth-bound knowledge to help with them. And I've seen too many of his sort abusing their position to get worldly wealth and favours – some given less willingly than others, if you get my meaning. …No lass, I'll not hold your ma's calling against you."

He held out his arm, gesturing for her to walk with him back out into what faded sunlight was filtering through the clouds.

"However, I do have a question for you. Would your pa be Johnne Allen by any chance?"

"Yes, he is! Why? Do you know him?" The odds on her father actually knowing some Highland warrior were beyond slim, and she could only assume that someone had told him about her father's talent with horses, though he rarely got the chance to show it. Did Grierson have a troublesome colt or filly that they needed a hand with? That was all Elspeth could think of. But then the Highlander answered, "No, lass. But I'd be grateful if you could tell me where you live so that I can come and speak to you both later…somewhere where it's more private, if ye' understand?"

Thoroughly bemused, Elspeth gave him directions to their croft, and then spotted her father across the square. She turned to tell her rescuer that he was here, only to find that McAllister had melted into the thinning crowd like a ghost. Almost wondering if he'd been a product of her scared imagination, she didn't say anything to her father until they were out on the road going home, but then found that he was as much in ignorance about the whole thing as she was.

"I think the last Highlander I knowingly spoke to was your Aunt Geillis' brother, who came to visit one year," Johnne told her. "I can't imagine what this man wants with me."

It was therefore with some concern that they waited for the knock at the door that night, because one thing that Elspeth was sure of was that this stranger wasn't going to delay coming. There had been an air of controlled urgency about him when he'd asked for directions, meaning that whatever it was wouldn't wait. Even so, they'd almost given up on him as the night deepened, when a soft knock came at the door.

In stark contrast to Jean's unwillingness to step over the threshold, Sorley McAllister preferred to come inside, and when he was sat by the fire, smiled, and said, "Please dinna look so worried. I'm bringing ye news you'll want to hear. Your daughter Mailie is safe and well."

For a moment, both Johnne and Elspeth were too stunned to speak, but Johnne recovered enough to ask, "Where is she, then?"

"In the Highlands with my people," McAllister said reassuringly. "She's had a rough time of it, but she's with a good man now who will guard her with his life. She told me about you, ye' see, and so I came down under the pretext of finding work to see if I could find you. Mailie was sure that your other daughter, Jean, wouldn't have told ye the whole story, but she was also worried that the person she found in Berwick to write to ye might well have never sent the letters and just pocketed her money."

"We've heard nothing. Not in ten years," Elspeth said through her tears of relief.

"Ten years? Aye, but that's a long time to be worried," McAllister sympathised, looking especially to Johnne as if guessing how deep a father's concern might run.

For a while Sorley filled in the gaps, telling of how Mailie's Patrick had died, and then also her soldier, culminating in how he himself had met her while she was hiding after the Battle of Worcester, and him guiding her and others away from the carnage. It had taken them the best part of two years to creep north again, all the time having to avoid those who would have taken them prisoner and then shipped them off to the colonies, but finally crossing the border only to find that it wouldn't be until they'd crossed the Highland Line that they'd be safe.

"I'd almost given up hope of finding you," McAllister admitted, "because I'll be going home soon. With winter coming on, Grierson won't be travelling as much, and he'll make do with the two men he keeps on permanently. I've managed to make myself useful this far, but I'm sure he'll be letting me go within a week or so, so I'm more than relieved to have finally met you. Do you have news you'd like me to take back to Mailie?"

"Oh God," Elspeth gulped, realising that Mailie would know nothing of what had gone on in the last eight years. And so with a shaking voice, she told McAllister of her own close brush with the McBurneys, and more recently of her mother being taken.

It said a lot for McAllister that he took their word for it that Jonet was innocent. More surprisingly, he asked if she was just being kept in the Manse.

"No' in an actual prison?" he queried.

Elspeth shook her head.

"Hmph! No' beyond our reach, then," he said with a wink.

"If we break her out, we'll all be hunted," Johnne warned him. "You and I might survive living rough, but after what that fiend will have done to Jonet, she won't cope, and I wouldn't wish it on Elspeth, either."

"I wasn'a thinking of actually breaking her out," admitted McAllister, "although that's no' impossible, I can tell you. But if ye' think you can pay to get her out with that bond, that would be far better because it will keep your names clean. No, I was thinking more of getting things like food and water to her. I can surely show you the way to creep up on such a place so that nobody would know you'd been there."

"Really?" Elspeth couldn't believe their luck. "I tried to get close when Ma was first taken, but those damned McBurneys had a couple of their ruffians lurking around the place like they were expecting us to try something."

"Oh, aye," McAllister said sagely. "Men like that would. But how many months has it been now? Several? Well, I'd bet my winter coat on them having got bored with guard duty by now, and bored men get careless," and he gave them a knowing wink. "My money would be on them going to the cellars to supposedly check on your ma, and in reality, helping themselves to yon Presbyter's wine to take the chill off the night patrol."

Elspeth gave a silent, 'Oh!' of understanding as it registered with her how many occasions she'd seen the same men staggering out of the taverns of Dumfries when she'd been there. At the time she'd assumed that they'd simply been spending the extra money Presbyter Veitch must have paid them, or possibly even the McBurneys, though why they would pay more to men already in their employ she naively hadn't considered. That they might have been well on their way to merry before they'd even got to the taverns now made far more sense of what she'd seen.

"Can you come tomorrow night?" she asked McAllister eagerly, only for him to answer with a grin, "What's wrong with tonight? Do you no' have food you could take to your ma?"

"Oh Lord, yes!" Elspeth gasped, immediately going and wrapping the warm bannock that she'd just baked into a cloth, and putting some hard cheese in another cloth, before slicing slivers of ham from the hock that was smoking high above the open fire, hung from a rafter of the thatched roof. Already she was thinking practically that it was no use taking her mother anything which needed cutting or spreading, and if it could be wrapped in a cloth and hidden beneath what little bedding she might have, so much the better, because Elspeth was in no doubt that the jailors would cheerfully rob her of anything which looked edible. Swiftly adding a little pot of soothing salve into the bundle, she turned around to find her father holding her heavy cloak out for her, and McAllister at the door.

"Shall we?" he said with a grin, before disappearing out into the night.

The first part of their night's walk was easy, for they had no need to hide themselves when they were walking country lanes at a time when nobody else was around. And if there was little moonlight to help them on their way, both Elspeth and Johnne knew these tracks like the back of their hands. Only when they got close to the tiny but spread out village of Irongray and its church did they slow down, and start leading McAllister over the fields.

Then as they crossed over the narrow lane going towards Terregles, and saw the bridge over the Cluden Water lower down, McAllister took over after Johnne had whispered to him that the Manse wasn't far away.

Indeed once over the bridge, it was just a short way to the right before they smelled the wood-smoke of the Manse's dying fires. The smell of tobacco gave away the presence of a man outside, and then they saw the glow from the pipe as he took another draw on it.

"How close is he to the cellar?" McAllister whispered.

"Not very," Johnne said, but more hopefully than with any certainty. "That big shadow you can see through the trees is the Manse. He's possibly sitting on the mounting block out the front, while the cellar opening is around to the side where visitors can't see it from the front."

McAllister reached out and gently took the bag from Elspeth. "You two wait here. If I can get you down to speak to her, I will, but at least she'll get this."

They couldn't believe how he melted into the night as if he'd never been there. Elspeth and Johnne were both country folk who could move quietly, but McAllister was at a whole other level of ability. He seemed to take forever, but that was no doubt their nerves making it seem so, and at least there were no calls of alarm. The tiny glow from the pipe continued for a while, and then they heard the guard get up and move around. For a dreadful moment they thought he'd heard McAllister, because he seemed to be coming towards them. But then they heard the sound of him urinating into one of the bushes, followed by him ambling back to his post.

Moments later, there was a faint rustling and then McAllister slid into the dip where they were hiding.

"Right," he said with triumph. "Food delivered! She's no' in a good way, but she's still got her senses – which is no small thing in the circumstances."

"Can we go to her?" Elspeth asked eagerly.

"Ah…that wouldn'a be a good idea, lass." McAllister had already taken her by the arm and was gently leading her away, Johnne in their wake. When they were far enough away to be able to talk properly without being overheard, he elaborated, "It's a bit tricky getting close to the grating over the cellar window. It's no' that big an opening, either. More like just a few bricks' worth removed wi' a couple of iron bars inset just to allow some ventilation in. Thank the Lord it's more of a wine and general store that she's in. I was dreading that it would be somewhere they'd need to keep the rats and mice out of, which wouldn'a have any opening at all.

"But the thing is, it's pretty overgrown in front of that opening, so in the daytime, folks would soon notice if the weeds had been crushed by a person going to the cellar. They might or might not come for you, but they'd surely take it out on your ma that someone came looking for her. I went in right by the wall, so that from the front, nothing looks disturbed. But Johnne, man, you're too stiff in the joints to bend far enough. And Elspeth, short of taking off your skirts and risking getting nettle rash all over, ye' couldn'a get close either."

"So this is a one-off?" Elspeth asked dejectedly.

Yet McAllister chuckled. "I wouldn'a say that just yet, lass. I have an idea. I'll come to you tomorrow night and bring someone with me." He wouldn't say more than that, and as soon as they got to the lane to the Allens' home, he bade them goodnight and vanished into the darkness.

When he came the next night, he had not one but two people with him.

"This is Alexander Black," he said of a young man probably less than a couple of years younger than Elspeth. "And this," he added, turning to a younger lad probably just into his teens, "is his cousin, Hugh Ferguson. You'll mind that Alexander's poor mother is Marione Corsan, who's likewise charged as your mother is of being a witch."

Alexander nodded gravely. "This time there wasn't sufficient evidence at the time of the accusations to hold my ma in prison, but my grandma is still in Kirkcudbright Tolbooth, and Ma will still have to appear in a trial. After Pa was taken for questioning, we decided that it wasn't safe for him to be in and around Dumfries – because that's surely where any trial is going to be – so I said I'd come and find work here so that I could keep an eye on things. How we're going to get the two of them free I do not know, but I'm watching and waiting."

He put a sympathetic arm around his young cousin's shoulders. "Hugh and his pa, James, are worried sick that my Aunt Jannet will get dragged into this mess as well. He's been working with McAllister at Grierson's but in the stables, and he'd told McAllister about our family troubles. So when McAllister found you, he knew we'd help. I found the way to Irongray back when Ma was there eight years ago. I got food and drink to her then, and it was her staying in her right mind all the way through because of it that meant she wasn't what the Kirk Session were expecting when they finally saw her."

Elspeth and Johnne knew what he meant by that. They'd seen so-called witches dragged out after questioning, their faces swollen and black, purple, and green with bruises, hair a filthy matted tangle from being unable to keep themselves clean, and even missing teeth, giving them a hook-nosed appearance as their gums folded in. Reducing a woman to looking barely human in public was another ploy by those who wanted them out of the way. It was so much easier to convince the gullible and unquestioning of someone's guilt when they looked nothing like the other women watching on at a trial.

"One or the other of us will come twice a week to take stuff to your ma," Alexander was continuing. "Hugh can sneak away once a week, we think, and as long as I'm not seen leaving the town too often at night, I should be fine, for I sleep alone above the stables where I work. There's none but the horses to know I've been out."

"We're so very grateful," Johnne Allen said from the heart. "Both to you two for offering to help us, and to you McAllister, for thinking to bring them to us."

At which point Elspeth had an idea. "If you need somewhere safe to hide someone," she said, "the old nunnery ruins near the stones hid me when I was being chased. If you take your mother or aunt down into the crypt, it's cold and it's dark, but nobody would know anyone was down there, and few dare to go there even in the day."

"Is it not haunted?" Hugh asked warily.

Elspeth smiled. "Yes, but the ghosts are those of nuns killed by wicked men. They hid me, and they'll hide any other woman in need too."

Chapter 13

It was at this point that a very damp-looking Gary wandered in.

"Fish not biting?" Anna teased.

"The fish ha' more bluidy sense!" Gary growled back, but not with any anger. "Only stupid buggers like me go and spend hours up to our bollocks in freezing water waiting for them." He gave a huff of disgust and dropped into the other seat by Anna's table. "So what are you two youngsters up to, eh?"

He had obviously left his dripping waders and outer clothes in the tackle room, and the dampness was mainly around his head and neck, the rest clearly having been kept dry by whatever he'd been wearing. The thick khaki socks which came up to his knees were dry, as were the knee-length tweed breeches and his ex-army issue sweater. He'd also obviously padded through to the kitchens in his socks, and despite it being the time when Emilio's helpers were starting to prepare the evening meal, had helped himself to a large and steaming mug of coffee.

"Covenanters!" Cameron said with a grin. "Anna says you know more than we do."

"And I'm guessing that wouldn'a be hard?" Gary riposted with an amused sideways glance at this guest.

Anna thought it was a good sign of what kind of man Cameron was that Gary would rib him like this. She was getting to recognise Gary's tell-tales, and one of those was when he became very formally polite to someone. It was, she now knew, a sign that he thought them a total arsehole. The stiffer Gary got, the more he was hanging on to the threads of his patience not to tell them exactly what he thought of them, or worse! So the fact that he was here in just his socks, and supping his coffee, was a sure sign that he positively liked Cameron, and if Anna was still at the stage of not yet trusting her own judgement about people after her bruising experiences of the last twelve months, she certainly trusted Gary's.

"Anna's trying to work out which bit of the whole period might apply to your errant ghosts," Cameron explained, "but she's a bit hindered by her lack of local knowledge – not that I'm either local, or an expert, I hasten to add. I was just reminding her of where Auldearn is."

Gary immediately sat up, like a hound getting the scent. "Oh? Auldearn? Aye, that's up right by Fort George where I was stationed whenever I was at home." But then he shook his head. "No, lass, you're far too early for what you're looking for. The Battle of Auldearn was way back at the start of the wars, even before the fighting broke out in England. You have to go to the other end o' the wars to get to the troubles around here."

Anna gave a sigh of relief. "Oh, thank God. I thought I was going to have to plough through every book on these perishing Covenanters to get to what I wanted."

Gary laughed. "In England it's the Wars o' the Roses that nobody can get to grips with. Up here it's a tad later and the Covenanters."

Anna looked at him quizzically. "You sound as if you've read up on both?"

Gary shrugged. "I'm no' some expert historian, if that's what you're hoping. It's just that I'm no' a great one for fiction, ye' understand? I much prefer factual things. So once that Kindle thing came along, it was a great. I could stuff my wee reader full o' eBooks and read them wherever I was. And being the good Scottish laddie that I am, I always wondered what made those Jacobite lads think that they could ever reach London?"

Anna was already catching on even if Cameron wasn't. "Ah! So that Romantic – in the sense of the movement, rather than just lovey-dovey stuff – idea of the silly Jacobites thinking that they could reach London, and everyone wondering why the hell they would ever have thought that, intrigued you?"

The grin of approval that Gary gave her almost choked Anna up. Not once had her own father ever looked at her like that, and she would have given almost anything to have him do so. She had strained everything she had to achieve *something* at school which would earn that approval, and yet her best had never been enough, let alone *good* enough. In that instant it made her see her father in a whole new light, as a man who had never *wanted* to be pleased by her, not that she had failed him. She could have gone on to university and achieved who knew what, it crashed in on her in that moment, and he would never have given her as much as the time of day.

Luckily her mental paralysis was covered up, and she had no need to explain why she was sitting with goldfish goggle-eyes, staring at Gary, because Cameron was already asking him, "Was that because of what Anna was telling me of the Scots getting as far south as Worcester in the English Civil War?"

Gary was nodding, adding, "And that was far from being the only time. You canna understand the Jacobite Rebellions without knowing what came before. There's a whole long century before 1745 which throws it into a completely different light." He leaned back in his seat again, now thoroughly comfortable in speaking openly.

"But for what you're looking at, you only have to go around the kirkyards hereabouts to see the dates on them, ye' see? All these martyrs' graves we have hereabouts? They're no' from the start o' things, they're from the end." He smiled at Anna. "I had no idea that you were trying to get through the whole era – and that's my fault for no' grasping that you wouldn'a have had any notion o' where to start. I've got so used to knowing what I know – if that makes sense – that I forgot that you wouldn'a.

"So forget the Bishops' Wars. They come right at the start o' the conflict, way back in 1639, or thereabouts. Back then, every man and his dog had signed up to the Covenant here in Scotland. It was a way o' demonstrating to King Charles that they didn'a appreciate him laying down the law, via his man Archbishop Laud, about the way they were to speak to God."

Anna waved a hand to pause him. "Okay, hang on a tick, Gary, please. For the love of God, will you explain who or what the Covenanters actually were, and what the heck the difference is between the Epicopalian Church of Scotland and the Church (or Kirk) of Scotland? I'm drowning here!"

She half expected Gary to get a bit exasperated at needing to explain something quite fundamental, but instead he just nodded and said, "Ach, of course you wouldn'a know. …So. Scotland didn'a become Protestant until well after England did, on account of Henry the Eighth's rule no' extending over the border. For us up here, the move to Protestantism didn'a come until Mary Queen o' Scots was a wee lass on the throne and Queen Elizabeth the First down in England, so quite a bit later. Now driving around up here, you'll see churches that are one or other of the two you just said, but in fact the division didn'a come until 1690, so verra much a final consequence of the Covenanters and all that.

"As to who the Covenanters were, that's oddly hard to define because it depends on when you're talking about. They come in different phases, ye' see."

"Oh bloody hell," Anna groaned, burying her head in her hands, and raising a chuckle from Gary at her despair.

"It's no' quite that bad, lass. 1560 is the year when Scotland goes from being wholly Catholic to primarily Protestant, okay? I'm no' saying that there weren't any Protestants in Scotland before then, ye' understand, but that's when the official religion changed. So by the time Charles the First starts throwing his weight around in the 1630s, demanding changes to the forms o' service and prayer books, folks up here had had seventy odd years to get used to their own kind o' Protestant worship, but at that stage *all* o' their churches or kirks were what we'd now call Episcopalian. In other words, they still had bishops. With me so far?"

"Just about," Anna laughed weakly.

"Great. So when Charles and his Archbishop Laud started causing ructions, that was when the Solemn League and Covenant was drawn up, and that's in 1638. It's basically a charter wi' a seal, but there were copies which got signed by lesser folks too. At that stage, damned near every man and his dog from within Scotland literally put their own names to copies of the Covenant, because it wasn'a just a religious statement, it was a political one too."

He scratched his close-cropped beard pensively. "It was a symbol of being dragged backwards, and being forced to answer to a foreign *English*, and all too Catholic-sounding, Church. In truth, I think King Charles was a total idiot for even trying. His father, King James, was no' called the wisest fool in Christendom for no reason – he may no' have been the brightest king we've ever had, but he was canny enough to know when to leave well alone. His son wasn'a."

"I'm guessing something changed, though?" Anna speculated. "You said that at the start everyone signed up to the Covenant? That sounds as though things changed significantly as time went on?"

And there it was again, that beaming smile of approval for having caught on, which reduced Anna almost to tears, and this time she realised that Cameron had seen her reaction too. So she was almost undone when he covered for her by asking, "Would I be right in thinking that what started as almost nothing more than a political challenge, to a king who was seen to have become divorced from his own people, turned into a monster which people felt might turn on them and bite them?"

"Aye, you would, lad," Gary sighed. "People never learn, do they? You canna invoke religion in politics without getting the nutters involved. Doesn'a matter which faith you choose. There are the silent majority, who just want to get on with worshipping in their own way, and then the rabid few who think they have a direct line to God – by whatever name you call him – and think that their way is the only way. I saw it overseas in this century, and it was no different in this country way back in the late seventeenth century. What started out as little more than a plea to be able to be left to worship in their own way, got hijacked by the extremists. Men and women died horribly, and gradually the ordinary folk became revolted by what they'd started, and support got withdrawn.

"That's being verra simplistic, of course. It was a lot more complicated than that for those on the ground. Presbyteries, in other words congregations who didn'a want bishops involved but to determine how they worshipped for themselves, had started back in the 1580s, while other Protestant kirks carried on being overseen by the bishops. By the end of that century, though, presbyteries had been legalised by an act of Parliament, and there were probably more presbyteries ruled over by regional synods than other kirks, and though the bishops still sat in parliament, on the ground you could say that they'd lost a lot o' clout. So to these free-thinkers up here, you can imagine how King Charles' reforms went down!"

"Hmm, lead welly time?" Anna guessed.

Gary laughed. "Oh yes! Now those Bishops Wars I was talking about? They came immediately after the signing of the Covenant in 1639 and 1640, and were verra much an internal Scottish thing. It was about supporters of the bishops, and therefore the King, against the supporters of what the Presbyterians had laid out in the document of the Covenant about what we'd probably call self-determination. But by then England was sliding into civil war, and armies from both sides in Scotland marched to help both sides in England. Well we all know how the Civil War worked out." And he saw Anna and Cameron's nods.

"Then with Cromwell in charge, the vast majority of those who'd originally signed the Covenant felt they'd got what they wanted. Aside from the poor Catholics, who by now were walking on thin ice, pretty much any kind of Protestantism was tolerated in England – Presbyterians, Congregationalists, Unitarians, Baptists, they all rubbed along – but in Scotland it was the Presbyterians more than any others who came out on top, and had the overwhelming numbers of followers.

"However, it all changed again when Charles the Second was restored in 1660. Only the year afterwards, he declared that Presbyterianism wasn't compatible with a monarchy – a bit *too* free thinking, ye' understand – and that he was restoring bishops to all the old sees. By this stage, there was bugger-all difference between the Episcopalian and Presbyterian prayer books, and probably not much in the services, either. So in a lot of the country it was just accepted, but for some reason, in certain parts it really rubbed people up the wrong way again, and that includes around here. *These* Covenanters after 1660 were now a minority within Scotland, but a forceful majority in places like here and around Fife. For them, nothing but the observances laid out in the original document of the Covenant would do."

He paused and took a slurp of his coffee.

"And so gradually it became to be seen to be dangerous to be a Covenanter – a bit like being seen to be a religious extremist these days. Now not everyone who hung onto the Covenanters' tenets was an extremist. Far from it. Many were just devout believers who didn't want to be dictated to by the bishops, who were inevitably drawn from the top tier of society – because in those days it was beyond rare for you to rise to the highest offices in any sector unless you were born into the right circles, Kirk or otherwise – and for that you can hardly blame them.

"Who doesn't, at some point in their lives, just want to be left in peace and without outside interference? Life can be hard enough at the best of times, you don't need some privileged idiot, with no idea how tough times can get for an ordinary person, laying down the law over something as intangible as how you speak to God! Bad enough over earthly things like taxes, but about what you feel and believe? You can see why it stuck in people's craws."

Cameron nodded. "You can only push people so far." That came so from the heart that Anna knew there had to be something personal in that statement, but he was continuing, "When they've reached the point where they feel they've got nothing left to lose, that's when it starts getting really dangerous. And I'm guessing that back in those days, a lot of people must have held on to the promise of a better life after death to get them through the worst of what they had to endure in the here and now?"

Gary agreed. "Life for the ordinary folk was bloody hard. Quite aside from any fighting, accidents or illnesses which these days we could knock on the head with a few antibiotics, could rob a family of the main worker almost overnight. And when they had no understanding of what had caused that illness, it could look very much like an act of God."

"All the more reason to stay on the Big Man's good side, then," Cameron said as understanding came. "And if you felt you were being forced into doing something which would bring God's wrath down on you …*phew*! You can see why people would have got a bit heated on the subject."

"It was one of the reasons why Presbyterianism found such fertile ground up here," Gary continued. "With so many people living in isolated glens – even in lowland areas like this – and in places where the great and good of the Kirk didn'a bother with them, being told that they didn'a need some bishop passing judgement on them and how they lived their lives was so appealing. For people who only ate meat when a cow or a sheep died, being told which days they could eat meat on was nonsense. Aye, it made sense for some fat abbot who stuffed his face wi' it on a daily basis, but no' for folk who half the time were making do wi' rough bread, what few vegetables they could grow, and a rough kind o' porridge on the days when there was nothing else."

Anna was listening, but flipping through her books at the same time. "So cutting it down to its most simplistic: before the Civil War, a Covenanter was almost anyone in Scotland who had simply signed a document about religious observances as a protest? But after the Restoration, the few hanging on were probably a bit more extreme in their beliefs? Less likely to conform to the government's demands?"

"Aye, that's no' far off. Covenanter in the sense o' the memorials around here pretty much means someone who was prepared to even die for their right to worship as a Presbyterian, and not be dictated to by clergy appointed by the bishops, who in turn answered to the king."

"So what dates do you think I should be looking at for our ghosts? Are they early Covenanters who just got unlucky, or are they among the much later ones?"

Gary paused to think before answering, "The sixteen-seventies into the sixteen-eighties."

Anna's head came up. "That late? Hmm…the restoration of Charles the Second came in 1660. …Why did you say there was there fighting up here?" Then her eyes widened as she realised, "Oh! But if you've just put the King *back* on the throne, you wouldn't want the people who had helped kick his father off still stirring things up, would you? Especially if that king had openly stated that he thought Presbyterians would turn against him, and especially not up here where it's harder to keep an eye on things. But that must have felt pretty ungrateful if you were the family of one of those Scots who died, or who were transported never to be seen again, after Worcester in 1651. They gave their last for a king whose son then treats them like *they* were the enemy. …Oh! Hang on. Are we talking about 1685?"

Gary did a quick reckoning. "That's the date when most were killed around here, yes."

"Why is that significant?" Cameron asked.

Anna gave a triumphant smile. "Because that's the year when Charles the Second died and his younger brother, James the Second came to the throne, and James was married to a Catholic. And I can't remember it all exactly, but if not a Catholic himself yet, was at least very close to becoming one. It was because of that that he lasted only four years before he was harried into exile, and the throne went via the female line to the very Protestant William of Orange and his Stuart wife, Mary.

"Nobody in England by that time wanted England drawn back to being under the thumb of the Pope, but if you were up here and sympathetic to a more Catholic king, would you want there to be lingering pockets of ground-level supporters of those who threw the last king out? Because you did say that Catholicism did linger on in the Highlands in particular, didn't you? And for the other side, the Covenanters, that must have been the last straw! King Charles tried to force bishops onto them, but now his brother might take the country back not just to bishops but to the pope. That's what changes in 1685!"

"And geographically," Gary added thoughtfully, "that would matter far more here, close to the English border. Presbyterian, and therefore Covenanter, rebels up on the far West Coast, for instance, would still need to be rooted out – although, yes, the Catholic Church always had more influence up there than the hard-line Presbyterians – but they wouldn't be seen as the imminent threat that a rising in Dumfries and Galloway would be. From here, a decent long day's march and they would be across the border. That had been proven all the way back in 1640 when an army from around Fife and Edinburgh crossed into England at speed. Now there were a lot of reasons to fear rebellion deeper into Scotland as well, but the proximity of the English was surely relevant too."

With a sigh of relief, Anna sat back. "That helps a lot. I feel like I know when I'm hunting for our mystery men now, and why they might be in such conflict."

Out in the hallway the long-case clock struck the hour.

"Oh heck, I'd better clear all this away," Anna sighed. "We've got three more guests who want to eat in here with their dogs tonight, as well as these two lovely lads of yours, Cameron."

As she began to pack the books and her notes into her bags, Gary asked, "Why don't you move across into one of the spare cottages, lass? You don't have to stay perched up in that eyrie now that you're here permanently. You're the manager. Give yourself a proper place to stay."

Anna paused. "But I still haven't had a proper contract through, Gary, and that's starting to concern me. I got that letter saying yes, I could be the manager, but I'd have expected to have had a formal contract come through by now. Why hasn't someone at the company sent one?"

Then turning, she saw that Cameron was looking very embarrassed.

"Oh, I'm so sorry!" she apologised. "That really wasn't professional of me. It's just…" How could she say, 'I forgot you were a customer and not a friend' without either sounding desperate or a total dimwit?

Luckily Gary rode in to her rescue. "Our owners are a bit slow off the mark communicating wi' us sometimes. Grand in all other respects, mind, but slow on the internal paperwork." He said it so blithely, as if it were the least of things and not to be worried about – a knack of diffusing situations that Anna wished she had.

Slightly odder, Cameron acted as if he was covering up a *faux pax* of his own, saying, "Oh, no… Erm, it's just that I was wondering if you had room for me to extend my stay?"

"There's no problem with that," Anna told him with some relief. Then wondered if he'd thought she was having to stay in rooms which would otherwise be used for guests? It didn't sound likely, given that he must travel a lot for business, and be used to hotels, but just in case she added, "We can easily fit you in for as long as you like at this time of year. Most folk are just coming for one or two nights at the moment, and we haven't got them booked in to specific rooms. Closer to Easter we've got a few more week-long bookings who've requested rooms they've had before, including yours, but not now. I was only saying about my lack of room because my room is one of the attic ones for the staff, and they're a bit cramped because it's up under the conical eaves and has sloping walls." There! Hopefully she'd covered any misunderstandings.

"Come on through to reception and I'll book you in," she said, grateful that Gary picked up the heavier of her bags as she led the way out.

Sat at the desk with Harris and Lewis at her shoulders, and breathing soft huffs of breath on her neck, she brought up the screen and then asked Cameron, "How long would you like to stay for?"

"Two weeks, if possible," he said without batting an eyelid.

Two *weeks*? Anna mentally squeaked, and was glad she'd turned back to the screen already so that he couldn't see her surprise. What happened to the busy businessman? Shouldn't he be jetting off to somewhere else in a hurry? Not that it wouldn't be nice to have him and his dogs around for that long. The only problem she could foresee there was her becoming too attached to his company. Funny how she'd never felt like this about Jensen.

The booking all done, he seemed surprised when Anna led the way out and across to the oval staircase, and began going up it, as if heading for his room. As they reached the top, he strode ahead up the last two steps and held the fire door open for her, after which she heard his, 'Oh!' of understanding as she passed his door and put her bag down on the narrow stairs at the back, clearly labelled 'staff only'.

"So you're up above?" he said, as she turned and took the other bag off Gary.

"On that side," Anna said with a smile, pointing to the opposite side of the corridor. "There's a small room up above here, and one up above your room that the other receptionists use if they're on last thing at night and then in again to open up at seven. You can't expect someone to drive home, get a decent amount of sleep and drive back in barely eight hours."

"No, I suppose that would be unreasonable," Cameron agreed.

"I'll see you later, then," Anna said, and picking up her bags, she began to climb the stairs. She could hear Gary still chatting to Cameron but thought nothing of it. Gary was probably sounding him out to see if he wanted to borrow any fishing gear.

In truth Cameron was fishing, but not for fish. "She seems like a really nice lady who's had a rough time of it," was his leading opening.

"Aye, that she has," Gary agreed.

"The ex-husband sounds like an idiot."

"*Ach*, him? He's no' fit to lick her boots! Great saft mammy's boy. He turned up here not so long back, wanting her to go back wi' him. But no' because he loves her so much. No, it was because he's in his mammy and daddy's bad books for letting her get away." Gary rolled his eyes in disgust. "But that's why I want to get her out of the main building. One of the other receptionists thought she was doing them both a favour by booking him in here."

Cameron was instantly horrified. "That can't have been pleasant for her."

"It wasn'a, and she handled it wi' a good deal more grace and tact than he deserved. Verra professional she was. But what worries me, and I haven'a said so to her, is what will happen now. He's gone back wi' a flea in his ear, and I don't think we'll see him again. The father, though, he's another matter. Sounds to me like one o' those bullying men who canna stand not to get his own way. I don't want him turning up here and causing a scene that Anna canna get away from."

Cameron looked at the cramped little stairs. "She's too vulnerable up there, isn't she. One sign isn't going to keep a man like that down here, and once he's up there he could knock her about, and if there's nobody in the rooms down here, who'd hear?"

Gary looked at him with approval. "That's exactly it. And I dinna want someone charging around the hotel who we then struggle to throw out. If she's out in one o' the cottages when he turns up, we can treat him like anyone else who barges in uninvited, and get the polis to remove him if necessary. Other guests need never know that he's come hunting one o' the staff. But if she's here and guests get upset and complain to our owners, she could get the sack. And where can she go then?"

1659

Elspeth

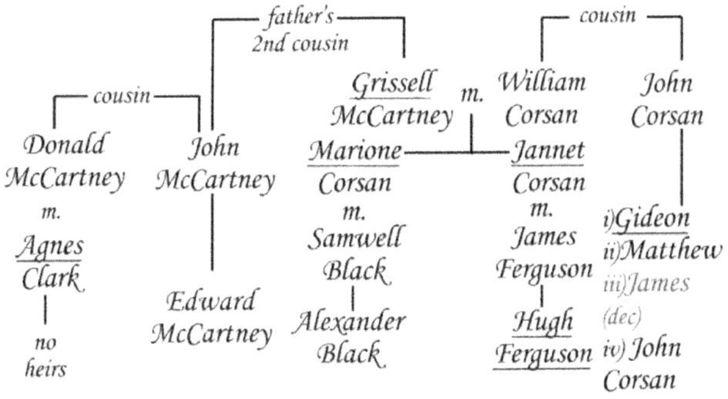

McAllister must have given Alexander and Hugh some serious training in the time he was around them, because in the months before Jonet was brought before the sheriff, and Johnne Allen was able to buy her freedom, not once did they get caught. Twice a week without fail, one or the other of them came and took food, drink, and healing salves to Jonet, Elspeth making the effort to walk as far as she dared towards the Manse with them to show that she wasn't expecting them to take all the risks if they got caught, but also so that she could run for help if they did. It brought her very close to both young men, sympathising as she did with their own worries about their mothers.

And those worries weren't without foundation, for Elspeth now found out that Hugh's mother, Jannet, had been investigate by the Justices of the Peace back in May at the same time as her sister

Marion – Alex's mother – and their grandmother, Grissell. Jannet might not have been imprisoned for long, but she was still going to have to stand trial, and her husband, James Ferguson, had taken what little hope he could from Johnne and Elspeth's experience of paying the bond.

"Pa has saved what he can from the harvest and kept our best pigs back from slaughter so that we have something to offer the sheriff," Hugh told Elspeth. "But it doesn't look good. Ma is accused of *flyting*. Was your ma accused of that?"

Flyting was an exchange of verbal abuse, but not simply a slanging match. It held the implication of two skilled rivals, fiercely verbally contesting who was best – in this case, the presumption by those bringing the accusations being that the women had been casting spells, when Gaelic words that few knew had been used. At the top end of society, *flyting* was very poetic and courtly though also ribald. At this end it usually included considerable profanities, and Elspeth feared that if Jannet Corsan had been provoked into taking God's name in vain, then that would go badly against her. Profaning in public already carried the heavy fine of twenty shillings – a whole pound, and a crippling sum for most ordinary people to find just for swearing at an enemy. What the court would fine Jannet if witchcraft came into the mix, Elspeth dreaded to think.

Pulling Hugh into a hug, she told him, "No. Thankfully with my ma it's Veitch who has a personal hatred for her. She spurned him when she was young, you see. But Hugh, please tell your pa to be careful. The sheriff isn't a vindictive man, but even he has to tread a bit carefully around the Kirk, and he can't be seen to go lightly on something like *flyting* if there are credible witnesses."

A few days later she mentioned the conversation to Alex as he took his turn with the provisions.

"You're right to be worried for Hugh and my Uncle James," he said sadly. "Aunt Jannet is a lovely woman, but she has a mighty temper on her, and she's had a shouting match with the Provost of Kirkcudbright's wife no less. Couple that with her and my ma helping Grandma, who's been investigated more than once, and our family starts to look very suspect indeed." He sighed. "It's bizarre that your ma, who's not done anything in reality, should be imprisoned at the Manse. Yet my ma and my aunt are accused of far worse, but because it's being done through the courts, are at least at home with us until the trials start."

Then a week later he brought sad news. "Grandma Grissell has died. She passed peacefully in her sleep at the last. Mind you, all the stress and the harsh questioning she's been through in this last year have done much to hasten her end. I find it hard to forgive the Presbyter for that, because he's been one of the ring leaders in this witch hunt."

"Oh, Alex, I'm so sorry. I know you loved her very much. But at least she won't go to trial now. An old lady like her wouldn't have had the strength to stand day after day in the court being badgered by those haughty men, let alone even heavier questioning."

Yet Alex shook his head. "But they might feel they've been cheated out of burning a notorious old witch. Grierson of Lagg has let Hugh go from his job, you know. He won't have the son of an accused witch under his roof, he told him."

"But he was there last week." Elspeth protested. "How is it different no…? Oh Lord! They're really going to go after your Aunt Jannet now, aren't they? I'm so sorry." Then she knew she had to make the offer. "Alex, if your uncle gets taken like your father was, we'll hide Hugh. It's the least we can do after the way you've helped us."

"Thank you. I appreciate that, because I wouldn't dare have him actually at our house – though of course I'd do whatever it took to hide him – because it's the first place anyone would look."

At the beginning of February, Jonet came home, but there was no celebrating for anyone connected with the Clarks. At the very end of the old year, Agnes' husband Donald sickened further and died, and all of a sudden Agnes' position became extremely precarious. Donald's avaricious cousin, John McCartney, began throwing accusations around that Agnes, like her sister Margaret, was a notorious witch. The immediate family knew it was all a pack of lies, but Agnes and Donald's croft was worth too much for John McCartney to leave in the hands of a young widow, who might live for many years before he could get his hands on it as the next male (but already married) heir in the wider family.

Nor was her sister Margaret any less in danger. She might not have been accused of something as serious as *flyting*, as Jannet Corsan was, but whereas Jannet's husband James Ferguson was moving heaven and earth to help her, a nasty rumour had begun to be whispered abroad that Margaret's husband Thomas had another woman. That Thomas had never been faithful to Margaret was old news. Yet this time the widow he had begun to seduce had some money of her own, and Agnes and the Allens feared that the dreadful Thomas had seen a way to get rid of a wife he'd long tired of, and swiftly, so that he could remarry. When it came to getting his hands on money, simple seduction would not suffice.

"It doesn't help," Alex told Elspeth, for he had continued to come and see her after Jonet was set free, "that out of the kindness of her heart, your cousin Margaret took in a woman called Bigis Cairns to act as a servant."

"What does she have to do with it?" Elspeth asked, already dreading the answer.

Alex sighed. "A woman called Janet McGown from Kirkcudbright is going to be tried in Dumfries as a witch. I think her trial date is the same as ours. She's a poor old soul who's lost everything. In truth, I think she's a bit mad – not dangerous or a witch, just old, confused, and has been through too much. Once upon a time she was well-off enough to have Bigis as her servant, back when Bigis was a young girl.

"Then when Mistress McGown lost everything way back in forty-four, she went to her old friend, my Grandma Grissell, and asked her if there was anyone who would take Bigis in. Well by then Grandma was already a widow and glad of the help on the croft. But in the last three or four years the croft hasn't produced enough to support Grandma *and* Bigis, and along with my father and Uncle James, your cousin Margaret used to go and do what she could to help. And one of the ways Goodwife Margaret helped was by taking Bigis into her household when her old maid left them."

Elspeth felt her blood run cold. This serving lass was the link between the Clark families and the

Corsans, and she could yet be the way men like John McCartney and John Corsan brought them all down.

"What kind of name is Bigis?" she asked, her voice shaking as the possibilities sank in.

"I believe her real name is Agnes," Alex said, "but she's always been known as Bigis for some reason. The worst of it, though, is that my ma and pa know of a great row between your cousin Margaret and her husband Thomas – and, so do too many of the neighbours – because she found Bigis beaten and terrified, and discovered that Thomas has been having his evil way with her."

He shuddered. "God help the poor soul, because it was probably for all of the years she's been under his roof, regardless of his other mistresses. Apparently, Grandma Grissell used to regularly slip Bigis some herbs when she feared Thomas had got her with child, though in truth she was probably a bit old for that to have happened. But you know what slant the men of the court will put on that. 'She tried to get rid of a child that God wanted her to have,' will be the way Veitch puts it to them, whether it ever existed or not, and because half of them are no better, they'll smirk and agree. They won't pause for one breath to think of what would have happened to Bigis if her belly swelled, and she was put out of a so-called Christian house. And now he's got this new woman, he wants to makes sure she's well out of the way, because she adored Margaret!"

"That wicked man!" Elspeth exclaimed. "My ma and pa never liked him. Well, they were right not to, weren't they."

"Aye. But now that Bigis is in the cells being tortured alongside poor old Mistress McGown, God-rot-him Thomas has testified that Bigis was a witch under his roof, and so without having to say a word against his own wife, he's made her the guilty one who knew about it but didn't stop it. I fear your cousin Margaret may be as deeply in danger as my own ma and aunt."

Elspeth cried herself to sleep that night, not just for her cousins Margaret and Agnes, but for the woman she had never even met, Bigis Cairnes – a poor soul who was an innocent with no guile, according to Alex – who hadn't understood that she should have complained earlier, and had only broken down when evil Thomas had decided that the new wife he had lined up wouldn't want his tame whore under the same roof, and told her to get out. Or more likely, he feared what Bigis in her naivety might let slip about what the master expected in his bed. Alex had demurred at telling Elspeth more, but he'd heard that Thomas liked some rather peculiar things; things no decent woman would want to do, and which Thomas would want this new woman securely tied to him by marriage vows (and therefore unable to refuse so easily) before he started demanding them of her.

The one bright spot was that she and Alex were now very close, and the way he'd been so disgusted with Thomas made her sure he wouldn't ask anything revolting of her if they ever got the chance to wed. Right now wasn't the time to be making wedding plans, though. And not just because of the impending trials. Young Hugh quite clearly had the most enormous crush on Elspeth, and she and Alex had no desire to break his heart by revealing that his cousin had won her affections, when he was facing some dreadful months in the immediate future.

Chapter 14

Cameron

Left to his own devices for the hour or so before he went down to eat, Cameron sat in his room wondering what on earth he was going to do. The way Anna had talked about the owners had embarrassed him, but not for the reasons she probably thought. How could he now come clean without seeming to be the creepy guy who had come spying on them?

When he'd first arrived, he'd expected to be rumbled pretty much straight away, and when he hadn't, had supposed that it had much to do with the professional way that all of the staff dealt with their guests. But looking at the screen over Anna's shoulder tonight, and then at their headed notepaper, it dawned on him that they thought their owner was most likely a company, and not a person. Why had Austin thought it okay to put Co. Ltd. after his name on the paperwork they had? He wasn't a company, and in no way had he limited liability! That had been one of the first nightmares that Cameron had discovered.

"Austin, if you're going to go around sticking your money here, there, and everywhere, with no limitations on what people can come back at you for, sooner or later you're going to take a massive loss, and through the courts where you can't wriggle out of it!" Cameron had remonstrated with him. "You have to go through the *proper* channels to get your companies set up and limited. Just sticking Co. or Ltd. on a letter isn't enough."

But Austin hadn't wanted to listen to that. He was too busy right now delving into some obscure piece of computer hardware that he thought he could improve. The fact that he probably could was something that Cameron just had to accept, because if he asked for any kind of explanation, Austin was incapable of speaking about it at a level that any normal person like Cameron could understand. What increasingly rubbed Cameron up the wrong way, however, was Austin's arrogant attitude towards what Cameron could do far better.

"He can't help it," their mother kept saying to Cameron, trotting out the by now worn-out metaphor of, 'He can't walk a mile in your shoes, because in his world, the only shoes that exist are the ones he wears.'

"I get that, Mum," Cameron remembered saying to her a couple of months ago. "But I can't help him if he won't let me! You're asking the impossible of me. There's no earthly point in me sorting all his stuff out, if he's just going to go out and do the same all over again. You begged me to give up my career to come and run Austin's finances, and because I care, I did. But you have to talk him into signing that document that makes me effectively his financial carer.

"Do that, and with the money he has pouring into his accounts, I can set him up so that even if he never invents another thing, he'll be set for life. Without that, though, I'm having to get him to sign off on every damned thing I'm doing, and some days he's in the mood to do it, and then there are whole weeks where he can't be bothered, and if I stand over him pushing him to do it, he throws tantrums and tells you I'm bullying him."

"That's how it probably feels to him," his mother had said, once again making every excuse for Austin's dreadful behaviour.

That had been when Cameron had really started to feel for his dad. When Austin had been in a special school, surrounded by other kids who all had their own disabilities, he'd at least learned how to behave moderately well. The staff had been kind but firm and consistent, and the family had seen a marked improvement in how Austin reacted, not only with them, but with outsiders too. But whereas other kids who'd been in Austin's class had had to face up to the realities of life outside of school once they left – even if they didn't cope terribly well – Austin, having made his first significant invention at seventeen, had not. Instead, he had been fêted as the young genius, and since all too many of the young geniuses of the computing world were to a greater or lesser extent similar to him, his random behaviour was treated as near-normal in those early days of him being out in the adult world.

The fact that companies now found this out-of-control man in his late thirties too much to deal with actually on-site was telling, though. Others might not be quite at his level of inspiration, but they weren't as hard to have around, either. Those companies who contracted out projects to him were happy to provide facilities and equipment for him to work with on his own, but he was too disruptive to have even amongst others close to his intellectual level, and on the way to being as divorced from reality.

A conversation between Cameron and his dad after that had brought the two of them closer than they had been in years. And with his dad now relieved that his own son didn't see him as the overly harsh judge of Austin, together they had once more tried to persuade his mother that something was going to have to give.

"Why don't you understand him?" his mother had pleaded, with his exasperated father snapping back, "Why can't you see that he's turning into a monster, Helen?"

"He's not a monster, Jeff!" Cameron remembered his mother weeping, and his father fuming,

"But he is! He has no control around anyone anymore! For the love of God, Helen, he's not a small man. What happens when he lashes out at someone and really hurts them? Do you want him to end up in a secure mental hospital?"

And as Helen had become more upset, Cameron had tried to help by saying, "Dad has a point, Mum! You can't close your eyes to how all this overindulgence has changed Austin. All his money won't save him if he hurts someone. If you would just back us up to get him to sign things over to us in a trust, we could easily afford to buy him somewhere quiet to live, with all the lab stuff he needs, and where trained staff could look after him. But leaving him in that apartment with ordinary families in the homes around him is asking for trouble.

"What if he lashes out at a child because it's screaming? He's never been able to take that kind of noise, not even when he was a kid himself. But at least when he was at school, *he'd* be the one to move away. Now, he's more likely to use his fist on the kid. He's a danger to himself and others, Mum, please, help us help him."

Yet it had finally been a crafty move on Cameron's part, waylaying Austin when he'd taken to his bed with a cold, which had got the documents signed, but not before his father had called it a day on the marriage.

"I'm sorry, Helen," he'd said on the day Cameron had last seen them together. "I can't do this anymore. I've waited until Cam was here because I want him to hear what I have to say. Cam's your son too, but he's never had a fraction of the attention that Austin had…"

"…But Austin needs…"

"No!" his father had yelled. "Enough! I'm sick of what Austin needs! You had another son. A son I am so proud of for never once holding it against us for all the holidays he had to forego, all the other things he missed out on as a kid. And he did miss out, Helen. I did my best to fill in the gaps while you were so busy with Austin, but there were family things that we just never did together, *could* never do together.

"Even now, Cam has done what you asked of him: given up his own life to help sort Austin out. And yet not once have you thanked him for that. Worse, you've refused to back him up when he's doing his best to help you do what you say you want. He doesn't have some magic wand, Helen. He can't make everything right *and* let Austin keep on behaving like a spoilt brat with that money."

And as Helen went to interrupt him, he ploughed on, "So I'm saying this now to Cam in front of you too: Son, if it gets too much for you, I won't think any less of you for walking away. Austin's your brother, not your child, and there's only so much even your mother should expect of you when it comes to caring for him.

"Helen: I'm done. I'm tired of having a wife who barely looks at me anymore. I took you on with Austin, knowing what he was like, but I could never have expected that with him only a few years off forty now, that we'd still be doing as much as we are. I didn't sign up for that. I want a life before I'm too old to even enjoy it, and Cam has the right to that too."

Now, Cameron sat gnawing a finger nail, worrying about how Austin was going to wreck what could be the best thing to happen to him; because in Anna, Cameron saw a kindred spirit. Of all the women he'd met down the years, here was someone who might just understand the weight of parental expectations, shoved on you when you were too young to know how to say 'no', or that a different existence was even possible. There had been a moment when he'd felt so bloody guilty as he'd listened to Anna talking about her parents virtually forcing her into marriage, because all he'd been able to think was, 'She'll get it!' Yet Austin's carelessness in setting things up, or in following up on what he had done before, now meant that things hadn't been done properly for the staff here, and that included Anna.

When he'd gone through the hotel's books, long before arriving, he'd been reassured that everyone had at least been paid regularly. That had been more to do with the bank's efficiency than anything, though, and now he realised he should have looked harder, and enquired more, about whether everything else was in order. When he'd logged in to the email account the hotel used to communicate with Austin, he'd been appalled at the number of unopened, let alone unanswered, emails, but as he'd frantically tried to get rid of the totally unviable investments and recoup something before Austin lost everything, he'd foolishly forgotten about *Nuns' Kirk Haugh*.

Almost dreading what he would find now, he went back in on his laptop and actually started going through them. The acceptance of Perdita Walliams as manageress had him groaning out loud. Her C.V. was clearly so made up, nobody in their right mind would have given her the job. The attached photo of a rather pouting, glamorous girl had obviously been the only thing that had caught Austin's eye, and the single line response of 'you've got the job, start whenever you're ready' was so careless it took Cameron's breath away.

The stream of angry emails after she'd left likewise had him in no doubt that Austin had been brutally direct on the phone to her too. Then he stopped. Wait. What was that this dreadful woman had written? Oh God, that it was another woman whom she'd spoken to. That could only mean his mum!

He checked the date of the email again and gave another groan. It was a day he wasn't likely to forget in a hurry either. He'd come back from having to pull the plug on a business, a day spent with a bank manager who was all sympathy for what Cameron was having to do, but who was adamant that there was no alternative. And Cameron had been dreading having to do the same with another venture Austin had sunk money into, only to discover that it was a charity, which made it even worse. He'd arrived with the documents for Austin to sign – if he was in the mood to, heaven help them – only to have his mum come haring down before he'd even got in through the door, having clearly waited to see his car pulling up outside.

"I thought you were supposed to be dealing with things!" she'd screamed at him. "I can't do everything."

"What are you talking about, Mum?" he'd asked, at which point she'd had a massive rant about a phone call that had upset Austin, and her having to take over, and when he'd tried to get details, she'd stormed out, saying, "Don't bother yourself! I've done it now!"

Absolutely shattered already by that day, Cameron had made a note to try and find out what it was all about, but had done nothing more than walk the dogs once he got home, then eat a microwave meal and fall asleep. The following days had been too hectic, dealing with things that the bank had told him were the priorities, and it had slipped into the abyss of all the other things which had been pending at that stage. Now, though, he was horrified. *Nuns' Kirk Haugh* was the best thing by far that Austin had thrown money at, and it was this amazing team who had held it together without a scrap of help or guidance from his family's end.

Who had called whom on that fateful day when Perdita Johnson had stormed out? The way his mum had spoken, he presumed that the ex-manageress had called Austin actually on that day, at which point, Austin had had a tantrum over being asked to make a decision. Then their mum had rung Ms Johnson the day after, going for blood from a young woman who had dared to upset her darling boy. All of which made it little short of miraculous that the hotel had simply picked up the pieces after Ms Johnson left, and carried on.

For that alone, he thought they all deserved a damned good bonus. And going through the emails he saw that Anna had done a great job of getting the young apprentices onto the books and hired properly, having found some contracts used by the previous owners and just changing the names and the hours as relevant. She'd been open about doing that too, to her credit. A covering email with each explained why she'd used the old contracts, presuming them to be drawn up in a way which would withstand legal scrutiny should it be needed.

"Oh God," Cameron groaned, burying his face into Lewis' scruffy fur as the big dog sensed his distress and came to nuzzle at his elbow. "I'm going to have to come clean to them, aren't I? I can't leave Anna worried to take over the cottage, and putting herself in potential harm's way, just because I don't want to look a twit."

With a sigh he turned back to his laptop and more out of habit than anything, opened up his personal email account. These days he got fewer of those than he used to, so it was a surprise to see one from the estate agents he'd put his Edinburgh flat on the market with. A few days ago, they had been enthusiastic about an offer they'd had from someone who was moving back to the UK, and who therefore wasn't part of any property chain. But now they were saying that this client would like to complete as soon as possible, within the week if that could be done. And all of a sudden Cameron knew what he was going to do.

On his own he would never have been able to afford to buy the beautiful period apartment right close to the city centre which he was now selling. His job had been good, but not that good! And in all truth the flat should have gone to his dad, not him. But his dad's aunt had seen things more clearly than any of the rest of them had at the time. She had married well, but had had the terrible misfortune to lose her only son in a car crash when he was in his early twenties, so once her husband was gone, there was nobody else to leave the lovely old place to.

I am not leaving it to you, Jeff, she had written in the letter which had been handed on at the time of her will reading, *because I do not want you to be pressurised by Helen into selling it for Austin's care. Helen will hate me for saying this,* and she had, *but Austin is not your son, and I fear that at some point in the future the burden of caring for him will drive a wedge between you.*

My dear Clifford was, as you know, a consultant at the Edinburgh Hospital for Sick Children, and he often used to tell me about families torn apart by a sick child. If there are other children, they inevitably get left to their father to bring up, and though you didn't want to hear it when we warned you of this before you married Helen, Clifford foresaw that you would be another of these families. Austin will need more than you can give at some point in his life, and if Helen will not relinquish control of him, then you will find yourself being forced further and further out of her life.

However, you at least went into the marriage knowing something, if not all, of what you were getting into. Poor Cameron was born into it and never had a choice. Therefore, I am leaving our apartment to him, with the only condition being that he does not sell it to fund Austin's care, and that he will give you a place to live if you ever need it.

Well, his dad needed it now. Jeff was currently living on a static caravan site, having delayed his departure from the family home until they reopened after the month's winter closure in January. But Cameron knew his dad couldn't stay there forever. It was meant for those retired people who could jet off to the sun during the winter months, with other static caravans on the site being let out to holiday makers, and Cameron had known from the start that his dad would hate it come the main school holidays when he was surrounded by hordes of screaming kids. So his plan, once his dad had announced his intention to leave, had been to put the big apartment onto the market and buy them each somewhere smaller.

Now, though, he was looking around the hotel, and having walked the dogs around the grounds, he knew that there was at least one more property on its grounds besides those used by the staff. Could *he* buy it? It would require a loan, of that he was sure. A viable business like this would cost more than the value of one Edinburgh apartment, even one of the best in the area…or so he thought in those first moments!

He double-checked the estate agent's email. God bless Aunt Jemima, because the apartment had sold for a nice margin over the six-figure sum. And when he went back into Austin's accounts, he couldn't believe what the former owners had off-loaded it for. It had been very short-sighted of the investment company, that he realised now. But with Covid-19 ripping through the country at the time, and hotels and every other hospitality facility shut for months on end, it must have looked as though it would continue long enough for the hotel to go from making a healthy profit to making a sizeable loss. Now their short-sightedness could end up being his salvation.

Granted, he would need to sink every penny of his savings into the hotel as well, and that wasn't to be done lightly. Without a mortgage, he had been careful to invest the considerable residue of his wages into ISAs and other secure investments. One man on his own, who was barely at home enough to enjoy it, had run up few bills, and if his old job had been demanding enough that he'd had little leisure time to go out on spending sprees with, he had also always thought of it as short term. Eventually, he had always hoped, he would be in a good enough financial position to give the job up and go and do something he genuinely loved, not marketing stuff he couldn't have given a damn about for other people. Quite how he'd been good at his job he'd never quite figured out, because it certainly wasn't because he had a passion for the work, and he'd been more than a little relieved to have a reason to leave when his mum had come begging.

"All I need to do is put the amount Austin paid for this place back into his accounts and get the deeds transferred over to me," he said to Harris and Lewis in hushed tones. "God! I don't want to rob my brother. But by the same token, this is leaving something priceless in the hands of a man who will dump it or ruin it without a second thought. Dad could happily live here now that he's retiring, and if I come here and help run the place, we can maybe both escape? You'd love it here, boys, wouldn't you?" At which both dogs enthusiastically wagged their tails.

Feeling as if the weight of the world had come off his shoulders, Cameron fired off several emails in quick succession. The first was to accept the offer on the apartment. The second was to the solicitors he'd engaged to help him unravel the chaos of Austin's finances, asking them to help him draft up a transfer of ownership of the hotel, and to put it into writing. Something which would stand up in court proving he was fully reimbursing his brother for it, alongside a couple more emails to the companies he had his investments with asking them to liquidate them. And finally, before he headed down to a meal he was suddenly looking forward to a good deal more than when he'd come up to his room, he put in a call to his dad.

"Your mum is never going to forgive you for this," Jeff warned his son after Cameron told him what he intended to do. "You were never supposed to think of yourself in any of this. It was all supposed to be about Austin. …Don't get me wrong, son. I think you're doing the right thing in every respect. If these people are as good as you say, then they don't deserve to have their livelihoods in the hands of someone who will never give them a second thought, like Austin. Sick though I am of saying this, he can't help it. But they don't deserve to be at his mercy either."

"Thanks, Dad," Cameron said with relief. He'd never doubted that his dad would understand why he was doing this, but it made a difference to hear him say so. His mum never would, he sadly realised. "But this was about you, too." He felt himself choking up. "I can't believe that Mum said she wouldn't sell the house and give you half without a fight. For God's sake, she's at Austin's more than she's ever there, anyway. What does she want with a three-bedroom detached house with a downstairs granny-flat extension? Austin's never going to go back there. He hates that house – and when, these days, does he ever do anything he doesn't like?"

He heard his dad's sigh. "I don't know whether to be glad that you're beginning to see the reality of life with Austin, or be broken-hearted that you're well on the way to becoming cut out of your mum's life. You deserved so much better than this, Cam. You're her son, too, and you should never have been considered just Austin's spare carer."

Cameron felt himself choking up. "Thanks Dad."

He heard a very heavy sigh come from the other end of the line. "Please don't hate me for telling you this, son, but right now you need to know. I don't want you being guilt-tripped into changing your mind, regardless of whatever happens to me." There was a dreadful pause. "Your mum never told me this until only a year ago, please believe me on this. I would never have bloody married her if I'd known for one second that she might think of something like this."

Cameron felt a cold knot appear in his stomach. Oh God, what had his mum said?

Clearing his throat, Jeff said, "She told me that she'd felt she had to have another child in case Austin's conditions deteriorated, because you're old enough now to know that he's got more than just mental problems going on. Granted, the physical stuff – like the hole in his heart – has become less of a problem as he's matured, not more, but back then it was in case he ever needed an organ transplant. Something like a kidney or a bone marrow transplant. And you were supposed to provide it without question."

And shoving the chair away from the desk, a horribly shocked Cameron had to dash to the bathroom to be very sick.

1659

The Trials

When the trials came around in April, they were every bit as grim as Elspeth had feared. Her own mother wasn't called to appear before the court since they'd satisfied the sheriff with the bond payment, but her cousins Agnes and Margaret were, and so too were Alex's mother and Hugh's. And if old Grissell McCartney was past them harming in life, in death her name was dragged thoroughly through the mud too.

The first case to appear in front of the court was Margaret Clark on the second of the month, though she was not allowed to give testimony, alongside Jean Thomson, Janet McGown and Agnes Cairns. In Margaret's case, even the Provost of Kirkcudbright turned up to add his voice to her condemnation, relishing his moment to crush her hopes. There were only six men and six women in all testifying against Margaret, but of the women, two were supposedly Jannet Corsan and the elderly widow, Janet McGown, and another was a notorious 'witch' from Kirkcudbright named Helen Moorheid, none of whom were allowed to appear, only their supposed 'testimonies' being read out for the court.

The fact that Helen had received a serious blow to the head as a child, as Agnes had told them years before, and had been seeing things ever since, seemed to count for nothing. But what shocked Elspeth when it came to Helen's own trial two days later was that

Helen's own sister's husband was one of her main accusers, claiming that she'd demanded he support her when her own husband had died; and that when he refused, she had cursed their family. That she was accused of killing her own eldest son in favour of the next son, and with that second son standing side by side with the uncle of whom he was clearly terrified, was just heartbreaking to watch.

Similar to Margaret, Helen had supposedly been denounced in turn as a witch by Jannet Corsan and Janet McGown.

"This is going around in circles, Pa!" Elspeth whispered into his ear in horror. "They're each being used to denounce each other. How could women in Kirkcudbright have known about women up here near Dumfries? This isn't a trial! There's nothing 'lawful' in any of this."

He wrapped an arm around her and pulled her close. "Not here, lass! Don't say another word or we'll never leave here alive."

That was on the first day, and Elspeth and Johnne joined James and Hugh to offer what little comfort they could when the court broke for midday refreshments. There was no way that Jonet could come to court to see her nieces being tried and not be in danger herself, because nobody knew what state either Agnes or Margaret would be in, and a simple cry for help could be misconstrued in all sorts of ways. Elspeth stood in her father's and James Ferguson's shadows with her arm around Hugh's shaking shoulders, hoping to remain anonymous, but when it came to Margaret's trial in the afternoon, she found herself biting her glove to stop herself from screaming at the injustice of it all.

She had never seen Jean Thomson or Janet McGown before, but both women came from the tiny hamlet of Borgue near Kirkcudbright. And Janet tore at Elspeth's heart, because like her own mother, Janet McGown had been under suspicion in 1644, and this time around had first been questioned all the way back in May of last year. All of the evidence was hearsay from neighbours, and the dreadful John Corsan one of her investigators.

Meanwhile, Jean Thomson looked suspiciously as though she was in the same position as Agnes. A middle-aged widow who might yet live for years, she had a very desirable sheep herd to bring in income to whoever owned them. Elspeth felt too ragged to summon the curiosity to find out who might benefit from Jean's death, but her guess was that it might be a friend of John Corsan's, and for that Jean had Elspeth's sympathy.

There had been a spate of accusations around the Kirkcudbright area the previous year, with two women dying, but until now Elspeth had been too taken up with her family's own problems to take much notice of who they'd been or why they'd died. Now, though, although she was still none the wiser of what poor Katherine Clacherty had done to deserve such a fate, Jonet Millar from Dundrennan suddenly took on a new importance. Somewhere in the tangle of investigations which had been going on since 1656, she had implicated Janet McGown, Agnes Cairns (known as Bigis), Jean Thomson, but also Margaret Clark and Jannet Corsan.

"How on earth did she know your ma, Hugh?" Elspeth asked, baffled. "Dundrennan is right down on the coast. I know they're saying that Jonet Millar was a travelling healer, but she never came up our way. And why would your ma have used her help anyway?"

But it was James who answered her. "I heard that her investigator was John Corsan," he said bleakly. "I only heard that Millar accused my Jannet a few months ago. This is Corsan using a beaten and battered old lady's befuddled testimony to his own ends, you mark my words. We never set eyes on her."

They went their separate ways that Saturday night, all of them knowing that they would get little sleep, for the court would not sit on a Sunday, and then the trials of Jannet and Agnes were to take place on the fourth. The following days were ones which Elspeth would never forget. Yet someone had to get up on Monday and go and find out their fate. The last thing Elspeth could face was the thought of a neighbour having to come and tell them the worst.

And so when the weak morning sun crept over the hillside, she put her bonnet back on and walked into Dumfries, hand in hand with her father. When they met Hugh and James outside of the court, it was to discover that more women were being tried that day. Alongside Jannet and Margaret, were the already infamous Helen Moorheid, who Elspeth now realised was never going to escape her accusers, but also two other women she'd never met, Janet McNaught and Jennat Callen.

Agnes, it seemed, was accused of cursing God's malediction, and quarrelling with neighbours over kale, meat, and purchases of wool, but it came out as though her neighbours had had to give in to her for fear of her feeling malice towards them, and consequently magically harming them. Knowing that one farmer had never liked Agnes or Donald, she wasn't surprised to see him and his wife giving testimony, but she saw others giving fearful glances to men sitting to one side of the chancellor, James Logan – a man she scarcely knew aside from the fact that he lived at a place called Fillis. Those men were John Corsan and John McCartney, Corsan sitting with his son Gideon, who was showing signs of relishing every moment of the trials, and McCartney with his son, Edward, who wasn't seeming half as keen.

All of James Ferguson's efforts to pay a bond had failed, and he and Hugh were devastated as they clung to one another while they heard the court proceed. As Elspeth had feared, the accusation of *flyting* was a grave mark against Jannet, but almost worse, no less than eleven women and nine men came forward to accuse her of witchcraft in one form or another. Yet to Elspeth's ear, most of those were just the kind of disputes between neighbours which would have soon been forgotten if someone hadn't been pouring oil on the fires of their anger behind the scenes.

They had an agonising overnight wait before they found out the sentencing, and all spent most of it on their knees praying for the worst not to happen. Yet when they got to the court on Tuesday, the mood was somber except for a small clump of officials who all appeared suspiciously satisfied.

"Oh God help us, I don't like the look of this," Agnes whispered the Johnne. "Why is John McCartney so smug and giving John Corsan those looks?"

When Logan announced that Margaret, Agnes, and Jannet were to be taken outside and strangled, then burned, on the following Wednesday, James Ferguson collapsed against Johnne, who just about managed to support him down to the ground, while Hugh turned and sobbed his heart out on Elspeth's shoulder. Elspeth herself was feeling as if her legs had turned to water, and it was only holding on to Hugh that was keeping her upright. Then from somewhere a little way away, she heard someone laugh, and so did Hugh.

Together they looked up through streaming tears and saw Gideon Corsan pointing at them to his father and laughing. John Corsan was shushing him, but only for public appearances sake, for he was looking far too smug to be genuinely disturbed at his son's callous response. And suddenly Elspeth realised that there really was a hidden agenda going on.

Working that out was more than her shocked mind could manage at that moment, though. How she was going to tell her mother that both of her nieces were going to die such horrible deaths defied her. Then she heard her father saying to James Ferguson, "Come home with us. You'll be amongst friends there and it's not as far."

He looked over James' bowed head and Elspeth saw him looking at the triumphant McBurney sons, who were already bracketing the Corsans and McCartneys, and knew he was worried that the younger pair of McBurney brothers might well go and torch the Ferguson's croft with them inside it, knowing that they would get away with it in the light of Jannet's conviction. The tiny cottage wasn't worth much, but abandoned fields could easily be claimed by the avaricious pair.

There would be nine women in all being strangled and then burned on the same Wednesday. For joining their three would be Jean Thomson, Janct McGown, poor Bigis Cairnes – who was already crazed with fear according the woman who took food to the cell – Janet McNaught, Jennat Callen, and Helen Moorheid.

The only thing that marked Agnes' fate as any different was that unlike the others, John McCartney hadn't been her chancellor.

"God have mercy on them," Jonet howled when they got home and told her. "That bloody McCartney has got what he wanted – Agnes' croft – at the price of her life. Damn him to the lowest layers of Hell! I hope his black soul weighs him down into the eternal fires like a millstone."

Yet Johnne had a different question. "Where was Alex? I thought he would be here to hold your hand, Elspeth?" He'd not been blind to the way Alex and Elspeth looked at one another, but was now wondering whether he'd been right in thinking that Alex would make her a good husband. Had he run away in fear?

However, it was young Hugh who answered before Elspeth could. "He borrowed a fast horse and rode for Edinburgh as soon as we heard the definite trial dates. He's petitioning at the courts there to get Aunt Marione's case heard in a higher court." He cast a covert glance over his shoulder towards his sobbing father, then said more quietly, "He warned Pa that offering goods instead of an actual payment could be deliberately misread as a bribe. He said that he should go to the sheriff *first* and ask if a bond would be allowed, not assume it, but Pa couldn't see what the difference was, even though Alex told him it would sound as if Pa was presuming on the sheriff or the provost's goodwill."

He checked over his shoulder again. "I think I saw Alex waiting on the sheriff as we left with a piece of parchment in his hand." His voice cracked as he added, "I truly hope he's saved Aunt Marione, but I wish he could have saved Ma too."

"Will he come here tonight?" Johnne wondered, but Elspeth already knew the answer to that.

"No, he'll go to his ma and pa first. It's only right that he lets them know how he's got on. Poor Marione must be going out of her mind worrying over her sister and what her own fate could be."

Sure enough, a week later when they made the grim journey into Dumfries to the Tolbooth to see the punishments carried out on the Wednesday, it was announced that Marione Corsan's case would not be heard until July, to allow for further evidence to be gathered. Whether that was good news or bad was hard to say, but truly awful news followed, which was the declaration that Bigis Cairnes had hanged herself in her cell.

How terrified she must have been to do that tore at Elspeth's heart, even though she'd never even met her. Suicide was a mortal sin, condemning her soul to Hell just as surely as the guilty verdict of being a witch was supposed to, but Elspeth suspected that it had been the more imminent prospect of the pyre that had been the deciding factor, and who could blame her?

Please, God, Elspeth prayed silently, *forgive Bigis what she did for she no longer knew what she was doing. No woman deserves to go through this, let alone innocent women like my cousins and Jannet Corsan. I can't plead for the others, not knowing one way or the other of their guilt. But if they've been snared by John McCartney and John Corsan, then I truly believe that they've done nothing to deserve this.* A whole week of sitting in a cell waiting to die such a violent death would turn the mind of many a stronger woman.

She was holding onto her mother for dear life, for Jonet had refused to stay at home on this occasion.

"If my poor brother was alive, he'd not stand for this," she kept saying over and over, "and nor would his Geillis! She'd have a word or two to say about this, and then they'd know what it was to be cursed by a full witch! And in Gaelic too!"

"Hush, Ma." Elspeth pleaded, feeling her mother shaking with emotions – both of fear and pent-up rage.

At the last moment she felt a familiar hand upon her shoulder, and turned to see Alex behind her, grey-faced with exhaustion and grief. He reached out and pulled Hugh to him, giving a nod of solidarity to Johnne Allen as he saw him supporting James Ferguson.

And then the women were being brought out. The state of Helen Moorheid, Janet McGown, Janet Callen, Janet McNaught, and Jean Thomson was so shocking as to rob Elspeth and the others of their breath. They must have been beaten to within an inch of their lives, for their faces were black with bruising and they were filthy, looking more like scarecrows than living women. One of the four whom Elspeth didn't know by sight had blood dribbling from her mouth, possibly from having had another tooth knocked out, and another seemed to have either lost an eye, or it was so damaged as to be invisible within the bruising. And then their own followed, just as violently abused, robbing them of the breath to speak initially as their shocked minds refused to process what their eyes were seeing.

"Who could do such a thing?" wept Hugh, and then they saw Rab McBurney standing by the executioner, dried blood still on his bruised knuckles. He was talking to his brother and Gideon Corsan, who was actually admiring the knuckles and laughing.

"There's something very wrong with that boy," Johnne said under his breath, then groaned as he saw Presbyter Veitch come and clap both Gideon and Rab on their shoulders, clearly offering words of praise. "The Devil surely looks after his own," he sighed softly, making Elspeth whisper her own warning of, "Pa! Be careful!"

He nodded, but wrapped the arm not around James Ferguson a little tighter around Jonet.

There was a grim silence to the crowd as the full enormity of what was about to happen sank in. Veitch stood up and offered up prayers, though what he actually said Elspeth could never have said. She was past hearing what he, or the sheriff, or the provost said. Instead, she made sure she caught Agnes' glance and then kept eye contact with her as if her own life depended on it. They had all agreed that they needed to be where their loved ones could see them, to let them know that they hadn't been abandoned or forgotten. Not in the very front row of spectators, which might have invited trouble, but close, only a couple of rows back.

Yes, it was dangerous to make such a public showing, but they all felt it was the least they could do. Her mother's eyes were all for Margaret, and Elspeth thought it wicked that neither of her grown sons had come. For Margaret's daughter Isobel there was some excuse, since she had married a man from Stranraer and lived too far away, but the sons were local enough to have come. Yet the tragedy was almost worse for Agnes, with nobody but the Allens to care if she lived or died, and Elspeth had vowed she would not let Agnes think she'd been forgotten.

She had not for one moment been prepared for the reality of it, though. For a brute of a man to come and put a cord around her cousin's neck and throttle her was so violent as to make Elspeth wet herself in shock. Hands tied down, Agnes couldn't even reach up to try and pull the cord away, jerking like a bird in a snare. Thank God they hadn't been able to face food this morning, because Elspeth was already retching and so was Jonet.

And then without checking to see if the women were truly dead or just unconscious, the pyres were lit.

As the flames licked up around them, the screaming started. The older women, Janet McGown, and Janet McNaught hadn't survived the strangling, but Margaret, Jannet, and Agnes had, while the others were too lost in the smoke to tell, though choking noises and the odd faint cry said at least one of them lived. The flames rose fast, the smoke swiftly blotting out faces, but it was too much for Jonet. Elspeth knew that her mother had feared this fate more than anything, and the sight of her nieces was more than her weakened heart could bear. With a scream of pain that echoed those on the pyre, she grabbed her chest and then went limp in Elspeth's grasp.

"Ma! Ma!" she wept, just about managing to prevent Jonet's head cracking on the cobblestones.

Johnne let go of James Ferguson, who fell to his knees, and dropped to cradle Jonet's head in his arms.

"No, Joni, no! Don't leave me. Don't leave me! Not now." he wept, but it was too late. Jonet was beyond anyone's help.

And it was then that they heard Gideon Corsan yelling with glee, "Look, Presbyter. You got her! You got her in the end! And she's taken the place of the witch who cheated you!"

Chapter 15

Cameron was still pale-faced when he went downstairs for dinner. Anna was nowhere to be seen, but Gary was sitting in the bar chatting to four men who had clearly come for the fishing, and was talking about the best places along the beat on the Cluden Water that belonged to *Nuns' Kirk Haugh*. Not wanting to disturb him, Cameron just put a hand on his shoulder, and when Gary looked up at him, asked, "Can I have a word later on?"

Astute as ever, Gary instantly took in Cameron's pallor and nodded, with a pat on the hand signalled that he understood that it wasn't over something trivial.

When Gary caught up with him, it was as Cameron was coming out of the dining room in search of one or more good single malt whiskies.

"I've got something I need to tell you, and it's important," Cameron managed to say with more calm than he was feeling inside. So he was considerably relieved when Gary looked around the hall full of people, some about to go in to dine, and others like Cameron coming out, and clearly thought this was no place for a confidential chat.

"Let's go up there," Gary said, with a nod of his head up at the mezzanine landing on the stairs, where there was a comfortable small seating area up above the back office at a lovely old oriel window – or at least a very nice Scottish Victorian version of what a Tudor oriel window should be.

Feeling more than a little guilty, no sooner had Gary settled down with his glass of Lagavulin than Cameron was pouring out his heart to him. And it was now that he fully understood what Anna had meant about Gary being such a good listener. Not once did he interrupt, or pass comment, until Cameron was done.

Sitting back and discovering that his own glass of Dalwhinnie was empty, Cameron gladly relinquished it to Gary as he said, “I think after that we both need a refill!”

While he sat waiting for Gary to come back, Cameron leaned his head back on the wall and looked upwards at the ceiling. There was a very odd atmosphere just around here, and it was considerably chillier than down below, despite the warmth from the hall drifting upwards. With the glass fire-screen just up a half-flight across the stairs at first-floor landing height, and a second at the top floor – understandably to prevent a fire from funnelling up the great oak staircase – it should have been as warm here. The actual windowpanes weren’t so big that they would drain every ounce of heat out of the small square seating area.

Even odder, he had the strangest feeling that someone had been listening in on what he’d said. Yet Brenda was downstairs, flitting between the reception desk and the bar, which he’d vaguely seen out of the corner of his eye, and there was nobody on duty with her. There’d been one couple who’d come down the stairs while they’d been talking, but they’d been engrossed in their own conversation and had gone straight past. A little after that, another pair had gone past heading up to their room, and had wished them goodnight, but then had been heard carrying on up to the second floor by the well-muffled footsteps he'd heard on the next flights of stairs, or rather, more by the creaking of the stairs than the footfalls themselves. It was most odd. Why should he feel spied upon?

"Here you go," Gary said, breaking his reverie by placing what looked more like a treble than a double whisky in front of him on the small coffee table they'd pulled over closer to them. "You bloody need it!"

Settling himself down beside Cameron, Gary clinked their glasses in a silent toast then said firmly, "Now listen, lad. Anna's no' going to think any the worse of you for what you've done. I can tell you that now. And especially once she knows about your brother's involvement in this bloody mess."

Gary took a mouthful of the whisky and let it linger in his mouth as he savoured it, then continued, "Now don't take offence at this, but your mother doesn'a deserve you! Your poor dad sounds like he was at his wits' end, and it sounds true to me that he didn'a know about your mother's twisted idea of having you as a spare – and God help us, but I've heard of other mothers doing similar, though why you would do that to a child of your own I canna imagine. Why anyone would assume that your second child would even be willing to give up body parts is beyond me."

He shook his head in disgust. "It's no' like asking to borrow money, is it? It's way more permanent than that. And what would have happened if the donating of a kidney or something had then wrecked *your* health? Would she have been as worried? Only I know of someone who got pressured into giving a brother a kidney, and then he died young with his health in ruins, while the brother lived on. She doesn'a seem to have thought of that at all.

"And it rings true that once he knew, your dad wouldn'a have known how on earth to tell you. It's hardly the conversation you just bring up at the dinner table, is it? And I tell you, Anna will understand that too. Most people – and thank God they are the vast majority – haven'a a clue what it's like to be so manipulated by their parents from day one, so that they have this weird control over you even when you're an adult. I have the funny feeling that like her, it will only be now that you'll get fully out from under your mother's manipulation." In this instance, Gary felt the more affectionate Scottish 'mammy' wasn't a word to apply to Cam's parent.

"You'll no doubt start looking back and realising just how many times you were twisted into doing what she wanted. People like that don't do it by screaming and shouting at you. They do it by making you feel guilty, or bad in other ways, for being 'selfish' or whatever, when in reality all you were doing was trying to ask for a bit of consideration."

Cameron gave a sigh of relief. "That's exactly how it's felt!" Then he gave a shiver. "Am I coming down with something, or do you keep feeling these strange little drafts around here?"

"Aye, it's an odd wee corner is this," Gary agreed. "It doesn'a seem to matter how many comfortable cushions and vases o' flowers the housekeepers put up here, nobody ever lingers long." He looked down at where Harris and Lewis were lying on the other side, not splayed out like they normally would be, but curled up with their backs to the wood of the bench-seats, gazing watchfully around. "Even your dogs are no' relaxing." And suddenly Gary was looking upwards with a thoughtful expression.

"What is it?" Cameron asked.

"Hmm, a conversation for another time, or at least after you've talked wi' Anna, but let's just say that I think this is part of an older building, or at least above where it used to be. Hmm… I wonder if that's significant?" He shook himself. "Go grab a coat and we'll walk over to my cottage; we'll be more comfy and more private in there. I'll ring Anna and get her to meet us over there."

He was about to say that he'd mind the dogs for Cameron, but the moment their master got to his feet, both hounds were up and at his heels. Clearly neither of them had any intention of staying in this spot any longer than they had to, and that made Gary even more convinced that the germ of an idea that he was having was right. Dogs were far more alert than humans to odd atmospheres, and while some might pooh-pooh the idea of them being sensitive to ghosts and the like, Gary had had too much experience down the years of things which couldn't be logically explained to be so dismissive. And even as he wandered down to reception and rang through on the internal phone line to Anna's room, he was wondering whether they might be able to get a better sense of where the ghosts lurked if Harris and Lewis could help.

Meanwhile, back on the mezzanine seating area, a ghostly figure detached itself from the niche created by the bench seating and the balustrade of the stairs, and stared furiously after Gary and Cameron, having been listening in on their conversation.

'A Ferguson!' it fumed in its other reality. 'A bloody Ferguson owns *my* house! *Ferguson Investments?* What, by Christ, is that? *Investments*, my arse! Just another way of that family taking what isn't theirs, I'll be bound. I'll no' have some bluidy descendant of that whoreson bastard lording it around in *my* family home! I'll have him out, so I will! I'm no' standing for this.'

And he stomped back up the stairs to the room he would forever call his own, plotting his revenge.

Outside, Gary and Cameron had barely got out to the forecourt, with Harris and Lewis taking the chance to water a couple of bushes, before Anna caught up with them.

"This is all very Secret Squirrel, Gary!" she said cheerfully. "What's up?"

Gary gave her a wink. "Our guest is no' exactly a guest, it turns out, but he needs to tell you this himself, and away from other flapping ears."

"Ooh! Mysterious." Then she saw how worried Cameron looked, even in the gloom of the lonely couple of lamps which lit the way up to the old stable block. "Wow! That serious?"

Gary wouldn't let them start talking until they were settled in his lounge, a large pot of decaf and mugs in front of them, and a whisky poured for each of them.

"I've been instructing Anna in the fine art of malt whisky appreciation, her being a Sassenach and all that," Gary teased gently. "But I thought it a bit harsh to start her off wi' Laphroaig and Lagavulin, so lucky for you, Cameron, I bought a bottle o' Dalwhinnie and one o' Old Pulteney to start her off with."

"Thank God for that," Cameron said, mocking wiping his forehead and making the aside to Anna, "Those two Islay malts just taste like TCP to me!"

She had to laugh as Gary feigned dramatic disgust, saying, "Now you've let yourself down, laddie.

There was I, thinking you were a full Scotsman, and you canna appreciate the grandest whiskies o' them all."

His joking relaxed Cameron, who riposted with, "I think I'm not the only one of our fellow Scots who'd argue that point with you!"

But then to his relief, Gary broached the main subject by starting to tell Anna what Cameron had told him of his parents and his childhood. He was barely a few sentences in when, to Cameron's relief, Anna was already starting to nod in understanding.

"Oh, I get it," she said when Gary paused to have a drink. "It's so insidious. As a kid you only know what *you* have as a home life. That's your definition of normal. Then when you go to school, and you start getting invited to other kids' houses, you gradually realise that not everybody lives like you do, but even so, you still just don't get how downright weird your home life is."

"Well, not all I have to confess can be blamed on my childhood," Cameron admitted, and taking a deep breath, told her about Austin owning *Nuns' Kirk Haugh*, why there hadn't been responses to the multiple emails, and what he was hoping to do in the way of buying the place.

When he finished, he sat back and took such a large gulp of his whisky he momentarily choked on it. He was half-expecting for Anna to be on her feet and halfway out of the door by the time he stopped spluttering and his eyes stopped watering, but no, there she was still sitting staring at him. Admittedly she looked a bit shell-shocked, but then it was a lot to take in.

"I can only say how sorry I am again," he managed to splutter out, and was surprised to see her waving his apology away.

"You've nothing to apologise for," Anna said firmly. "By the sounds of it, you've been run ragged for the last six months, fire-fighting one looming disaster after another. I'm not surprised we were low down on your list of priorities. *Nuns' Kirk Haugh* must have looked the most stable of the lot from your perspective, so why *would* you have put us first?"

"That's very understanding of you," Cameron gulped, but if anything, feeling even worse for both Anna and Gary not having cussed him out at any point. He certainly felt as if he deserved to be.

"Look, there's no harm been done," Anna said reasonably. "Our bank has paid all the suppliers and our wages out of the money we ourselves were putting in in the way of takings, because that was left alone by your brother when he bought the place. So in that sense, we've had no interference from him at all."

"But your contract?" Cameron protested.

"I was getting worried about it," Anna admitted, "but not to the extent of losing sleep over it. I'm afraid I was starting to take the attitude of, 'If they want me out, they'll have to tell me, because I'm not giving this up unless they do.' …I've come to realise that I'm very happy here, you see."

Cameron felt a surge of relief. "Then please, move over here to whichever cottage you want. I'll get a contract sent over for you in the morning. You're here for as long as you want the job."

Anna's face broke into a grin. "Then I'll take the one next door to here. We should have a second chef starting next week, and she can have the other end one of the three. The chap who I think we'll end up taking on as the sous chef is a local, so he can use one of the tower rooms if he's got a back-to-back shift.

He's not happy about where he is at the moment because he's in the position Emilio was in a few months ago of holding the fort alone, with the difference being that instead of the other staff trying to help him as much as possible, he's got a bully of a manager who just keeps bawling him out. Brenda knows the hotel, and says that we've had guests come here who wouldn't go back there because they don't like listening to him ranting at his staff, so the guy's complaints sound genuine." She gave a clap of her hands. "So we're now set up for the wedding season. Bring it on!"

"So, you're all good with things now?" Cameron asked cagily, not quite believing his luck.

"With these chefs coming, and you getting us proper contracts for them, yes, absolutely." She became more serious. "But what about you? It sounds as though you've had one almighty shock this evening, and believe me, I know how these revelations about your parents can rock your world. Are you all right?"

"I…I'm not sure," he admitted, having been totally unprepared to have her worry about him.

"Only while I was up with Aunty Rita, although I was barely there a week, she got this friend of hers over the one evening to talk to me. Dr McCreary usually deals with service men and women with things like PTSD, but he's got years of experience and he sat me down and asked me some pretty telling questions – and I didn't realise quite how telling until after he'd gone and I thought about them some more.

"Honestly, Cameron, I had never once thought of either of my parents as diagnosable narcissists. Well, you don't, do you? But it was when Dr McCreary told me that about one in two thousand people have Narcissistic Personality Disorder, and I thought, 'wow, that's a lot of people out there like that,' that it dawned on me that my parents could be amongst them. I mean, one in two thousand isn't exactly common, but when you think of all the people you rub up against in life, it stands to reason that at some stage, any one of us is going to bump into one or two. But it also brought it home to me that those narcissists presumably have families, and so why *couldn't* mine be one of those?

"Dr Mac said that the overriding characteristic is what he called a 'grandiose sense of self.' They have a lack of empathy and caring for others, coupled with a need for endless reassurance and being told that they are special, to cover up their own insecurities and angst. Some people just have mild traits, others show all the traits and have convinced themselves that they hold some special place in the world, and ought – indeed unquestionably *deserve* – to be recognised by all and sundry as such.

"That's my father! They, and he, have an endless need for attention, drama, and they love tension. While everyone is at each other's throats, my dad knows he can exploit them and make himself the centre of each nasty cauldron of misery. But my mum is also one in a different way. She goes more down the passive-aggressive route than he does, but it's still as manipulative, and it's while I've been listening to you talking about your mum that I've thought she sounds very like mine."

Cameron sat open-mouthed.

"It's a mental illness," Anna continued gently. "A genuine, recorded illness, but it's hell for those who have to live with them, and unlike some conditions, it's rarely – if ever – that they'll seek help, let alone get cured, not least because they cannot conceive of there being something wrong with *them*. For instance, narcissists can have near-impossible standards for those around them. In my mum's case it was her wanting me to be some weird kind of 1950s stay-at-home housewife, *and* a career girl, *and* getting out there dating every guy around in the search for the ultimate son-in-law for *her*! Looking back now, I couldn't have done everything she wanted with double the hours in the day, let alone what it would have done to me in the process. And please note, the acquiring of a suitable son-in-law for her and dad was the overriding concern, not me finding a man I could be happy with.

"Now doesn't that sound like your mum with you? She wanted you to be your brother's carer to make *her* life easier, but she also wanted you to run all of his business interests for him so that *she* would never have to look twice at them. And on top of that, she wanted you to do it in such a way that never upset Austin, so that *she* didn't have to deal with his tantrums.

"Do you see? When you take a step back from it all, it wasn't *Austin* making those demands of you, was it? Whatever kind of pain in the neck he's become, because nobody could be bothered to help him set reasonable boundaries, he's not the one who put pressure on you."

"Bloody hell!" Cameron gulped, the full impact of what she was trying to get him to see pounding in on him.

"And talking to Dr Mac, these types can be very charming when you first get to know them. Your mum was probably that very alluring mixture of the bright and vivacious lady who could light up a room – when she chose to be – and yet seemingly very vulnerable and needing support on the other. Given that your dad sounds like a really nice guy, he was probably sucked in without even realising how much he was giving up for her until it was too late."

Cameron shook his head in dismay. "I was born within a year of Mum and Dad getting together. Oh God, she orchestrated that, didn't she? What he said about her wanting to have a 'spare' for Austin…she entrapped him with me, didn't she? Once I was on the way, how was she going to cope with Austin and a new baby? He had to stay for my sake!"

"And being a decent guy, he probably did that willingly," Anna consoled him. "At that stage, was Austin already at the special school?"

Cameron mentally counted back the years. "Yes, or at least he was in a local state school for kids like him. It was my dad who paid for him to go to a private residential school as the best thing for him."

"And you dad's decision was probably made on that basis," Anna reassured him. "But for your mum, *her* specific need to not be run ragged between a troubled six…seven…eight-year-old and a baby, had *primarily* been satisfied by him. I'm guessing that your dad had a good job so that it was always going to be possible to do that for Austin?"

Mutely, Cameron nodded.

"So, she hunted your dad, not him courting her, I would guess. There wasn't much of the mutual attraction going on there, he probably realises now. No wonder he feels so bitter."

"Poor Dad, he didn't stand a chance."

"No, I don't think he did. But, in case you think later that this is stretching a point a bit, how *thin*-skinned is your mum? Only Dr Mac said that there's nobody as sensitive or as quick to take injury as a narcissist. They're shockingly insecure at heart, you see, and I saw that in my dad. He was always worried that he was missing out on something, and he couldn't take *any* sort of criticism. Something as simple as suggesting that he looked tired, and could do with a day off, would be met with him lashing out in a verbal tsunami of rage. How *dare* I criticise him. How dare I offer him advice when *I* was the child and he my father. How dare I comment on *his* work when I only worked in a supermarket. There was nothing he couldn't twist into me insulting him."

Cameron by now was looking as though he'd been run over by a truck. "That's Mum," he said weakly. "God! That's so Mum! Every time I made some suggestion for making her life easier, it got thrown back at me like that. *I* was the one who didn't understand what it was like looking after Austin. *I* didn't know what it was like to love someone you couldn't help – that was a really nasty one she used a lot, as if *she* was the only one who loved or cared about him."

Anna gave a thin smile to Gary. "He's beginning to see it now." She turned back to Cameron. "Another trait I recognised when Dr Mac told me was this: they're lovely to strangers. Oh, they can charm the pants off a stranger! And that person will go away thinking 'Poor Mrs Gracie,' in my mum's case, or 'Poor Mrs Wiseheart,' in your mum's. But it's contrived. It allows *them* to be as vile as they like to the immediate family, safe in the knowledge that nobody will believe them if they complain. The partner or child will have nobody sympathetic to turn to, because all the sympathy is with the narcissist, not their victims."

"I used to get that," Cameron said weakly. "All

my friends' mums used to feel so sorry for my mum. I never felt that I could complain that I never got what I wanted for tea, or the Christmas or birthday presents I really wanted. All I ever heard at those other houses was how they didn't know how my mum managed, especially once Austin turned eighteen and was home all the time. But I was a teenager of just turned thirteen who never got to be a teenager from then on. Oh, I could go to other kids' houses for the odd overnight, but I soon learned never to say anything about the tantrums *Mum* threw. And God knows, she could match Austin one-to-one with those!"

"Which probably didn't help him any," Gary said knowingly. "Someone with his problems needed someone who would stay calm around him, not wind him up. It's no wonder he's become such a handful. Your idea of getting him somewhere out of the way, nice and quiet, and with a couple of professional nurses who know how to keep him calm, would probably the best thing for him."

"But your mum is never going to let you do that," Anna said sadly, "because then you've robbed her of her role as the martyr mother. And she does what Dr Mac called 'weaponising compassion'. That whole, 'Austin can't help it' routine, which you've said she uses over and over, turns your compassion for Austin into a weapon she uses against you. And there's a whole raft of other sayings that I recognised and I'm betting you do too.

"…'You're being over sensitive,' is one. …'You're making that up.' …'You're overreacting.' …'You're being irrational.' And note that it's always *you* who's in the wrong with these. And the ones that now make my flesh crawl just hearing them: 'We talked about this, don't you remember?' That's a cracker, because they get you doubting your own sanity trying to remember conversations that actually never took place. And the other crippler: 'There *you* go again, being *so* ungrateful to me', … or 'your father', …or 'to us' – delete as applicable."

"And then there's the isolation tactic. When you were a kid, I bet Austin was always used as the reason why you couldn't bring other kids home, even when he was away at school?" Cameron's jaw was just hanging by now.

Anna nodded sympathetically. "I got that too. They'd disturb my dad, or she and Dad were going to have someone over and Mum couldn't have the house messed up. Always something vaguely plausible, but really about keeping you from having the kind of close friends who, even if they couldn't actually help you, might lend *you* a sympathetic ear.

"So tell us, Cameron, even as an adult, when was the last time you went out with a bunch of friends? Even just people from work? How often did you tell your mum that you had the weekend off and were planning to do something, only for her to ring up at the last minute with some crisis which made you cancel, and go to see her instead? Some crisis which she would use Austin as the excuse for, and which once you got there you couldn't necessarily see the connection to?"

At that point Anna felt that she had better stop, because Cameron was as white as a sheet.

From his point of view, never in his wildest dreams had he ever thought that someone would see through his mother with that much clarity, indeed to an extent that he never remotely had himself, and someone who had never even met her at that. That doctor Anna had talked to was right. His mum would never admit to anything being wrong with her, so she'd never accept help. Even in leaving, the fault would be his. That she had driven him away would be too impossible to even consider. But it explained so much.

No. It explained *everything*! That was what shook him so deeply. It wasn't just something where he thought, 'Oh, that sounds familiar, but the other stuff isn't mum.' It hit every marker, ticked *every* single box, and as his hand shook as he brought the glass of whisky up to his mouth, he knew that though he'd never wanted it to happen, he was going to have to cut his ties with his mother. If he didn't, he might not survive with his own mental health intact, because after all this time she was never going to change.

1659

Aftermath, April - August

It said a lot for the shock of seeing the reality of a witch trial that the ordinary people of Dumfries helped Elspeth and Johnne find a hand cart to take Jonet's body home on. Suddenly there was no talk of witches, she was just a neighbour who'd been taken ill and died. Nobody wanted to see a repeat of those dreadful, shocking few hours.

Alex immediately had his hands full with his Uncle James and Hugh – because as had been the case with Jonet – Marione and Samwell hadn't dared to go to her sister's trial in case they got swept up in the hysteria and died without even having a trial. Marione still had her own accusers to face, but staying away meant leaving Alex to cope alone with his distraught uncle and cousin as Jannet died. Father and son were almost catatonic with shock, but they followed the Allans home, not least because that house was nearest and Alex couldn't have got James any further anyway. The two men, widowed on the same day and at the same time, were suddenly united in grief, and it was left to Elspeth to wash her mother's body clean and lay her out properly. She was part of the way through doing it in the privacy of the loom shed – for it would not have been proper for Alex or Hugh to help her – when old Christian came puffing up the slope to the croft to help her, and surprisingly, two other older local women came too.

"I'll not leave you to do this on your own," Christian said stoutly, and the others agreed. No woman was left to enshroud her own mother alone except in the direst of circumstances, and clearly the older women had decided that today was not that time. Something had changed on this day. A line had been crossed, and the quiet, law-abiding, folk of the shire had come to their senses and decided that enough was enough.

When Veitch declared that he would not bury a witch in Irongray's kirkyard, he found himself with a very depleted congregation the following Sunday, and that at time when not attending was noted and could be dangerous. Meanwhile, Gabriel Sempill, the minister at Kirkpatrick Durham, adopted a more Christian attitude, and at least offered to come and say the words over her, when Johnne, Alex, and Hugh went and dug a grave for her in the nun's tiny kirkyard at the old nunnery, for which he got much quiet approval. And though John McCartney did in the coming weeks get his hands on Agnes' croft, he had the sense to not make much of it publicly, seeing which way the wind was now blowing.

For Elspeth, the world would never be the same again. Her hair, which had been a mass of dark curls, was now snow-white, having turned overnight with the shock of what she had witnessed. Both she and Johnne got on with the day-to-day jobs, but could rarely find any words to speak to one another, mostly exchanging harrowed glances when they looked to where Jonet used to sit by the fire, or when Elspeth did some task her mother used to do. Johnne could no longer bear to sleep in the bed they had shared, and so he took over Elspeth's bed, and she returned to the truckle bed beneath which she'd had as a child, not caring anymore that it was too cramped for an adult to sleep on long-term. She believed she was past feeling anything anymore.

Alex came frequently, but he and his father were still working furiously to save Marione, and they had James and Hugh to worry about too. And so it was to help all of them, that by the time Marione's trial approached, it was decided that for the next month or so James and Hugh would come to stay with Johnne and Elspeth, the pair of them sharing the bed that had once been Johnne and Jonet's. It took some of the strain off Alex and Samwell, and allowed them to go into Dumfries when the trial came around.

Nobody expected the others to go in for it. Not after what they'd been through. But it also meant that if Alex and Samwell had to take drastic action and make a run for it with Marione, they wouldn't be leaving Hugh and James unguarded.

With that in mind, two days before the trial, Elspeth took Alex and Hugh up to the old nunnery. As they got to the tumble of the outer walls, Hugh froze.

"Are you sure it's safe, Elspeth?" he asked, despite the fact that it was as lovely a summer's day as you could wish for, and the sunshine was warming the sandstone to a friendly glow. "Grierson's son said he saw terrible things here a few years ago."

Elspeth stopped in her tracks. "How long ago is 'a few years ago'? Eight, by any chance?"

Hugh had to think, but then nodded, "Yes, it would about then."

"Then that was the day he and the cursed McBurneys hunted me down like a fox," she snapped, and saw him making the connection. "Yes, Hugh, the nuns did scare them witless, but it was to protect *me.*

And I'll tell you something else while we're here. See over there?"

"The Apostles' Stones?" he gasped.

"Well, my ma, Agnes, and her ma took me to the stones to thank the fae for sending the fox who took the hounds off my scent for long enough for me to get here. But I thought I needed to thank the nuns too. And when I came here, I saw the nuns' ghosts again, but the fae I saw with my ma was standing here *with* them!"

"Y…you saw a *fae*?" Hugh's eyes were nearly out on stalks in awe.

"I did."

"And…?"

"And what, Hugh?"

"Did it look…well, human?"

Elspeth thought back to that night. "Taller. Slimmer. But not skinny, if that makes sense. More willowy. And she really was almost a ghost, so please don't ask me what colour her hair was or her eyes. All I could say is that her eyes were more catlike in shape than human. But one thing I do know, and that's she was angry that I was being hunted like that…with dogs, and by drunken men who would have beaten and raped me if they'd caught me."

"Then I'm glad she was there," Alex said, taking her hand in his and holding it tight. "I would hunt them to the ends of the earth if they'd done that to you."

"Ye'll be needin' a hand wi' that, then?" a familiar Highland voice said from behind, making them all jump in shock.

Where McAllister had sprung from was a mystery, but there he was, smiling cheerfully at them.

"Are you working for Grierson of Lagg this

summer?" Hugh asked. "Only I'm not allowed there anymore,"

His expression fell as it came back to hit him all over again as to why.

"I heard, lad, I heard," McAllister said, coming and wrapping a fatherly arm around him. Sometimes these days, Hugh seemed older than a lad only just coming up fifteen because of what he'd seen and been through, and then on others he really was a youngster who needed – indeed craved – a father's guiding hand. That James Ferguson was like a walking ghost himself was understandable, but not much help to Hugh.

"I brought Alex and Hugh here to show them where it would be safe to hide Marione, and possibly Hugh's father," Elspeth explained with a thin smile, and was rewarded with McAllister's clear gaze settling on her with great pity in his eyes.

"That was a terrible thing for your ma to witness," he said gently, "and you too. I see the change in you, Elspeth, and ye' have my deepest sympathy. Indeed, that's partly why I'm here. Ye' see, when I told Mailie about what had gone on, even before I left she could only think o' bringing all o' ye' to safety in the Highlands. She and her man are no' rich, but if ye' can help them farm the land, ye'll no' starve. And there'll be no bigoted wee man o' the Kirk to persecute ye' there, either."

Alex stepped forward and shook McAllister's hand. "If that invitation extends to me and my family, I'll gladly come. I've been fretting over how I could possibly ask Elspeth for her hand when my ma could be a convicted witch, even if she gets away with her life. It would put Elspeth in such grave danger when coupled with what happened to her cousins, you see."

"Ye'd be verra welcome," McAllister declared.

"And I reckon the sooner I can get ye' all away, the better." He turned and looked at the ruins. "So, Elspeth, do ye' feel this is safer than hiding at yon stone circle? Who are these pious men more afraid of? The fae, or the ghosts of the nuns?"

"Probably both in equal measures," Elspeth admitted, "but in the stone circle there's really nowhere to hide except behind the stones themselves. I'm not a tall woman, and even I can look over the top of the stones, because they're not that big. And if they come hunting us on ponies again, all they have to do is ride *around* the circle to get to us, because we'll be seen from almost a field away – they never need to chance going within it. Here though," and she waved her hand at the nunnery, "you can get down into the old crypt and the under-croft, and be out of sight."

It was nothing but the truth. The distant Apostles' Stones formed a large circle, but none of the stones were that big in themselves, and some had toppled to lie on the ground. Worse, you only had to get up to the top of the field they were in to see the full spread of the circle, because the land rose sharply from the river. Potent the stones might be, but no adult would easily hide behind even the largest stones for long, making the monastic chapel the much better bet.

"Show us," McAllister said, and took her arm as she led them under what had once been a stone arch between the nave of the nuns' kirk and its choir. Once in the choir, the taller walls threw long shadows, and there was a distinct atmosphere here that the sun did nothing to dispel.

"These are the stairs down to the crypt," Elspeth said, pausing at the top. "The ones over there go into the under-croft. The roof's not fully on that anymore, because the wall's crumbled away on the far side where the land slopes more. But you could get deep into the shadows there and not be seen."

McAllister nodded, but ducked his head to go down a few steps into the crypt. "Aye, but this is properly covered over," his voice echoed. "Oh yes, this is the place I'd hide someone. If ye' stayed quiet as a mouse, nabody would ever know ye' were here." He came back up and looked to Alex and Hugh. "We need to bring everything ye'd want to take wi' ye' up here tomorrow," he said firmly. "Bags and baggage can go in the under-croft. That way, if anyone does come, they'll think that's where ye'll go to hide. But put a couple of warm blankets down here in case ye' have to make a run for it."

Alex sighed. "I'll have to leave you to do it, I'm afraid. Pa and I have to take Ma into Dumfries tomorrow. She isn't allowed to wait until the day of the trial in case she doesn't turn up."

Hugh looked pale, but remembering what was at stake, managed to nod firmly as if he wasn't near to soiling himself in fright.

"I'll be with you," Elspeth said encouragingly, and that seemed to give him heart.

The following morning, Alex, Samwell, and Marione, stopped to break their fast with the Allens on their way into Dumfries, and to speak to James and Hugh, for who knew if they would ever meet again? In the couple of months since their families had been bereaved, much of the fight seemed to have gone out of the wider demands for witches to be brought to justice. That didn't mean it wouldn't happen, though, and Elspeth was quick to caution everyone,

"John McCartney got his hands on what he wanted, which was his cousin's croft, and that's set his wretched son Edward up for life without depriving his older son by his first wife of any of his own lands. And with his own lands at Senwick being right by Kirkcudbright, now having Agnes' home much closer to Dumfries, where he can go and demand that his son put him up for a night or three, makes it easier for him to travel up here and fawn around the greater men of the shire he'd love to be an equal with. I won't say that makes him content, because I doubt if that man would be so, not even if he was made a laird with a castle to call his own, but he's not as dangerous as he was.

"But forget John *Corsan* at your peril. He sat in judgement on our loved ones without turning a hair at what he was doing. And he's far from satisfied with what he's got as yet! His words were some of the worst which condemned your ma Jannet, Hugh, and he blackened the names of Janet McGown, Jean Thompson, and your grandma, Grissell, and he was behind the death of that poor woman Jonet Millar, who got strangled..." She couldn't help but gag on that word, "and burned in Dumfries in May *last* year. We should have taken heed back then what might happen. The only reason it didn't cause such a scandal as our families' deaths this year, was because she was just one woman, and therefore everyone believed she really must have been as bad as he said. It took them murdering *eight* women on one day, and another dying on the spot, and in public, to wake everyone up.

"Well, whatever it is that John Corsan wants, I don't think he's got it yet, because that vile son of his, Gideon, is still at home, and the youngest one too. I presume that like McCartney, he wants somewhere for that creature he calls his son to have as his own. Your croft, Hugh, is good as far as it goes, but yours, Alex, would be a far finer place for him to get his hands upon because of the land you have – and if he can get both, well…! And what better way to do that than have your ma declared a witch, thus making it near impossible for you to stay in the area?"

Alex had gone paler and paler as Elspeth spoke, and now gave a shudder. "If it's the croft he wants, he can have it. I'd rather work my fingers to the bone and keep Ma and Pa in their old age, than have it easier with our good fields but with them gone." He turned to McAllister. "I fear I must presume on you to help my family as much as Elspeth's. Can you get Uncle James up here the night before the trial? I have a terrible premonition that in spite of all that I've done to get Ma's case heard in Edinburgh by a less biased court, we're far from safe, and what Elspeth's just said makes too much sense to be disregarded."

"Of course I'll help," McAllister said immediately. Then he dived back into some bushes growing beside the ruined walls, and came out with a wicked looking dirk in a sheath, which he thrust into Alex's hands. "I taught ye' how to use one o' these, lad. Dinna be afraid to do it if it will save your ma's life! Once we're across the Highland Line, they can call ye' all the names under the sun, but they willn'a find ye', no' if the Highland folk dinna want them to. And most o' my family will shake your hand for defending your own folk from men like that."

They returned home with that promise, McAllister retrieving his pack and coming to Elspeth's home to see Johnne and James Ferguson.

That night, as McAllister shared some *uisge* with all but James, who was curled up in the bed, he said softly, "Yon poor man is fair wracked wi' grief to the point of no' being any use at all. We'll need a pony for him, even if the rest o' us walk."

Hugh pointed to the wall, on the other side of which was the lean-to where both the Allen's work pony and theirs were stabled. "We have two. …You are coming, Master Allen, are you not?"

"Aye, I'm coming," Johnne said, his voice so sad it broke Elspeth's heart all over again. "I can't breathe here without feeling my Jonet. If I stay, my grief will eat me up." He looked to where the hanging across the bed hid James, everyone knowing that he recognised that James was already in that dark place. But pulling himself together, Johnne said, "I want to be able to dangle Elspeth's children on my knee in my old age. From now on, she and her family to come are my future, not anything here. Jean has made her bed, and must now lie in it; whereas I would dearly love to see Mailie again."

McAllister chuckled as he topped up the *uisge*. "Well ye' can do a fair bit o' that dangling straight away wi' Mailie's youngest, though the older ones are a bit big for that now."

That made Johnne sit up a bit straighter, and Elspeth was relieved to see that he clearly meant every word about him being able to find a future in his grandchildren. How easy she would find it to get on with an older sister whom she hardly knew, but was effectively going to be beholden to, was another matter, but she would bend over backwards to make this work to see her father coming alive again.

They spent the rest of the day packing what they could into tight bundles that would strap onto the one pony. Hugh had already brought what few precious items he and his father had to the Allens' for fear of leaving them unprotected at their humble croft, while

Johnne was more concerned with taking the best of his tools with him.

"If we're to start over, I'll be needing these," he said more than once, but by the time the sun was sinking into the west they had everything ready.

"I'd like to get you all up to the nunnery tonight," McAllister declared, "because I've no idea how early they're going to start Marione's trial tomorrow, and something tells me I need to be there, just in case."

"That's all good by me," Elspeth said, and jollied Hugh and James into moving, while her father got the ponies ready.

It was a strange and sad feeling to be closing the door on their home one last time – something a few years ago, Elspeth could never have imagined doing. Now, the only thing that broke her heart was that there would be nobody to put flowers on her mother's grave. And with that in mind, while McAllister led the forlorn procession up to the nunnery, Elspeth ran down to Christian's tiny cottage and begged her to make sure her ma's grave didn't become overgrown with weeds, especially as it wasn't in the regular kirkyard where others would see.

"We dare not stay," she sobbed to the old lady who had been their friend in their darkest hour, "but I can't bear the thought that people will think we didn't care about Ma."

"Don't you worry," Christian said, patting her hand. "I'll ask my daughter to tend it once I'm gone. She understands." And in that moment Elspeth remembered that Christian herself was no mean healer, and that of course she would have passed what she knew on to her daughter. In different circumstances it could have been Christian and her daughter who had burned, so naturally they were sympathetic. And if they hadn't spoken up, it was only out of terror of what would be done to them if they did.

It was a grim and chilly night in the under-croft for them all, for McAllister wouldn't let them light a fire for fear of giving their presence away. And come the morning, before he set out, he made sure that James and Johnne were safely in the entrance to the crypt. There'd be no need for them to go right in unless the worst happened, but the speed at which James moved at these days meant that he'd never reach safety in time if they needed to run for the crypt from the under-croft.

In the end, young Hugh decided that he would go with McAllister.

"Uncle Samwell is stronger than my Pa," he reluctantly admitted, "but if Aunt Marione dies like my ma, who knows how he'll take it, and I should be there for Alex the way he was for me."

And so he and McAllister vanished off into the morning mist, which promised a rare day of hot summer weather once the sun burned it off. For a while Elspeth sat on the wall watching, but realising that the trial wouldn't even have begun yet, she decided to go for a walk to the Apostles' Stones. If they were leaving, never to set eyes on here again, then she wanted to walk amongst the stones one more time, for since her escape she had come here far more often – usually when she wanted to think in peace and quiet. It had become a special place for her, and she would miss it.

She'd completed a circuit of the stones, touching each one as if shaking the hand of an old friend to say farewell, when to her horror she heard a sneering voice.

"Not at the trial, little witch?" And there, perched on a far finer horse than she'd seen him on before, was Rab McBurney.

She darted one way, getting to the other side of one of the largest stones, but on this faster and more nimble horse, he was there a moment later. Wherever she tried to dodge to, he was with her in a heartbeat. And then as she was just a step too slow, he caught her by the hair.

Holding her tight, and by too great a handful for her easily to pull free, he dismounted and pulled her to him. To her disgust, she could already feel how aroused he was, and she feared that this time there'd be no quick escape, no McAllister to appear out of the blue to save her. Tripping her down onto the ground, he was on top of her before she could recover, fumbling with her skirts with one hand as he pinned her down with the other across her throat.

As she started to see stars as she fought for breath, she suddenly saw the fae behind him, standing over him with what looked like an ornate bow and arrow.

'*Do you want his blackened soul?*' she sort of heard the fae asking, but not of her.

Then into her swimming vision came two of the nuns, one of whom Elspeth was fairly sure had been her saviour before.

'*No, you can have this one,*' the one whose 'voice' Elspeth recognised said. '*He is past redemption. He will never learn, that is now clear.*'

The fae glided silently around to behind Elspeth's head, and then she felt a sudden chill on her hair as if very cold breath was brushing her.

Rab had hitherto been too intent on undoing his breeches one-handed, but now looked up, a lust-filled leer on his face.

He froze. The leer momentarily stuck in place. Then in a heartbeat it collapsed to be replaced by stark terror accompanied by a scream.

Just for an instant, Elspeth thought she caught a glimpse of a very different face to the serene one she'd seen. This was dark, with a widening maw full of razor-sharp teeth. Being flat on the ground, she couldn't see the eyes, but she didn't want to. Rab, on the other hand, couldn't fail to see, and seemed unable to turn away.

"No*ooo*! NO*Ooo*!" he shrieked, scuttling backwards off Elspeth, yet still caught in the fae's gaze like a rabbit in a fox's. Breeches clutched up enough in one hand to let him move, he struggled to his feet, all the time backing away, and when he was upright, swatting at this fearful apparition with his spare hand.

Then in the lightest of gusts, the fae passed over Elspeth without touching her and straight into Rab. Where she went beyond that was impossible to tell, but Rab gave a gurgling choke and keeled over as if struck by lightning.

'*Come child, you do not need to see this*,' a kindly 'voice' said, and Elspeth turned to see the two nuns beckoning her away. '*No. Do not look back. Keep your eyes on us. The fae exact a terrible revenge on those who do not heed their warnings, and that man had plenty of those.*'

"What did she mean, 'Do you want him'?" Elspeth asked worriedly. "You can't kill, can you?"

'*Certainly not. That would go against everything we held and still hold sacred. But we can frighten, and in frightening hope to teach people to mend their ways. Sadly, that man has not changed one iota since he pursued you here years ago. Indeed, he has chased three other young women to the Stones and had his way with them.*'

"I never heard of that," Elspeth said, horrified. "But then his father is a powerful man who is very good at threatening people into keeping quiet. Could you not have saved them the way you saved me?"

'Ah, but child, you forget – they trapped you in our kirk, not the Stones. And you had time to hide there. Clearly, he and his brother remembered their fright and have since avoided our home. Therefore they chased those poor girls straight to the Stones, giving them no time to hide or call for help.'

"Could the fae not have helped?"

'The fae are fickle with their favours, and these days they find it harder to manifest into this world at speed the way they once did. Today you came to their world, offered your thanks, and in effect invited them to you. That made all the difference. The fae won't risk helping those who might betray them.'

"Oh!" Elspeth hadn't thought that her mother bringing her to the Stones and giving thanks would make such a difference, but clearly it had. "Those poor girls. To be hunted like that and then have nobody take their part. I dare say that if any got with child, Bailie McBurney or his brother made sure that they kept quiet – I doubt they even paid their families to raise their bastard grandchildren as other great men have done, just threatened them."

'Just so. The father we cannot reach, unfortunately, nor the brother at the moment, but that does not mean we are not aware of them and the evil they do.'

"Do you mind that I've brought my father and another man to the nunnery?" Elspeth thought to ask, suddenly worried that she hadn't thought to ask their permission. However, the nuns smiled benevolently.

'We are not remotely threatened by the grieving, and one in particular is crushed by his grief. I wish we could offer comfort to him as we would have done in life.'

"I don't suppose you can bring the ghosts of his wife and my Ma here so that they can see them?" wondered Elspeth. "It might do much to ease both of them if they could see that their souls were safe even if their bodies are gone."

'*We will see what we can do*,' the older one said, '*but for now, return to them, for your friends will be here soon*.'

How the nuns knew such a thing, Elspeth couldn't imagine, but by mid-afternoon Alex was leading his parents in, Hugh hot on their heels and McAllister a little behind them, turning frequently to scan the fields behind them.

"What happened?" Johnne asked, coming to wrap one of the blankets around Marione's shivering shoulders, though it was far from cold.

Alex flopped down onto a fallen stone capital from one of the columns in the nave. "We won a reprieve, that's all."

"But that's good…isn't it?" wondered Elspeth, who hadn't dared tell anyone of what had happened to her as yet.

However, Alex shook his head. "The court said that they didn't think there was enough evidence – which there isn't – in spite of several prominent men offering their statements. They were all too vague, God be praised. But the provost could see that Presbyter Veitch was spoiling for a fight, and even he has to be careful of going up against the Kirk. Sadly, Sheriff Campbell is away, because he would have the authority to fully dismiss a case. So what we've ended up with is Ma's case being thrown out of the main court, but being referred back to the Kirk Session that's to be held later next month at Irongray Manse."

"No!" gasped Elspeth and Johnne in unison in their dismay.

"But that puts her right into Veitch's grasp," protested Elspeth.

Alex nodded. "It does. That's why we're making a run for it in the morning."

"No, lad," McAllister said firmly. "Now. Not tomorrow. We go *now*, while they still think we've run for the croft and are sitting there licking our wounds. Come on, let's get the ponies. It's mid-summer, we still have plenty of light, and when it goes it will just give us a few hours to rest and then we can move again."

Somehow, hearing Marione's voice behind them as she prayed at where the altar stone had been – and sounding so like his wife's – brought James Ferguson back to earth a bit, and he said he could walk for a while to allow her to ride.

"We'll cut across the fields to Auldgirth," Alex decided. "That way we can cross the River Nith there, and have the river between us and any who try to follow us. It's not much, but it's better than them being able to ride us down without warning."

"Lead on," McAllister told him, "I'll just check behind us." But then Elspeth realised that he'd looked across towards the stones and seen Rab McBurney's body, and was going to investigate.

"No, McAllister, leave him," she hissed urgently, tugging at his sleeve, and motioning him to hang back with her.

With her voice shaking as she relived that morning, Elspeth told McAllister what had happened as best she could. To her amazement he accepted the interference of the fae and the nuns.

"You believe me?" she gulped.

"Of course I do. Ye' canna live in the Highlands wi'out having a few…unearthly moments, especially when you've reached my age."

At which point he crossed to the choir and walked back up to where the altar would have been, had not Rab and Thomas McBurney come some years after their fright here – and very much in broad daylight – and dragged the stone with their horses down to the river, where it now languished in the shallows. Going down on one knee on the spot in front of the scar in the pavers where it had been, he began to recite something in Latin, which it dawned on Elspeth must be part of the Catholic mass – a service she had never seen performed in any local church. Even more astonishing was the appearance of all thirteen of the nuns' ghosts, summoned by someone saying words they must have been so familiar with in life.

McAllister didn't recite it for very long, making Elspeth assume that he only knew part of it off by heart enough to repeat it.

"My apologies, sisters," he said, looking up and seeing them, "It's been a while since I had chance to attend mass."

'*You are forgiven, my son,*' the prioress told him benevolently. '*It is so good to know that not everyone has forgotten our ways.*'

"Ach, they may have down here, but not up where I'm from," he said, talking to her as though it was the most normal thing to hold a conversation with a ghost.

'*Take care of these poor souls,*' the prioress told him. '*They have suffered greatly at the hands of mere mortal men who presume to know God's will. I fear they will torment many more before they are done, but at least they will not get their hands on these souls again.*'

"No, I promise you they won't," McAllister said

sincerely, and a ghostly hand reached out and made the sign of the cross on his forehead.

'*Go with our blessings*,' she said, and they vanished as if they'd never been there.

"Well that was something," McAllister said in awe, and Elspeth felt that not much overawed him. Then shaking himself said, "Come on, lass, let's catch the others up. Dinna worry, I won't say a word. I know your pa would be horrified that he never noticed you were gone until it was too late."

"Thank you. He's had as much as he can bear right now, and in the end, I came to no harm."

As Elspeth and McAllister hurried to catch the others up, they suddenly became aware of a flare of light in the distance.

"What's that?" Elspeth wondered.

"Fire," McAlister said bitterly. "Looks like ye' won't have a home to go back to."

"No, that's not our house," Elspeth said with certainty. "It's too far away, and it's in the wrong direction. …Oh no! But it's the right direction for Hugh's home!"

"Then we'd best be moving faster. For now, they probably think that Hugh and his pa are with Samwell and Marione, licking their wounds, but it won't take long in the morning for them to realise that they're wrong. Come on, let's get going."

"But where are we going to?" Elspeth wondered. "You've never said where it is that Mailie lives apart from in the Highlands."

"Argyll," McAllister said with a smile, "the bonniest place in all of Scotland. Your sister lives in Kintyre now, and trust me, none o' this lot will ever find ye there!"

Chapter 16

At coming up midnight, Anna had to leave the men to it. She was on duty at seven in the morning, and if she didn't get at least six hours of sleep in, she knew she would feel ragged for the whole of the day. Cameron was well on the way to being legless on Gary's whisky, but she'd noticed that while Gary was happy to top Cameron's glass up, he was much more circumspect with his own, and as he showed her out, Gary said, "He needs this. He needs to let go. Don't worry, lass, I'll watch over him. He'll have a killer hangover in the morning but nothing worse, I promise."

She took Harris and Lewis out on their leads for Gary for a last inspection of the undergrowth, and once satisfied that they at least would settle down and sleep through the night, she went back into the hotel and gratefully fell into bed.

In the morning there was no sign of either man until midday, at which point Garry appeared first, heading out with the two dogs for a brisk walk, and as fresh as a daisy. The same could not be said for Cameron when he tottered in and took the lift up to his room. If his head was as bad as he looked, Anna felt sorry for him.

"Is he okay?" she asked Gary when he appeared, booted and suited for his evening shift.

"Oh, he'll be down for the evening meal," Gary said blithely. "He'll probably be starving by then. I tried to tell him that the proper cure for a hangover is a Mars bar and a can of Irn Brew, but he wasn'a having it."

"I don't think I've heard of that one," Anna admitted, only for Gary to respond,

"Aye, but you're no' from Glasgow, are you?"

"Well known there, is it?" she asked with a laugh, to which he replied,

"Oh, aye, practically issued on prescription! Verra cheap on the NHS are Irn Brew and Mars bars. If it's really bad you might need a paracetamol, but that's after a real bender."

Anna folded up laughing, but secretly made a note to offer Cameron some more paracetamol if he looked like he might need it.

"Aside from the thumping head and feeling queasy, is he okay, though?" she pressed Gary.

Stepping around to behind the desk and into the more private area by the back-office door, Gary admitted, "The poor lad was sobbin' his heart out by two o'clock, though I haven'a told you that. Let him keep a scrap o' dignity over it, eh?"

"I wouldn't dream of embarrassing him," Anna assured Gary.

"Aye, well there's a world o' hurt there and he's only just woken up to how much he's been keeping a lid on everything. The good news is that his father sounds like a decent bloke, and if the two of them can get away from the mother, I think they'll be able to recover something like a normal relationship."

"Then I have to admit I'm a tad envious," Anna confessed. "That's never going to happen for me with either of mine. Dad more than Mum, but nonetheless, without his express permission I don't think I'm ever going to see her again, or at least not in a very long time."

Gary gave one of those snorts which Anna was becoming familiar with as an expression of contempt. "*Hmph*! Your father is one of those on my list of people to give a damned good hiding to if ever I catch them alone in a dark place. I canna do that to your mother. Brought up too well and taught never to hit a woman, me." Then a twinkle came into his eye. "But I bet your Aunty Rita could raise welts on her without even touching her! A grand woman for the scathing dressing-down is Rita."

Anna laughed again. "Oh, I think my dad could attest to that. Even over the phone she could make him turn puce."

"Aye, well I never got to have the kids I'd have loved, and neither did she. It cuts us both when we see good people like you and that lad upstairs being thrown away like garbage. They don't know how lucky they are to have you."

"Aunty Rita has said that before," Anna admitted.

Gary smile became a bit broader. "Well thanks to you, I've had a good reason to be phoning her a bit more often of late."

"Oh, have you?" Anna said delightedly. "And is she thawing? Maybe coming around to the idea that you two are meant to be together?"

"You cheeky wee matchmaker!" Gary laughed, but she could see that he was pleased that she was on his side in this.

However, when Cameron finally appeared, and had emerged from the dining room looking a decidedly better colour, Gary's mind had turned to another matter.

"Harris and Lewis," he said to them both, as he and Anna joined Cameron by the inglenook fireplace, where tonight the two big dogs were sprawling in front of the log fire as if born to the manor. It was a quiet evening with few guests lingering in the hall-lounge, and so with Gemma having taken over for the evening from Anna, she and Gary felt capable of taking their ease in the public area.

"What about them?" Cameron asked, sipping at his coffee, the very thought of whisky tonight being enough to start his head pounding again.

"Well last night when we were up by yon' window, they were very edgy. Once we got over to my place, they flaked out with not a care in the world, but up there they were definitely on guard over something. Now don't laugh, but I've heard that dogs are a lot more sensitive to spirits or ghosts, or whatever you want to call them, and I was wondering, how would you feel about walking the lads around the hotel and seeing what they react to?"

"That's a good idea," Anna immediately agreed.

"Not tonight, though," Cameron pleaded, making Anna suggest,

"How about after eleven tomorrow? We've got that bunch of workmen booking out tomorrow morning, so that'll be five bedrooms we can go into for a start off. We've a lot of people coming in tomorrow afternoon for the weekend, but if we're done by about three, we've got almost a clear run through every room. The only ones we can't go into are Pepper and Cinnamon on the first floor, and Dahlia on the second, and since those are at the far end at the back, where the ghosts have never been seen, they're hardly a priority."

It proved to be a good plan, and in short order they soon wrote off the rooms over the dining room and kitchen on both upper floors. The two big dogs went in, sniffed around, but showed no sign of being in any way bothered. At Gary's suggestion, they had first taken the dogs up and down in the lift to discount the rooms at the back on the second floor, but after that they had tried to be methodical in working their way up through the building from the ground floor upwards. Neither dog had been any happier about the mezzanine level on the stairs than they had been at night, but had perked up with the first-floor back range, and had been positively waggy-tailed over the four rooms through in where they were staying in the small tower. The same went for Thyme on the first floor and Daffodil on the second, both of which had another room buffering them from the main staircase.

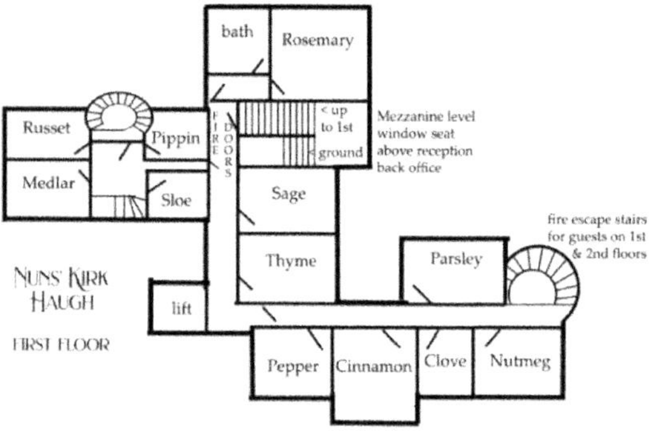

The first sign that the dogs weren't happy came as they let them in to Sage, the room closest to the stairs on the first floor aside from Rosemary and its bathroom on the far side. Both dogs had to be coaxed to go in which was a first. So it was very obvious when they had to be lured into Sage with treats, and even those wouldn't get them into Rosemary. Neither dog would set a paw past the door from the landing into its inner lobby and the door to the bathroom, much less either room itself.

"Well as barometers of the spooky, I'd say they're working pretty well," Gary said as he held the fire door to the next stairs open for them all.

What none of them was expecting was for Harris and Lewis to get two thirds of the way up that first half-flight and then freeze, growling softly at something only they could see.

"What's the matter, lads?" Cameron asked, gently stroking their heads, but they were not to be distracted.

"What are they looking at?" Anna wondered, squinting to try and see if there was some trick of the light that was spooking them.

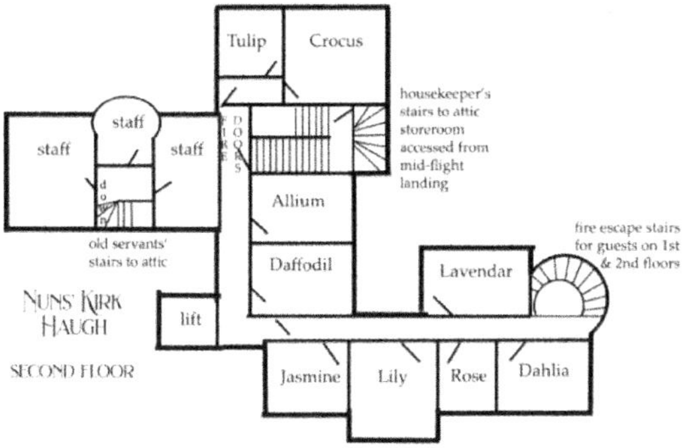

"It's the housekeepers' stairs!" Gary suddenly realised. "God, why didn't I think of that."

The housekeepers' stairs ran off the mezzanine landing between the two half-flights up to the second floor, putting them directly over the sitting area Gary and Cameron had used last night.

"I know it sounds daft," Anna said, "But I don't think I've ever been up there. I've never had any need to. Sally keeps things so well run at her end, I've never thought to question what's up there beyond knowing that all the spare linen is kept there."

"Aye, well those stairs are old," Gary told them, easing past the dogs to go and stand on the upper, smaller midway landing, which the usually closed off stairs ran from. Once upon a time these lesser stairs would have stood open to the main ones, but now a lockable wooden gate closed them off except for when Sally and her ladies were accessing their stores. Now, though, it stood open – being late morning – and for the first time Anna stuck her head in and saw that these were much rougher stairs, which went up a few steps and then twisted back on themselves. Substantial wooden posts acted as the main supports, and though they, the treads, and the handrails, had been stained to match the wood of the main stairs, it was clear that they were a different wood beneath.

"How old are these?" Anna wondered.

"I have no idea," Gary said softly from right beside her, "but I'd take a guess and say at least as old as the previous house, and maybe even from the time of the original tower house."

"Is it too fanciful to think that even if they aren't in their original place in the old tower house, that they might have been reused in virtually their original state for the interim house?" Anna wondered.

"Would you two please come out of there," they heard Cameron calling. "The lads are getting really distressed about you being there."

In deference to the dogs, they left the old stairs, but even so, they had to take the dogs back down a half-flight and over to the lift to get them up to the second floor again. Nothing on earth was going to persuade either dog to go beyond where they'd got to on the main stairs upwards from the first floor, and of course, never having had to go beyond the first floor if accessing Cameron's room from the main flight, it had never been apparent before. When they walked them along the second-floor landing towards the front of the building again, this time they baulked just by the door into Allium, and would not be persuaded to even get as far as the stairs' fire door, much less into either Crocus or Tulip.

"Now isn't that interesting," Anna said to Gary, as Cameron left them to take the dogs downstairs via the lift, and out for a good walk as their reward. "And do you know, they've made me wonder? Did I not hear anything much that night when Mrs What's-her-name complained, because the ghost was tramping *not* up the main stairs on onto this landing next to my room, but *down* them and then up those other stairs? If he went up the housekeeper's stairs, then he'd have been right by her room! Because when the ghost frightened our young couple, it could be the other ghost, and him coming a different way – which is why I heard at least *something*."

Gary looked at the stairs, at her, and then at the doors to the rooms. "I tell you what. You go into Crocus, then I'll go down the main stairs and up the housekeeper's. Let's see if you can hear me."

Passing Sally with an arm-full of clean towels, Anna gave her a grin and said, "We're on the hunt for the ghosts!"

As Sally went into Crocus' dinky en-suite shower room to put the clean towels in, Anna called out, "All set, Gary, I'm closing the door now."

For a moment she was rather disappointed that she heard nothing, but then suddenly she could hear a man's heavy tread quite clearly through the wall. For a few moments he sounded really close, and then faded a bit as if getting higher up.

"Jings, that wasn't it, was it?" Sally said worriedly from beside her.

"No, that's Gary going up the stairs to your linens room."

"Good Lord, that sounds creepy from in here!"

"I know. You can understand why the guests have been spooked. Imagine hearing that after midnight!"

The sound of Gary coming back down was no less eerie, but Anna rushed out to meet him with a beaming grin. "That's it! That's definitely it!" she told him triumphantly. "Now let me nip across into my room and see if I hear anything at all when you do it again."

Sure enough, having called Gary via their mobiles to tell him she'd arrived, this time Anna didn't hear a thing.

"Well, that clears up one part of the mystery," she said as she met him on the first-floor landing. "Now comes the harder part. What are we going to do about it? Our ghosts are hardly regular. They don't appear at a set time of year or on full moons or anything, so I can't keep guests out of those rooms just in case."

"No, that's no' possible," Garry agreed. "I suppose we could go to the main library and see if there's anything in their archives about the history of this place? Where that would get us, though, I don't know."

"I think it's more important to identify these two men than getting a comprehensive history of the building," Anna decided. "If we know *who* they were, we can maybe work out what's causing them to manifest so strongly at some times, and then not at all for the most part."

She turned and looked around, thinking. "It's actually quite a small footprint where the ghosts are attached to…if we're convinced that the dogs have nailed it down for us, and I think they have. Can we have a go at drawing or pacing it out? Only all of a sudden, I'm wondering whether we're looking at the footprint of an old tower-house? Or at least the actual tower part of it."

"How does that help us, though? I mean, what specifically about that are you thinking of?"

Anna gestured for him to follow her back down to the reception area, and went and picked up a glossy hard-backed book that was left for the guests' perusal. It was something of a gazetteer of all the old tower-houses of the county, and had been dug out of a cupboard in the back office where it had been consigned to by her predecessor, after Anna had mentioned to Brenda about her walk around the outside of the hotel, trying to work out eras for the different parts. Initially, Anna hadn't thought it would help her much, because although *Nuns' Kirk Haugh* was mentioned, the eighteenth-century engravings of the place hadn't seemed to match what she knew of the current building.

Now, though, she opened it up at the relevant page and pointed to the one image.

"See that? That big square tower which is the tallest part of the old building? Well do you think that that's of a similar size to the footprint of the main bit of the front? The bit with the huge foundations?"

Pulling his reading specs out of his shirt pocket, Gary peered at the illustration. "Aye, it could be. What are you thinking?"

Anna gave a little shrug. "I'm far from sure, let alone any kind of expert, but having narrowed the

haunted bit down so much, it occurred to me that maybe the owner who built the house as we know it, didn't want to go to the expense of fully pulling the main old tower-house down. Do you see? He might well have thought, 'This is a good, solid set of walls, why rip them down to the foundations only to have to rebuild them?' Because if you discount the much later huge bay window in the conference room at the front, don't you think that if you *rotate* this image, you could more or less overlay it over the floor-plan we have of the main front, and part of the side, of the house?"

Gary peered in a bit harder, and then Anna picked the book up and walked over to the plan of the ground floor on the wall, which was up for the benefit of guests knowing where the fire exits were.

"Look at it, Gary. If you square off the conference room and our reception area and stairs, doesn't that look like it could be the base of the tower bit of the tower-house? And then our hall-lounge with the inglenook fireplace looks much like this slightly lower, two-storey building that's alongside it on the old illustration."

"Good God!" Gary gasped. "Yes! And then it looks like what's now our wing over the kitchen, which has the first-floor bedrooms at the back over it, is much of a size with that wing that's at right-angles to the tower and its side bit. …But hang on, why then, have we not had any hauntings in those back bedrooms?"

Anna grinned. "Foundations! Think of where they are, Gary! Right where the land does a dive down the bank! What if they didn't put good enough foundations in along that bit? I mean, that looks like it was the working section of the tower-house anyway, doesn't it, what with all those chimneys. So what if they weren't built to the same standard as the tower and its sort of fortified house – the posh bit – but then that proved to be their downfall? Literally!"

And looking at the illustration, Gary could see what she meant. The longer, lower, two-storey building at right-angles to the main house looked as though it might have had more than one door to the outside, but none of them were exactly an imposing entrance. That door was on the main tower. But what they did have were several chimneys, artistically throwing out smoke in the image, which hinted that a kitchen range might be somewhere in that plan, if nothing else.

"That bit's certainly not defensible," Gary said, his military training kicking in. "That side-range any well-trained force would go through like a knife through butter, even considering their weapons of the day. Whereas the tower and its side bit? You could hold that against all comers! Especially if there wasn't a connecting door between that and …what is it? The west or south range? …Yes, that's definitely orientated right.

"And I'll tell you something else, Anna. If I was that builder in the Jacobite era, when you might not know who your friends and enemies were, I too would have the tower looking out over the river, and the domestic buildings effectively tucked into the loop of it. Because if your enemies were going to sneak up on you, you'd want the river there to slow them down before they got to the vulnerable bits."

He turned and grinned at Anna. "I think you've got it, lass! If they built that domestic range without good enough foundations, chances are that the first year they had any kind of abnormally torrential rain, they would've started spotting cracks in the walls. Twenty years down the line and it could have been downright dangerous to go inside. And of course, over the centuries in between, the river has probably cut a bit closer to the house, and they probably had considerable erosion on the bank. That could all help undercut poor foundations, and explain why the current ones are so substantial, the Victorians being rather better engineers. How long did you say there was between the tower-house and the current building?"

She grinned at him. "That's the important bit! This more detailed account of the building – which I didn't know of when I did my first walk around the outside – says that the fortified tower was *possibly* built in 1605, but that the tower-house as we first see it in these engravings, was built in 1679. Although thinking of it now, our leaflet says that the tower house changed hands in 16**8**9, so maybe whoever started building it ran out of money in the 1680s? That's when that Captain Fergusson buys it.

"But he only had it for a few years, because he died in 1715, when the McCartney family get it. It was then 'improved' in 1787 – though whether that was the McCartneys or not, I'm not sure, but would it be so strange to think that *that* acquisition might have hinged on which side they were on in the Forty-Five? Winning side, you get the house of someone who wasn't. Losing side, you lose your home too?

"But 1787 is when the fancier bits you can see on the tower in the second engraving were added. Let's face it, they would have been of no use at all from a military point of view by then – even I can see that! Who would put arrow slits in by the time of the Georgian era, except to make the place look older than it was?"

"Oh, I agree that they're no' the real thing. Totally in the wrong places, anyway."

"Right. And then the house as we know it really appears in **18**77 when Major Grant restored it from being near-derelict. But what I'm now thinking is that at each of those changes, the core of the house – the tower – didn't change *that* much. The first version of the tower was probably basic to say the least, and I'm now hyper-aware that these experts only *think* that the tower bit was built in 1605.

"They're not that sure, are they? And the only reason I can think of in that period where anyone would have felt under threat from anything, other than avaricious neighbours, is the Gunpowder Plot. But all the ramifications of that are felt far away down in England, near where I used to live – which I know about having visited Coughton Court, home of the Throckmortons – not up here. So what if it started its life as something more like a fairly substantial gatehouse to the nunnery?"

She half-expected Gary to shoot her down in flames over that, so when he simply nodded and said,

"Carry on. I'm beginning to see where you're going with this," she felt buoyed up enough to continue.

"So I was thinking…Lincluden down the road got sold around 1590, though that's still a ruin, not a house. But that's only a decade or so from when someone presumably made a house out of our nunnery, or part of it. And, the same would apply to the nunnery as to the large house, wouldn't it? That steep bank down to the river would be a construction nightmare.

"I'm hardly as well read-up on history as you, but I do know that churches are built facing east-west. And from the old churches I've wandered around on the odd occasion, anything that looks like a tower is always at the west end, while the altar is at the east. So given that the morning sun shines straight into our dining room, do you really think that our main hall is big enough to be over the old nave and choir – that is the proper name for the east bit, isn't it? – of the nunnery's kirk?"

Gary thought for a moment. "It's no' the width so much as the length," he decided. "Width-wise, aye, I've known country churches and wee kirks which are no wider. But you have a fair point about the slope of the land. I dinna see those medieval builders sticking the most important part of their kirk, in other words the choir with the altar, right where it's likely to fall into the river. They built far better than that! You only have to go anywhere where a river floods, and see all the old medieval churches sitting up on high ground like ancient lighthouses, to know that. So that would mean that you have a big, imposing tower, or at least the surviving base of one, but then squash both the nave *and* the altar in *before* you effectively get to our dining room door. They'd look insignificant compared to it, and I just don't see that being right."

Anna gave a sigh of relief. "Great, I'm glad you think that. So…could our main block, and what I'm now thinking was the tower part of the tower-house, be instead some fairly heavily fortified gatehouse to the nunnery? Because in some of the old abbeys down south, the gatehouse was where prestigious guests would be put up, rather than shoving them in with the scruffy pilgrims, or whoever, in what was loosely called the guesthouse. I remember going on a couple of trips to old monastic abbeys with friends from work who were doing history at uni, who were more into that stuff than me, and them telling me that the actual guesthouses were nothing much more than a basic dormitory. So, if there was a visiting prior or the like, they got what amounted to a private room in the gatehouse.

"Now thinking on that. Wouldn't it make sense if you wanted to build your fancy house, even if you were going to strip out a lot of the existing stone blocks from parts of the nunnery, to use the basic gatehouse building as the starting point? Okay, you'd probably block up the gateway itself, especially if it was big enough to bring something like a cart through, and instead make a nice driveway as we have now. But if you've got solid walls and a couple of upper floors already there, why wouldn't you add to it instead of starting from scratch?"

"That all makes sense," Gary agreed, "but how are you fitting that with our ghosts?"

"Ah! If we can find out about the owner who did this work in the early to mid-seventeenth century, then he was probably the first person to make any major alterations to what had been part of the nunnery – or at least only the second, if the place really was started as early as the beginning of that century. And he was probably the one involved in the Covenanter fights, if you're telling me that the real conflict came only a little later in 1685. Because earlier – even more than in 1685 – unless there was murder and slaughter in the ruined nunnery, there's no reason for a Covenanter, of all people, to be in what had to have been a Catholic monastic place, is there?

"And even if it was still a Catholic place, albeit rather hush-hush by then, do you see a devout believer actively desecrating an altar? *Any* altar? …The part where the nuns were, maybe, if they thought the Roman Church was the fount of all evil to that extent…"

"Oh, aye, and they did! 'The Whore of Babylon' they called Rome and the pope, amongst other less than polite names. There was no 'we're all Christians together' attitude at all."

"Oh! That acrimonious?"

"Definitely! But I take your point about desecrating a consecrated altar stone, even if they trashed the rest of the place."

"Okay. So, if it was all on the ground floor where our ghosts are haunting, then yes, you could say the nunnery was ruined by then, and fighting took place within its precinct as a no-longer-sacred space. But not when our ghosts are on the upper floors. That implies a still-standing taller building, doesn't it?"

"Oh! I'm with you now. He's our starting date, yon builder man. And he must be real close to the Killing Times in 1685, as you say."

"Exactly. And the **17**87 changes to the building are well after even Culloden, let alone these Covenanters we're chasing. And what we're after is some kind of connection to this place in that early stage of it being a tower-house. That's why we've got no haunting going on in the rest of the place – it's all too late! We need to know more about that builder."

Chapter 17

Investigating the seventeenth-century owner of the house had to wait a couple of days until Anna had another full day off, but then accompanied by both Cameron and Gary, she went down to Dumfries and started trying to find records. Luckily, Gary had had the foresight to book a seat at one of the computer terminals, apparently having gone delving into history before, and knowing that county record centres tended to get heavily used by local people wanting to research family history. And once one of the library staff realised why they were there, she was all willingness to help them.

In short order, they had found some Victorian histories of the area, but the librarian was quick to point out that most of them were history as the Victorians would have liked it to be, rather than well-researched to modern standards. What did come as a shock was discovering the name of John Corsan coming up in an unexpected context in an online search.

"Bloody hell!" Anna squeaked, bringing Cameron and Gary over to her side from where they'd been pouring over an old book on grand houses of the area.

"What's up?" Gary asked cautiously.

"I've found a John Corsan. Could he be one of the Corsans connected to our house? Maybe the father of that Jean Corsan who married the captain? He's the right generation. Only I've just found someone of that name in the same era here in Dumfries, and he's involved in *witch* trials!"

"Shit! That's a turn up for the books." Cameron gasped. "Didn't see that one coming, did we?"

"When?" Gary asked. "The 'when' is everything in this period."

Forcing herself to take a couple of deep, calming breaths, Anna answered, "The trials take place in Dumfries in 1659. Granted, that's a good twenty years before the Killing Times you were talking about, Gary. But I can't stop myself from thinking about what I heard the one ghost yelling at the man he hated. 'Don't you touch my women folk!' was what he yelled. Now if you were a man of that time, and someone you loved had gone through a *witch trial*, vicious things that *they* were, wouldn't that be the sort of thing you'd shout? And what's more, the two names Ghost One – for want of anything else to call him – called out were Corsan and McCartney. …Meaning I'm now wondering if that's the same McCartney family, if not the same generation, as the ones who later owned the house?

"And if they were so closely connected as to be cursed by our first ghost, was John Corsan maybe the pre-Jacobite owner, and if so, how did it end up with only a daughter to inherit? That book we found was pretty authoritative, and if it says work was done on the house in 1679, then I'm thinking that's a fairly firm date for us to work on for tracking down our builder. And I'm thinking that something happening in 1685 in the Killing Times is awful close to 1679, but also to that first Jacobite rebellion of 1689?"

Cameron almost choked over that. "What are the chances of that?" he spluttered. "The same surname? I know you said that there was a Colonel Douglas in the area, Gary, and that his name is mud with those who remember and honour the Covenanters who died for their faith, but who the heck were Corsan and McCartney that our ghost is so enraged by them?"

"That's rather the point," Anna told him. "You'd have expected the ghost to be fuming over the way the infamous Colonel James Douglas treated the Covenanters he hunted, wouldn't you? Or the man I've read about called 'Bloody Clavers', another commander. But that's not who he's seething about at all."

"That is quite a turn up for the books," Gary agreed. "If this was all about the Covenanters and nothing more, then yes, Colonel Douglas is the most hated man in this area by far. He hunted men down," and looking at Cameron, he reminded him, "and he shot them without giving them even time to pray. That was pretty much as bad as it got in those days. Everyone expected to die, and sooner rather than later for a huge variety of reasons. But most folk thought they'd have at least some chance of making their peace wi' God before they went. To actively deny them that was…well I canna think of anything that equates to it in our secular world."

"That bad, huh?" said Cameron, pulling a face of horror.

"Oh, verra much so," Gary said solemnly. "Let's face it, the memory of that has been passed down for over three centuries to the people who still go and put flowers on the Covenanter martyrs' graves, or pay for the upkeep of the monuments to their memories. You don't do that over nothing. But if yon man was also involved in witch trials, that's really grim stuff, and could account for someone hating him down the years."

Cameron sat down at a chair opposite Anna with a huff of surprise. "You don't realise how much you don't know of the history of even your own country, do you, until you come up against something like this."

"Would you like to see one of the Covenanter memorials?" Gary asked. "Only seeing as we're here in Dumfries, it might be an idea if I showed you the one in St Michael's kirkyard. It's literally just down the path from the grand mausoleum the Victorians put up to Robbie Burns."

"What? *The* Robbie Burns?" Cameron gulped, and seeing his expression, Anna laughed.

"Is there *another*?" she joked with fake innocence, then seeing the way Gary sucked in through his teeth in mock approbation, laughed again holding her hands up in surrender. "Sorry! Just the Sassenach here! Only asking."

"Nay, lass, there's only one. And in truth, I bet he's revolving in his grave at the overweening grand monstrosity they've removed his bones to. Burns himself was quite happy where he was, but to the Victorians, it wasn'a grand enough for a man they'd elevated to being the national poet. I canna show you anything like as grand for those poor women, but the Covenanters you can see for yourselves. Come on, let's go and get a breath of fresh air – we're at the end of our allotted time-slot at the computers anyway, so the archivist will be chucking us out soon."

The fact that Gary had avoided touching so much as a single key on the keyboard made that statement more than a little amusing for Anna, but she grabbed her coat without saying anything beyond thanking the woman on duty, and then hurrying out after Cameron and Gary.

It wasn't a long walk down the main street of Dumfries to get to St Michael's, and instantly even

Anna and Cameron could tell that this was one of the older graveyards in the city.

"It's over here," Gary said, leading the way around the church itself. "See that grand edifice over there?" He pointed to a huge white marble, domed affair. "That's Burn's tomb."

"Good grief," Cameron laughed. "I can see why you called it grand. There's no mistaking it, is there?"

Gary just rolled his eyes in disgust, then led them around the east end of the church a way to where they could see something which looked suspiciously like a pyramid.

"Now that's something I didn't expect to see in a Scottish kirkyard," Cameron said in surprise.

As they got closer, they could see the inscription.

"Wow!" Anna gasped. "Two men shot in 1667, and then another who died in 1685. But this isn't contemporary to them, is it, Gary?"

He shook his head. "And that's why I wanted you to see it. It's what muddies the water so much with those who died for their adherence to the Covenant. At the time they were definitely *persona non grata* to the Kirk of the time, which was reinstating bishops and didn't want rebels stirring the pot, so you don't get memorials erected at the time. And I'm talking about even memorials put up probably a century or more after the event, let alone grand things like this. So you can see why you can't take them as absolutely accurate."

Anna looked down solemnly at the slabs behind the neat iron railing. "Didn't Brenda tell me that there are more memorials in the area?"

"Oh yes," said Gary. "In fact, if we get going now, we've got time to drive over to one of the nearby kirks."

And so piling them into his truck, he drove them out to Kirkland of Glencairn and the church there.

"Gosh, it's a bit gloomy, isn't it," Anna observed, looking at what was clearly a much later, grey stone, and forbidding, church building. "Very 'thou shalt not!' I can't imagine them giving a few rousing choruses of 'Shall We Gather at the River' in the congregation when this was built."

It had started to drizzle, and although the kirk was out in pleasant countryside, something about the dour, hefty family tombs here really gave Anna the creeps. For all their disavowing of all things fancy, the leading Presbyterian families had found a way to over-awe their neighbours even in death, with massive tombs of scarcely decorated sandstone. A bit of fancy white marble, with the odd stone angel, would have been welcome here just to relieve the gloom.

The Covenanter graves were within an iron railing again, with three slabs lying on the ground, and then the memorial slab upright at their head.

"Twenty-eighth of April 1685," Cameron read aloud. "Isn't that a bit late for what we want?"

"Aye, it might be," Gary agreed, "but given Anna's reasoning of the house being our starting point in 1679, when we have that contemporary engraving of a house to *prove* it was already there, it's no' that far off …especially compared to the gap between 16**67** and 1685 on the martyrs' tomb in Dumfries. Our house comes smack in the middle of all that. And I wanted you two to see how long these grievances carried on for, you see, and why it's not that easy to just say, 'Oh, if it's a Covenanter then it must be *then*'. It's no' like Culloden – one battle, one date."

"Point taken," Cameron said, leaning in to peer closer at the carved stones, well decorated with white lichens. The three tombstones lying down were virtually illegible, making him ask, "Are these contemporary and just the memorial later?"

Gary sighed. "They're a wee bit closer to the time, but a lot o' these Covenanter graves were carved by a stonemason called Paterson, who became known as 'Old Mortality', because Walter Scott later made him into a lead character in one o' his novels. But Paterson wasn'a even born until the eighteenth century, while these men died in the seventeenth. And if you allow for him having to learn his trade, by the time he was travelling around lowland Scotland giving these unmarked graves proper headstones, you have to be thinking of the middle of the century – perhaps the 1840s and 1850s."

Anna immediately caught on. "And unmarked graves? How did he know where to look, then? Okay, some of them must have had family members still tending them, but you're already talking a good seventy years after the event. That's hardly going to be their children, but more likely their grandchildren or even great-grandchildren who he must have spoken to. And how many of *those* burials are actually recorded in parish records? If what I've read is right, these were people who were refusing to attend their *parish* church, and going to unlicensed meetings out on the hillsides. So would the minister even have allowed their martyrs to be buried here?"

"Exactly," Gary said with a nod. "If the family paid up, he might, but it would be *verra* unmarked. No' so much as a wooden cross. So by the time you get into the early nineteenth century, and all the Romanticism whipped up by people like Sir Walter Scott, you're hardly talking about un-muddied waters. And it's the 1850s before Scotland becomes a desirable place to visit, thanks to Queen Victoria and Balmoral, and that's really when Scotland's past starts getting a make-over."

"It's all a bit distant from the events, isn't it," Anna sighed. "That's what the librarian was warning us about."

"Aye," Gary agreed, "but the other thing I wanted you to see here is how it's Colonel James Douglas again who keeps appearing on these tombs as the evil one." And he pointed to the inscription where Douglas' name appeared once more. "Yet despite his movements being better documented, we have nothing to connect him to *Nuns' Kirk Haugh*. No mention of his troops shooting anyone there, aside from Hugh Ferguson's much-later tomb – which suffers from the same distance from the past as these – and you'd think if there was more than one man shot, they would be remembered when you look at this here."

"Oh dear, Douglas could have been added onto our tomb just because he *was* on all the other tombs, couldn't he," Anna added sadly. "And of course, the victims were just ordinary people, weren't they."

Only for Cameron to demand, "What difference does that make?"

"All the difference in the world," Gary told him. "Even to the men they held their lands off, they were little more than an entry in a rent book, and you have to be really lucky to find something like that for anything before the nineteenth century. *If* you can find any parish records, you'll get their births, marriages, and then deaths, but again, going back three and a half centuries, it's about what's survived, which generally isn't a lot. There are the odd surviving muster rolls from the Forty-Five, and a few estate records, but they're a verra long way from covering all o' the country. History, my lad, is written by the upper classes back in this era."

"Then we're stuffed," Cameron said dejectedly. "We've got a hotel with rooms that periodically get haunted and we can't get rid of the ghosts!" Then he brightened. "Heck of a marketing opportunity, though, if only we can work out when they're likely to appear. Oh yes! Paranormal weekends are all the go these days. We could even have one of those TV crews in."

At that, he turned and began walking back to Gary's truck, but Gary and Anna exchanged worried looks at that announcement.

"That's to be discouraged," Gary said softly to Anna, as they picked their way through the long, wet grass, trying not to trip over other gravestones. He was expecting her to agree by saying something to the effect that it was because of the difficulty of predicting when any sighting would happen.

So he was deeply approving when she said, "It's bloody disrespectful is what it is! Those spirits are in torment. They shouldn't be used for somebody's titillation. I want to help them rest in peace, not drive them into distraction."

It was enough to have Gary wrap an affectionate arm around her shoulders and give her a hug. No wonder Rita was so proud of her half-niece, Anna was the right sort. And as that thought hit him it did Anna, who turned to him only for both of them to say in unison, "Rita!"

Anna grinned at him. "If we can't trace them through normal means, we'll just have to go alternative," and with Gary giving her a wink, they rejoined Cameron at the truck but said nothing. This would be something better done when he'd gone to Edinburgh or somewhere on business. The last thing they wanted was for him to have some daft notion of séances in the hall – that really might open up a whole new can of worms they weren't prepared for!

However, Anna was far from done with ghosts. In between shifts, she had made a concerted attempt to make the two cottages alongside Gary's more pleasant to be in. The dreadful Perdita had simply dumped furniture in them that had previously been stored in the main hotel's cellars as being too faded or worn to be used there. Nothing showed how ignorant she'd been of what guests would expect in a self-catering cottage than this, for the mattresses were lumpy and the sofas downright uncomfortable, not to mention that the rugs were shabby and almost worn through in places. At least the original self-catering cottages further down the drive hadn't been tinkered with by Perdita, and so were still in the good order which had come in Margaret's time as manager, but they could hardly rob the more comfortable beds and furniture out of them for the staff.

"If I'm going to expect a chef to live in the end one," Anna said to Brenda and Gary when they were discussing this, "then the very least we need is a comfortable bed. You can't ask someone to work their socks off catering for a wedding and then sleep on one of those."

Gary had been a lot more fortunate, having arrived under Margaret's management, but at that stage the two other cottages in the stable block hadn't been used in several years, the previous chefs having lived locally enough to go home between shifts. But things were changing, and so one of the first things

Anna had asked Cameron, once she knew who he was, was whether he could allocate a modest budget to set the cottages up better. And given how they'd held things together for him, Cameron could hardly refuse.

It meant that having done the morning shift on the Tuesday following their visit to Dumfries, Anna decided in the afternoon that she'd finish stripping stuff out of the end cottage. Gary had got Alan and Greg, the two gardeners, to help him move the heavy stuff out of both on the rainy Monday, when they couldn't make the repair on the riverbank path they'd been intending to do. But things like the tatty curtains and old mirrors still needed to come down and be stored somewhere until they could get a refuse pick-up by the council, all of it being only fit for the recycling and refuse site. And with the new chef starting at the weekend and the new furniture for this place being delivered the day before that, Anna wanted to mop all the floors through one last time before the thick wool rugs she'd bought went down. All three cottages had lovely old oak floorboards, so as long as they were clean and there was something a bit warm over them, she wasn't worried about getting anything like fitted carpets down – but she did want Harriet the chef to feel welcome.

The three staff cottages were part of what had once been a stable block, with them once upon a time housing the grooms, while two more sides around the square yard formed by them had the remains of old stable stalls in them. The remaining side was a bit of an oddity, with its own low tower forming what must once have been quite an ostentatious entrance to the stable-yard, and it was here that Anna was putting the stuff to be taken away. That was primarily because it had clearly been used as a storage area for animal feed, and was passably dry, but also had large doors which opened onto the track where Gary parked his truck and she her old car.

Lugging another armful of musty curtains over there, and gratefully dumping them onto an old Formica table that had probably been in her cottage since the 1950s, Anna paused to stretch and rub her back. And it was in leaning back that she looked up and saw it. A stone angel!

"What on earth are you doing there?" she gasped aloud as she stared at the carving. It was nicely done too, not just some rough work hacked out of stone. A true stonemason had made it, even Anna could see that. But why would you have something that good in a stable?

Moving over to the main doors to the track, Anna unbolted them and flung the double doors open to let more light in, then went back to the ones she had come in by and opened them too. It wasn't the brightest of days, but despite that, she could suddenly see a lot more, and what she saw startled her even more. The stonework on this internal wall of the tower was fine stuff, and it was old – much, much older than the brickwork that the cottages were made of. And then she looked across the yard and wondered why she hadn't noticed it before, because the back walls of the cottages were totally different to the front. These were in the same old stone as the tower, as were the two stable walls around the square courtyard. Granted, the window openings were modern, which was probably why she hadn't taken much notice of them from the inside, but they weren't inset in brick as at the front.

Going and standing out in the old stable-yard, she turned slowly around, taking in the building in a way she'd never done before. Of course, arriving as she had with winter coming on, any time she'd been inside Gary's, he'd mostly had the curtains closed and the lights on. And it was only in the last week or two that she'd spent any amount of time over here in the daylight, and even then, she'd had other things on her mind than architecture. But now something about the place was really tugging at her. It was as if it was trying to get her to see something, but she couldn't quite make out what.

Then out of the corner of her eye she saw a light go on, making her turn around. It was in one of the bedrooms on the top floor of the hotel, but it suddenly dawned on her just how the hotel and the stable block were orientated to one another. These days, because she came to it up a sweeping path, she'd never appreciated how the block was so directly in line with the hotel, nor that it was much closer than she'd thought.

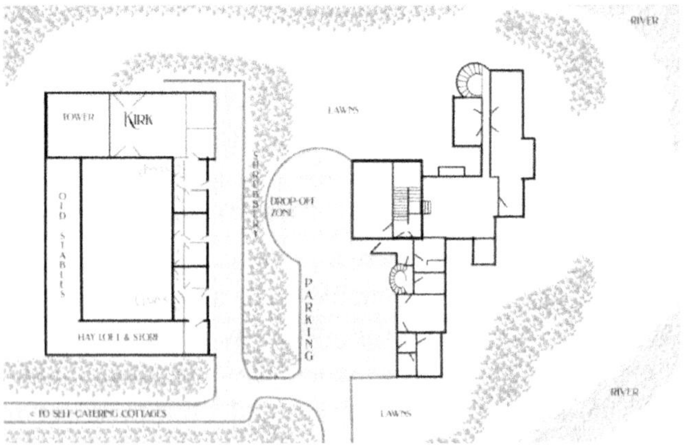

Some previous owner had planted a line of large rhododendrons and other shrubs to save the high and mighty visiting the house in its heyday from seeing one of the working bits. So even from one of the first-floor bedrooms, all you could see was the uppermost bit of the tower and bits of roof. But even that had disorientated her, because she'd assumed that the tower was the closest bit of the stable-block to the house, and the cottages were behind it, if viewed from one of the upper rooms.

Yet that wasn't the case at all. The cottage part was facing the hotel, with the tower being at the back roughly west-north-west… Anna stopped and gasped. That surely wasn't right!

Turning around, she tried to work out where the points of the compass were.

"If that's a light on in Crocus," she reasoned with herself, "then that's facing west, because I know that side gets the sunsets. So this tower is at the *west* end of these stables, not the east as I assumed. …Oh, good grief!"

She turned around again, clasping a hand to her mouth in shock as she realised that the remaining stable wings formed something looking suspiciously like a southern cloister. A very basic and rather rough cloister, admittedly; but then all the modern structures, excepting the tower, were probably built on the foundations of what had been the nunnery's domestic buildings, rather than being full survivors themselves.

The tower, on the other hand, suddenly made sense. It wasn't some imposing folly, stuck on a random corner of the stables by a Victorian owner with aspirations. It was the surviving western tower to what had been the nunnery's chapel or kirk! And the walls which ran eastwards from it towards the hotel were the last remaining vestiges of the northern and southern walls of that church's nave.

These days, the brick wall which formed the front of the cottages cut straight across the ancient nave, probably replacing whatever original end wall to the choir had been there and terminating the nave forever, and if anything else remained, it was underneath those massive rhododendrons and the tarmac of the turning circle outside of the hotel's main entrance. But that meant that the lounge of the cottage she was preparing was butting onto the old nave.

"Oh! The front windows are modern, because they're in a modern wall, but it's why the *back* window has such a huge, deep sill."

And that's why that cottage had such an eccentric layout, too. She'd not understood why the little bathroom was behind the lounge, of all places, whereas the kitchen was behind the bedroom – although least not leading off it – but now it made sense. There was no way they could put a back door in if the kitchen had been installed behind the lounge, because that was blocked by a buttress of the old church, possibly a chunk of wall from a monastic building which had had to be left to prevent the kirk's wall from bowing out.

Instead, the bathroom had a side window so small, narrow, and high up, Anna half wondered whether it was the bottom of an original window in the nave's wall, because it seemed to be cut off at ceiling height, rather as if it didn't belong to the building. And, she now realised, it was always so gloomy in there because it gave into the kirk space rather than outside – hardly likely to give offence when there had been nothing but the carriages left in there, but almost certainly making use of an original lancet window. The kitchen had a door out into the stable-yard, which if hardly picturesque, at least gave a safe fire exit, which was probably all anyone had ever been worried about, even for staff in the twenties and thirties.

Anna hurried back into the cottage, a worrying thought now forming. Turning around in the lounge, she then went through into the bedroom. Yes, it was as she thought, there was no reason why the bedroom couldn't have been the lounge and vice versa, because they were the same size and both had fireplaces. So why have such an odd arrangement …unless?

"Oh, bloody hell! Is the lounge haunted too? Could nobody get a decent night's rest when it was the bedroom?"

Nobody had been in here for so long there was nobody she could ask about that. But if she was right, then putting Harriet into here was a really bad idea. It had taken her such a search to find her, there was no way that Anna was going to risk having Harriet running screaming from the place in her first week because of spooks in her lounge!

"Gary!" Anna yelped, dashing around and knocking on his door, praying that he was up already and preparing for his night shift. "Gary! We've got a problem!"

1678

Hugh

Hugh Ferguson sat on his shaggy pony at the side of the road into Dumfries and looked across to the Apostles' Stones. It was eighteen years since he'd last been here – back then a mere boy, and now a grown man of nearly thirty-three. Much had happened since then, not all of it good, but nothing remotely as bad as what had happened here.

"A penny for your thoughts," a cheerful voice said, and Jamie McAllister reined in his own shaggy garron beside him.

"I was thinking of the last time I was here with your father," Hugh told him, as they tried to stop the two hefty ponies from nipping one another.

"Aye. Bad times," Jamie sympathised, having heard his father, Sorley, tell the tale of what had caused the families to return to Argyll with him. "I canna imagine what it must feel like fer ye'. Are you sure you're all right, man? Nobody would think any less of ye' if ye' asked to go wi' the other half of our troop further west."

"No, it's fine, Jamie. Well…not fine, exactly, but I'd rather be here with you and your brother than over there on my own." Jamie's older brother, Archie, was riding up ahead with the senior Campbell who'd accompany this armed force of Highlanders, which had been raised to come south and instil some order in Dumfriesshire. "I've not forgotten that Elspeth and Mailie's oldest sister Jean lives out that way. One of my nightmares is that I find myself talking to some woman and it turns out to be her! What on earth would I say to her?"

"Hmph, that could be tricky," Jamie admitted, though with a mischievous twinkle in his eye that said that if it was him, he'd make full use of the moment to tell Jean what her lack of family loyalty had cost them. That readiness to tell the truth and shame the Devil – very much as Sorley always did – was one of the things that Hugh liked best about Jamie. The man didn't have a false bone in his body, and having grown into someone who trusted very few people, Hugh held those like Jamie whom he counted as friends very close.

"Those bloody McBurneys and God-curse-him Gideon Corsan tried to hunt Elspeth in that stone circle," Hugh reminded Jamie. "It was her good luck that she ran to the nunnery instead."

Jamie squinted into the lowering sun, appraising the stones before saying, "No matter how connected to the fae that place is, there's no' a lot of cover there, is there?"

"None."

At that moment Archie rode back to them. "Campbell says he's fine wi' ye' going to look at yer auld home if ye' want," he told Hugh kindly. "I told Himself about what happened to yer ma here, and he's all sympathy." He gave a disparaging sniff. "Wouldn'a have happened amongst decent God-fearing Catholics in the Highlands, I can tell ye'."

Hugh gave him a weak smile, though he knew that there had been a few witch trials over in the west and north. Nothing remotely like the number around here and over in Edinburgh and up into Fife, mind you. In the Highlands you had to really be overt about your practices, and cross some powerful people, to end up in the situation his mother had died in.

"Can you give the Campbell my thanks for his consideration, and that I'd really appreciate going to look at my old home, but it's not necessary right now."

Archie gave an approving nod and heeled his garron back up to the front of the column.

"Ye' could ha' gone," Jamie gently reprimanded him

But Hugh answered, "I know. I'm just not ready yet. Just being here is a lot to deal with, Jamie. I can't go and put flowers on my ma's grave, because there was nothing left to bury by the time the Kirk had done with her. Just her remains dumped in the old nuns' crypt…and I will go there and pray for her soon. But I'd like to go and put some on Elspeth's ma's in the kirkyard there. …You know, be a bit respectful first."

"Aye, that does ye' credit, Hugh," Jamie said affectionately. "Come on, then, or we'll be last in camp and end up wi' the worst spot to bed down!"

It took Hugh two weeks to summon up the courage to go and visit the places he remembered as a child. Two weeks in which his local knowledge was invaluable to the young Campbell laird leading their section of the greater party of several thousand men. In theory, the Highlanders had been summoned by the government in Edinburgh to try to dissuade the Covenanter prayer meetings out in the countryside known as conventicles, and to establish some kind of order which the local lords had singularly failed to manage to do.

The reality was that here in the south-west there was little or nothing in the way of overt public disorder. Markets were held without any fuss, normal business went ahead without any interference, and the courts carried out their usual hearings. The only thing that hinted that all was not well was the refusal of many parishioners to attend any kirk where the minister did not follow the Covenanter tenets, with some such ministers getting a very rough ride indeed.

What it really boiled down to was that for most Presbyterians in the shire, King Charles II was not a king in the Covenant's terms, let alone in his desire to reinstate bishops everywhere. And to them, a king who would not agree to protect the Scottish Kirk's right to worship as it would, had no right to impose his will on them. That that particular king had been restored to the throne seventeen years ago, and with still no sign of a legitimate heir, was further cause for concern, because that meant that the next in line for the now-united thrones – if not united countries – of England and Scotland was the King's brother, the Catholic James, currently the Duke of Albany and York. And a Catholic sympathiser on the throne came perilously close, in the Covenanters' eyes, to having an English, Catholic, king dictating how the folk of Scotland would worship.

All of that made it remarkable that the folk of Dumfriesshire accepted the Highland Host at all – made up as it was by more than a few practising Catholics – and that the respect was returned. There were no reports of clashes between Highlanders and locals, armed or otherwise, and for the most part, the local women went unmolested as long as they didn't linger around the Highlanders' camps. Meaning that all in all, the Highlanders were only an inconvenience in terms of the need to feed and quarter several thousand hungry men and their ponies throughout the shire.

For Hugh, however, it meant that there was still a certain amount of danger to a lone couple of Highlanders riding out to an abandoned croft. Resentment at the army taking fodder the crofters also needed was a sore point, as was the amount of grain requisitioned. And it wouldn't take much for some fiery local lads to see the chance to pay them back for what they undoubtedly saw as theft, albeit government sanctioned.

"Which do you want to go and look at first?" Jamie wondered as they trotted out of Terregles, where their troop was quartered in a trio of farmer's barns.

The more senior members of this part of the Host were quartered at Terregles Castle, the most recent member of the Maxwell family to inherit it being careful to be obliging to the government after a predecessor, Sir John Maxwell, had suffered greatly for supporting King James I & VI's mother, Mary Queen of Scots, against Queen Elizabeth. That had resulted in substantial damage to the castle itself, which the next laird, William Maxwell, had had to repair and upgrade. Now a younger distant cousin, also called John Maxwell, having succeeded in rising to be Earl of Nithsdale and laird of the castle, wanted to avoid a repetition of that disgrace – hence him putting up with troops of Highlanders in his own barns and those of his home farm.

However, Archie had told Hugh and Jamie that the current Earl was personally inclined very much for the King, and wary of Covenanters both in religion and politics, perceiving them as a menace to peace and prosperity. It meant that, so far, Hugh had seen little visible opposition to the soldiers, but away from where the Earl or his men might see, all the Highlanders knew that they might get a much colder reception from the ardent Presbyterians. Hence Hugh and Jamie's caution at venturing out, and presenting a vulnerable target for any group of local men who might outnumber them severely.

Bracing himself, Hugh answered, "Unless there's been a new bridge built since I was here – and I seriously doubt that there's been the money to do that – then the quickest way to get to our old croft is going via the bridge at Irongray. Part of me fears what I might do if I see old Veitch, because he was as much to blame as anyone for the deaths in our family."

"Surely he'd be an old man by now?" Jamie wondered.

"True," Hugh sighed. "If anyone in his family is still in the Manse, it's probably his son – someone who was a lad when I left, but who must be a grown man by now."

Archie had been unable to get time away to come with them, but Jamie had recruited two other men he knew from home to come with them.

"No point in courting danger," he'd said with a wink, as Dougie and Tormod joined them. "A group o' young local lads might think themselves the big men taking on two Highlanders out where – as they think it – they've no business being. But only outright idiots would take on four o' us."

And Hugh was grateful for Jamie's consideration, because right now his emotions were dragging his normally honed senses of survival all over the place. After arriving in the Highlands with Sorley McAllister, Hugh had quickly realised that unless he wanted to marry a local lass very rapidly, and then help tend her folks' fields and cattle, the best way to keep a roof over his and his father's heads was to join the local militia. In truth, this was less a militia as he'd known it in the south, and more of an armed force organised by clan fealties. In their case, being in southern Argyll, that meant to Clan Campbell, based near Inveraray. Hugh had joined as the most lowly of recruits, but with words of commendation from Sorley, who, it turned out, was highly regarded by the Campbell himself, even if he'd not been nobly born enough to hold a high rank.

In the intervening years he'd watched Elspeth wed Alex, and them fear they would never have children after the shock that Elspeth had suffered. Only when Mailie had died in an unexpected, and very late, pregnancy, and Elspeth and Alex had taken on her two youngest since there was nobody at home to watch over them, had Elspeth fallen pregnant herself. She and Alex had had only the one daughter, and Hugh had always been welcomed into their little family whenever he wasn't off somewhere fighting.

That was until disaster had struck. A couple of years of terrible harvests had shown just how precarious crofting in the real highlands could be, and Mailie's husband had only been able to grow enough to feed himself and his two oldest boys. Alex had never fully settled in the Highlands, though he'd tried his hardest, so it was no surprise that he took Elspeth and the three children south and east to the coast to find work. Only then had Hugh realised how much he had put off finding a wife of his own.

For him there was nobody else but Elspeth, and not seeing her on a regular basis had been the final push to him enrolling permanently in the service of the Campbell. Better to be far from home than wandering around the settlement seeing her ghost at every turn. And yet Elspeth's ghost had followed him down here. This had been her home too, and without realising it, Hugh found his pulse quickening in the hope that Alex and Elspeth had found the east coast more inhospitable than expected, and returned here.

At his old home there was little to see. Ivy and wild clematis, known as Old Man's Beard, had tangled their way over the crumbling lime-harled walls of his cottage, the roof having long gone, making it little more than a few mounds covered with new spring growth.

"At least it's not been disturbed," he found himself saying with relief to Jamie. "Elspeth said she saw it burning when she left with your father, but for this much growth to be here there can't have been anyone disturbing the place since then."

"That looks like a family of foxes have made their home here," observed Tormod, making Hugh exclaim,

"The fae! Elspeth said that the fae appeared to her as a fox!"

"Then the fae have kept your home safe," Jamie said, totally accepting that the fae both existed, and would do something like that. "You told me that Elspeth showed them respect. Well, it looks like that has been rewarded."

However, when they got to what had been Elspeth's home it was not as undisturbed. A sullen looking man stood in what had been the Allens' yard and refused to tell them his name, only that they would have to answer to 'the laird' if they harassed him. The Griersons at Lagg were still the nearest thing to a laird in the area, but Hugh was fairly sure that the man wasn't one of his. Grierson might be a stickler for the law, but he'd never been known to hire roughs to do his work for him. Whoever this 'laird' was, it was someone other than him.

And then as they rode up to the old nunnery, it all became clearer. The walls of the old cloisters were down almost to the foundations, and there was next to nothing left of the east end of the kirk. Where the crypt had been looked as though it had been filled in with the rough stuff that was of no use, and the flagstones of the eastern part of the nave had been lifted, going by the tangle of weeds across the space. Only the west tower stood guarding the old way in, but with many other walls gone, it sat isolated, its function lost.

"Where's it gone?" Hugh cried in dismay. "Where have the ruins gone?"

"Into that, I suspect," Jamie said regretfully, pointing to where building work was going on on what would soon be a substantial tower and side-house.

"Dear God," Hugh gulped, trying to get his bearings and then pointing. "See? There, where they're working on the roof? That's the old gatehouse! Those massive stones they're making into the house foundations must be the remains of the old under-croft. I suppose it was in the wrong place to be reused for this house, although I would have thought they'd have been better leaving it be when it was shoring up the bank. A few heavy rains and that other building they're putting the foundations in for will slide down into the river."

"Is there anything at all left o' the old choir and crypt?" Jamie wondered, standing in his stirrups to look around. "Have they desecrated yer ma's last resting place wi' all o' this? Yon's a great square tower, but it's surely too short to account for all of a kirk? But if yon other tower was the kirk's, then there must have been a gap between gatehouse and kirk we're no' seeing anymore? And where's the graveyard? Have they flattened that too? Is Elspeth's ma's grave under yon stones?"

Hugh looked to the side and saw that where there had once been humble mounds in neat lines, there was now a huge pile of earth from the building work. Jonet's grave was as lost as his own ma's bones were in the crypt, which had to also be beneath one of the piles of rubble.

"It wasn't a big kirk," Hugh admitted, "and yes, you're right, there was a gap where a yard must once have been, but there were also the standing ruins of other buildings. It looks very much as though they've robbed the stones out of the chapter house and dormitories, as well as the nave and choir, to have enough stone to build that wing next to the gatehouse. My ma is forever buried now, I fear. I'll never be able to retrieve her bones and sneak them into a proper grave." He felt himself choke up. "It isn't even consecrated ground anymore, by the look of it."

Then it hit him. "Oh no!"

"Hugh? What's wrong?"

"The nuns…They told Elspeth that their blood had gone into the flags of the nave floor up by the altar, and that while that was there, they were anchored to the place. It gave them the ability to appear, I think. Well, if the flags have been broken up, or at least separated for use in other places, then the nuns' power here is gone! They won't be able to protect anyone who comes here anymore."

Jamie gave a snort. "Sounds to me like someone did that verra deliberately. Someone who had cause to be afeared o' vengeful ghosts."

"And here he comes," Hugh sighed.

"What? Yon long streak o' pish strutting out wi' his man hanging at his heels?" The second man looked shifty, but also scrawny and unlikely to put up a fight, proven by the way he suddenly turned and scurried back inside.

"The very same. He's older and thinner, but that can only be Gideon Corsan. How, by all that's holy, did he get to be so rich as to be able to build his own tower-house?"

"Let me do the talking," Jamie urged. "Better if he thinks we're all Highlanders." Then called out loudly, "G'day, sir! We're just on patrol. Nothing to be worrit about."

Gideon paused far enough back to ensure that he didn't have to look up to these men on horseback. "You have no reason to come here," he said pompously. "There are no rebels on my land. We're all good attenders of the kirk at Irongray. No creeping off to some conventicle in the hills for any man who works for me. I see to that. Won't have law-breakers working for me! Won't have it, d'you hear?"

"Oh, I hear ye' loud and clear," Jamie replied, though his accent meant that Gideon didn't pick up on the sarcastic tone. "And who might the man at Irongray be? Just so as we know who to refer to, ye' understand."

"Why that would be Presbyter Veitch."

"An old man with long-standing loyalties, then?" Jamie made it sound such an innocent assumption, but Hugh found himself holding his breath for the answer.

"Aye, a man of many years, but with a son coming on to following in his father's footsteps at Irongray," Gideon said with as much pride as if he'd been claiming royal connections. "We're loyal to the Veitches around here. Not like some."

"Ach well, that's good to know," Jamie said affably. "My thanks for your time. We'll no' be keeping you from your building. Aye, but it's going to be a grand place once you've done. Your sons must be proud to be inheriting such a place."

The reference to sons made Gideon blink, then around a corner of the building work as if summoned by Jamie's words came a young man brandishing a musket.

"Away with you, filthy Highlanders! And leave us alone." he yelled, bringing the musket up to bear.

"Woah! Steady, lad! No need fer that," Jamie protested, but Hugh, who had moved his garron to the far side of Jamie, Dougal, and Tormod's, so that Gideon wouldn't be looking straight at him, heard the click of the flint and the whiff of the burning match.

All of his militia training kicked in, and he dug his heels into the garron's side, plunging forward to come upon the musket from slightly to the side. Before Gideon's son could change his aim, Hugh had a foot out of a stirrup and kicking out hard at the barrel to deflect it. With a bang that echoed off the stones, the musket went off, but with the ball flying over the heads of the three riders. Only just, though. Dougie clapped a hand to the top of his head as he felt the ball knock his bonnet off, but he wasn't the main casualty. The young man went over backwards with the combined recoil and the force of Hugh's boot, crashing him hard into the unfinished wall which already towered over him. As he slid down it, insensible, a red smear from his head followed him down.

"John! No!" Gideon howled, running to cradle the lad's head in his arms.

"He brought that on himself," Hugh said coldly, unable to feel a scarp of remorse for this spawn of one who had murdered his mother, nor for defending Jamie, his as good as adopted brother. "There was no need for muskets. No need at all."

"And we'll be reporting that back to the Campbell, too," Jamie declared. "So dinna even think about trying to make out that this is our fault. Come on, lads, let's leave this man to deal wi' his son."

"I won't forget you." Gideon roared as they rode away. "I'll get you for this, I swear to God I will!"

1678

Hugh & Gideon

Gideon Corsan was as good as his word over reporting Hugh and his friends to the sheriff, but they had been faster reporting back to John Maxwell and Captain Campbell, and since he was also related – albeit distantly – to the sheriff of Dumfries, it meant that no action was taken. That only inflamed Gideon further, though, and he was vocal in his condemnation of these 'foreigners' lording it in the shire, as he put it. Most of the ordinary people ignored him, too busy making sure that they stayed out of trouble and getting on with their lives, but Gideon had a willing audience in the form of Thomas McBurney.

The death of his brother Rab all those years ago had left him as the sole heir, and therefore a richer man than expected, but it rankled the way the families of those witches had vanished into the night on the same one as his brother died, and he was sure they were connected. There hadn't been a mark on Rab's body. A normal, healthy young man had dropped down dead for no explainable reason in a mystical place on the night the witches left, and that was enough of a connection to make Thomas a rabid witch hater. Not that he could explain why Rab's breeches were around his ankles beyond the obvious, but Thomas couldn't believe that a mere woman could have overwhelmed his brother. No, witchcraft had to be involved.

And their experience hunting Elspeth and running into the shades of the nuns had left McBurney with a hatred of papists, too. Indeed, when John Corsan had been looking for a spot to build a better house – one more befitting his new family's status – it had been Thomas who had connived to get his now elderly father and uncle to allow the Corsans to take over the old nunnery.

"Rip the vile place down!" Thomas said when he came to give John Corsan the good news. "Remove all traces of those vile witches from the earth. For witches they are, merely ones that answer to Rome."

So when the Highlanders arrived, some of them sporting Catholic symbols in the form of saints' pilgrim badges or crucifixes, to him they were little short of worshippers of the Antichrist himself, and that made him instantly on Gideon's side.

"Never fear, my friend," Thomas told Gideon, "You shall have your retribution on those responsible. You've not been plagued with the witches' ghosts at the tower, have you? …Good! So we'll get rid of this plague too. They'll not stay here telling *us* how to pray." And Thomas was a vehement Covenanter by now, ever up at Irongray Manse, even if the older McBurneys walked a more circumspect path.

Moreover, pay back *was* required in the pair's eyes, because hot-headed Young John was now sitting staring vacantly at the wall of his bedroom, needing a maid to watch over him at all times to remind him to do the most basic of things, like eat. Yet that maid was already one of their vengeances.

"Does the maid still suit?" Thomas asked with an evil grin.

"Oh, she does very well," Gideon replied, momentarily gratified at the thought. "Taking Thomas

Milligan's widowed daughter to Veitch to get her off his hands when she came home a-begging was a moment of divine inspiration on your part, I must say. It keeps Milligan beholden to us for favours, and keeps the daughter of that witch of a first wife of his away from his second.

"God have mercy upon us, Thomas, at least your wife and mine had the grace to die trying to give us sons. Can you imagine being in Milligan's position where his new wife has more money than he, too old to breed, and so recalcitrant too? 'Tis surely a wife's duty to do as her husband bids in the privacy of their chamber? Not spread it abroad that he asks too much?"

"Indeed," Thomas smirked. "Did not Presbyter Veitch say as much only last Sunday?"

Gideon nodded with a sanctimonious leer that had nothing to do with godliness. "Another man who knows how to deal with an unruly woman. You were most generous to let him have the use of her before our need became the greater."

Thomas shrugged. "With his son away for the foreseeable future, an old man like the Presbyter should not be left without his creature comforts in his declining years. A man must have his bodily needs cared for if he is to attend to our spiritual ones."

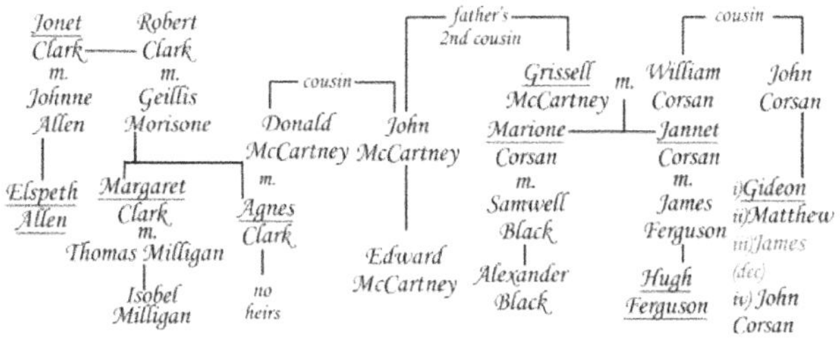

In one respect Hugh and his friends had been wrong, and Hugh had soon realised it once he had time to think. Gideon wasn't old enough to be the lad's father. They had to be brothers, but where the elder John Corsan – who had been complicit in the trials – had got to puzzled him until he learned that too much indulgence had, in the last year, brought on a seizure. It had left him currently confined to the house he had taken from Marione and Samwell after theirs and Alex's flight from the shire, his town house having stairs too cramped for him to be able to manage anymore. All he was waiting on now was for Gideon to finish supervising the building of the grand new house at the nunnery, for the croft was too mean a place for him to want to be there for long. Sometimes old John went back to his townhouse in Dumfries if business demanded his presence, but mostly he watched his builders, scrutinising them for every broken stone or delay, not trusting Gideon to do the job for him.

"We know where that old goat is, then," Dougie said with a wicked grin. "Any trouble from the Corsans and we can go and have a strong word wi' him, and all his lording it over folks won't do him a scrap o' good."

Moreover, Gideon and Thomas wouldn't have been quite as smugly sure of their triumph had they known that the plight of Margaret Clark's daughter, Isobel, had reached the Highlanders' camp.

"Are you sure it's her?" Dougie asked Hugh, as the four friends huddled together around their small camp fire. "Are you sure she's Elspeth's cousin?"

"As sure as ever I can be," Hugh replied. "Elspeth's cousin Margaret, who burned alongside her sister Agnes and my ma, was married to an evil bastard named Thomas Milligan, of that I'm certain. I remember how disgusted we all were that he testified against his own wife. You don't forget things like that. And as best I can recall, Elspeth and Johnne were equally disgusted that Margaret's two sons followed their father's lead, while her daughter – and I'm sure her name was Isobel Milligan – lived over Stranraer way with her husband, so was too far away to do much.

"I vaguely recall Elspeth saying that she was ever grateful that her own father never shoved her off as a young lass into the arms of a much older man as happened to Isobel – indeed that was the very context I heard Isobel's name mentioned in, otherwise I might not have known it. The thought of a young Elspeth with some old brute who cared not a jot for her was what made it stick in my mind all these years. So it's not beyond the realms of possibility that Margaret's Isobel has been widowed in the intervening years and forced back into her awful father's household, yet is not beyond remarrying and having children, if given the choice."

"Aye," Tormod sympathised. "It's a cruel world for any widow of a man who is only a farmer's worker. If the man doesn'a work, the woman doesn'a have a roof to call her own. Did you ken the woman Isobel's father married after her ma, Margaret, was murdered?"

Hugh could only shrug. "All I heard before we left was that whoever she was, she'd been left money by her first husband, and that was what Milligan wanted to get his hands on. If what we've since heard from some of the locals is true, though, she didn't have much say in whether she married Milligan or not after Margaret's death. Just like Isobel, her family handed her off like an old milch cow to the highest bidder, while they got their hands on the large croft she left behind.

"But I tell you this, my friends, if Elspeth's poor cousin Isobel spent any time alone with old Presbyter Veitch after Milligan threw her out a second time, then he would have used her cruelly. That old goat had some carnal appetites, if the rumours we heard when I was a lad had even a scrap of truth in them. As I remember it from when I was young, no woman ever went into his kirk alone for fear of what might happen, and I can't imagine he's improved with age."

"Heavens," Tormod sniffed in disgust. "I know some of our priests are no' exactly angels. Do ye' remember, Dougie, when young Georgie McDonnell came home greetin' because Faither Jacobus had had his hand up the wee lad's kilt?"

"Aye, I do," Tormod said with a grin. "And I remember the leathering Georgie's pa gave the priest wi' the laird's blessing! Funny how yon priest managed wi' his fist instead o' a lad after that. And ye're right, Dougie, our priests might no' have all been guid, but by God, at least our lairds were no' scared witless o' them like the locals here seem to be. Ye'd think these Covenant men had a wee personal chat wi' God every Sunday afore they preach, the way folks are so scairt."

"It's politics, not God," Hugh told them resignedly. "The Kirk has got into bed with the men in power, and it means that many won't say a word against them for fear of what else they might bring down upon themselves."

"I say we take a ride over to yon scarecrow's

house when we know he's no' going to be there," Jamie said with a grin and a wink. "It might be that if we can get Isobel on her own, that we can offer to take her back up north wi' us. After all, we may no' have the usual militia's compliment of wives and women following in our wake this time, but she'd no' be the only woman travelling wi' us, would she?"

Hugh's mood lifted. "Yes! That would be a good thing. She can travel with the wise women and healers. ...If she wants to go, that is. I'll not be yet another man who forces her to go where she doesn't want. She's had too much of that already."

It took another couple of weeks to put their plan into effect, but finally they heard that the local court would be in session in Dumfries, and therefore that both Gideon and John senior would be away from home. They had also discovered that Gideon was forced to live with his father, along with his brother John, while the building work was underway. Yet when they got there, there was a different surprise for Hugh. A horse was tethered just out of sight of the house, and it wasn't fine enough to be one of the Corsans'.

Wary in case some kind of trap had been laid for them, the four dismounted and crept forward as silently as only Highlanders could do, Dougie and Tormod being determined to come along and see this through. Lying flat and peering through a tangle of ferns and bracken shoots, the four saw a woman of middling years come out, closing the door oh-so-carefully behind her, as if wanting to remain unheard. With backwards glances to the house, she then took to her heels and ran towards where a vegetable plot, with its tall frames waiting for the new beans to climb up them, hid her from view.

"Is she caring fer the lad, then? Ye' said that the old man wouldn'a have a lassie tending to him?" Jamie whispered to Tormod, who answered,

"Aye, that's what I heard. The auld de'il has no' got the proper use of one side o' his body, but there's nothing wrong wi' his bluidy tongue! He can lash out at folk as well as he ever could, and there's just some crachit man attending him – the only one who seems to put up wi' him."

"I doubt it's 'putting up with' in his case," Hugh said knowingly. "The poor bastard is probably someone who has no choice in the matter. Somewhere along the line he's crossed John Corsan and come out on the wrong side, no doubt. No wonder he's grim. Tending a man like that would try the patience of a saint, let alone one having no choice but to do it."

"Looks like the lassie's scairt that he might betray her, though," Tormod added sadly. "Ye'd think two folks like that might find a common cause."

Yet any further speculation was halted by Hugh's aghast exclamation of, "Good God! What's *he* doing here?"

The horse's rider had appeared from behind the copse of apple trees, and Isobel flung herself into his arms.

"Who is he?" Jamie asked, having to give the stunned Hugh a poke in the ribs to get an answer.

"That's Edward McCartney. …Or at least I'm fairly certain it is. He looks like Edward anyway."

Dougie leaned over Jamie to hiss at Hugh, "Wasn'a it a McCartney who was involved wi' yer ma's trial?"

"This man's father," Hugh replied grimly. "John McCartney got his hands on Agnes and Donald

McCartney's croft – that's Agnes who was Elspeth's cousin. John McCartney is – or was – Donald's cousin, and when Donald died, he wasn't prepared to wait for a young widow like Agnes to die of natural causes. He was hand in glove with John Corsan, who wanted his own cousins' croft – that's my Aunt Marione, Uncle Samwell, and Alex's, plus the land from ours – and Elspeth always said that those two had some kind of secret arrangement to find reasons to get those who stood in their way condemned as witches.

"It gets even darker when you realise that John McCartney was also related to my own maternal grandmother. Poor Grandma Grissell may have died in her sleep, but it was after being tormented for years, though before she got to trial, thank the Lord. So may God help me, but I'm related to John Corsan and his sons, but also to John McCartney and his sons, one of whom is the man we're looking at."

"God preserve us!" Dougie whistled softly. "It's awful personal for ye', is it no'? A part of yer family on both sides condemned the others to death."

"And I want a word with him," Hugh declared resolutely. "Come on, my friends, it's time to get some answers."

Yet as they appeared out of the undergrowth, virtually at the feet of Edward and Isobel, there was none of Gideon's belligerence about Edward. He swung Isobel around behind him to protect her, but there was none of the bluster and confrontation in his manner. Even more surprising, he peered hard at Hugh, then said in shock, "Good heavens! Is that you, Hugh Ferguson?"

Isobel's head appeared around Edward's arm. "Hugh Ferguson? Really? Oh, blessed be! Please tell me that cousin Elspeth survived? Please let there be one of us who made it away from this cursed place."

Taken aback, Hugh could only manage, "Aye, Elspeth's alive and well."

Isobel's sob of relief he expected, Edward's heartfelt, "Thank the Lord!" he didn't.

The three Highlanders took in Hugh's confusion and sheathed the dirks they had drawn, just in case Edward had wanted to make a fight of it.

"I think you'd better explain what's gone on," Jamie said, gesturing them all back to the far side of the fruit trees, and to where a goodly thicket of hawthorns hid them even further.

No sooner had they got to where they could speak normally then Edward was turning to Hugh, saying, "You have every reason to hate my father, but please believe me, I never wanted cousin Donald's croft. Not like that, anyway."

"You took it nonetheless," Hugh said dryly, yet Edward shook his head.

"Take? No. I had it forced upon me. There wasn't a night I spent in that place where I slept easily," shuddering violently at the thought.

"Hold on a moment, though," Jamie interrupted. "*You* weren't the one who accused them, were ye'? Did ye' give testimony to the court?" Edward shook his head vigorously. "Then why do ye' act as if ye' were so guilty? Surely ye' were no more than a lad, just like Hugh here was at the time? Ye' couldn'a have stopped anything if ye'd tried, no' against the local big men."

"That's true," Edward said with faint relief at Jamie's understanding. "But I felt so dreadful over what my father had done. …And they cursed us, you know. …Cousin Agnes, and her sister Margaret, and your mother, Hugh. While that monster Presbyter Veitch was shouting out his condemning prayers, I heard them through the others' screams. They cursed us all. My father and John Corsan, and their sons and theirs to a fourth generation!"

He gulped and gave a shiver. "Then Margaret and Agnes screamed something in a strange tongue. …Gaelic…I later found out it was Gaelic. But by all that's holy, they put every ounce of hatred they possessed into it. …I…I don't think they finished it. Their voices were shattered by the choking they'd already had, and then…and then the smoke got to them. …But it was potent! It was the most terrifying thing I've ever heard, and all the more so because even then, I knew that Agnes, at least, had done nothing to deserve that fate. My father sent one innocent woman to the stake, and probably the others too, all out of greed."

"I'm glad you, at least, know that," Hugh said gruffly, more moved than he'd expected by Edward's obvious distress.

For the first time Isobel spoke. "It was after the trial and you leaving that Edward came to see me. He felt someone other than my dreadful father should come and tell me the truth of what had gone on, you see. He knew my brothers would just follow Father's lead, but that I'd been closer to Ma than them." She looked up at him with genuine affection. "He took a big risk coming to see me, because my husband at the time was in debt to both Father and his, and he'd have told them in a heartbeat if he'd known."

"But that's when I started to believe the curse," Edward said with another shiver. "I'd been courting a lass from Dumfries when the trials took place, but the moment they happened, her family told me I wasn't welcome anymore." He sighed sadly. "I'd been naïve to think it could come to anything, because they weren't high enough socially for my father's liking, and he laughed at me for being so lovelorn, though perversely his pride was offended that anyone should turn me away. They weren't people he had any hold over, though, so it brought them no lasting harm.

"Yet the girl he picked out for me wouldn't have me at any price, either, and made a lowlier marriage to someone she openly said wasn't a 'murderer's son'. And after that had happened a few times, Father insisted Isobel and her husband come to help me work the croft, because even he couldn't expect me to run the whole place with just a glaikit lad to help me. Yet no matter what we did, things just kept getting worse and worse. Crops failed for no reason. Sheep sickened and died, or ran off into the hills where we couldn't find them. It just went on and on. And then George – that's Isobel's husband – stuck a fork through his foot." He grimaced. "I've never seen someone die such a long and agonising death as he did."

"Even so," Isobel added, "we hoped that once he was gone, that I'd be able to marry Edward and his father would leave us alone. How stupid were we? The old man thought I'd poisoned George deliberately. And no matter what Edward said, he kept on that I was a witch just like my mother, and my own father damned me for the same."

"That's when he dragged her off to bloody Veitch," Edward said grimly. "When he then said that I was too weak to have the croft, and that he was taking it back off me, I got my bags packed the same night. I couldn't wait to leave there. He shoved me off to another, much smaller, croft he'd got hold of in the meantime and pretty much disinherited me. Since then, Isobel and I have tried to see one another when we can. With Veitch it was easier because he was always off here, there, and everywhere, sticking his miserable nose into other people's business.

"In fact, we'd just got to the point where we thought we could run away and not be hunted down, when old man Corsan took bad. He has his man to help him get around, but they dragged Isobel in to do the washing and cleaning for him. And then bloody Young John went and got that knock on the head, and they've been running Isobel ragged ever since." The look he gave Isobel as he said that last fair broke Hugh's heart, because he knew he looked at Elspeth the same way.

"So is your father sometimes now at Agnes and Donald's croft?" Jamie asked.

"Oh, that's the strangest of all," Edward told them. "He went there full of himself, thinking he'd show me how useless I'd been – though with a man and lad to do the rough work – and that of course I should have been able to manage, but he had one accident after another. He'd made the space up in the roof into a sleeping loft, then fell down the ladder and broke his leg and arm within three weeks of getting there." Hugh and the Highlanders instinctively sucked in through their teeth and winced at the thought of how painful that must have been.

"He had to have extra help after that. Then the barn burned down when nobody was around, just as he was getting back on his feet after three months or so. Three months after that, three cows got struck by lightning out in the top field, and three months after that the grain came up filled with tares and teasels." He shivered. "If I'd never believed in the witches' power of three that my mother told me about before, I did after that!

"And I've never seen teasels growing anywhere near there before or since," Edward continued, reflexively crossing himself, which told Hugh that this was someone who didn't share his father's Covenanter beliefs. "After that he sold it, but do you know, the new people got it back to the healthy, fertile place it was when Donald and Agnes had it within just a year. It was just *us* the croft wouldn't abide being there!"

All the Highlanders nodded solemnly. They understood uneasy spirits and places haunted by those who'd been wronged, whatever the Kirk might preach.

"So would ye' like to start over somewhere new?" Jamie asked craftily, and got instant nods and yeses from both. "Then when we get the word we're going home, be prepared to come and meet us on the road, and we'll take you up to what's left of your family, Isobel."

1678

Hugh & Gideon

In truth, Gideon Corsan might bluster and pose when he was around men like Thomas McBurney, and when he felt he had to keep up a public front, but to his own desperation, he found himself longing for Isobel Milligan to look at him just once without seeming as though she wished him damned to the deepest depths of Purgatory. Why, he often prayed at night, did it have to be her whom he looked at, only to have his heart nearly leap out of his chest in delight? There were younger, more comely, women available – though in truth, 'available' had meant to just about anyone except to him, his brother, or the McBurney sons.

And given that Thomas Milligan had virtually handed Isobel's mother to the witch trials, subsequently, when their one son became a widower, he'd had no luck in finding a new wife, while the older son's two boys seemed to have one misadventure or misfortune after another. He wasn't sure whether Margaret Clark had cursed her husband Thomas and her sons, but it was certainly starting to look like it. And he knew beyond a doubt that she, her sister Agnes, and the other witches, had done so to him and his father, and to John McCartney, though somehow John's Edward didn't seem to suffer quite the same blight. Clearly, he also held a passion for Isobel, and wasn't having any more luck than Gideon with regard to the possessing of her; but that wasn't much consolation when that was the worst that had happened to Edward, compared to the endless misery Gideon felt he endured.

In the years since those nine witches had died, he'd come to understand what it must be like for lepers. Nobody openly said anything or did anything, especially knowing that he was seemingly mightily approved of by Patrik Veitch – though Gideon had progressively distanced himself from actively helping Veitch in any way, as the full impact of being seen by his side at the trial had sunk in, leaving that to McBurney – but apart from Veitch's most ardent supporters, the ordinary people around him let him know in quiet and subtle ways that he had crossed a line at that trial. It left him as isolated as if he had some dreadful disease that they were terrified of catching off him. Belatedly it dawned on him once he was fully an adult that, although people fully understood that a lad of his age at the time could not have had any influence at the trial and its aftermath, his laughing at the witches' fate had been a mistake. It had marked him out as cruel and, though not a soul said so to his face, positively devoid of Christian sympathy.

At the time he'd done it because he'd thought it was what his father wanted him to be like. And heaven alone knew what a harsh parent John Corsan was to his oldest son, while Matthew, the favourite when they were children, had long since escaped before he got tarred with the same brush. Young John, as the youngest of four sons, had frequently got away with being a regular lad, getting into mischief and being irresponsible, but Gideon was expected to do 'better'.

The problem was that Gideon struggled to understand what that 'better' was. And the longer it all went on, the more he found himself torn. Behave as his father wished and he very occasionally got the praise he so desperately craved. Yet in the doing, it always seemed to end up being something which continued to deprive him of the few friends he had left, until he had none at all unless you counted the bitter and twisted Thomas McBurney – and even Gideon could only stomach so much of his presence. All of which made Gideon a very unhappy man.

Some years ago, he had been forced into a marriage with a woman he couldn't stand the sight of – a sanctimonious older girl, who had withered what little ardour his youth lent him with her pious and condemnatory prayers before bedtime. Therefore it had hardly been surprising that they had not had children in the early years of their marriage, when it took Gideon having to get taken with strong spirits just to fulfil his marital obligations. Then when she did get pregnant, he had scarcely been able to conceal his relief when she and the child had died of some strange complication during a premature birth.

Veitch swore some witch had cursed them, deliberately depriving such an upright man of an heir to do God's work.

Conversely, Gideon got on his knees in the kirk that Sunday, and silently offered up heartfelt thanks for his narrow escape, for once actually glad if it was a witches' curse! Because if his wife had been a harridan with just the two of them, what she would have been like with an adored child to beat him with (verbally and morally, if not physically) had been the stuff of his nightmares for months already.

And then he'd met Isobel. Isobel who brought a whole new level of torment to his life. At which point he really began to believe that those witches' curses at their trial had more power than he or his father had believed. The only consolation was that he wasn't the only one of those who'd been there to suffer endless bad luck. That had been up until he'd caught the way the object of his desires looked at Edward McCartney.

Why, oh why, could she look at McCartney with such affection and sympathy, and yet turn such a frozen glare upon himself? Moreover, why did Edward also look at him as though he was the vilest human to ever walk the earth? What right did Edward-bloody-McCartney have to lord it over him?

The more Gideon thought about it, the angrier he became. And that anger was only fuelled when he learned just who the man had been with the Highlanders on the day that his brother took the fateful blow to the head. Another thing, as if fate hadn't been cruel enough already, which his father blamed him for. He hadn't even known that Young John had been daft enough to bring the musket to the building site. What on earth had prompted that?

Yet his father, who hadn't been there and seen that the four soldiers had posed no threat at all until Young John had come screaming in brandishing the damned thing, took the line that Young John had fully understood a danger that Gideon was too dim to understand. And typically, that weasel man-servant, John Renwick, had tailored what he'd been too cowardly to see for himself at the time to fit what the old man wanted to hear. Therefore yes, Gideon was angry that the man who had kicked Young John so hard was bloody Hugh Ferguson, of all people, but was just as angry at his fool of a brother for starting the trouble in the first place.

The next brother in line to Gideon, Matthew, had been such an obvious candidate for the Kirk, that their father had somehow found the money to send him all the way to St Andrews to study, and the third had died while still a lad. Well Gideon had no desire to spend every day with dust-dry books, but how he envied Matthew the freedom to be far away from the family and the censorship that their father had brought down upon them all. Only once, back in 1661, had Gideon left the shire of his birth, and that to escort Matthew to his college, and at the time he had been glad to return, having seen how the Chief Advocate had been soft on the witches brought to trial before him during the time Gideon was in Fife with Matthew. But that had been before the reality of the events of the previous years had fully sunk in, and just what it was costing him to be eternally seen as Old John Corsan's heir and duplicate. Now he wished he'd stayed with Matthew and never returned.

"Please, Lord," he prayed every Sunday after Young John was struck down, "Let my father find someone else to oversee the building of this cursed tower-house, and find some pretext to allow me to go over and join Matthew, even if it's only for a while."

Yet had he known how that prayer would be answered, Gideon might never have repeated it so often, and the results of his going were ones he could never have anticipated.

By the time they had been in Dumfriesshire for the summer, Hugh was similarly longing to get out of the shire. Word had gone around the locals of who he was, and though he was grateful for their sympathies and their apologies, more and more he found himself wanting to scream at them, "If you knew my mother was innocent, why didn't you *do* something?"

He couldn't. He knew he couldn't, and worse, he knew why they hadn't acted, but that didn't make life any easier. At least Jamie and Archie both understood full well what he was going through, but as Archie told him, "Ye're here as a soldier, my friend, and that means ye' have to abide by the rules, grim though that is. The Campbell canna have one o' his men taking the law into his own hands, not even for a past grievance as deserving o' vengeance as yours."

Worse, Hugh was increasingly drawn to Isobel, not least because the more he got to know her, the more he realised how like Elspeth she was as a person. In looks she was taller and slimmer, but in her heart and soul she was a kindred spirit to her older cousin and her aunt Agnes, if not her fiery mother. Yet, against all expectations, Hugh also found himself liking Edward McCartney. Unlike Gideon Corsan and Thomas McBurney, Edward had played no part in Hugh's mother's questioning and death, and the more Hugh spoke to Edward, the more he realised that having a father like John McCartney had to have been a torment to someone who actually had morals and principles.

It meant that when the time would come for them to leave, Hugh felt he had no choice but to help Edward escape as well. It wasn't in his nature to promise one thing and do another, but if he'd been willing to set that and his conscience aside, potentially he might sweep up Isobel and simply not tell Edward they were going until it was too late.

But no, just the thought of doing that was enough to have him cringing at himself. And how ironic that these ardent Presbyterians, who made such great play of their morals and faith, and their abiding by the Bible, could behave in such an ungodly way. Yet could look down upon him – whom they considered barely Christian at all for having bent his knee on occasions in the church of the Whore of Babylon, as they were heard to refer to the Catholic Church as – when he himself felt so constrained by his own faith and his belief in the Ten Commandments.

Not that Hugh was a devout Catholic such as Jamie and Archie were. He'd not thought in much depth about faith at all, in truth, but was happy to conform by going to whichever church or wee kirk he was sent to, or followed his friends and family to. And for the life of him, he couldn't understand why these men and women who took to the wilds to hold their prayer meetings were so vehemently opposed to having bishops. Didn't the Presbyterian Kirk have various tiers of meetings to decide what did or didn't happen? So how was that any different for the farmhand who only had one or two kirks within walking distance anyway, and therefore would never see the great Presbytery Session meetings that went on in places such as Edinburgh and Glasgow?

There were men whom Hugh did have a burning desire to wreak vengeance upon, though, and they were John Corsan the elder, John McCartney, Gideon Corsan, and Thomas McBurney. And the longer he was in Dumfriesshire, the worse his feelings got. So by the time he'd seen the two elderly Johns being driven into Dumfries for some meeting or other with Captain Campbell and others, and saw how the local people still cringed around them, even though they were now both little more than crippled versions of themselves, it was all he could do not to draw his dirk and finish the two devils incarnate off, and be damned with the consequences.

And with that in mind, he began to make plans to slip away when the army withdrew north once more. He could trust Jamie and Archie to take Edward and Isobel to safety, and just as it had been easier in a strange way not to see Elspeth so in love with his cousin Alex, it would be easier if he didn't travel back, and then have to watch Isobel and Edward being welcomed into the fragmented remains of their families when there was no chance of happiness for himself. How that worked out, though, was in a way he could never have dreamed of.

Chapter 18

Thankfully Gary was at the door by her third knock, and looking worried as he took in Anna's expression.

"Can you come and help me move what there is of my stuff into the other cottage, please? Now!" she gasped. "I'll explain why as we're doing it."

More than a little perplexed, nonetheless Gary tugged on his battered old trainers and came with her. As she opened the back door to the middle cottage which she'd been intending to have and then the one to the end cottage, she told him what she feared, then took him into the tower and showed him the angel.

"Bugger me!" Gary breathed in awe when he saw it. "You're no' wrong about that, lass! That doesn'a belong in any stable I've ever come across."

Then he looked even more startled when Anna pointed out what she'd found about the orientation of the place, concluding with, "So if I'm right, and previous inhabitants of the end cottage were quite literally spooked enough to swap the main rooms around, I can't possibly put Harriet in there, can I? I mean, I'm not exactly jumping with joy at possibly having a ghost in my lounge, but at least I'm braced for it. She isn't."

Shoving up the sleeves of his old army sweater, Gary gave a huff and said, "Right, let's get on with it, then," at which point Anna could have hugged the life out of him. No arguing. No treating her as if she'd lost her mind, as her father and mother would have done. Just acceptance that she'd made a sensible decision. And it was, Anna realised, because even if there was no ghost after all, they simply couldn't afford to take the risk of losing a chef, not with the first wedding only four weeks away.

They didn't have time to do anything besides cart Anna's stuff across and take down the other old curtains before they were both due on duty, but at least Anna had already done the floor cleaning in what she'd thought would be her new home.

"The rugs can go in when they come tomorrow," she said with relief as, changed into their formal clothes once more, they walked together over to where Anna was taking over from Polly for the evening.

"You can stay in my spare room tonight," Gary told her. "If you go back up to the room at the top, the others will start wondering what the heck is going on. And the last thing we want to do is get Cora and Polly wittering on to guests about us having to change rooms about because they're haunted."

"Nor Cameron," Anna said in a voice heavy with disappointment.

"You weren't impressed with his reaction, were you?" Gary sympathised, and she shook her head, halting him on the other side of the glass doors through to reception so that Polly wouldn't hear her.

"I'm not comfortable with the way he has no idea of how bad this could get. It's as if he has no feeling…no sixth sense, if you like, of atmosphere. Would he even have picked anything up if it wasn't for Harris and Lewis? And if that's the case, I don't want him around Aunty Rita if she comes to help us."

"Your aunt won't take any nonsense off him," Gary chuckled. "I certainly wouldn't worry about her being upset if he disrespects her beliefs. She's more like to traumatise him than the other way around!"

Anna laughed with him, but added, "It's more if he wants to sit in on what she feels needs doing, but then starts playing silly sods while we're doing it. Do you see, Gary? He might think it's all a bit of a joke? After all, *he* hasn't been the one to experience the ghosts, has he? And in fairness to the dogs, we can hardly put him into one of the affected rooms. I'd feel awful doing that to them. So he's not going to experience it, meaning he's not taking this as seriously as he should. I don't want him doing something stupid like calling out an invitation to any other spirits we've got hanging around the place. That could be mayhem. Because for all we know, the only reason why others aren't manifesting is because they haven't been given a way in…but he might give them one!"

"Holy crap," Gary muttered softly as he held the door open for Anna, having noticed that Polly was looking at them curiously, and not wanting her to start asking what they were being so secretive about. "No, lass, we really don't want *that*!"

To Anna's secret relief, the following evening Cameron announced that he'd be leaving on Sunday night. Blissfully unaware of the concern he'd caused, he was more regretful of having to go back to Edinburgh.

"I've got to sign papers on the flat, and while I could do them electronically, there's other stuff I need to do in person over there, so I might as well go," he said, looking glum. Then he shocked Anna by saying, "Can I leave Harris and Lewis with you and Gary?"

Blinking and realising that it would be hard to say no when he was still ultimately her boss, Anna nodded. It was only then that she realised that he'd started leaving the pair in the room while he came down to eat, but of course, even though they'd got used to the room they were in, that wouldn't be able to continue. That room was needed for guests coming in, not least for the looming wedding, when the hotel would be stuffed to the rafters – something Cameron had known he'd have to move out for already. So the dogs would have to move to somewhere strange without him if he wasn't back in time, no matter what she said, and that cut her more than she expected.

Managing to paste a smile on her face which she hoped didn't look too fake, she managed a cheerful sounding, "Of course, that'll be no problem!" And it wasn't where the dogs themselves were concerned. Anna had always wanted a dog of her own, and had become very fond of the two big hounds. But she was less than sure how they would cope with seemingly being abandoned by their beloved master, and when she told Gary last thing that night, when they were alone at the reception desk, he was of much the same mind.

"Bugger! Why did he have to do that right now?" Anna growled. "Why not take them with him? Because unless you have them over here when you're on at night, I'll have to have them in my cottage when you're working, if at no other time…"

"…and just when you fear you might have ghostly tenants of your own!" Gary caught on immediately. "Fer feck's sake!" Even though he did it under his breath, Anna knew it was a measure of how unimpressed he was with Cameron that he would swear in front of her.

It turned out that he was leaving them in part because Cameron was going to pack up his flat, and couldn't do that with the hounds under his feet, not to mention where he would go afterwards temporarily, city centre hotels not being known for their welcome of huge dogs. But however good the reason, Anna and Gary were still unimpressed with the way he'd not given the dogs time to come over and spend more time with them before he walked away, even if he'd brought all of their bedding and toys across with them. For the first evening, the pair of them paced and whined, wondering where Cameron was, to the extent that Anna once again resorted to Gary's spare room. Shunting them between cottages when they were so distressed was only going to make things worse.

It was the following night, with both Anna and Gary off duty, that Anna sat on the one of Gary's sofas with Harris' head on her knee and looked across to where Lewis was with Gary, and said, "Is it my imagination, or has he grown in the time he's been here? I'm sure his tail end didn't used to reach the far sofa arm."

Gary looked down at the big shaggy hound and stroked his ears. "Aye, I think you're right. But in that case, he can't be that old." He gently lifted Lewis's lip and said, "Those are really white puppy teeth to my eye. Adult teeth to be sure, but only just. Jeez, how long has he had these two? Is that why he doesn't seem that clued up about looking after them?"

Cameron had left all the dogs' information with them, just in case they needed the services of a vet for any reason, and so Anna got up and went and retrieved them.

"Oh Lordy!" she gasped as she read Lewis' details. "He's only about nine months old. I thought he was smaller than Harris because he was crossed with that poodle, but he's not fully grown, is he?"

"I doubt it. What about Harris?"

She rolled her eyes in exasperation. "Looking at the different vets' names on his vaccinations and stuff, he must have been got rid of by his first owners when he was about Lewis' age. *Hmph*! Got bigger than they thought, I expect. So he's gone from whoever bred him to them, then off to the rescue, then to Cameron for… Oh for heaven's sake! What's the matter with the man?"

"What?

"Well, when he said that lady was pestering him to let Harris breed, I thought it must have been over several months. But now I wonder if she knew Harris when he was in the rescue, and when they wouldn't let her have him just for a day or so to breed from, she got onto Cameron as soon as she knew he was having Harris." She came over and ruffled Harris' fur with tears in her eyes. "He's not even two, Gary. He's still just a big pup himself."

"Poor lad," Gary immediately sympathised. "I think I'm going to be having a strong word with young Cameron when he comes back, boss or no boss!"

And yet ten days went by with not so much as a phone call from Cameron.

Harriet the chef came and was an instant hit with Emilio, to everyone's relief. However, Sally was rather less happy, taking Anna on one side the second day after Cameron had gone.

"If he's coming back here for another long visit," she said grimly, "then you're going to have to put him out in one of the cottages the fishermen use down the track. The room stinks, Anna! I put it down to the dogs always having just left the room when I went in while he was there, but doing a proper deep clean now, he's not dried them off properly when they've come in from the wet. The room just honks of damp dog. I've gone through bottles of Febreze and left the windows open as wide as I dared without freezing the other guests in the next-door rooms, but I'm only just getting rid of the smell. Please tell me that at least one of the wedding guests is bringing a dog, so that we can put them in there. Hopefully another dog owner won't notice any lingering scent, but another guest might."

"That was pretty thoughtless of him," Anna sighed. "And of themselves, Harris and Lewis aren't smelly dogs, so they must have been wet and muddy as hell to do that. Message received and understood, Sally. I'll juggle the wedding rooms, and luckily, we've got no guests booked into *both* cottages at the same time for a while after that. If he comes back, I'll give him the smaller one long-term, and I'll upgrade the guests who'd booked that one into the bigger one. They're unlikely to complain at that."

However, once Sally had gone, Anna felt a wave of sadness come over her. Somewhere in a quiet corner of her soul she'd dared to hope that she had found someone who might just care for her. Not in a whisking her away to a life of luxury, daydream kind of way, but someone who would stick up for her if her father ever came here, for instance, or worse, if Jensen's father came. Someone who wouldn't just clear off when the going got tough. Someone who'd been through the mill enough himself to understand her. But if Cameron could be so careless with Harris and Lewis, it didn't bode well for him in his human relationships.

Oh, she got that he'd been as damaged by his mother as she had by both of her parents, but at least he'd had a normal dad who'd tried to do his best for him. That was more than she'd ever had. Yet she could instantly empathise with Harris and Lewis' distress, while he hadn't seemed to even consider it.

No, keep it polite, keep it professional, she lectured herself. *Stay friendly, but don't place any hopes on him being the one you always hoped you'd find. Look what a bloody disaster Jensen was! And you thought you loved him. Well he didn't love you, did he? So you're a lousy judge of men when it comes to your love life. Focus on keeping your job here. If this is anything to go by, he'll come back a few times, then you'll hardly see him again, and if you gain two gorgeous hounds out of it, you're better off sticking with the dogs and forgetting having a boyfriend, let alone the 'h' thing.*

That was easier said than done, though, and at first Anna couldn't work out why she was so upset. She knew that as soon as she'd finished her shift, she was going to end up in tears. Not that that was a new thing for her, but in the past, she'd been up in the sanctity of the turret bedroom where nobody could hear her sob, and it had been solely over the train wreck that her wedding had been. That awful wedding and what had led to it was something she'd have been more surprised if she hadn't had a few wobbles over, especially as it wasn't even six months in the past as yet.

But in the last few weeks she'd hardly sniffled over that at all, not even when her hormones were doing their monthly worst to her. Indeed, looking back, she could now see that Jensen's appearance and awful behaviour had cauterized her wounds faster than anything, and since then she'd been even more settled here. So as she trudged back to her cottage, thankful that she'd already told Gary earlier that she felt the need to be in her own place tonight, half the problem was that she couldn't understand why she felt one sniff away from bawling her eyes out.

With his usual tact, Gary hadn't questioned her, and was keeping the dogs with him tonight, and Anna had never imagined she would be so grateful this soon for Harriet being the chef on duty tonight. Harriet's bedroom was on the other side of her lounge wall, and if she'd been there tonight, Anna would have felt it necessary to go into her own bedroom so that the chef wouldn't hear her sobs. But doing that also felt too much like being a teenager again, howling out her misery into her pillow so that her mother and father wouldn't hear.

"What the hell is the matter with me?" she hiccupped, going to pour herself a very large red wine from her new stash of supermarket specials. With virtually no bills to pay compared to her flat, being able to treat herself to a few bottles against the time – as she'd thought of it – when she might want to invite some friends over, had been a new luxury she'd not had before. Never had she thought she would be drowning her sorrows. Because she was smart enough to know that that was what she was about to do.

Sitting in her one and only armchair – because she had already been thinking of taking a few days to go south and get someone with a van to empty her flat and bring that furniture up here for her – she wished she'd got more than her MP3 player with her. Putting the stereo on and belting out some of the songs she loved always made her feel better. At which point she began to realise what it was. Back down south, she had seesawed between 'just getting by' and being utterly miserable. Whereas here she was actually *happy*, and happy in a way that she'd never known before, which was why she'd dared to be hopeful.

Moreover, Jensen had never invaded her work space. Oh, he'd come and met her from work – which was where the envy of some of her colleagues had come from – but he'd not actually *seen* her working. When it came to work, her world and Jensen's were a million miles apart and never connected. Which meant that it had been one aspect of her life that he'd had no hold over or connection to.

And now she realised that simple exhaustion had played a bigger part in her tearful episodes since their break up than she'd recognised. Working full time in a physically stressful environment was hard enough, but then for over six months she had been run ragged by Jensen and his family with the wedding preparations. When had she had a single weekend to de-stress in that frantic year, she now wondered, looking back? Then realised that the answer was never, meaning her frazzled state had been physical as well as mental.

In total contrast, Cameron *was* her work. He'd been part of it initially as a customer, and then afterwards as the owner of where she now worked. He had invaded that space which, even when Jensen had been at his worst, had never been invaded before – not even by her parents, because God forbid that they should interact in any way with mere supermarket staff! And somewhere along the line, the fact that Cameron had seen her being efficient and capable, and had appeared to respect her for it, had led her to believe that for once, here was a man of her own age who actually *saw* her, and liked what he saw.

In truth, that might still be the case, she told herself sternly as she went and topped up the large glass, rather surprised to see how far down the bottle of red she was already. *You can still be a manager he likes working with*, she mentally chided herself with. *Nothing's changed there. You were just a fool thinking that there was something more to it than that. Mark it down to you being on the rebound from what went on with Jensen. That would derail any woman, let alone someone like you who, let's face it, Anna, has trouble with relationships because you don't know what 'normal' really feels like, do you?*

You've hardly played the field. And that was fair enough when you were working with folks whose idea of a night out was going out and getting so legless, they didn't know how they'd got home, or who they'd slept with. But it means you've not got much experience to fall back on, have you? Nothing to compare to. So calm it down, woman! Flirt with him if he seems to want that, but don't be such an idiot as to pin all your hopes on him. Yet that didn't stop the tears from suddenly flowing again, and her finding herself truly sobbing once more.

So much so that she didn't notice the temperature drop until a voice that seemed to be more in her head than actually heard said, 'Don't fret child, you are safe here,' in a very old-fashioned and hard to understand accent.

Cuffing her eyes dry with her sweater sleeve, Anna looked up and gave a stunned squeak. Hovering in the middle of her lounge were three nuns. Or at least women who looked like they might be nuns in that they had something resembling a wimple on, and long, flowing garments that weren't fitted enough to be dresses.

"He*ee*…" she coughed, cleared her throat. Then tried again. "Hello. Who are you?"

The leading figure cocked her head on one side, bird-like, as if similarly struggling to understand Anna.

'This is ours,' she declared in that voice that wasn't a heard voice, then seemed to realise that something about the room no longer looked familiar. Frowning, she turned and said something to the other two, but Anna caught nothing of that, and then they disappeared.

"Bloody hell!" she gulped, taking a good swig of the wine, and then nearly choking on it.

When she'd stopped coughing enough for her eyes to stop watering, she looked up to see three totally different women in the room. Yes, they were still ghosts because they were transparent enough for Anna to see through them a hint of what was in the room behind. But these were what she would class as normal women, or they would be without the terrible marks around their throats and something which looked like burns on their faces and clothing. Also, she could now smell smoke, and a very unpleasant smell which she found she didn't want to think of the source of, given their burns.

"Oh my God! You're those poor women from the witch trial." she gasped, her own misery suddenly forgotten.

'My name be Margaret Clark,' came another mental voice, which seemed to come from the woman on the left. 'We can no' rest. Help us! Please!'

Chapter 19

Feeling faintly ridiculous holding a conversation with someone who had to have died over three hundred years ago, nonetheless Anna also felt a strong connection to these women. In a different time and place, her Aunty Rita could have been alongside them. Indeed, if what Rita had said about her having the same talents, then she herself could have been a suspect at the least.

"Did you die here?" she asked, trying to annunciate clearly so that they'd understand her.

"We died at the Tolbooth in Dumfries, but our remains were brought here," another said. "I be Agnes Clark," she nodded to the first speaker, "her sister."

"And I be Jannet Corsan," the third said, and something about the way she said her name made Anna think that it was closer to Jeanette rather than Janet, though she couldn't be sure. But it was the surname that made her start.

"Corsan?" she gasped. "But that's the name one of our male ghosts keeps shouting! That's not you or your husband, is it?" She had a horrible moment when she thought it might be this woman's son or husband who'd died here. Good grief! That could be a laying to rest to test even Rita's talents.

Yet the third ghost seemed to spit in fury. "He's none a' mine!" she snarled. "My faither's cousin. God rot him! Betrayed his ain fer money and greed!"

"Blimey!" Anna swallowed hard. No love lost there, then. Then felt her eyebrows going up even further as the Agnes ghost declared, "He kilt us all. Him and my man's wicked cousin, John McCartney. Kilt al' nine o' us on one day! Send him doon, lass! Send him doon to the De'il he serves to get his just rewards! Only then can we rest in peace." And they were gone, as if exhausted by the effort of reaching out enough to communicate with her.

Flopping back in her chair, Anna declared, "Well that rather puts my worries into perspective. At least none of the men in my life have tried to burn me at the stake!"

What on earth was she going to do about it, though?

Time for a call to Aunty Rita. Yet when she rang Rita's mobile it was engaged, and suddenly Anna had a vision of Gary calling Rita to tell her about what had been going on, and that, at least, made her smile. If her problems were getting Rita talking to Gary, she'd invest in more tissues and bear it, because both Rita and Gary were due some happiness, and together.

Suddenly exhausted by the day, she forced herself to drink a pint of water to make sure she didn't wake up headachy and dehydrated, then fell into bed, and if she dreamed of the ghosts, she didn't remember it in the morning. However, she did get up with a new resolve. Finding John Corsan's name in connection with those witch trials was the most solid lead she'd had up to now, and so she decided that she would pursue that.

She had to go in for the morning shift, meaning that, although there was a sniff of spring in the air by now, it was still pretty dark at six o'clock as she made the dash across to the hotel and opened up the front door. The workmen who had returned had booked an early breakfast and would be leaving by seven to get to their job, but the other guests weren't due down until closer to nine, which gave Anna a couple of hours before her shift properly started to do some online digging on her own laptop, which she'd taken across with her. Having the three women's names was a help, but she really had to focus and remember that back then a married woman kept her maiden name, while her children took their father's. So she couldn't simply look for a married couple called Corsan.

On the other hand, the woman called Agnes had said that her husband's cousin was called McCartney, so there was a chance that that might have been her husband's surname too. What she wasn't expecting to find as fast as she did, was another reference in the University of Edinburgh's database on Scottish witches where she'd first found John Corsan's name. And when she put Agnes Clark in there, she got an immediate hit. Moreover, there was an interactive map, which when she zoomed in on Dumfries, gave the cases which had come up there. The initial time-span was over a century and a half, but once she'd narrowed it down, she soon found Margaret Clark and Jannet Corsan, seeing that indeed it wasn't spelled 'Janet' in the old records.

"Good job I didn't go looking for 'Janet' first," she muttered, hurriedly making notes of what she'd found. "I'd have thought I was on the wrong track when I didn't find her."

But what really shocked her was delving into the files on each of the women, and seeing that they'd been partly damned by revelations by, and associations with, the other women who were being accused of being witches. And John Corsan's name was linked to some of them, too! Yet as she went from one to another and back again, she began to get a nasty feeling that she was looking at some perverse, seventeenth-century version of the playground game of Chinese Whispers. Half the time accusations going one way were mirrored by accusations going back the other, going round and round in circles.

"There's no bloody *proof!*" she declared in disgust, leaning back and drinking the coffee which had almost gone cold while she'd been so absorbed.

"Trying to find some Scottish ancestry?" Sally's voice came with a laugh as she walked over with her own coffee. She plonked herself down in the second chair on Anna's side of the desk. "Can't do anything until the couples in Thyme and Parsley check out," she said, "and the others only need a spruce up today."

With the workmen in the back run of rooms also on the same floor, Anna knew what she meant, so turned her laptop so that Sally could see.

"I'm still ghost hunting," she explained, "so I started looking for men with the name Corsan in the seventeenth century, because that's when Gary thinks the uniform and weapons date to." There was no way she was telling Sally that she'd been chatting to ghosts in her cottage the night before. That would be inviting comments to the effect of it being time she went and had a chat with the local GP.

Even so, Sally said, "You're taking this very seriously," in a worried tone of voice, as if wondering whether Anna was a bit obsessed.

"I don't think we can afford *not* to," Anna responded. "Remember the mess you and I had to clear up in Rosemary? Regardless of any personal beliefs, we can't keep having that happen." And being very careful to refer to Cameron formally, Sally and the others by now knowing who he was, added, "Mr

Wiseheart has some daft idea of marketing ghost hunting experiences," with a roll of her eyes. "But honestly, Sally, that could be disastrous."

"Why?"

"Reviews! How many times will folk post a negative review on Trip Advisor when the ghosts don't show? And how many times can that happen before the business starts taking a hit over it? It's one thing running a ghost walk around an old town, when you can have an accomplice ahead of you, blowing a bit of dry ice around to create a chill where you want it, or blowing some smoke. And if it all feels a bit phoney, folk will just have a giggle and move on for what you pay for something like that. But we'd be asking people to pay hundreds of pounds for it to be worth putting on a whole weekend of something like that, and that's when folk start wanting value for money."

"Which we couldn't guarantee giving them." Sally sighed in realisation and with a shake of her head. "You're right, Anna. It's not a good idea, is it?"

"No," Anna said firmly, and with her voice more disapproving than she'd intended, added, "Mr Wiseheart may be a very good marketing man, but he's never had to stand in front of irate, disappointed customers and try to calm them down. By then, he's hiding behind his desk cooking up his next campaign. After all, as long as he's delivered what his customer asked for, it's not his problem if what they wanted was a non-starter. But here, it is! Here, he's expecting us to protect his brother's investments, and I don't think he's appreciating the difference."

"I thought you quite liked him?"

Damn! That was a question Anna hadn't wanted her to ask, but she was saved from having to bluff her way through by Gary arriving with Harris and Lewis in tow.

"I did up until he just dumped those two on us and buggered off!" she said with feeling. "Gary and I worked out that they're not much more than pups, and I tell you, Sally, they've been really pining for bloody Wiseheart. I could slap him for that!"

That raised even a covert eyebrow from Gary at that, but luckily Sally getting up to go and start sorting out clean towels and bed-linen disrupted the conversation. Giving the two dogs a corner each off her breakfast croissant as their treat, Anna now told Gary about the witches and finding their records.

"It's beginning to look as if this Corsan chap is a right nasty piece of work," she ended with. "I know it's not a lot, but I think if we can at least try to track down who these women might have been married to, we might just find our other ghost."

"Well you'll have help wi' that," Gary said with a sly smile. "Rita's on her way down!"

"Good grief. That's fast!"

His smile broadened to a grin. "I mentioned yon lad's daft idea about promoting the ghosts, and that he almost certainly wouldn'a be here until after that big wedding in just over a week's time. That it might be better to see what we could do *before* then, both for the wedding guests' comfort, and while the coast's clear, so to speak."

"Gary, that's very crafty, and a damned good idea." Anna approved. "And hopefully our boss will do us the courtesy of letting us know when he's coming back, but if he doesn't, then without the lads, here, we can stick him into one of the smallest rooms like Clover or Rose, and he'll just have to suck it up."

"I thought you were really taken with him?" Gary was now looking concerned. "What's changed?"

"Oh, I still like him, and I'll have no problem working with him. It's just that I did some soul-searching last night before the witches turned up. I made myself face up to the fact that I got badly scorched less than six months ago, so it would be really stupid to go dashing into anything while my feelings are still all over the place."

She gestured to where Harris now had his nose proprietarily on her foot, and Lewis the same with the foot Gary had on the floor. "He's been wounded too, but it's making him careless of others. Even at my most emotionally battered, I couldn't have left these two behind. If it had meant strapping a couple of black bags of stuff onto the roof of my old car to make room for them inside, that's what I'd have done, even if that's not really approved of."

Taking in the way she immediately leaned over to fuss Harris, Gary realised he'd underestimated how easy it was to hurt Anna at the moment. She was transferring that hurt too. The dogs' obvious distress was feeding her own, but she was putting her own feelings of abandonment onto them as well, making him glad the Rita would be here by tonight. She was so much better than him at dealing with those sorts of emotions, and right now what Anna needed was a surrogate mum she could talk to. So when he went to collect Rita from the station, he was quick to fill her in on this new development.

"I think she's scared herself with how easy it was to be attracted to young Cameron," he said regretfully, "and he – silly sod – has done nothing to help that sudden jolt by buggering off and not even ringing to see how things are. That's why you're staying in my spare room, so that you'll be close at hand for private chats, not dodging customers in the hotel." He'd seen her out of the corner of his eye open her mouth to protest at the words 'spare room', and then snap it shut when he made Anna the reason.

Nicely played, Gary, he congratulated himself. *She couldn't argue with that one, could she?*

Anna was back on reception for the evening, so he took the truck straight around to the cottages, and let Rita put her bags in the bedroom before taking her outside.

He began on the front, pointing out where Harriet's cottage in the middle ran to, and where Anna's began, but then took her back through his kitchen and out into the yard.

"Verra smart of Anna to see that the tower doesn'a fit with a stable block," he said, having put his outside light on, and then going to the other blocks and putting theirs on so that Rita could fully see the layout in the gloomy late afternoon. "If I noticed it at all, I would've just put it down to being a bit o' a cobbled together building, because it was out o' sight o' the main house. Come and see the angel," and he led her inside, shining a torch up onto the stone angel.

"Gosh! She's a beaut'!" Rita exclaimed in approval. "Oh yes, you're both right, that doesn't belong in any sort of service building, stable or otherwise. That's a church angel, and no mistake."

"Anna gave me her keys so that you can go in and see what you make of the atmosphere in there," Gary said when he'd given Rita enough time to have a poke around in the store. He'd never picked up on anything in here, although that didn't mean she wouldn't, but she gave a little shake of her head in dismissal, and followed him out.

In Anna's cottage it was a different matter. As soon as they'd got out of the hallway, which Anna and Gary had guessed was part of the more recent, altered frontage, and into Anna's lounge and then across the hall to the spare bedroom, Rita gave a shiver, making Gary ask, "We were right to not put our new chef in here, then? Anna said that with this being the larger room, there was a danger that Harriet might use it in preference to the other one Anna's in."

Rita turned around to face him, eyes wide, and said, "Oh yes! I wouldn't want anyone unprepared to be in here. I don't find the atmosphere here as…I hesitate to use the word malevolent, but maybe 'confrontational' explains the main house better at times? This is less…aggressive. Very unhappy, though. Very! Even if you hadn't told me about the three nuns *and* the three witches on the way over, I would have guessed at several spirits here, not just one or two. Jings, Gary! You've found me quite a clean-up job to do here."

"Technically it wasn'a me but your niece," Gary responded with a chuckle. "I haven'a seen or heard a peep in all the time I've been here."

Expecting Rita to make some joke about him having the sensitivity of a plank, he was surprised to see her taking that seriously and frowning as she thought on it.

"Interesting," she murmured. "…Did you say something about Anna being upset when she came over here last night?"

"Aye. She told me she needed some time alone to think, and I could see that she was a bit teary, but I thought it was to do with her working through what that big tit Jensen did to her. She's had a few weepy moments just as you warned me, but she's kept them well hidden, and they've decreased rapidly since he came up and made such a spectacle of himself, which is why I wasn'a terribly worried about her. I thought she'd tell me in her own time as she's done before." He didn't want Rita thinking he'd gone all blokey on Anna and hidden away whenever tears were close.

That wasn't the line of her thinking, though. "Strong emotions again. Hmm…and I think it's significant that it's when *women* have them – or at least over here it is." She turned and gave Gary a squinty-eyed stare. "How's your PTSD been of late? No nightmares?"

"Err… No' like it used to be, no." Then he caught on to where she was going with this. "But, yes, I have had my share o' nightmares in the time I've been at the cottage. And no, I've never had as much as a peep out o' any ghost. So you're right, it's when a *woman* gets upset over here that it calls to those women in the past." He thought for a moment before saying, "In which case, I don't think revenge is the big thing, do you?"

Rita nodded approvingly. "Justice, almost certainly, but not blind revenge, no. There's not the hankering to do someone harm in the way those two male ghosts go at one another in the hotel. And that makes this space a bit safer for Anna. I wouldn't like to put a man into this cottage until we've calmed things down a bit, because I reckon those ladies in the past have had good reason to hate men, and they might be up for doing a bit of serious frightening. But if they were real witches, then they'd have known that what you hand out can rebound back on you rather nastily, even if back then, there wasn't always the full teaching of it coming back at you three times worse, as we believe nowadays."

"I won't be swapping places with Anna then, and letting her stop in my place wi' you," Gary said, quietly relieved that he had a good reason now not to let that happen, should Rita have been thinking of it. However much she shied away from it, she'd have to share his cottage with him while she was down here, and he knew she loved Anna dearly enough to not want to leave her to deal with this on her own.

"No," Rita agreed. "That wouldn't be a good idea." She wandered through into the other rooms, pausing when she got back to the bathroom. "This is next to the tower, isn't it?"

"Aye. Directly."

She nodded. "I could feel it straightaway. You probably don't get much haunting going on *in* here because of the frequent running water – spirits don't like that – but I can feel an atmosphere like an undertow in here. Not as strong as in the spare bedroom, but it's clearly running through from the other side of the wall. Can we go back outside and let me see the floor of next door?"

Letting her out of Anna's kitchen door as the fastest way, Gary went and unlocked the store, expecting Rita to follow him in, and turned to see her inspecting the doorway.

"These aren't original," she pronounced, gesturing to the large doors on either side. "They've gone in through the kirk's side walls to create them." Then walking inside, she took the torch off Gary and shone its beam over the walls of the tower, stopping at the western one. "Ah! See that arch in the brickwork? That would be the original west door to the monastic kirk. Probably only used on high days and if special guests came, but the main door nonetheless."

She turned to the opposite tower wall. "And there you are! The line of the archway into the nave. What a pity we seem to have lost the chancel arch when they remodelled for the cottages. Look at that keystone in the arch – you won't find anything as fine as that in anything medieval apart from a church, and I do think you've got a medieval monastery here in terms of the build, even if the ghosts are its last inhabitants time-wise."

Passing under the arch, she scuffed the old straw and dust out of the way. "Oh look, Gary! Aren't those *huge* flagstones! That's a very posh floor. Do you think we could clean it up tomorrow? Only if I have to do any summoning, I'd rather do it here than in Anna's spare room."

"I'll get the bass-brooms out," Gary sighed good-naturedly, foreseeing Rita doing a lot of this asking, but expecting him to do as he was told. Not that he minded. If it kept her here, he'd sweep as many floors as she wanted.

Chapter 20

With Anna taking the next day as her day off before a long weekend of being on duty, all three of them set to work clearing out the old nave to Rita's instructions, and by the end of the day it smelled strongly of the lavender floor cleaner Anna had bought and liberally used. The old flagstone floor positively gleamed in the stark electric strip-lights that had been installed, but now Rita wanted them switched off and the place only lit by candles. Gary had even moved all the stuff in store across to the nearest stable with Anna's help, and so the space now lay empty and revealed in its full glory.

"What a lovely old place this must have been," Anna sighed appreciatively, now that she could see where two old windows facing one another had been blocked up.

There were the remnants of the deep sills, if little else aside from the lines in the stonework, and it was on these that Rita set up some beeswax tapers, three on each. She then put a lone pillar candle almost by the western arch, one in the centre of the room, and another up by the wall to Anna's cottage, all in lanterns since they were on the floor where there were strong drafts.

"What a lovely scent," Anna commented as the wax warmed on them all, and began giving it off.

"Nutmeg, cinnamon, and cloves in the tapers," Rita told them, "but the pillar candles I had made for me with some myrrh and frankincense in." She gave a wink. "Always had a feeling I would need them one day."

"Are we doing *it* now, then?" Gary asked, slightly concerned that Rita was jumping in feet first.

"If you mean, am I going full bell, book, and candle on you today? Then, no. But I do want to get a feel of what I'm dealing with. And I want to give those women who came to Anna a sense that they are being taken seriously at last, if for no other reason than I don't want them pestering her if they fear she's ignoring them, as everyone else down the years must have done."

And Rita was nothing if not thorough in her preparations. She had brought a small sprayer with her, and had prepared holy water by saying the Lord's Prayer three times over fresh spring water she had brought from home, which she then anointed the door frames with, getting Anna and Gary to repeat the prayer along with her over and over as she did it.

"You can't be too careful," she told him sternly when he looked slightly askance at her. "That's the way people get into trouble. Not every spirit is kindly or in need of help. Some want to come in on spiritual smash-and-grab raids, and trust me, I've had to clean up after enough of those to not want to be dealing with one here."

At least Anna was prepared for this, having seen Rita do this once before – though only the once – but for Gary it revealed a side of Rita he hadn't really understood until now. And he had to take it seriously because she and Anna were, but his slightly startled looks every so often told Anna that in one way Rita had been right – Gary wasn't fully prepared for what living with her might be like. But she also could tell that Rita had been very wrong if she thought that it would send Gary running for the hills. Gary was made of sterner stuff, and just because he wasn't familiar with all of this didn't make him scared of it.

When she was satisfied that all was ready, Rita gestured for them to bring three of the stored ancient dining chairs into the centre of the nave space, and sit on them in what might pass for a circle around the central candle.

"No insult meant to you, Gary," she began, "but I'd have preferred to be doing this with three women in deference to the women we're going to try and contact. But you here willingly, is better than another woman dragged here and not wanting to be, and the significance of three as a number hasn't been lost on me. Three nuns' ghosts. Three witches manifesting. So there'll be three of us. Someone is trying to tell us something. Let's go along with it, eh?"

With Rita leading, she took them into a semi-meditative state, instructing them in how to set up their own personal protection. Then when she was sure they were as prepared as they could be, she called upon the Goddess, higher beings (by which she meant angels or something of that ilk, or even the fae), and their own higher selves – something Anna had a vague grasp of but which meant nothing to Gary as yet. And now wasn't the time to start asking, because even he had started to feel the drop in temperature, and was glad that the one nod to the modern that Rita had insisted on was that they bring over and switch on a small fan heater, blasting warm air at their feet and rising around them. Sitting here in what was to all intents a medieval church in very early spring, with a frost coming on as the afternoon waned, was a chilly experience all by itself, let alone the chill of the portal opening to somewhere else.

"We're here to *try* and help," Rita began with as she invited those who had appeared before to come through, and Anna noticed her emphasis on the 'try'. Rita was making no wild promises she might not be able to keep.

Almost as if they had been queuing up on the 'other side', Anna was shocked to see many more women than she'd expected were gradually filing 'through' what appeared to be some kind of gateway, however ethereal it seemed from where she was sitting. Not quite fully 'here', it was definitely still a spirit-way towards them. First through were several nuns, though she didn't quite get to count them, followed by several women with the tell-tale scorched appearance and damaged throats – some hazier than others – plus a couple of others whose place in all of this she couldn't guess as yet.

"Can I ask who has been here the longest?" Rita began, obviously making sure that she took control of the situation.

"We have," said a woman with a wimple, and wearing what looked to be a lovely handcrafted crucifix, even if it wasn't dripping with gems and gold, and with two others like her gliding forward to appear fully in their vision. "We died here at the hands of wicked men who claimed to be from the church in Rome."

Anna saw Rita start at this, then she said, "Much as I sympathise with how dreadful that must have been, Sister, I don't think we'll be able to do much to help *you*."

Yet the elderly nun was already shaking her head before Rita had finished.

"We do not come here for ourselves," she said with the assurance of one who knew how this would work. "We are here merely to watch over our poor sisters, women wrongly murdered," and she gestured to the women not dressed as she was.

"And was that long before these other women died?" Rita asked, Anna guessing that she was trying to work out just how closely they might be connected. Had they even known one another?

"The last of our sisters passed over in the rebellion against Queen Mary," the leading nun said, which the modern listeners could only assume was Mary Queen of Scots. "They presumed that because we remained Catholics, we were complicit in plots to unit Scotland wi' France. We weren't, but we died anyway."

Rita took an audible deep breath. "That's tragic, but am I right in thinking that you died over a century before these women who died as witches?" For which she got a nod. "Very well, then, who are you others?"

To their surprise it wasn't one of those who had clearly been murdered who came forward first. Instead, it was a woman with greying hair and a face long-etched with worries, dressed in woollen homespun.

"I be Jonet Clark," she said, her distress rolling off her in psychic clouds. "My dear man was Johnny Allen. I lost all three o' my girls thanks to those wicked men. My eldest was got on me by an evil Presbyter named Veitch, who then told her she was his and turned her against Johnny, who was a good, good man. She drove Mailie, my middle girl away, and I lost track of my dear Elspeth and Johnny when I passed. T'was so sudden, you see? Such a shock?

"By the time I knew what had happened, she was gone. She's no' deid here. I canna feel her near here. Nor him. But where are they? Where did they die that

I canna feel them? I canna rest until I know Elspeth didn'a die as I did."

"So who are we looking for," Anna dared to ask. "Elspeth Clark or Elspeth Allen?"

She saw the spirits looking a bit askance, as if it ought to have been obvious, but nonetheless Jonet answered, "Elspeth Allen."

"I'll look on the compu…in our records, I promise," Anna told her. "I'll do my best, though I can't guarantee that I'll find her."

"I thank ye' fer trying," Jonet said sadly. "Nabody else has even done that."

"Who is next?" Rita called, and one with a very blackened face came forward who Anna recognised as one of those who'd appeared to her.

"I be Margaret Clark," the woman announced in an angry tone. "I was nay witch. None of us were! But my aunt here," and she gestured to Jonet, "who was my father Robert Clark's sister, and my own sister." She indicting another who Anna also recognised. "She did less than any o' us! My ma and I," a slightly hazier figure slid up to beside her, "stood accused o' *healing* in Kirkcudbright. Healing, ye' understand, no' *cursing*! No' *flyting*, like Jannet."

It was a good job that Anna's ear had become more tuned in to the local accent over the months, and she recognised the name of the little fishing town on the south coast of Dumfriesshire which gave out onto the Solway Firth.

"Yet you died in Dumfries?" she queried. And seeing Margaret's scowl at the question, she hurriedly added, "I only ask so that I can find you in the records. I… We… thought you must all be living in Dumfries, you see."

Another figure glided in between Margaret and the three – the third woman Anna had had appear to her before. "Easy, Margaret," she cautioned. "These folk dinna know us fra' Adam. Ye' have to allow them to know who we are. How else can they help us?"

The one called Margaret gave an impatient snort, but waved the newcomer to carry on.

"*I* be Jannet Corsan," she began in a more reasonable tone. "I fear we have confused ye'."

"Just a wee tad," Rita answered with a smile. "So before we start writing down each of your stories, can you tell us please, are any of you related or connected to the men who haunt the tower across the way?"

There was another impatient huff and a ghostly mutter of, "Why worry about them!" from Margaret.

But Jannet moved a little further forward and told them, "We canna reach across there anymore, ye' understand? But we feel them. The connection was broken when the nunnery was broken up, and that was before either o' those men died, though 'twas after us. Our remains were brought here, ye' see, though not out of any deference."

She looked sadly back to the nuns. "Evil men brought our burned and broken remains here, and threw them into the crypt, cursing us but also the souls of the nuns, who they saw as whores of the Catholic Church." She tutted, and even in her hazy state Anna and Rita could see the glisten of ghostly tears in her eyes. "Such a wicked thing to accuse good women o' being. But that is how we come to be tied to here, and to them."

She seemed to take a deep breath even though she had no need of it. "One o' those men who haunt the other side is my son." At that even Gary joined Anna and Rita in gasping.

"Your *son*?" Rita checked.

"Aye. A good lad as ever there was, and heartbroken by what happened to me, and then what was inflicted on the women he loved," Jannet explained. "He hates the other for being John Corsan's son, and for never lifting a finger to help. John Corsan's faither was my faither's cousin, y'ken. And my faither, William, married Grissell McCartney, my mither.

"Yet together, John Corsan and John McCartney plotted and schemed to get their hands on our various crofts – taking the crofts o' their ain kin, ye' understand? – to make themselves richer, and bigger men in our community." And there was another tut and a shake of her head in disgust. "So much effort for something that wouldn'a last."

Frantically scribbling all this down in the notebook she'd had at the ready, Anna thought to ask, "Did this John Corsan have only the one son?" It got her a nod of approval from Rita, for if she was going to try and put these ghosts to rest, it would be all the harder if she was calling the other male ghost by a name not his own.

The more reasonable of the two sisters, Agnes, came forward to beside Jannet to answer, "He and his poor beaten wife had four sons, but only three grew to be men. Damn him, he scarce looked at his two daughters, 'twas all the boys. The youngest, John, was a wild thing but foolish. He died younger than he might, but having done nothing compared to his brothers. Matthew, the middle surviving one, we saw return after our deaths, and a zealot and a fanatic he was! He was martyred for his faith, if that's what you can call such a twisted thing as his was. But the oldest was Gideon, and Jannet and I think 'tis he who fights down the years with dear Hugh. Ever Gideon is trying to reach us over here, though we know not why, and ever Hugh fights him to defend us from his ghost as he did in life."

"Feck!" muttered Gary in shock. "Well that explains the acrimony between them. Hugh doesn'a want to move on in case his ancient enemy finally succeeds in getting to his ma. And the Corsan lad has some twisted hatred of women in general by the sound o' it."

"Gideon was no lad," Agnes cautioned him. "He was a man full grown by the time he died, as was Hugh. And his hatred we believe was not so much for *all* women, as any woman who didn'a behave as the Covenant said we ought."

"Gideon Corsan was an evil cur who laughed as we burned!" the ghost they recognised as Margaret Clark hissed. "*Laughed*! And him not fully yet a man back then, yet so warped and twisted as a lad as to think a burning nothing more than an afternoon's entertainment for him and those wicked men like him."

"Ach, Margaret," her sister Agnes remonstrated. "What chance did he have wi' a faither like John Corsan? That swine could ha' warped a saint, the way he treated Gideon as a lad."

Margaret glared back, her stare none the weaker for being ghostly. "Aye, sister, but some men bluidy grow up! He didn'a, did he? We felt him, did we no'? Back when those other lassies passed over in such torment. He was there."

"Excuse me," Anna said faintly, hoping that they wouldn't take exception at her, especially if she was going to have them literally next door to her, and maybe even, heaven help her, in her spare room or lounge. "But what lassies are you talking about? Could you give us some clues, please? We're over three hundred years on from you, and there aren't many records left anymore. We need all the help you can give us."

The impatient Margaret just tutted and seemed to wander away a little, but the leading nun came closer again to stand beside Agnes and Jannet.

"We give thanks for God's mercy, for we have felt very few die in such terror over the years since then," she began. "Many in pain, but almost all through sickness, not torture. But back closer to when these nine joined us we felt three women die. Not here. But not that far away either. And the man Gideon's presence was felt there as well, as was Hugh's but in a very different way. They were what alerted us, but such terror in death echoes where we are now, if you understand me?"

"I do," Rita said instantly. "Beyond the veil the connections are more intense, or at least they are when someone dies a violent death. I've come across this in other places, you see. Such strong emotions at the time of passing leave a heavy imprint on time. Far more than a normal passing at the end of a life, even if it hasn't been particularly well spent.

"So we're probably looking for three women who died within a few decades of your time in this world, and most likely closer than that. In our time, Dumfries and Galloway is hardly such a hotbed of violent crime that we have many instances to choose from, and three together is going to stand out – especially if one of your sons was there. That really cuts down the time-frame. You did mean that all three passed at the very same time, didn't you?"

Anna knew that she was clarifying this partly for her and Gary's understanding, as well as getting more information from the ghosts.

"Oh yes!" the leading nun confirmed immediately. "They all died together, or as close as made little difference down the years. Certainly on the same day. And strangely, I and my own sisters do believe that the one called Gideon had strong feelings for one of those." She and those in the present felt Margaret give a huff of exasperation and storm off into the 'other' place, along with what looked like four others, but Agnes and Jonet, along with a couple of the others remained.

"That's divisive amongst you," Rita said perceptively.

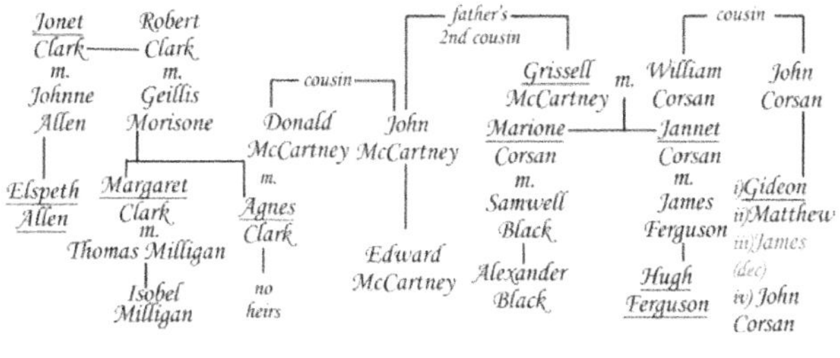

"Aye," sighed Agnes. "Understandable fer Jannet when she's Hugh's ma. And her sister Marione had to flee wi' her family." She saw Anna frantically writing and seemed to understand that she would need to make things plainer for them. "Jannet's sister was Marione Corsan, and Marione married Samwell Black, and her surviving child was Alexander. Alexander Black, if ye' are looking for him in records. And their mither was Grissell McCartney, whose faither was a cousin to God-curse-him John McCartney, who caused their deaths." She gestured to one of the lingering ghosts who was more indistinct but still very much a presence.

"But Grissell was married to William Corsan, and *he* was first cousin to dreadful John Corsan, making Grissell John Corsan's cousin by marriage, and William young Gideon's uncle. That's what makes this so painful for us. John Corsan kilt his ain cousins! And he made his son, Gideon, part o' that, even though Gideon was no' a grown man yet. That's why they canna forgive or forget.

"My ain man Donald's cousin was John McCartney, who wouldn'a wait to get his hands on our croft when my Donald died. Those two Johns were in league wi' one another, no doubt about it. But what cuts fer my sister Margaret is that unlike our Aunt Jonet, whose man Johnny Allen stood by her through thick and thin, Margaret's man threw her to the wolves. It's why I can forgive John McCartney's son Edward for being forced into our croft, which he never wanted himself, and Margaret's sons fer not aiding her when they had a wicked brute like Thomas Milligan fer a faither. But Margaret canna even forgive her ain sons fer standing by and watching her burn."

She turned and waved a ghostly hand to the other woman still waiting who, like Grissell, was faint but definitely there. "And our ma, Geillis – who married our pa who was Jonet Clark's brother, and is how Jonet is our aunt by marriage – canna forgive what happened to our Margaret and her brother's wife who she loved like her ain sister. And like my sister and Ma, Jannet's ma – Grissell McCartney – canna forgive what John Corsan did to *her* daughter Jannet, nor his son fer standing by him while he did it. It means the three o' them dinna want to recognise that there's pain on Gideon's side too."

"Agnes speaks the truth," the leading nun agreed. "The one called Gideon is as angry as Hugh, and although Hugh's is the purer grief – for he thinks only of others – in the other one there is still something which is crying out on someone else's behalf. I cannot tell you who, but he surely grieves for someone he lost too, even if it is as much for his own loss as hers."

"Gosh, that's a lot to unravel!" Anna said, still scribbling furiously in her notebook to try and make sure she got as much as she could written down so that it wouldn't be forgotten later on.

Yet Gary threw in one last, but perceptive, question. "Were both Hugh and this Gideon soldiers?"

"Does that matter?" the nun asked, bemused, only for Gary to reply,

"In my world, yes it does. I'm a former soldier myself, and I understand the huge difference between what I had to do under orders, and what I might have done of my own accord – and believe me, the two do not even come close to joining up!"

That seemed to give the ghosts pause for thought, but it was Agnes who finally gave Gary the answer of, "I believe that Hugh became a soldier after his ma's death. We feel his desire to protect the weak. To stand up for those who canna do it themselves."

"But no' for Gideon?" Gary double-checked and got several ghostly shakes of their heads.

"So I'm going to be looking for Hugh Corsan and Gideon Corsan," Anna asked, taking her cue from Gary.

But was shocked when Agnes immediately cried. "Oh no! No!"

"Who isn't…?" Anna asked, pen poised to write the answer.

"Gideon is John Corsan's son, so yes, he is a Corsan," Agnes said, still seeming a bit surprised that they couldn't work this out for themselves. "But *Hugh* is James *Ferguson*'s son."

"Oh! Of course." Rita exclaimed. "His mother may be a Corsan, but he would have his father's name."

And at the same time Anna gasped, "The same name as the Covenanter on the tomb!"

"No! *No*!" came Jannet's cry as she shot forwards again, her ghostly form almost on top of Anna. "Never say that! My Hugh hated and still hates everything that the bluidy Covenant ever stood for!"

Holding her hands up in surrender, Anna gulped, "I meant no offence. …It's just that that's what it says on a tomb …well something like a tomb, anyway, that's in the grounds here. It's on the inscription, not what I believe."

Placated, the ghost of Jannet faded away, and feeling that they'd all had about as much as they could cope with for one afternoon, Rita promptly set about closing the circle down. When she was sure that everything was secure, they blew out the candles and repaired to Gary's for a stiff whisky each.

"Well, that was an eye-opener and no mistake," Gary said, taking a goodly swig of his Laphroaig, and Anna had the feeling that he wasn't just talking about the ghosts' revelations, but discovering just what Rita could do, too. Luckily Rita was staring into the flames of his wood-burner, deep in her own thoughts, and didn't see his slightly sideways glances her way.

"It was, wasn't it?" Anna agreed hastily, wanting to keep the conversation on the ghosts until Gary had

had chance to process how he felt about Rita's hitherto hidden talents. "I must admit it was a shock to realise that the one ghost is Hugh Ferguson, though I'm kicking myself for not having made that connection sooner."

And before Rita could blink and fully turn to her to speak, she ploughed on with, "I think I vaguely thought something like that, but then wondered how on earth we'd know which ghost he was, if you get my meaning? Seemed to be taking a bit of a chance to say, 'Are you Hugh?' when one or other showed up, in case we got the wrong one, and just made everything worse."

"Yes," Rita instantly agreed. "You were right to think like that. If these two men have been adversaries for more than three hundred years, the last thing you want is for one of them to think that you are on the other's side. Good grief! Who knows what mayhem might ensue if that was to happen."

"But at least we have two names to work with now," Anna said, trying to sound optimistic, but knowing that in truth she'd not come across either name in the searches she'd done so far. And unless they could find out exactly why these two ghosts wouldn't leave without the other going too, she knew that she'd be juggling room bookings on into the summer. Meanwhile, it didn't bode well for any bride and groom sharing the Rosemary suite, because how could they possibly know which ghost might turn up, or if they would take offence at the nuptials going on there?

1679

Hugh & Gideon

In February the order finally came for the Highlanders to return home, primarily because the logistics of keeping all these men on during the winter was proving too much of a strain on the locals. It meant that the Host had got as far as Glasgow without Hugh finding a way to disentangle himself from the army, when he was called to Captain Campbell, and told that he was needed to ride with a message for John Graham of Claverhouse. Hugh never did realise that he had been skilfully manoeuvred by Archie McAllister, who was determined to keep his father's foster-son (as Hugh had become in the family's eyes) from making a dreadful mistake, and possibly even finding himself on trial for murder. Archie was all sympathy for what Hugh had been through, but he had enough distance from the matter to know that slitting the culprits' throats would solve nothing, and rather more importantly to his mind, would do nothing to assuage Hugh's lingering grief.

Therefore, while Edward and Isobel were subtly shifted forwards to amongst the first of the army's hangers-on heading for home, he managed to get Hugh sent in a different direction in a way that it would be hard for him to refuse. Moreover, within the longer letter sent from the Earl of Nithsdale to Graham of Claverhouse – now the recently appointed sheriff of Kirkcudbrightshire, and therefore a neighbour and fellow upholder of the peace in the shire to Earl Maxwell – there was a small note from Captain Campbell asking him to make use of this messenger, 'for his family has suffered greatly at the hands of men in this shire, and I would not have him ruin his life in taking revenge. He is a good and trustworthy man, and I trust to your good judgement when it might suit to send him back to us in Argyll.' That Hugh would never again see Argyll was something that Archie and Captain Campbell could never have anticipated.

It meant that as Hugh rode to intercept Claverhouse riding south out of Glasgow, he had no idea that his archenemy in the form of Gideon Corsan was also heading for the same place. In Gideon's case, he had finally seen a way to at least temporarily escape the clutches of his father, for old John Corsan had suddenly developed a burning desire to see his second son, Matthew. It wasn't a loving, parental longing to see his beloved son before he finally died, but rather because he believed that he could demand of Matthew that, as a man of God, he would in some way absolve him of his many sins before it was too late. Why Veitch wouldn't do, Gideon could only put down to his father knowing that Veitch's soul was as black as his own, and that any absolution granted by him wasn't worth having.

"You must fetch Matthew home to me!" the old man had slurred shrilly through his dragged down, one-sided face at Gideon.

And while Gideon knew full well that what the old tyrant meant was to send a messenger, or at most a servant, given that it had been said in the presence of Presbyter Veitch and Thomas McBurney, Gideon suddenly realised that he could wilfully misinterpret it as he himself being sent to get his brother. Those two would repeat the old man's words verbatim if questioned by others, meaning that it was Gideon's escape route.

"Thank you, God," he repeated over and over, as he threw a hastily packed saddlebag onto his horse, and then cantered out of the yard with as much speed as he dared subject his horse to, before his father could send someone out to summon him back.

Finding Matthew would, he hoped, take a goodly while, and so he was taken aback to run into a party of men heading out of St Andrews at speed, and to find his brother amongst them. Worse, there was a fanatical gleam in his brothers' eyes that Gideon recognised all too well from their father.

"We did it!" Matthew exalted, clasping his hands together as if in prayer, and yet shaking them heavenward as if brandishing them in triumph.

"What?" asked Gideon, feeling his heart sinking into his boots.

"Archbishop Sharp is no more." Matthew announced with nothing short of glee.

"No more? Oh Matthew, you mean he's *dead*?"

His brother turned on him in genuine horror. "Don't tell me you support the priests? Those men who would foist *bishops* onto us?"

And for the first time, Gideon stopped to wonder what it was that he *did* believe in. In truth, he wasn't that keen on the idea of some lordly bishop telling an ordinary man like him how to say his prayers, but equally he wasn't so appalled by the notion that he would kill for it. But clearly Matthew would!

"No, no." he managed to bluster, grateful of the growing dusk which masked his own horrified expression from his brother's gimlet stare. "I'm…I'm just shocked that *you* would think to do such a thing. You always upbraided me so when we were children for fighting…" He left that dangling to be seized upon in a wholly different way.

"But this is fighting for *God*." Matthew cut in before he could say more, sending a shiver of worry down Gideon's spine, but at the same time a feeling of relief that Matthew didn't seem to want to question him further. As Matthew marched, continuously praying his thanks aloud if softly, Gideon walked a pace or two behind and to the side of him – leading his horse which had now become the small company's baggage pony – and offering up very different kinds of prayers.

Lord, why did you send me into a family filled with fanatics? he asked, distraught. *Why does this always keep happening to me? I thought I'd finally got away from my dreadful father, and it turns out that this brother of mine could have been made from his rib just as you did with Adam, he's that much of a copy of him. So just when I think I'm getting away from Dumfries, and all those accusing looks – thanks to bloody Hugh Ferguson coming back and dragging up everyone's bad memories again – I find myself in with a bunch of men, of whom at least one and possibly more, are murderers! Why, Lord? Why? What did I ever do to so offend you?*

Utterly lost as to which way they were heading in the first place, by the time he had been on the road with them for a week, Gideon also knew that alone he'd never find his way home. For good or bad, he was stuck with them unless he wanted to risk travelling alone – and Gideon belatedly realised during that time, that he was far from being the man of the world he'd once thought he was. Travelling a well-used road in the company of others was one thing, striking out across country to who knew where was quite another, and one he was totally unprepared for.

At Rutherglen, south of Glasgow, they met with a larger party of Covenanter rebels, and to Gideon's intense relief he discovered that the party that he and Matthew were in were merely following the actual murderers, who had already raised a large force whom they were now joining. Matthew might not have made the distinction between those who had wanted Archbishop Sharp dead, and the one or two men who had actually done the deed, but Gideon belatedly remembered how the women who had died in Dumfries had been condemned as much by association as by anything they had done. And he had no desire to end up being hanged as a traitor if his brother got accused, and dragged him down with him.

Given that it had taken him all his time to work out who had secret deals with whom at a local level, Gideon had paid no mind at all to national politics. So he hadn't the faintest idea whether or not Archbishop Sharp had been another truly evil man of God, like Veitch, or the real thing and totally undeserving of such a cruel fate. Yet now his entire focus was on making sure that he didn't end up accused as an accessory to his murder.

Therefore, as the Covenanter force he was with confronted Graham of Claverhouse's force at a tiny place called Drumclog, he allowed himself to become separated from his brother in the mêlée. Please God he might now find someone who wanted to head south, and let him make a run for it with them. Yet God or fate – and by now he was past making the distinction in his distress – had other plans. Led by the minor laird's son, Robert Hamilton, and the zealot graduate from St Andrews, William Cleland, the Covenanter men had completely baffled Claverhouse, who was used to set-piece battles, and not fighting an angry mob of over two hundred men, some armed with nothing but pitchforks, who never did what he anticipated them doing. A full battle had commenced, and it wasn't going the way Gideon expected at all, for the soldiers weren't getting the upper hand.

Swept up in the mob frenzy, all Gideon could do was keep jabbing the half-rusted sword his brother had thrust into his hand towards the next man to appear in front of him. In truth, he doubted he gave anyone more than a scratch. He just wasn't that competent with a blade. Neither were the men on either side of him, as best he could tell, and yet against the odds they seemed to be breaking the soldiers' lines.

I hate you all! he thought, as he sobbed and stabbed his way forward. *Why me? What did I do to so offend God that I deserved this? …I honoured my father and mother, even when he didn't deserve it. I may have coveted Isobel, but she wasn't any man's wife by that time. I've never killed until now. …And I surely haven't possessed enough of anything to be culpable of the sins of greed or of gluttony! Why, God? Why?*

And then in the briefest of windows through the carnage he saw him.

Bloody Hugh Ferguson!

If his own father had created the wounds that had ensured that Gideon had never had a normal coming into manhood, able to at least *try* to court any girl he was interested in, Hugh Ferguson had been the most recent blight on his life. Hugh, who had all the sympathy of the people in the neighbourhood, even though his loud-mouthed witch of a mother had been the instrument of her own downfall. Hugh, who had reappeared just as Gideon had settled into something resembling being a respectable widower, his father's sins no longer hanging quite so heavily around *his* neck. Hugh, whose very presence had dragged up all those hitherto half-forgotten memories amongst their neighbours of the witches burning in front of the Tolbooth in Dumfries, while his father and John McCartney sat watching, smug as two cats that had got the cream. Gideon really hated Hugh Ferguson!

For Hugh, the moment his eye caught Gideon's was a shock. What, by all that was holy, was bloody Corsan doing here? Hugh had never had him down as having the backbone or balls to do his own fighting, yet there he was, screaming blue murder like the rest of the rabble, and with a sword as bloodied as Hugh's own.

Then to Hugh's horror, he saw Claverhouse's horse impaled with a pitchfork and in its pain, get the bit between its teeth and bolt from the battlefield. With their leader gone, the last of the soldiers holding to any formation folded, and as they saw the Covenanters shooting men who had tried to claim quarter, the sergeant leading Hugh's small patrol made a decision.

"Run, lads!" he bellowed. "Run for your lives! These bastard-God-fearing men will slaughter you like lambs, else."

Whereupon Hugh found his free arm being grasped by Big Tavish – a lone Highlander amongst them whom he'd made friends with – and being hauled bodily out of the fray. Tavish was a huge lad, almost half Hugh's age but making nearly two of him in bulk, and so when Tavish wanted him to move, Hugh got moved whether he wanted to or not. Yet he couldn't stop looking over his shoulder to where Corsan was, and saw his enemy was as furious as he was to be deprived of the chance to fight.

When they stopped for the night, huddled within a copse of stunted hawthorns, the rest of the men who'd made it out with Hugh were all for rejoining the rest of the force, or at least what was left of it.

"Don't worry, Hugh," Tavish said with a wink. "You'll get your chance to gut that far-too-holy swine soon enough. He was still standing when we left, so he'll be in the thick of it when we catch up with them again. And next time we'll be ready for their tricks. Claverhouse learned his soldiering in places like Holland, all nice and neat like toy soldiers. Next time he'll learn to fight like a Highlander, and then the bloody Covenanters will feel our steel!"

"He needs to," Hugh growled. "I may not be able to make Corsan's father and McCartney pay for what they did to my family, and to Elspeth and Isobel, but I can surely make sure Gideon does."

In the end, Hugh, and those with him, managed to rejoin Claverhouse's main troop in time for the next confrontation at Bothwell Bridge on the upper reaches of the Clyde, some three weeks later. And as Tavish had said, Claverhouse wasn't a man to make the same mistake twice, but in this instance the overall leader of the army was the infinitely more powerful and experienced Duke of Monmouth. The oldest illegitimate son of Charles II, Monmouth had recently married the Buccleuch heiress, Anne Scott, and having taken her name as well as her lands, as Duke of

Buccleuch as well as Monmouth, he had a vested interest in returning the Lowlands to law-abiding peacefulness.

One look at the well-disciplined force waiting for them this time, and the moderates within the Covenanters knew that they were going to take a beating, even though they had the advantage of numbers. Yet when they tried to treat with Monmouth, he refused to talk unless they laid down their arms first – something the radicals in their midst would never do.

"Told you we'd get them," Tavish said with relish, as he and Hugh watched the eight hundred dragoons who were with them now, storming the bridge. "We're just here to do the mopping up."

The dragoons were part of a force of nearly five thousand strong, but in terms of numbers, the Covenanters outnumbered them by an extra thousand, or so Hugh learned later. Yet all of Monmouth's troops had been drilled and trained, if not all were that experienced. By contrast, the Covenanters were a rolling mob of men and lads spoiling for a fight, but with no training or discipline at all. Worse, amongst them were those who had had their first taste of battle at Drumclog, meaning they were either soiling themselves in terror at the thought of going into a mêlée again, or overconfident of what they could achieve and egging others on with impossible expectations. Hugh and Tavish could see several of the former already edging their way to the sides of their force.

"Those bastards are going to run," Tavish observed. "They've no stomach for another fight."

"But will Corsan stay and be in the thick of it?"

Hugh fretted. "He seemed pretty committed to the fight when I saw him."

Yet Tavish shook his tangle of flame-red hair, or what he hadn't sheared off at the sides to prevent it from getting in his eyes in preparation for the fight to come, giving him the appearance of a wild beast with its hackles up.

"Aach, no!" he said with conviction. "You said he was a follower, a bully who hung on to yon other man you hate?"

"Yes, Thomas McBurney."

"Well, bullies don't stand and fight, come what may. They only get their dirks bloody when they *know* they can win and not get hurt. Do you see that happening here? …No. So your man will turn tail and run like the coward he is. All we've got to do is make sure that we're amongst the men our captain or the Duke sends to hunt them down."

And Hugh realised that Tavish was right. All the emotions at seeing Corsan had overwhelmed everything he'd learned at Sorley McAllister's hand and then later. These days he was an experienced soldier. Corsan wasn't. Riding roughshod over grieving older men, and young women and children was one thing, going hand-to-hand with a man who could hold his own against other trained soldiers would be quite another. And so like two hounds with the scent of the hare in their noses, Hugh and Tavish edged to where they could see the edge of the Covenanter line on their side. If Corsan was on the other edge, that would be annoying, but at least here they could see him when or if he ran their way.

When all hell broke loose, at first they thought they'd missed him. After all, he was just one amongst thousands. But as their comrades began herding what would become over a thousand prisoners together, and fragmented groups of other men began to flee, it was easier to see individuals. The young lads who weren't even old enough to grow a beard, the soldiers let go, focusing on those men who still held onto something that looked like a proper weapon, whether a sword or pike. Those were more likely to be ringleaders of what were probably local uprisings, and worth questioning by those in charge.

And so Hugh and Tavish had just finished chasing, and then hog-tying, three men who looked halfway competent with their weapons, when they saw another group dodging in and out of the copses of oaks, alders, and hazels along the upper Clyde's bank. Several other groups had headed that way already, and now Hugh realised that there must be a small stream over there, whose course was offering a low-lying escape route.

"Over there!" he called to Tavish and another companion called Murray, thrusting the rope for his prisoner into the hands of a man called Gow.

"Get these to the captain," he yelled at Gow, who yanked hard on the rope, tying one prisoner to another to avoid any one of them making a run for it. And it was as Hugh, Tavish, and Murray began sprinting towards the burn that he saw Corsan. He wasn't at the front, but he wasn't the last of them, either.

"He's with them." Hugh called to Tavish as he increased his speed, but Corsan must have heard him now that the noise of the fighting had dimmed down, and they were more distant from the main bodies of men.

With a look of horror, Corsan spotted Hugh pounding towards him, then registered that Hugh not only had a sword, but also a musket slung over his shoulder. A musket that when he got a decent long line of sight on Corsan, he stopped to load. And Gideon was shocked to see how fast Hugh could load the damned thing.

As Hugh brought the musket up to his shoulder and fired, Gideon dived for the water of the burn, not that it was deep enough to cover him fully, let alone swim in. Even so, he felt the musket ball clip the shoulder of his heavy coat, driving him face down into the flow.

Alongside Hugh, Tavish and Murray also fired their muskets, Tavish hitting another of those running square in the back, and dropping him straight on top of Corsan. Yet before they could pursue the others or check on their kills, from behind came the bawled order of their sergeant to come back and fall in line. A larger hunt for fugitives was taking place, and Hugh had no choice but to obey or be assumed to be deserting the field himself, for with little in the way of proper uniforms to spare, from a distance he might easily be mistaken for one of the other side's.

Swearing furiously under his breath, Hugh joined Tavish and Murray in trudging back to their line.

"Ach, dinna fret," Tavish said amiably as they sat by their camp fire that night. "Did ye' see the size o' that one I dropped on top of him? Even if yer shot didn'a kill him, the bastard will have drowned when he couldn'a get his head oot o' the water. Ye' did it, Hugh. Ye' got your revenge on one o' them."

1679

Gideon & Hugh

For Gideon, the plunge into the stream saved his life. It was midsummer, and the water of the burn was far from icy cold. Indeed, having been sweating profusely as he ran, at first its cooling effect was welcome, and at least he was able to assuage his terrible thirst. Who knew that the smoke from so many muskets could dry your mouth to parchment? Having the other man fall on top of him momentarily panicked him, but then he realised that two large stones in the watercourse had taken most of the corpse's weight. If he turned his face to the side, he could still breathe reasonably well, and so although he couldn't move much, he wasn't going to drown just yet, either.

He was just thinking that he'd recovered himself enough to try to heave the body off him, when he heard the tramping of marching feet going past. Feigning death, and trying to breathe as shallowly as he could, he hoped his terrified trembling wouldn't be noticed as, just upstream from him and the body, soldier after soldier nipped out of the ranks to fill a water-skin, or even just to cup a few mouthfuls of water in their hands to do as he had done, and wet their parched throats. By the time he was sure they had all gone, he was shaking with cold and shock more than fear, and he knew that if he wasn't to sicken and die, he had to get out of the water and get dry and at least partially warmer.

Shifting the body was harder than he thought, partly because his arms and legs were suffering badly with cramp after holding still for so long. But eventually he managed it, and crawled like an ailing dog up onto the far bank. For the rest of that night he stayed hidden in the undergrowth, stripping off as much of his clothing as he could and wringing it out, but then putting it back on at dawn in case he had to make a run for it. He would have loved to light a fire for comfort, but knew that that would be signing his death warrant. Instead, he burrowed as deeply into the leaf litter as he could, to keep what little warmth he had.

Come the morning, he felt ill beyond belief, not helped by having had nothing to eat since the previous morning, and back then he'd barely been able to stomach much out of blind terror. The only blessing was that he'd discovered that Hugh's musket ball had done little more than graze him, the thick wool having robbed it of some of its power. Now that it had started to scab, it was stiff and very sore, but it wasn't going to immobilise him unless it turned septic.

Weak, dazed, and confused, he waited as long as he dared, then hobbled back across the stream to the battlefield, where he scavenged what he could from dropped packs. It wasn't anything special, just a few double-baked biscuits, some dried meat, and a few withered apples from last autumn, but it felt like a feast and kept him on his feet. He saw a few other men doing the same, and they all steered clear of one another, but all sharing the same haunted look of men who'd gotten into something far deeper and nastier than they'd ever expected.

He returned to his little hollow as soon as he could, and spent the afternoon and night fitfully dozing. He never fully slept for fear of being caught, but at least by the next morning he had something closer to his strength back. Certainly enough to decide to start making a move for home – if he could call it that.

He was under no illusions as to what his father would say. And the evil old goat probably wouldn't hear a word said against his saintly Matthew. But Gideon was returning with a new resolve, which was to hasten his father's end in whatever way he could, so that at last he might end his own days in something like peace.

The money he wasn't bothered about, however much his father might have stashed away with men of money in Dumfries – because of course, old John Corsan would never let even his own sons know how much he was really worth – and if he'd left all of that to Matthew, so be it. But if he could sell those witch-cursed crofts, and buy himself somewhere where nobody knew who he was, he might just get to a point where he wasn't such an outcast. His youngest brother he would do what he could for, but if it proved impossible to find anyone to care for him, then a pillow over his face might prove the kindest option.

That wouldn't be murder in Gideon's eyes. If he himself was left a dribbling idiot, he sincerely hoped that someone would put him out of his misery sooner rather than later. What kind of life was it to not even know if you'd soiled yourself? Let alone never being able to walk outside and smell the fresh air – and Gideon knew how a sickroom could reek of farts and poorly washed underclothes from going in to his father's room, when he'd had no option but to go and hear what the old man was blathering on about. No, that wasn't for him. In spite of all his sins, Gideon would still prefer to meet his Maker rather than linger on like that.

It took Gideon weeks to find his way south and west, living under hedgerows, and roughly noting where south was by looking at the sun. His climb over the southern uplands was the worst, for he never dared drop down to the valleys where the roads ran, and the countryside was bleak with few places to take refuge. Every time he caught sight of a road, sooner or later there was a troop of soldiers going up or down it, and they were the last people Gideon wanted to meet, especially given that as time went on, he became more and more dishevelled. In his current state, he couldn't imagine anyone believing that he was the son of a leading person in Dumfries society, not a vagrant – *he* certainly wouldn't have, even up to a few months ago.

Yet finally the scenery began to look a bit more familiar, and then fully recognisable, and at that point he sat down and wept with relief. Something he had never done before. Like some thief in the night, he made his way to the door of his father's house, and then let himself in, both cursing Colum McKay – the man who did the grim job of nursing his father – for leaving the door unlocked, and blessing him for the same, because it meant he didn't need to rouse anyone to get in.

He soon found out why the door was unbarred. McKay was as drunk as a lord on rough home-stilled whisky. (Though not from any produced at any of their homes.) But then, if he had to wipe his father's arse and clean him up, Gideon knew that he'd be in that state by noon, let alone the end of the day, because old John was nothing if not a crabbit and foul-mouthed old cur, never grateful for anything anyone did for him.

Please, Lord, Gideon prayed, as he got clean clothing from out of the chest at the foot of his simple bed in the main room where McKay snored loud enough to wake the dead, *never let me get like my father. I don't want to die. But I don't want to end up like him, either!*

Indeed, he realised that he was coming to some significant conclusions about what he didn't want, even if what he *did* want remained so far out of his reach as to be invisible. He never wanted to live into foul old age like his father – dependent on terrifying those who cared for him to the extent that they dare not take their revenge upon him. And he certainly didn't want to cling to a life not worth living as his brother did. But that still didn't answer the now pressing question of what he was going to do next.

At least having had the chance to scrub himself clean enough to now pass for travel-stained, instead of totally tattered, scrape his straggly beard off and comb his hair as best he could, and then put on his oldest clothes so that they didn't look too fresh, he felt able to walk up to the door in the morning as if he'd only just arrived. The remnant of the night spent in the warmth of the stables had only strengthened his resolve, for the pallet where Isobel had been sent to sleep lay empty and a haunting reminder of the fact that he'd discovered too late that she'd run off with bloody Edward McCartney and those damned Highlanders. The only blessing there was that Gideon hadn't seen hide nor hair of them with Hugh when the battles had come, so please God she was somewhere safe, even if he couldn't overcome the jealous wish that someone might have filleted bloody

McCartney and got him out of the way so that Isobel might make a run for home – not that Gideon had the faintest comprehension of the reality that this was the last place Isobel would run to.

Too hung-over to bother with questions, such as where Gideon had spent last night to be getting there that early, McKay let him in when he knocked, Gideon not wanting McKay to know that he was aware that anyone could have walked in last night. At some point it might be useful to be able to point the finger of blame at McKay for some seemingly unknown person getting in and doing for his father, but at a time when he had a good alibi, of course.

Typically, his father's first words were, "Where is Matthew?"

"On the run with the killers of Archbishop Sharp," Gideon was able to retort in all truth.

"No! Don't lie, boy." old John snarled, or as best he could, groping for the blackthorn stick he'd regularly beaten his sons with when they were younger. McKay might not be the sharpest of men, but he'd only had to have old John lash out at him once with that wicked thing before moving it far out of reach, up onto the top of the cupboard in the main room.

"There'll be no more beating of me for doing nothing more than telling you the truth," Gideon snapped back, belatedly wondering why he'd put up with this for so long, when clearly his father was in no position to harm him with anything but his tongue. Yes, the old man was dangerous in that he still had his cronies in the district, but like him, they were now becoming old men and their power wasn't what it had once been.

"It's time you learned who the man of this household is nowadays," he said with scarcely disguised glee. "People have been saying you cannot be long for this world ever since your seizure. Would they question it if you finally went now?" And he left that threat lingering as he turned and walked out of the room, gratified that for once the old devil was lost for words.

Hugh spent the autumn of 1679 as part of the intensified hunt for the killers of Archbishop Sharp. He wasn't as convinced as Tavish that Gideon must be dead, but consoled himself with the knowledge that at least he was part of the hunt for men like him. He was even more pleased when in November, a proclamation was issued against all those who had taken part in the uprising at Bothwell Bridge.

It turned out that immediately after the battle, Monmouth – always a reasonable man – had offered a remission to anyone who had taken part, aside from those actually involved in the murder of the archbishop. But now Monmouth was back south of the border, and the King's brother, James, Duke of Albany and York, had come to take his place. Monmouth, being a Protestant himself, had at least been sympathetic to the Covenanters' beliefs, if not with them in their more extreme actions. James, on the other hand, was now known to be a Catholic, and utterly opposed to them. Therefore Monmouth's remission, which had been conditional upon those concerned signing a bond of peaceable behaviour, was revoked, and every last one of those who had been present at the battle, combatant or not, was now going to be subject to the full severity of the law.

What Hugh and most of the men he was marching alongside were less than happy about was the news that King Charles wasn't in the best of health, which meant that not only Scotland, but England as well, might find themselves with a new Catholic king, and with nobody to restrain him as Charles II had done so far with his younger brother.

"We shouldn'a be ruled by a man in bed wi' the Whore of Babylon," Gow grumbled, as they trudged their way knee-deep through a tangle of heather towards a rumoured nest of fugitives.

"Arse!" swore Murray, as his foot plunged into a hidden dip of peaty sludge, grabbing Hugh to save himself from plunging head first into the heather.

As Hugh and Gow hauled him out, holding him while he emptied out his boot as best he could, Gow added, "I'm no lover of those who think the way to change is by murder. You don't have to be a man of learning or a kirkman to see that that's a dangerous path to walk. Many o' those who got swept up in that rabble we faced were just lads who didn'a know better. Those wild preachers fair whipped up a storm. Carried folk along on the promise of a fairer life …or at least a better afterlife than others have promised them."

"I hear you," Hugh said grimly. "I've no issue with hunting down rebels and murderers, but it doesn't sit right with me to hunt down some young lad who only followed a friend or relative to that fight. They don't deserve that. Compared to them, our side got off almost unscathed. It was hardly as though they inflicted a grievous wound onto government troops, was it?" He tutted in disgust. "I don't see signs of massed rebellion fomenting here in the Lowlands, do you? All we've picked up so far is a few half-starved and terrified stragglers."

Murray nodded. "And I'm none so keen on the thought of the Duke of York becoming king, either. What might happen to us if he decides that Scotland is a hotbed of Protestant dissent against him, and decides to do more than issue proclamations? I have to say, I would baulk at fighting against my own folk just to prop up someone like that, but worse would be having to fight a whole English army just to save my skin and my family's," and Gow and Hugh nodded.

"I wouldn'a be so keen maself," said Tavish, having waded his way across the boggy ground to them and heard Murray's words. "Me, I'm a Catholic, but I've no wish fer us to end up wi' the kind o' persecution and counter-persecution happening up here as went on in England under Mary Tudor and Queen Bess. I fear that much o' this army will begin slipping away if we get sent to butcher our own."

It meant that when they came across three young lads huddled in a hollow, all looking half-frozen and scared out of their wits, the four soldiers simply pretended that they hadn't seen them. They stood with their backs to the lads and wondered aloud where the ringleaders might have got to? And in between coughs and sneezes, a quavering voice said that they'd heard someone preaching hellfire and damnation upon the Duke, and something about Wanlockhead.

"Well they're not going to last long up there in the winter, and with no shelter," Hugh, as the man with local knowledge, told the others. "The wind fair blasts through there, and there are no settlements big enough to take in more than a single man. They might have been going there, but my bet would be for them to be heading onwards into Dumfriesshire." Which when they reported back to their captain that they'd seen signs of men heading south, tallied with other information he'd had.

It resulted in Hugh and his friends spending the winter quartered back down south, but he got no closer to home or finding Gideon Corsan for the rest of that year.

1680-4

Hugh

Hugh spent the winter quartered with the rest of the men closer to Edinburgh. If their leaders didn't want to fully disperse those men whose homes were far away, in case they didn't come back, they were far from idle. In an era when there was no long-term levy to maintain a standing army of any size in Scotland, a few men like Hugh were kept close, but had to help out with those who were providing their food. It meant heavy work on the fields as well as them doing things such as cleaning and repairing the army's stock of flintlock muskets. It was also a quiet time for news of the Covenanters they were hunting, for they too went to ground as the worst of the weather settled in.

Yet if Hugh hoped that when the spring came around it would be proven that the radicals had given up and gone home, he was sorely disappointed. As soon as was practical, he and his friends were out on the road again, albeit no further than Queensferry on the Firth of Forth, and this time sent to act as an escort for a man being brought in for questioning, but also to hunt for one of the Covenanter ring-leaders, one Donald Cargill, who had evaded capture. Busy tramping around getting drenched and searching under bushes, it took a while before Hugh learned that the captured man had had damning documents in his possession, which revealed that the two leaders of the remaining radicals were declaring that King

Charles Stuart II was a usurper and a tyrant, and an enemy of Christ and the Covenant.

"By God!" Tavish swore, as they were sent to eat after being formally told this. "They're asking to be hanged as traitors. Do they seriously think that our government – let alone the English one – can stand by and let them carry on making proclamations like that?"

"I don't think they were so much proclaiming as plotting," Hugh said disgustedly, "but the end result is going to be much the same, isn't it? And God help the poor sods who get swept up with their preaching and end up dying for it."

The four friends – Hugh, Tavish, Gow, and Murray – were no happier when they marched out for Dumfriesshire again a couple of weeks later in late June. The two main leaders of the radicals, Richard Cameron and Donald Cargill, had been joined by Cameron's brother, Michael, who had been brazen enough to read out their manifesto and nail it to the market cross in the small town of Sanquhar in north-western Dumfriesshire. Vehemently puritanical and conceding nothing, he and it summoned the people to return to God, presumably by bearing arms against the King and the Duke of York and Albany, for whom they held a particular hatred for being a Catholic.

"Here we go," Tavish said gloomily, as they prepared to yet again tramp along the roads searching. "It'll be back to persecuting Catholics if the Duke becomes king, because the Scottish government won't risk him having a private army of believers at his personal beck and call up here, you mark my words. They'll want the likes of me well and truly cowed, not buoyed up by having a king of our own persuasion.

Bad enough him being able to command the English without his own force up here."

"If you need to make a run for it, we'll cover for you," Hugh said softly, feeling sympathy for the younger lad, who'd done nothing but fight bravely for the King and government. "I'll not see you hanged or burned, Tavish. Seeing that happen to my ma was once too often for this lifetime."

It reminded his friends that a different kind of persecution also loomed dangerously near, for this rag-tag end of what had once been a national movement, were also threatening a return to witch-hunting in a violent and obsessive way.

"I bloody hate these Covenanters!" Hugh spat viciously. "I bet that if God-rot-him Veitch is still alive, that he'll be one of those who've been hiding the zealots over the winter. The manse at Irongray is certainly big enough when there's only him and some frightened-near-to-death housekeeper. And if his son has returned and taken over as minister, then from what I recall of him, he'll be no better."

Mercifully, before they got close enough for this to become very personal again for Hugh, they met another force of some hundred men under Bruce of Earlshall returning to Edinburgh with prisoners.

"The two Camerons are dead." one of the other soldiers told them triumphantly, as Hugh's group and some others got detailed off to act as additional escorts, Bruce not wanting to chance some radical group wanting to free the prisoners. "Cargill's an old man now. He'll preach fire and damnation, but he's too old to lead in the field."

Yet Hugh and his friends were sickened by the sight of the procession that they were guarding. The only man of any consequence captured was someone called David Hackstone, who was tied sitting backwards on a horse, while on the horse in front of him were displayed Richard Cameron's decapitated head and severed hands.

"This is gross and unnecessary," Murray muttered, as they all pulled scarves up over their noses and mouths, despite it being July, just to filter the stench coming off the grisly trophies.

They remained in Edinburgh while Hackstone's fate was decided, and it was then that they discovered that he had been the leader of the party who had murdered Archbishop Sharp in St Andrews.

"Please God this is the end of it, then," Hugh prayed, "And we can go back to our homes." Though where home was for him these days, he was less than sure. He might return to Argyll, but without Elspeth there, would it feel like home? Nor was he sure of how he would feel if Edward McCartney was there with Isobel, and the pain of seeing them still very much in love. Could he cope with watching her having Edward's children?

Then he revised that thought, for Isobel was of an age with him, and had to be coming up around forty by now and past bearing anyone's child, so he would not have to witness that particular torment. Yet would being around her make his feelings wane as he saw her for herself, and not a surrogate for her cousin Elspeth? In truth he didn't know, but he yearned for Elspeth as keenly as he had all those years ago

But an end it wasn't to be. At the Mercat Cross in the capital, a scaffold was erected, and on the thirtieth of July they had to form part of the troops brought in to ensure no violence from the crowd, given that the executioner – in a planned and deliberate process – took his time taking off first Hackstone's right hand, then his left. Following that, Hackstone was hanged, taken down again before he actually died, his bowels then taken out, and his heart after that, which was then held aloft and shown to the people.

"Jesu! It's enough to make you believe he really did have God on his side to live so long through that," breathed Murray in horror, as they saw that the heart continued beating briefly as it was held up. "Surely no man could bear such pain without divine help?"

"He shouldn'a have killed the old archbishop, I'll grant you," Gow growled, "but they did for the old man swiftly enough. He didn'a suffer. Not like this. This goes beyond sending a message. This is bloody and vile vengeance!"

And marching out of the city again, they deliberately avoided looking at Hackstone's and Cameron's heads affixed to high poles, where all were supposed to see them and take warning.

Now there was a palpable sense of fear in the air as winter came around. The radicals had gone too far for the government to ignore any further, and large-scale hunts were organised when possible. And to Hugh's dismay, women were not exempt. Two women were hanged in Edinburgh's Grassmarket in January for giving shelter to some outlawed preachers, though he never learned who, and to his intense relief, this time he wasn't part of the company who had to ensure nobody tried to rescue them.

It was of little comfort to him that theirs, at least, was a regular hanging. Though he went there only as close as one of the side streets – feeling that somehow there ought to be someone there praying for their souls as nothing more nor less than women, who were someone's daughter, or wife, or mother – and was too far back to see their faces clearly, but he still had nightmares for weeks afterwards. In his dreams the unknown women's faces became his mother and his grandmother Grissell, but sometimes Elspeth's cousins Margaret and Agnes, and on a couple of really bad nights, Elspeth herself and Isobel.

Waking from those, he'd just have time to make it outside before heaving violently, and had the shakes for the rest of the day. Tavish, Gow, and Murray covered for him then, pulling and pushing him into line, and making sure he was properly dressed and armed, but all three were now really worried. How would Hugh cope if they had to take a woman prisoner?

Nor did matters calm down into the next summer, for Donald Cargil was found and hanged with four others in the May of 1681. Sent along with their company to once more become part of Claverhouse's garrison, the friends spent the rest of that year and throughout the next, chasing what felt like ghosts across Kirkcudbrightshire and Dumfriesshire. The near mountainous, high hills with their deep rolling valleys, and their tree-clad streambeds at their floors, provided too much cover. All the fugitives had to do was get over into the next valley, and there were so many ways they could escape into others that by the time the soldiers got to where they had been, there was no chance of telling where they had gone.

Too many of the ordinary people here were still sneaking out to conventicles in the hills, still deeply committed to the Covenant and its ministers, and willing to hide those preaching what they perceived as the true Word of God no matter what the cost. With non-attenders to the parish kirks having their names taken and passed on to the authorities, the main kirks were these days well-attended, meaning only the truly reckless could be easily singled out. But the hostile congregations talked amongst themselves, overtly went to sleep during services and ignored the minister, made none of the expected responses, and loitered threateningly at the kirk door until the minister could summon the courage to walk past them.

Yet with major plots taking place against the King and his brother in England, 1683 was a quieter year for Hugh. The Cameronian followers were temporarily side-lined in the minds of a reshuffled Scottish government which had its own problems. Not least was the fact that within it were men like James Douglas, Marquis of Queensberry who was also the Lord Treasurer – a firm Protestant Episcopalian – alongside others like the Earl of Errol, the high constable, whose Catholic family had so far been kept out of government because of their faith. With the Catholic James, Duke of Albany and York as the most senior man in Scotland on his brother's behalf by now, these changes had finally happened, but not everyone was happy about them. Nor did that halt military harassment to enforce the law, especially concerning the attendance of the kirk, and Hugh, along with the rest of his regiment, spent a grim year feeling more like armed sheepdogs than soldiers. More than once he found himself standing between other soldiers and a woman with her children.

"She's just abiding by what her man tells her," he said over and over again. "What do you want her to do when he beats her if she *doesn't* go to the conventicle, and we threaten her if she *does*? He's with her day in and day out. We only turn up occasionally.

Can you stop him raising his fist to her when we're not there? No. So leave her and the bairns be."

The fact that the more vehement followers of the Covenant all too frequently were the worst at leaving their wives with visibly blackened eyes, or hobbling along holding ribs which were obviously bruised or worse, did nothing to soften his feelings towards the local ring-leaders, let alone the national ones. In fact, Hugh was well on the way to becoming a true Covenanter hater where the most zealous were concerned. And now being quartered around Kirkcudbright brought back too many memories.

He and his parents might have lived closer to Dumfries, but Kirkcudbright wasn't so very far away that he hadn't been there in the short time that he'd been a stable lad for Grierson at Lagg. The old man whom Hugh had known, and who had dismissed him from his service for having a witch for a mother, had died in 1666, but his cousin Robert had taken over and was a vehement upholder of the law against Covenanters. Yet Hugh only saw another laird at Lagg willing to punish common folk for things they had little control over.

For Hugh and his friends, what affected them more personally was that at a local level there was rivalry and disagreement between their commander, John Graham of Claverhouse, and Colonel James Douglas. Douglas was the second son of the late Earl of Queensberry, making him the brother of William, the current duke and earl of Queensberry, and meaning he was uncle to William's son, the politically important and currently part of the government, James, Marquis of Queensberry. Disregarding Claverhouse's own wishes, Douglas got forced on to them in early 1684, and made second-in-command of their regiment. Claverhouse was by far the better soldier, but the barely battle-seasoned Colonel Douglas had political influence to spare, and the men under them feared being tugged back and forth between Claverhouse's desire to do what made sense, and Douglas demanding that they do as the politicians in Edinburgh wanted. And they only had to ride past the enormous mansion house of Drumlanrig Castle, which the Douglases were currently having built, to know how much wealth and standing they had.

"If the Douglases want it done, Claverhouse has no chance of stopping it," Tavish observed darkly.

The final nail in the coffin of reason, as Hugh saw it, was that Robert Grierson of Lagg had married Colonel Douglas' sister. As commissioner for Galloway, Grierson presided over the military courts in that shire, set up to try rebellious Covenanters, and had already ordered more than one execution without needing to wait for a higher authority to give their permission. For somebody who was a staunch and devout episcopalian, he was perversely contemptuous of those Presbyterians who begged to be allowed to pray before their deaths, and fiercely policed his own tenants, ensuring that they neither attended conventicles, nor gave shelter to the wandering Covenanter preachers. Robert Grierson was ruthless.

And if Grierson himself was too young to have had any part in the witch trials when Hugh's mother had died, as far as Hugh was concerned, the whole family was tainted, while Grierson's apparent relish at persecuting ordinary folk only proved the point. It had Hugh thinking: heaven help any poor woman who comes before him as commissioner. One whiff of 'healing', when the damned man thought someone should not have survived, or perversely even more reprehensible, invoking prayers to heal without a Kirk-man there to lead the prayers, and she would find herself hanging at the crossroad, or worse, alongside those who would have persecuted her just as hard because of what their Covenanter preachers told them.

And that was how he came to get involved with the family of Grissell Rae. Very much as had happened to Elspeth's mother, Jonet, Grissell had been imprisoned in 1671 and dragged in front of a court in 1672, but the woman who had stood both accused beside her and accusing her, had died in prison and the case had gone no further. Then just four years ago in 1679, Grissell had found herself being put to the question again, and although once again insufficient evidence had been found to take her to a full trial, Grissell and her husband, John Asman, were living in a state of permanent fear on their small croft which lay between Castle Douglas and Kirkcudbright.

It was as their daughter staggered home, heavily laden, from the market at Kirkcudbright that Hugh came upon her, and he and Tavish stepped in to save her from the rough jostling and lewd comments of their fellow soldiers.

"Stop it!" Hugh commanded, and by now being one of the oldest men in the company, his word carried some weight with the youngsters. "For the love of God, what is the matter with you? She's of an age to be your baby sister, not your lover. Leave her alone!" And with Tavish, Gow, and Murray coming to stand behind him, all four of them known as men who'd seen some real fighting, nobody pushed their luck. A blow from Tavish's fist had laid one man out cold for a day after he'd ridiculed Hugh for his nightmares, and that hadn't been forgotten.

"Have you far to go?" Hugh asked her kindly, after the others had marched on and he'd swung her heavy pack up onto his shoulder, while Gow had come to relieve her of a bag so weighty it had been scuffing on the ground.

"Barncrosh," she said nervously.

"Ach, that's just off this road," Hugh said with a smile. "No trouble for us to see you there. What's your name, lass?"

"Grissell, after my ma."

That made Hugh's heart feel as though it was about to leap out of his chest. Grissell wasn't a rare name, but it wasn't that common either. And his beloved grandma's name? What kind of coincidence was that? It meant he knew his voice sounded choked as he asked, "And what's your family name, Grissell?"

"My pa is John Asman."

"Ah, so you're Grissell Asman. My grandma was Grissell, too." Hugh kept the smile pasted on his face, but all he could think of was his poor grandmother dying wracked with fear, and terrified for what was going to happened to her daughters. So when they got to the small cottage, very like his old home, and saw her mother coming out looking petrified, but still pulling her daughter to her as if to protect her from these strange men, and with hands twisted into unnatural claws, his heart leapt so hard it threatened to choke him.

"Oh, dear Lord! Not you too." came out of his mouth without thinking.

The older Grissell flinched as he thrust the pack into her husband's arms and came to gently take her hands. He now knew why they'd sent the girl to market, in spite of the dangers of a very young but comely lass being on the road alone with soldiers in the neighbourhood. Elspeth had told him often enough of the even greater danger of her mother being seen in public after she'd been accused and tortured, let alone him having to go to market for his own mother while his father worked the fields, and for the same reason – the marks of being 'questioned' were not easy to hide, screaming 'witch' for all to see.

His voice shaking with rage, Hugh turned and spoke over his shoulder to his friends. "*This* is what they did to my Aunt Marione! The one who escaped to the Highlands with McAllister and the Allens. She could scarce hold a besom to sweep the floor with, much less anything like a needle to sew with, after Veitch and the McBurneys had done with her. She'd done *nothing*. It was all to let bloody John Corsan have their croft!"

Tavish in particular came and looked at Grissell's hands in horror. Gow and Murray had seen rather more of what could happen to an accused woman, but even they'd not seen it this close up, and they were both looking deeply uncomfortable. Then all three looked shocked as Hugh, voice shaking with emotion, declared, "I couldn't save my ma. But I helped save my aunt's family and another. If you need me, I will help you too! I'll be listening for your names, and if I hear anything untoward, I promise I will come and warn you."

"What's your name?" John Asman asked worriedly, clearly wondering if this was a particularly contrived and clever trap being set for them.

"I'm Hugh Ferguson. My pa was James Ferguson, whose croft was the other side of Castle Douglas. But my ma was Marione Corsan."

There was a sob of understanding from the older Grissell. "The women who died in Dumfries! Your ma was one of them?"

Hugh blinked back tears, nodding as he struggled to say, "She was."

Immediately his hands were clasped as best she could by Grissell, and young Grissell came and hugged him, both suddenly choked by the realisation that at last here was someone who truly understood their torment. "We'll take your help, and be grateful," the older Grissell managed to croak out, to which Hugh gave a nod and clasped her ruined hands in silent bonding.

As the four soldiers left, Gow and Murray hustling Hugh in particular along, so that their sergeant wouldn't wonder where they'd got to, Murray said, "Have you lost your senses? Do you know what they'll do to you if you're caught helping them?"

Only to have Hugh reply, "Never again, my friend! Never again will another woman die like my ma while I have breath in my body! You don't know what it's like. What it's like to see a woman you know and love being brought out, beaten black and blue, tied to a post, and throttled. And for her not to have the blessing of dying like that, but to have to watch an evil swine like John Corsan hand the flame to the executioner who lit the bonfires, and the flames start to blacken them and burn!

"I can't do it! I can't stand by again. I was a boy, too weak to fight my way forward back then, and too taken unawares to be anything but a shaking mess. I won't blame you if you won't help me. You don't need to be part of this. I know what it might cost me. But for me there's no choice. No choice at all!"

Chapter 21

With Anna telling Rita that so far, she'd not come across any Hugh Ferguson or Gideon Corsan in the records she'd managed to search, Rita came to a decision.

"I think I'm going to have to contact the male ghosts in person, "she said with a sigh. "You just don't have the time to keep on digging, and with the risk that even so, you might not find anything. The number of records that could have been lost in over three centuries could mean there's nothing surviving to even find. Something has made these ghosts more active than they've been in years, and we need to know what. Even if I can't put them to rest just yet, because one won't leave without the other, if we can just find out what triggers them to appear, it'll be a big step forward."

Gary's, "Aye," sounded more than little doubtful, making Rita look at him sharply.

"Oh, I dinna question your abilities," he said hurriedly. "I'm just hoping to God that it's something we can do something about, rather than just us not using the best room in the hotel." And as Rita's expression softened, he continued, "Knowing, and it being any use, are two verra different things, are they not?"

"Point taken," Rita sighed, and followed his glance to Anna, who was staring gloomily into the flames of the fire, clutching her whisky but not drinking it."

"Sup up, lass," Gary jollied her. "After this evening's shenanigans, there's at least another whisky wi' your name on it. I'm no' that short of bottles!"

That made her grin at him, but after she'd headed back to her own cottage, Gary was quick to tell Rita of his fears.

"This lad Cameron's a nice enough chap," he explained, "but as I told you yesterday, he's a world o' problems of his own, thanks to his family. She's never said as much, but I think she was real taken wi' him right up to the point when he cleared off and left Harris and Lewis here." The two big dogs had taken an instant liking to Rita and were currently snoozing at her feet. "Anna feels their abandonment verra keenly."

"Of course she does!" Rita said with an affectionate rolling of her eyes at him. "She's a sensitive, the same as me. She picks up atmospheres and tensions without even knowing she's doing it. Actually, I want to give her a bit of training while I'm here, because she needs to ward herself a lot better, because I think that's also part of the reason why she was so emotionally battered by those idiot in-laws of hers."

"And speaking o' them… I dinna mean to teach my granny how to suck eggs here, Rita, but for Anna, this is more than a job now. It's her way of finding a new life for herself."

"Obviously!"

"But if young Cameron starts to feel that this hotel's suddenly become more trouble than it's worth, there's nothing to stop him from putting it up for sale, or changing its use from a hotel to something else."

Rita's expression became worried. "Lord, I hadn't thought that much further on."

"Aye, well you see now why I'm pushing the need for a *practical* solution. Anna's no' been here long enough to simply walk into another hotel manager's job. No' yet, anyway, being only a few months on the job, and if she then gets shoved out by the owner selling up. Or worse, him thinking that a tougher manager would sort the problems faster. Who's going to read her C.V. and think, 'The owner was a daft tit who couldn'a tell hay from a bull's foot'?

"Because Anna can hardly say that he wouldn'a listen to sense over the place being haunted, can she? No, it'll be taken as Anna being no good at her job and being let go before she wrecks the place. And that's a verra far cry from what's really taken place, when Anna's tried to get him to see that exploiting the ghosts will only make things worse."

"Oh dear," Rita sighed. "He really didn't get it?"

Gary shook his head. "No' remotely. But then he wasn'a there like I was when I heard that shot going off, and had to force the door open to get to Anna and that great wet blanket, Jensen. I tell you, Rita, someone's going to get badly hurt unless we can sort this. Just getting walloped by that king-sized mattress would do an elderly person some damage, let alone if it thumps them back into the wardrobe wi' the mirror on it, and it shatters. I dinna need your talents to see the verra real and practical problems if we canna sort this.

"And while Anna has confided in me that wi' the manager's wages coming in, she can afford to hang on to her flat in Worcester for a wee bit longer, realistically that can surely only be for the time it takes to sell it? The hotel might give us the cottages, but we pay our own bills, so it'll be like running two homes when the winter comes around and she needs to heat her flat to avoid burst water pipes and the like. Nor is she being paid that much that she might pay that mortgage and find somewhere other than the cottage here to live in if things go wrong.

"So if she had to move to another job up here, that would mean affording somewhere to live as well. But completion within eight weeks is the legal norm on this side o' the border, so she'd need to put that flat on the market pretty soon to be sure o' getting the sale sorted by the end o' the summer, and she knows that. Meaning her knowing that her job is *totally* secure, and that she'll no' have to go cap in hand back to that bloody awful supermarket asking for her old job back, is way more of a worry than we've allowed for. Christ, Rita! We canna let that happen to the lass."

Rita reached over and hugged him. "We'll do it," she said firmly. "We'll not let Anna down like her parents did…even if this is bit outside of anything a normal surrogate parent might have to do," and Gary went to bed with a happy glow, Rita not having hugged him like that in a long time. A bridge of sorts had been crossed, and hopefully Rita would find it hard to go back.

Anna at least had the next morning free, though she needed to go and take over at lunchtime for the rest of the day, so they convened at Gary's for breakfast, at which point Anna pointed to her notes and said, "I was reading these again in bed last night and realised something interesting. Our lady ghosts never once mentioned William Corsan – who was the dad of Jannet and Marione if my notes are right – or Robert Clark, who was Agnes and Margaret's dad, loitering here. The women spoke of them as if they were fond of them, so where are they in all of this?

It's as if they simply died and moved on to the next plane, or whatever, whereas it's the women who seem stuck here."

Gary groaned. "Now my head's hurting. Who the hell did you say William Corsan and Robert Clark are again?"

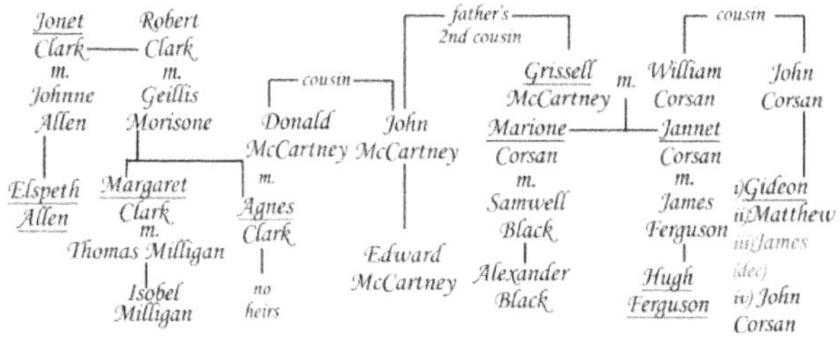

Anna laughed. "If you Scots will have ladies hanging on to their maiden names after they've married, no wonder you get confused! But truthfully, Gary, I had to start drawing a family tree to work it out. So, Robert Clark was Geillis Morrison's husband – though I'm betting that if I find her surname in any records it's not spelled like that. And their daughters were Margaret Clark – who was one of the really angry lady ghosts – and Agnes Clark, who was the reasonable one at the end who was trying to help us with the names. But he was also Jonet Clark's brother.

"William Corsan was similarly Marione and Jannet's dad, and married to Grissell McCartney, and it's Grissell who is another of the angry but more distant ghosts and is the one who makes the connection to our 'baddie', John McCartney, for some of them. But do you see what I mean? We have the two mums, Grissell and Geillis, who are positively spitting tin tacks over everything, but not the dads.

Where are they in all of this? And is it relevant? Because I find it hard to credit that *both* fathers wouldn't give a stuff about their daughters being burned at the stake! One, maybe…if he was another like *my* dad. But not both."

"Aye, you would expect at least one to be a normally affectionate father," Gary agreed.

Yet Rita had already started thinking on this and said, "I wonder if it has anything to do with what Jannet, I think, said about their remains being brought to the ruins of the nunnery and thrown into the old crypt? Are the women linked to here because they weren't put to rest in a normal kirkyard? In other words, on consecrated ground, or given that the nunnery would have been that relatively recently to their time, on ground which *remained* consecrated and undisturbed down the years?"

"Now that's an interesting thought," Anna agreed. "I wonder if we could find the graves of William and Robert? Maybe even try to find these women's remains and have them interred in the same graveyard?"

"I hate to burst this bubble of optimism," Gary interrupted, "but even if Cameron was willing to have a major excavation in the car park for the ladies, I think the chances of tracking down the graves of two verra ordinary men from that far back would be nigh on impossible. Don't forget, the cost of a carved headstone would have been beyond the means of the average crofter. If they had any marker at all, it would probably have been a simple wooden cross, which has long since rotted away."

"Didn't we see some from the right era in that church you took us to?" Anna asked, perplexed, but Gary grimaced.

"No' exactly. Pretty much every one o' those was from into the next century. There's a big difference between looking for gravestones for someone who was buried in the **16**80s and someone buried in the **17**80s." He took in her crestfallen expression and hurriedly added, "I'm no' saying you're wrong that the men went into a regular kirkyard, just no' to expect that you can find proof, let alone any exact stones."

"Point taken, Gary," Rita said, unruffled by the setback. "The main thing to take from this is that the absence of the two fathers probably means that we're on the right trail if we think that the women's ghosts are here because their remains are here. And perhaps it's significant that while we could feel the anger of both Geillis and Grissell, we didn't really *see* much of them, did we? They were very faint, never quite coming forward to speak to us. So, maybe Grissell and Geillis *are* buried with their husbands, and it's just that strong mother-daughter bond that pulls them here? I'm comfortable with that as an explanation, especially if it was the mothers who taught their daughters things like the incantations which got them killed."

"Gosh! A touch of guilty consciences, you mean?" Anna wondered.

Rita shook her head. "I wouldn't go that far, though it's a fair point to consider. But in those days, there would normally be a much stronger bond between mother and daughter, because they would be passing on specific crafts and skills, while the sons would be more engaged with their fathers and learning about working the land, and such. It's easy to forget how divided men and women's worlds were back then, when these days, women go out to work and can do most of the jobs men can. But in a world before contraception and modern machinery to do the heaviest tasks, there wasn't much crossover."

Gary topped up their coffees as he asked, "So remind me, who are our main lady ghosts?"

Anna checked her notes. "Going over these, I'd say we've got four," and seeing Rita's frown, grinned at her, clarifying, "but only three of those were actually burned at the stake," making Rita smile in satisfaction at her theory of threes being proven. "We've got the two sisters, Margaret Clark – the angry one – and Agnes Clark – the reasonable one. The other one who died like them and seems really distressed is Jannet Corsan, and you can understand her distress if she's the mum of one of our male ghosts."

"Who's the fourth one?" Gary asked.

"Ah! Once I had her name, I did a quick dive into the witches' database last night and found her faster than I expected. She's J**o**net Clark, the two Clark sisters' aunt. But according to the database, she herself was hauled into Irongray Manse and questioned by the minister there, but I don't find her dying with the others." She flipped a page back and forth. "Didn't find his name on the database, but when she spoke I noted her mentioning an evil Presbyter called Veitch, so presume that must be him?"

Anna gave a huff of disgust before continuing, "Poor woman, she got hauled in for questioning twice in her life, the second time when her nieces were being questioned in 1659, so I'd guess that she died before she could be tried. Maybe even died *of* being questioned?"

Rita leaned in to peer at Anna's notes. "Ah! But if she was suspected of being a known witch, she might not have been buried in the Presbyter's churchyard.

He might have denied her family that. She may well have been brought and buried here as a compromise to her family, because a Benedictine and therefore Catholic graveyard would surely not have been their first choice. As they saw it, she would at least have been on hallowed ground here, not left with her spirit to roam in some shallow grave out on the moors."

"Blimey, that's a creepy thought!" Anna said with a gulp. "Did many people get just dumped where they fell?"

"Not many," Gary enlightened her, "not least because the Kirk was verra good at getting the money out of folk for burial fees. But I know of Covenanters who were simply dumped in a grave where they fell. That's where you later get those commemorative slabs cropping up in remote places."

"Right!" Rita said firmly. "So we know that our four ladies all have their remains somewhere on site. All of them were at the very least *questioned* as witches – and a grim process that was back then – and three went through a full trial. I don't know whether you agree, but I think if angry Margaret knows her persecutor is gone, she'll be satisfied, and if Jannet knows her son can rest in peace at least, she'll happily pass over properly. And if this Gideon was as instrumental in Agnes and Jonet's deaths, once he's gone, their main link is to the other two, and they'll be glad to rest."

Anna buried her head in her hands with a groan. "But I saw other women ghosts in the background, didn't you? Who are they? Are they connected? And that means that our main problem is still what it always was – the two male ghosts who hate each other's guts."

Gary patted her on the shoulder. “Aye, lass, but at least now we have a name for them both. That’s a lot further forward than we were a couple of days ago.”

At that, Anna had to go to work, but Gary took Rita up to the rooms and showed her the housekeeper’s stairs as well.

“How did I miss these the last time?” Rita wondered, looking around her as if seeing something beyond the physical, and Gary could see the goosebumps on her arms where she had her thick sweater sleeves pushed up, the hotel being warmer than the cottages.

“I think Anna’s right about this being part of the old tower-house, don’t you?” he said.

Rita nodded. “More so with these old stairs than the main ones, actually. Just by the feel of them, I’d say that these are where they’ve always been. Possibly the rougher stairs to the old tower’s top floor where the servants mainly lived. Going on that picture Anna showed me, would you agree that the better rooms of the family’s would have been in the two-storey house at the side of the tower?”

Gary nodded. “Aye. The ground floor o’ the tower, where our front room and reception are, was probably always a fairly busy place, where folk coming

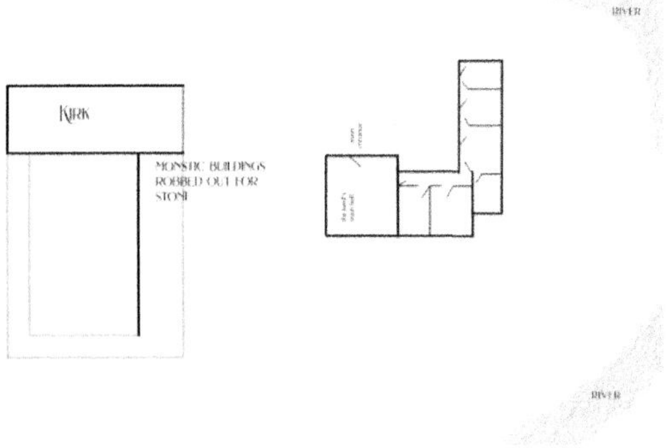

to see the laird would ha' been met. The ground-floor room, or rooms, to its side where our hall and fireplace are, would ha' been where some cosier reception rooms for the family were. Then on the first-floor in the tower was probably a fairly grand room or two for entertaining, and across in the other bit were the main family bedrooms. Also, I think we wouldn'a be too adrift in assuming that the wing at right-angles to them in the engraving, which was where our modern kitchens and dining room are, was where most o' the servants worked and slept. And Anna's right that *that* wing fell down, or had to be pulled down when its foundations got eroded."

"Good! Because if there's a 'safe' place to have a session with these ghosts, I think the housekeeper's room is it."

Gary's eyebrows shot up. "I dinna think Sally will be any too happy about that."

"*Hmph!*" Rita dismissed Sally and her worries. "At least she and her two ladies don't spend the night there, do they? They only go up during the mornings to get linen and put it away. If necessary, they can have an emergency store of stuff while we sort things out. You can't do that with the guests – especially when you've got the place fully booked for that wedding! We've got less than ten days now to sort this, Gary. I haven't got time to dance around people's sensibilities and panics."

The reminder of their very limited time settled it for Gary, and while Rita carried on checking the rooms out by dowsing over them, Gary went to break the news to Sally. As expected, Sally was none too happy, but also surprised Gary by being philosophical about it.

"No, Rita's right," she said with a shiver. "At least we don't do much but flit in and out of there – after all, we can always go into the conference room when nobody's about to do any folding and sorting we need. It doesn't *have* to be done upstairs, it's just a bit unprofessional if we're seen by any guests. But just for once it wouldn't hurt.

"And we're braced for it, I suppose. As long as the ghosts don't start throwing the towels and duvet covers around so that they get crumpled and dirty, it's less of a problem for us. Tell her to let me know when she wants to do this, and I'll make sure we have what we need for the following day down out of there, just in case."

By the time Rita and Gary joined Anna for an evening meal in the front conference room while Anna was on her break, so that they could have Harris and Lewis with them, there being no guests who wanted to use the room either, Rita had something like a plan of action.

"Gary tells me that you're on in the morning tomorrow, Anna?"

"Yes."

"So tomorrow afternoon would be a good time?"

"Oh yes, Aunty Rita, though only after three, and better after four. I'm not on until the following lunchtime after then, so plenty of time to recover."

Rita turned to Gary. "Does that work for you?"

He laughed. "I'm no' so out of practice that I canna do wi' a bit less sleep! Especially for a good cause." Anna missed his flick of the eyes in her direction which Rita caught the full meaning of, and for which he got a full-blown smile. *Yes*, he thought with satisfaction, *it's about time you realised that I'll always be here when you need me, and when those you love need me, too. I'm no' like your late husband – letting you down just when you need me most.*

Oblivious to Gary's thoughts, Rita was carrying on with, "Great. Then if we can meet up in reception and then go up to the housekeeper's room at three? …I'll go up there as soon as Sally and her ladies have finished, and do some preparations. Make sure you have a proper breakfast." She looked pointedly at Anna, knowing that if she was going on duty very early in the morning, that she'd been known to only snack through the morning, rather than having something solid inside of her.

"But then have something before you come upstairs, but nothing heartier than a sandwich and a cuppa. The food is to make sure you stay grounded, but not so much that an over-full stomach distracts you." This time her steely glance was to Gary, knowing that he was one for 'filling up the gap', as he put it, at lunchtime. "I don't need you so grounded that you can't feel a damned thing!" she warned, wagging a finger in his direction, and getting a cheeky grin back

1684-5

Hugh

Hugh was good to his word, and made a point of listening for the names Asman or Rae, but to his relief they seemed to fade from the scrutiny of those in power. That wasn't necessarily because the local men had ceased to care about witches, but had more to do with the Duke of York and Albany's priorities. In towns like Dumfries and Kirkcudbright, the tolbooth jails became over-crowded with non-conformists who'd just been in the wrong place at the wrong time, and swept up at conventicles. They weren't leaders or trouble-makers in the political sense, and yet the magistrates couldn't just let them go, either. Transportation to the Americas became the governmental solution, but at a practical level it wasn't much help.

"That's all verra well," Tavish said, as the four friends shared their ale on the evening they heard about this, "but where are they going to send them from?"

Gow and Murray looked at him perplexed, but Hugh knew what he meant, saying to the other two, "We're here in Kirkcudbright, yes? Sitting looking at the quay. Do you see anything bigger than a fishing boat? Even out beyond Kirkcudbright Bay and into the Solway Firth? …No, you can't. Tavish and I have seen the ships going to the Americas being laden in the port at Glasgow, and they're huge! They have to be to survive the massive waves out on the ocean for weeks."

"You couldn'a get one o' those in here," Tavish enlightened them. "The water's no' deep enough, nor anywhere along this coast. So what's supposed to happen, eh? Are we going to be marching all o' them from Kirkcudbright and Dumfries up to Glasgow? Cos' I dinna give much chance on the same number getting on the ship as left here!"

Hugh nodded. "How do you think the young lads in our company would hold up, marching for a couple of weeks – because let's be frank, we're not going to hold any kind of pace dragging families with young bairns along – and them hearing and seeing women like their mothers weeping, and cursing them for dragging them away from their homes?"

Gow sighed in realisation. "They'll turn a blind eye."

Murray groaned. "On a dark and rainy night – and the Lord knows we get enough of those up here – they'll just not patrol as hard as they should, and that's all they'll need to do. Just let them slip away. And if every group of lads only lets one family escape, that's still an awful lot of prisoners we could lose between here and Glasgow!"

"And that, my friends," said Hugh grimly, "is why men like Grierson will hang, not transport. He's no fool, whatever else we think of him, and he knows that transportation will never work for men and families sent away from here, not least because the chances of them even reaching the ship are slim. And God forbid, in his eyes, that they might return to offend again. So to keep control – as he sees it – he'll hang anyone he thinks is a troublemaker, or even someone who has merely helped a supposed troublemaker."

"Dear Lord help them," Murray intoned, truly meaning it as a plea to the divine. "That's bad. That's *really* bad!"

Hugh nodded. "It is. And that's why I offered to help the Asman family. Because if they're swept up with the Covenanter faithful, those lunatics might think that God will look kindly upon them if they take a known witch down with them. In their warped view, it won't help them in this world, but it might bring them untold rewards in the next. That's what will drive them on."

Gow looked askance. "Do they no' need *proof* that this woman is a witch? The court, I mean."

But Hugh's sour expression answered, even before he said, "There was damn-all *proof* against my ma! Just accusation brought by neighbours – and most of them had been threatened by those bastards Corsan and McCartney to make them, let alone by Thomas and Rab McBurney, the bailie's sons, who were vicious wee shites as boys, and ten times worse as grown men. When Elspeth's ma's heart gave out at seeing her nieces burned at the stake, it was only when night came that a few old wifeys dared to come out and help her lay her ma out. Until they couldn't be seen, they were too terrified that they might end up similarly accused, and who could blame them? No, Gow, you can forget proof when it comes to accusations of witchcraft. It's down to the whims of the men who have the local power."

"Christ ha' mercy upon them." Tavish said with feeling. "Verra well. If we think that the Asman wife and his girl are in danger, I'll help ye'. If it's got that bad, and I'm heading for home to save my own skin, I might as well save some other poor sod in the process." And Hugh knew that even if Gow and Murray balked at refusing orders when the time came, Tavish would hold to his word.

That May, the government produced a list of nearly two thousand so-called fugitives from justice in the Lowlands and around the east coast, giving them until the first of August to take an oath of loyalty to the King and government, or risk the consequences. Yet all that did was increase the mistrust and fear within communities, and resistance to the government in all its forms within what was becoming known as the 'Remnant' of the Covenanters. And it only strengthened in the face of the increased military activity which Hugh and his friends were part of. Therefore it was in the July, when they were escorting sixteen prisoners to jail, at a point between Sanquhar and Thornhill, that they were ambushed.

As the first shots rang out, the soldiers dived for cover, for in the rolling hills and deep valleys, it was hard to see where their assailants were. The great folds in the land with the tree-lined river and stream valleys were nigh on impossible to patrol, and spotters in the bracken high above near the hill tops had the perfect view of the road to pick their places to attack.

"Do ye' see them?" Tavish called across to Hugh, who had found cover behind a particularly thick clump of bracken.

"Not a damned thing." Hugh softly called back.

And yet at the first shots, the sixteen prisoners took to their heels. Their hands had been tied, but the uneven terrain had meant that their feet couldn't be hobbled without making it impossible for them to walk. The rescuers had chosen their site well, for the River Nith cut a deep, wooded valley at this point, overlooked by high, rounded hills. But the Nith had many streams coming down to meet it along this stretch, giving the escapees plenty of shallow channels to hide in, let alone there being a deeper and longer valley, just a little to the south, which cut far into the southern uplands, and – if you went far enough – even allowed access to the main valley running into Scotland from Carlisle in the west. The ambushers weren't the best of shots, but they didn't need to be. With musket balls flying around and ricocheting off boulders, it was more than the soldiers' lives were worth to try to pursue their prisoners. Although the aim was often wide, one poor soldier a few men over from Hugh was killed when the musket ball caught him in the eye when it clipped off the boulder an inch or two away from him.

By the time they dared to emerge, their prisoners were long gone apart from two old men, incapable of making much of a run, and it was hardly a challenge to take them on through the tiny hamlet of Thornhill down to Dumfries. However, their return to Dumfries was as bad as they'd feared if not worse. Blame was laid at the soldiers' feet for this and other escapes by prisoners, Claverhouse was appointed by the government to a Committee of Public Affairs to reinforce the laws, and the sheriffs were upbraided in a government proclamation for lack of diligence in tracking down 'fanatical and disorderly persons', and for not taking action against those who harboured them.

It led to several grim months for Hugh and the rest of his company, as they found themselves regularly stopping and searching travellers, who most of the time were doing nothing more than going about their business, visiting markets and the like.

And with most of the soldiers being barely literate, the number of men dragged into Dumfries or Kirkcudbright tolbooths for nothing more than possessing 'papers', most of which had nothing to do with religion, made the soldiers hated and feared.

"They interrogated me last week for this." complained a local man, as Hugh stepped in to stop three annoyed young soldiers from dragging him in, after they'd been pelted with rotten eggs by his shrieking wife.

"Ye' filthy auld witch." one of the soldiers yelled back at her, as he wiped the stinking mess from his face. "Ye' weren't taking those to market, were you?"

Which made her screech back, "Two whole days, you bastards kept him, last week! Two whole days for nothing! We lost selling our cloth because of you! I hope your mothers are proud of raising such weasel-faced turncoats as keep honest folk from making a living!"

Hugh had to grab the soldier's coat and spin him around as he lurched forwards, clearly intending to drag the wife off the cart and give her a beating.

"Leave it." Hugh commanded, then tried to explain, "The man they sell to only comes down to Kirkcudbright once a month. I know it wasn't us who stopped them the last time, but that's three or maybe four more weeks they'll have to manage without the money they would have earned. It's not much, but it would probably have bought something like the seeds they need to plant for their winter grain, and if it rains, those seeds might get planted too late to do much."

And then the fateful words came back at him from one of the other three.

"Might'a known you'd take the Remnant's side! Coming from here, and all. Your old pals getting caught, are they?"

They turned and stalked off, the lad who Hugh had pulled away spitting angrily into the dirt, and stabbing a finger in Hugh's direction, threatening, "I'll be watching you, Ferguson! I hope you've your prayer book stashed somewhere safe, 'cos if I catch one whiff o' you at your Covenanter prayers, I'll be up to the captain, d'you hear? I'll no serve alongside the likes o' you!"

Adding insult to injury, the crofter and his wife roundly cursed them as they sent them on their way, Hugh's attempt to save them further misery seemingly counting for nothing. They were damned soldiers and nothing more, and just because they hadn't persecuted the crofter this time didn't mean that they wouldn't do it the next time. They seemed to think that it would depend on something as arbitrary as which was the wind was blowing, rather than there actually being some good men amongst Claverhouse's regiment.

As they marched onwards, Murray told Hugh, "You have to stop this. You can't keep taking the part of the locals. It's not our decision to make. We only follow orders!"

"He's right," said Gow, wagging a warning finger at Hugh. "You'll end up in hot water, else. This isn't your personal fight, and I don't want to see you swinging from a rope at the tollbooth."

Yet Hugh was unrepentant. "Where do you draw the line, then?" he asked them. "What does it take for you to stand up and say, 'This is wrong! We shouldn't be doing this,' or even, 'No, I'm not doing that?' I know you all. You all know right from wrong. You don't need a Roman priest, or an Episcopalian minister, or a presbyter, to tell you that. You *know*! So when does your conscience force you to act?"

Gow shook his head. "There's conscience, and then there's being a bloody fool. Sometimes, you just have to recognise that there's something bigger than you, and you canna stop it even if you tried."

Hugh stopped and looked him in the eye. "Something bigger? Is there something bigger than God? Because you don't have to be a Covenanter to have read the Bible."

"But God's no' exactly looking after His own, is he?" Murray pointed out sadly. "Looking at what's going on around here, you might think that the Big Man is on the side of the Douglases and Claverhouse, no' the wee man on his croft."

"Or He's testing us to be better men?" Hugh countered. "You can use that argument both ways, my friends. And while I truly hate, with every bone in my body, the way the Covenanters condemn folk left, right, and centre, and I'd agree that they're not exactly following the Word of God when it comes to others, let alone their attitude to women they think are witches, does that justify us behaving as badly?"

He shook his head regretfully. "I can't stand by, do you understand? Too many stood by while my ma burned, too scared to stand up and say, 'Enough!' If they had, the likes of the McBurneys, the McCartneys, and the Corsans couldn't have got away with what they did. There weren't *enough* of them compared to the rest of us. But they split people up. They relied on them not banding together. And alone, they could frighten families into keeping silent.

"And that's all it takes, isn't it? The majority of people staying silent to save their own skins, when if they all stood up together, they wouldn't be in half as much danger. Look at how this Remnant of the Covenant have got us run ragged. It's not because they're clever. It's not because they're trained and well-armed. They're succeeding because nobody is giving them up to us! Because whether they're right or wrong, they still have families around here who care and don't want to see them shot. And we can't win against that. This time around, the majority of the folk around here are keeping their mouths shut for the right reasons."

"Jesu! Don't let anyone else hear you say that." Tavish gasped in alarm, giving Hugh's arm a shake. "If you willn'a listen to Gow and Murray, at least listen to me when I say I ken *why* ye' feel this way. But for the love o' God, if ye' must act, at least don't *talk* about it. Help when ye' can, but remember: ye' canna help anyone if ye're dead. And ye' might end up with us swinging from the rope alongside ye'! Because nabody will believe *we* didn'a know."

Hugh took a calming breath and nodded.

When they set out on a patrol going north into the wilder lands around Sanquhar, he was less than surprised to notice that Tavish seemed to have a bulkier pack than normal under the heavy plaid he was wearing against the chilly autumn day, and the steady drizzle that was accompanying them. As they got to the scrubby uplands and the heather, and even the tiny farms and cottages became few and far between, Tavish said quietly, "If ye' come again to Argyll, ye' know where to find me."

"You're leaving?"

Tavish nodded, sending a shower of fine droplets off his tangled locks. "I canna do this anymore. Ye' were right what ye' said. At some point ye' have to think o' your eternal soul, and my conscience willn'a let me persecute the ordinary folk anymore. Soldiering to fight a war is one thing. Going up against men as armed as yersel'. But this harassing of folk who dinna ken how to fight, and women and bairns, that's no' what I came to do."

"You're a good man," Hugh said warmly. "May God go with you."

"And with ye', too, Ferguson. Take care."

And with that Tavish slid down into a stream gully and vanished from sight as if he was part of the very landscape.

On the way back they found some of his things, for his absence had been soon spotted even if he hadn't. But Hugh noted that it was anything that would have marked him out as a soldier of Claverhouse's. Beyond here, Tavish was a tartan-clad Highlander, returning home after the summer working in the south.

"God speed, my friend," Hugh prayed, suddenly feeling very much alone.

And more alone he now found himself. Without Tavish's genial presence, Gow and Murray were still friendly, especially when others were around, and they knew that Hugh couldn't risk saying anything which might arouse suspicion. But it was very clear that they no longer spent time alone with him, when others might wonder what had been said in private. Though in fairness, it wasn't all down to Hugh himself.

As soon as they were back in camp, and their captain knew that Tavish had run, he was asking all of those who had been friendly with him what they knew, and of course that meant primarily Gow, Murray, but above all Hugh.

"Did you know he was going to run?" the captain demanded, when Hugh was marched into the townhouse where the senior officers were quartered.

"No, sir, I did not," Hugh answered honestly. And as the captain looked at him in doubt, he felt he had to add, "I knew he was unhappy about how things were working out here."

"Unhappy!" exploded the captain. "It's not a bloody soldier's job to be 'happy' about his orders. He's to get on and do as he's bloody told!"

Then another figure, who'd been at the far end of the room, turned around and Hugh felt his blood run cold. It was only Claverhouse himself! Yet the commander turned a questioning eye on Hugh and said bluntly, "Clarify! In what way unhappy?"

Taking a deep breath, Hugh knew that he was going to have to answer or take a flogging, though he might get that anyway. "Tavish was a Highlander and a Catholic, sir," he began. "He's been worried ever since it's been clear that the Duke of York will become king, and given the present king's health, maybe sooner rather than later."

"What's that got to d…!" the captain began to snarl, only to be silenced by a sharp wave of Claverhouse's hand.

"Carry on, soldier," their commander instructed, glaring at the captain to keep quiet.

Swallowing hard, Hugh continued, "Tavish wasn't a fool, sir. He knew that having the Catholic duke becoming king would be deeply unpopular with a lot of folks in Scotland, and also that the government wouldn't want to risk the lairds in the Highlands who are Catholics, in effect becoming the Duke's private army." He saw Claverhouse blink in surprise, but also nod in agreement.

"Tavish was worried, sir, that when the duke becomes king, that there would be a purge of Catholics like himself from the army, just in case they were found to be plotting with the new king against the government."

That really raised Claverhouse's eyebrows, but Hugh wasn't so overawed that he didn't notice that Claverhouse didn't shoot him down over it as his own captain clearly wanted to do, saying instead, "Carry on."

"Well, sir, we've seen how the local men have been treated by the lairds, provosts, and magistrates. Only last week we met a man who was dragged in and held for two nights just because he had 'papers' on him. That they were bills of sale for goods he had every right to sell meant nothing to those who brought him in, but it was the fact that it took so long to set him free that did the damage…sir. They lost the sale of the wool they've woven, you see, and that's going to put them behind on re-sowing their runrigs, because without that money they can't afford the seed grain."

Hugh took another deep breath and ploughed on, praying silently that he wouldn't end up with his own neck stretched for speaking the truth.

"It doesn't sit well with the locals, sir, but you probably know that without me telling you. But for Tavish, it wasn't such a leap to see that if an unpopular king got the throne, then he, and men like him, might be treated with just as much violence. With nobody bothering to ask if they'd actually *done* anything, or even spoken so much as a word in support of the man who is the current Duke of York.

"He was genuinely afeared, sir, that he might get his neck stretched for no other reason than following the faith he was brought up in. That's why he ran. He's not disloyal, sir. He just feared that too many would condemn him without even caring to look and see that he's been a loyal soldier all these years."

"You see, Douglas?" Claverhouse said, as a hitherto unseen and even more richly dressed figure turned to look out at Hugh from the depths of a wing chair. "I told you that going in like an enraged bull would come back and bite us! …Soldier, do you know how long this Tavish had served us?"

"Ten years, and loyally too, sir."

"Indeed," Claverhouse intoned dryly, while looking sideways at the man who could only be Colonel James Douglas. "You see, Douglas? We are in dire danger of doing as much damage to our own side as good." He sighed, and shook his head as his nominal second-in-command, but politically his senior, waved a dismissive hand in the direction of Hugh.

And Hugh was no fool. He took in the way Claverhouse briefly closed his eyes in exasperation and with a pained expression, and understood that while Claverhouse was the commander and Douglas his second, there was only so much Claverhouse could say to the man when he was so politically connected.

"Thank you, soldier," Claverhouse said in dismissal, at which the captain began hurriedly shooing this reprobate underling of his towards the door, only for Claverhouse to say, "And Ferguson?"

"Yes, sir?"

"Stop thinking! It isn't good for a soldier like you."

And Hugh took the hint. Claverhouse had taken what he'd said in the way it had been meant – simply answering his commander's questions as honestly as he could – but others would seek a hidden agenda. And those men, who had not thought the matter out as clearly, might see Hugh as a threat.

Chapter 22

When Anna and Gary joined Rita in Sally's space up under the eaves, she had already done substantial preparations. Carefully putting some masking tape around the doors of the big old linen cupboards to prevent the incense smoke from drifting in, she had then proceeded to do a thorough cleansing of the room with a white-sage and herb smudge-stick. If she was going to call at least one of the ghosts to her, the last thing she wanted was for some hitherto unknown spirit to gate-crash the party. Not that there were any 'white ladies' lurking around *Nuns' Kirk Haugh* as far as Anna or Brenda could tell her, but it didn't pay to be complacent about such things.

She'd also commandeered a trio of the reasonably comfortable dining chairs from the conference room, so that they'd have something to sit on. Upright chairs were good, because with Gary not being used to meditations, and being between night shifts, she didn't want him getting too comfortable and nodding off at the crucial moment. And she was glad to see that Anna had put on a lightweight sweater under her formal jacket so that she could shrug that off and be more relaxed.

"Right then, are we all ready?" she asked, as they sat down in the centre of the room, having once again lit the three pillar candles, though this time they were set evenly spaced around the room. "I was thinking that we should call upon Hugh first, unless either of you have any good reason why not?"

"No," Anna said. "No objections to Hugh. In fact, I was going to say I think it might be best to do him first, if only because we can tell him we've spoken to his mum, and that she's worried about him. We've got no personal connection to Gideon Corsan, have we? Only women who seem to hate his guts, and that's not a positive place to start negotiating with him from."

Gary nodded. "I'd been thinking along the same lines, but also that as a fellow soldier, it might come down to me appealing to Hugh as someone who's been through a similar thing to desist. I canna make that kind o' connection wi' Gideon," and was quietly smug that Rita was clearly surprised that he had thought it through to that extent.

With that in mind, Rita carefully opened the gateway to the other side and called Hugh's name. At first nothing happened, and Anna was beginning to think that they might have got it wrong that he was one of their ghosts. Then the temperature dropped a bit lower, and suddenly there was the sensation of someone else being in the room if not speaking as yet.

"Hugh? …Hugh, can you hear me?" Rita called, keeping her voice soft. "I come to tell you that I've spoken to your mother. To Jannet."

One moment he was distant, the next, right there in the room with them, making Anna gasp as she recognised him from her encounter when Jensen had fainted on her. It all made sense now. Hugh, who'd seen his mother burned at the stake, and also somehow lost the women he'd loved later in life, had picked up on Jensen's antipathy towards her and been drawn to defend her.

"Thank you for saving me." she blurted out, then caught Rita's sharp glance her way, and could only give an embarrassed shrug.

Yet it was the right thing to have said. Hugh's ghost drifted towards her, becoming more distinct all the time.

"Ye' should watch that man," his disembodied voice said. "He doesn'a care what happens to ye'. I've seen his sort afore doon the years."

"Dinna fash'," Gary said in the broadest version of his accent that Anna had heard, in the hope that it would be closer to the broad accents of Hugh's time. "I threw the shite out ma'sel'. He didn'a linger long."

"Good," Hugh said firmly. "Dinna let him return!"

"Oh, I don't think he'll be back," Anna reassured him. "He does nothing without his father's say-so, and I doubt the old man will want to waste money chasing after me. I'm not worth it."

She meant it in the sense of just an unnecessary drain on Jensen's father's wallet, but it got her a funny look from Rita, but more surprisingly the waspish comment of,

"There was another like that aroond here!" from Hugh. "Hated women!"

"Are you talking of John Corsan?" Rita asked tentatively.

There was no mistaking Hugh's snort of disgust. "Evil auld goat!" he growled. "He was the one who made my ma suffer. T'was a judgement on him that his end was long and slow and full o' indignity. He deserved every minute o' it. I'd ha' made it more painful too if I could ha'!" He gave a ghostly shudder. "But the evil auld swine met his end afore I did, and my reach wasn'a far enough in life as it might ha' been in death."

"The thing is," Rita said firmly, feeling the need to take charge of this situation. "We've been speaking to your ma. She's very worried about you. She's not happy that you are chasing Corsan in death as you did in life. But the thing is, Hugh, she canna pass over fully until she knows you are safe, and so she's lingering here too. You canna feel her because there's a separation between your two places in our present time, but she felt you pass and so knew where to seek you."

She hoped that that would make sense to him, having also broadened her accent from her normal speaking voice. What she really wanted was for his concern for his mother to override his desire for revenge, so it was a surprise when he said gravely,

"Ah, but it's no' just ma mither. She was no' the only woman the bluidy Corsans wronged."

Anna instantly flashed a worried look to Gary, who had also developed a concerned frown.

"There are other women?" he asked warily. "Women who John Corsan wronged?"

"Women who God-curse-him *Gideon* Corsan led to their deaths!" Hugh snapped back.

It made Gary clap a hand to his eyes muttering softly, "Oh, bollocks! That complicates it."

While Anna groaned in anticipation of more ghost hunting, "Did these women die here? Here at *Nuns' Kirk Haugh*?"

"*Nuns' Kirk Haugh*?" Hugh repeated, but looking confused. "I ken no *Nuns' Kirk Haugh* in these parts."

Of the three of them, it was Anna who caught on fastest.

"Oh! Of course! You wouldn't know *this* place by *that* name. I'm so sorry, we didn't think about that. This place you've been in all these years is now called *Nuns' Kirk Haugh*, and for us it's had that name for a long time, but it was probably nearly a hundred years after you died before it got the name. It was called *Blackpark House* before that. The house became almost a ruin, and a man called Grant restored it and gave it a new name."

Rita signalled Anna to stop with the history lesson and asked firmly, "Did the women you talk of die *here*? Here in these buildings? Are they still with you?"

To her relief, if neither of the others', Hugh immediately shook his ghostly head. *Thank God for that!* she thought. *Not another lot of ghosts to deal with.*

"They died on the coast," Hugh told them, and they could see how upset he was about it. "They were tied to stakes in the Firth, or at least one was. My dear Isobel was scourged through the town in front o' everyone as a warning."

"I'm no' doubting your word," Gary began gently, "but if we're to help, we need to have everything clear." He saw Hugh's ghostly nod. "Grand. Then for the benefit o' this Sassenach lassie," and he gave a nod and a wink in Anna's direction, "we're talking about the Solway, yes? No' somewhere like the Firth o' Forth – she wasn'a taken to Edinburgh or elsewhere, is what I'm asking?"

"No, no, just across the bay at Wigtown." Hugh seemed to pull himself together to add, "See, they were found in the hills where others were seized, havin' been to a conventicle. Isobel and young Grissell weren'a there, ye' understand…at the conventicle. T'was just their misfortune that they were close by when Major Windram and his men scoured the area."

Hugh buried his head in his hands in grief. "Why did they listen to bluidy Corsan and no' me? I knew he was wrong to lead them inta the hills. I told them we'd hide further east!" He wrung his ghostly hands in anguish. "I thought Isobel was safe until only a few months afore they got caught. I'd sent them north wi' the Highlanders, ye' see? Wi' friends o' mine who'd ha' kept them safe. But bluidy Edward McCartney turned out to be a weak reed. I thought he'd ha' married Isobel at the first chance, but no, the stupid holy-willy declared he'd no' marry her except in a proper Presbyterian kirk that abided by the Covenant. Well, there were fewer and fewer o' them as they headed north and west, so the damned fool decided to come south again towards Ayr."

Another disbelieving shake of his head. "The fools married, but in Sandquhar, of all places. The one damned place where we'd patrolled time and again and found Covenanter Remnants! I canna fathom why they then thought that they might find somewhere closer to Dumfries to live, but by the time they'd come doon the main road as far as Thornhill, they were mistaken for a husband and wife previously taken and questioned as witches."

"Oh no!" gasped Anna, "They weren't taken and questioned too, were they?"

Hugh nodded miserably. "He was, the damned loon. I ken no' whether it was the beatings he got from auld John McCartney, but he didn'a last long under question. Started gibbering all sorts o' tomfoolery – and I know because my troop were sent to bring them to Dumfries for further questioning. God preserve us, but the man could yammer on! Most o' it utter nonsense by this point, but somehow he managed to implicate Isobel too. Nothing they could take as proof as yet, but for all the emphasis on finding Covenanters, nabody in these parts ever gave up on finding witches, either. It's like they bluidy presbyters thought they could prove their holiness by dragging some other poor wretch doon wi' them.

"So there was a couple, ye' ken. John Alexander and his wife Marion Hopkirk, who'd been detained and questioned only five or six years afore this, though there'd no' been sufficient evidence for a trial." He gave a humourless smile. "After my ma and the seven other women burned together, and another hanged hersel' before they could do it to her – no' to mention Elspeth's ma, Jonet dyin' o'shock at the burnin' – the courts wanted a wee bit more than some presbyter's rants, ye' see?"

Anna gave a little gasp as she realised who the other ghosts must be, but dared not interrupt him as he added, "But Edward and Isobel were mistaken for Alexander and his wife, when they come across them wi' Edward callin' on …well, *something*! He said later t'was the Lord, but if he was rambling even half as much then as later, I can understand why there was confusion. And then stupid Edward said something to the effect – according to the guard I spoke to at the Manse they were being held at when we got there – that Isobel's mither was 'Marione'."

Hugh threw up his hand in exasperation. "Isobel's mither was *Margaret.* Margaret Clark! The Marione who nearly got hanged and burned wi' my ma was *ma* aunt, Marione *Corsan.* Nought to do wi' Isobel at all. To me, aye, but no' her. And absolutely naught to do wi' Marion Hopkirk at all. But all they kent was the words 'witch trial'.

"Had they cared to look harder, o' course it would ha' become clear that her ma was another woman who died at the same time. So she'd ha' probably stood accused anyway, yet they didn'a. But then, o' course, because o' the misidentification, Isobel was immediately suspect as the daughter o' a *pair* o' questioned witches – on account o' ma uncle, Samwell Black, also being accused, though no' brought to trial – and by the time Edward had finished, she was in real danger o' being tried as one!"

Hugh's gulp was almost a sob. "I couldn'a let that happen. I just couldn'a. So one dark night I ran wi' her. I learned later that that same night Edward died, struck down wi' some sort o' seizure or fit. Might even ha' been his heart, 'cause the man was a ball o' nerves and twitches all the time. But ye' can see how all of a sudden, there was only the word o' those who'd heard Edward's ranting, to testify that he was no' exactly sane anymore, and who could therefore clear Isobel's name…if they could even be bothered or dare to."

"Good grief." Anna sympathised. "Poor Isobel! Not a shred of proof and yet already condemned in some men's minds!"

Hugh's gaze turned on her, and for the first time there was real warmth in his smile. "Ye' understand," he said with such relief and gratitude it made Anna's eyes fill with tears.

"Aye, we do," Gary agreed, gently drawing Hugh onwards with, "So, you ran with Isobel, and I presume you found her somewhere to stay in safety?"

"I did. In ma time patrolling, I'd come across another woman accused but no' tried."

"Have you a name for her, please? And also Isobel's surname – her family name," Anna asked, "only it will help me find them in the records."

"Isobel was born Isobel Milligan, then was forced to marry George Hopkirk – so again, ye' can see why she sounded suspect when Edward blathered that out, because it sounded like she was kin to the wife witch they'd questioned. I never got as far as finding if she was properly married to Edward, so you'd best seek her as Isobel Milligan."

"Thank you, that really helps. And this other family?"

Hugh gave a huff of disgust. "He was another who'd save his own skin by condemning his wife. He was John Asman. His poor wife was Grissell Rae, who'd already been dragged in and questioned brutally as my aunt was. The man his-self was content to go to kirk as bidden, but he had an older son and a married daughter who were staunch for the Covenanter Remnant, and given to attend conventicles in defiance o' the law. Mad zealots that they were! So having a wife who'd been questioned as a witch was about as big a rift as you could get in a family – the verra same had happened in Isobel's, in fact."

The three modern listeners nodded in sympathy.

"I'd thought that would make them understanding o' Isobel's plight," Hugh continued, "but when I got there, I hid Isobel just to be on the safe side and went to the Asmans' croft alone. Thank God I did. I never even got to the door afore I heard the psalms being sung. I crept closer through the bracken on the hillside, and saw a coffin being loaded onto a cart to be taken away. Asman walked away wi' the minister and his pals, and it was then that I heard a lass sobbing. It was Asman's daughter, Grissell, who

I'd met first, and now I went down and found her hands bound and tied to a post in the barn. She'd been whipped and left there to 'contemplate her sins'!

"I couldn'a believe that he could be so cruel as to no' let her attend her own mither's burial, but she told me that the last thing he'd said to her in front o' the minister was that she didn'a have her mither to protect her anymore. She was terrified she was going to be tried as a witch herself!"

"Poor girl," Rita said angrily. "How old was she?"

"She couldn'a have been more than seventeen, even then."

"Shameful," Rita growled. "She was little more than a bairn."

"I willn'a argue on that," Hugh conceded with another smile. "So instead of hiding Isobel with them, I found myself on the run wi' two women accused of being witches. That's when I recalled that nabody had lived at my auld home for years. The roof might ha' been off, but I could prop a couple of the auld beams up within the walls to make a shelter, and as long as we didn'a light a fire until after dark, we'd be fine for a few days. Certainly long enough for me to come up wi' a better plan."

He grimaced. "It would ha' worked, too, if not for bluidy Corsan! O' course he heard about Isobel once word got back to Dumfries, and I'd been slower getting south wi' Isobel, because she was exhausted and I kenned I needed to find somewhere off the hills for her to rest up. I meant to take her north to Argyll, where I knew it was safe, ye' see, but whichever way we took to get there was dangerous and she might need to run at times, which she couldn'a do without rest and some decent food inside her.

"So he kenned I was on the run, too, by the time we got into the shire. His evil auld goat o' a father had already died, but Gideon knew where ma home was as well as him, if no' better. And Gideon had persecuted the love o' my life, Elspeth, who had to run to Argyll wi' her faither and mine, and my cousin."

"She's not one of the women who died here, is she?" Anna asked worriedly, already thinking that Hugh had some pretty understandable grievances from what he'd said already. If he'd lost the love of his life here as well, getting him to rest without knowing her fate might be nigh on impossible.

Yet Hugh shook his head. "Nay, she didn'a die here. But I lost her because of what happened here before, all the same. She married my cousin Alex, and they eventually went far away from Argyll, where we'd taken refuge." His ghostly voice broke nevertheless as he added, "I never saw her again. 'Tis why I never married. There was never anyone but Elspeth for me. But Isobel was her cousin, and so like her that for a time I thought I might be happy wi' her."

His next sigh came as if from the soles of his boots. "For her, though, there was none but Edward. Edward who would ha' shit his-self if a mouse had run up his leg, much less wi'stand a proper questioning."

It was a mental image which had Anna and Gary smothering giggles, even though they knew Hugh hadn't meant it to be funny.

"And poor little Grissell? I take it she was Grissell Asman?" asked Rita gently, giving the other two chance to compose themselves, and bringing Hugh closer to events again. "Did you care for her?"

"Only as a poor lost lass. Though I'll no' lie – her having the same name as my much-loved grandma gave me a turn when I first met her, and it carried on tugging at me."

Rita blinked as she remembered just who the Grissell McCartney they'd spoken to in the kirk was to Hugh. "Heavens! Yes, that must have felt very much as though you'd been guided to her to help," she agreed, and saw Hugh's vigorous nod in agreement.

"That 'twas it exactly. I knew what my ma would ha' said, and that was it. I could almost hear her at my ear saying, 'Ye' have to help her, Hugh'. And I did! I was intending to give Isobel a few days o' rest, and had gone out to get a couple o' hares for the pot to give them both a hot meal o' something more than shrivelled root vegetables.

"And that's when he found them. I never got to find out what he said to make Isobel go wi' him, but I suspect young Grissell went because she was too scared to stay there and wait for me alone. No' because she was taken in by him."

Hugh's ghostly form bent over, hands on knees, as he shook his head, still distraught by the memories. "Why bluidy Corsan decided to take them o'er the district border into Cruel Lagg's jurisdiction I ken not. Even then, everyone kent he was given to trials and hangings, no' just imprisonment let alone deportation. Where I'd left them, if they had been caught, at least it would ha' been to Dumfries they ha' been taken to, no' bluidy Wigtown!"

"Was Wigtown that bad?" Anna asked.

"As a place?" Hugh answered. "No. No' that bad at all. 'Tis a fair enough town. 'Twas who sat on the trials there that made the place bad. Our commander, Graham o' Claverhouse was a fair man. Harsh, but fair. He'd do what the law demanded, but no' a jot more. But his younger brother had been made sheriff o' Wigtown, and must ha' felt he had much to prove to live up to his brother. And then there were Provost Coltrane and Major Windram – I wouldn'a have trusted them as far as I could spit, and was proven right. But the worst was Grierson o' Lagg, the local laird. He'd been hanging or shooting Covenanters for months already, and a man wi' no' an ounce of pity in him.

"Well, Corsan was no Highlander, able to melt his way into the heather. I'm no' saying I was quite that good, but I'd spent a lot o' time wi' Sorley McAllister, the man who rescued us twenty years afore, when we needed a friend, and I was way better than Corsan. He left a trail a blind man could ha' followed. Stupid bastard even got spotted in Newton Stewart buying supplies the next day!"

"If the women were that weak, how did you not catch up with them?" Gary wondered.

Only for Hugh to growl, "Oh, *he* came wi' horses! Well, no' exactly horses, but the working ponies from this place!" and he waved a furious arm at the surroundings. "I was on foot, and fleet though I was in those days, even I couldn'a quite keep up that well. And o' course, I'd returned late in the dusk, not wanting to give the game away, whereas he, the fool, rode up wi' two spare ponies in broad daylight in the morning when many folks were about, to what was supposed to be a deserted croft! He might just as well ha' lit a bloody bonfire to show where we were.

"I had to go to ground and avoid those wondering who had been hiding at our place, and that slowed me down, too. So all in all, I was easily two days behind them, and by the time I caught up, they'd already been taken again."

"Corsan, too?" Gary wondered, but got a snort of disgust.

"Nay, not him. He'd left them as I had, to go and get food, but nothing like as well hidden. Wi'out Corsan, nabody would ha' found them, because I left no signs. 'Twas only him having a thing about being denied taking Elspeth fer his ain that had him coming ferreting around our croft, and him knowing that I was on the run too, and where my home used to be.

"Nabody else remembered me well enough for that. And I knew *that* for certain, having been part of Claverhouse's regiment around here for years by then. Aye, they knew I'd been a local, but none cared where, or could ha' found the place with that much ease, as he did. Nay, 'tis all on his head that Isobel and Grissell got caught."

And how on earth are we going to get him to let go and leave when he had that much at stake? Anna wondered worriedly

Chapter 23

Rita must have been thinking the same as Anna, because she leaned forwards and asked gently, "Did Gideon Corsan actually condemn them? Did he testify against them?"

"He didn'a have to!" was Hugh's retort. "Once in Wigtown they were put into the thieves' hole along with three others. One was an auld wifey called Maggie McLachlan, and the other two, young sisters who'd gone to visit her. What damned those two was that the brother who came between them in their family had made a run for the hills to join James Renwick."

He realised that the name meant nothing to Rita, Gary, and Anna.

"Renwick was the leader o' the Cameronians – the last dying dregs o' the radical Covenanter Remnant – who lurked around Sanquhar, drawing folk in wi' his fiery preaching."

"Oh, good grief!" Anna gulped. "We're back to Sanquhar again. So if Isobel mentioned under pressure that she'd been there with Edward, that would have made her look incredibly suspect."

Hugh shot her another grateful glance. "It did. Well, the two sisters, Meg – Margaret – and Agnes Wilson, were only eighteen and thirteen, but then that made young Grissell look less abnormal too. The Wilson girls' faither went all the way to Edinburgh and paid a great fine to get Agnes set free, and came back wi' a reprieve for Maggie and Meg."

Anna could tell that that hadn't gone as hoped for, though.

"Lagg wasn'a having his law overridden in his ain shire, though," Hugh continued bitterly. "They got scourged through the town, Maggie, Meg, my Isobel, and young Grissell, though she was no' much older than Meg Wilson. They even accused them o' being at Bothwell Bridge! Young lasses at a place like that? *Pfhaa*! …I was *there*. *I* fought for the government at Bothwell, so I *know*! But the government had long since declared all who were there were condemned by association, and that gave Lagg and those other foul swine the reason they needed to take the law into their ain hands."

"Bloody hell, a fixed trial," Gary groaned, and looked worriedly to Rita and Anna. This was getting worse at every turn.

As if it was a relief to get this off his chest to a sympathetic audience after all this time, Hugh was already plunging on with, "And they used a *witch's* fate for those women! In Edinburgh, I saw Covenanter women hanged alongside the men! Aye," he'd seen their shock, "that was no' good, but in a *proper* Covenanter trial, wi' legal men in control and all, there wasn'a any distinction made. But there was *here*! Only witches are ever drowned. They didn'a die as martyrs for their faith, they died as witches in every way but name," and he covered his eyes with his hand, overcome.

The three listeners all felt his pain. To have seen his mother strangled and burned would have left psychological scars that would have totally crippled most people. To see someone he loved then being subjected to another grim fate, but one which linked back to witch trials, even if it wasn't openly one, must have ripped open his old wounds in the worst possible way.

"No wonder he can't rest," Anna whispered to Gary, who whispered back,

"PTSD and then some! Poor bastard!"

"Witches aren't persecuted to death now, not in this day and age, Hugh," Rita was saying to him gently. "In our time, there's even a move afoot to get a declaration of innocence for the women killed as witches. It can't bring them back, but it can clear their names, however late."

"Then maybe you'll get justice for mine," a grief-stricken Hugh said.

"We'll do our very best," Rita promised. "Did Grissell drown as well as Isobel?"

Yet that caused another sob. "Isobel didn'a drown. She died o' being scourged before they could take her to the water. She'd no' been strong, y' see. All that walking over hill and glen wi' stupid Edward for months. While she was wi' the army, they got food. No' great food, I'll admit, but enough to keep a body together. But once it came doon to Edward providing, they really went short. She was skin and bone when I found her, already a near ghost o' the woman I'd known."

"I'm guessing that scourging means a whipping?" Anna asked in an aside to Gary, feeling a bit sick.

Gary leaned in to reply quietly, "Aye, but usually a scourge has things like knots in several flails. It's far worse than just a whipping. And I've never heard of it being used on women, only as a punishment in the navy and army in the next century on from him." He looked to Hugh. "Please tell me that someone picked her up and tried to care for her?"

Hugh looked even more miserable, if that was possible. "She fell and couldn'a get up, so the soldiers doing the scourging just left her. I tried to get to her, but bluidy Corsan beat me to it. He was wi' the soldiers guarding them, ye' see, whereas I was in the crowd kept back by them. The bastard carried her back to the tolhouse. Back to prison!"

He gave a savage growl. "But I thought he'd at least get her tended to, so I followed the soldiers as they took Maggie, Meg, and Grissell doon to the water. Where Isobel was, I couldn'a reach her. Couldn'a break in as one man alone. So I thought to try and save at least one o' them from the worst being handed out. Maggie was aye old and unlike to be able to run, but Meg and Grissell were still young lasses, and I hoped…

"God rot their miserable souls, the soldiers stood watch over the women as the tide came in, though thankfully none o' them were men I'd fought alongside – that would ha' been too cruel. Never just one or two men either. I could ha' taken a couple if I'd picked my moment, but half a dozen and all armed? I couldn'a get close, and there were those 'guid folk' who thought to placate Lagg and the Presbyter – because those two were effectively on opposite sides o' the Covenant, but both powerful men if they took against someone – by watching, too. And there was also how I'd get them away in their weakened state? Running for it – and we'd ha' *had* to *run* – just wasn'a possible for them by then. Weak, and wi' freezing cold, sopping wet wool clothes dragging them back…"

He shivered at the memory. "I ran back into the town to see if I could find even something like a handcart, in case I could get one o' them out at night, 'cause I knew that Isobel wouldn'a be walking, and after being up to her neck in cold water, neither would Grissell, even though she hadn'a had the worst o' the scourging. …No' a damned thing!

"…Then I heard that Isobel had died. …Couldn'a help *her* now. …Ran back to the water and saw that the tide had come in faster than I'd expected. Auld Maggie went under as I watched, and I saw the soldiers tormenting young Meg, demanding that she recant and accept the oath to abjure the Covenant. …She wouldn'a. And wi' her and the soldiers between me and young Grissell, she drowned when they weren'a even *watching*. Poor wee lass!" and he totally broke down sobbing.

But then as if from far away came another voice, shouting, "You lie, Ferguson! You bluidy lie!" and the bang of a musket resounded in the confines of the tower room. "Don't you dare speak *her* name, y' cur!"

Hugh spun around, and for the first time they saw a ghostly musket appear in his hands which he brought up and fired back.

"No! Hugh, please, no!" Anna squeaked, but she was drowned out by the crack of the musket, which in the confines of the room was positively thunderous for all that it wasn't in the real world.

With their ears ringing, Anna, Rita, and Gary faintly heard running feet and then Sally and Brenda knocking frantically on the door, Brenda calling, "Gary! …Anna! …Somebody answer me! …Are you alright?"

Gary recovered fastest, and was already on his feet, getting to the door and opening it to reveal their friends looking shocked and worried at the top of the old stairs.

"No harm done," he told them calmly, at which point Anna belatedly realised that of course this wasn't the first time Gary had been around guns, or even been shot at, probably even knowing the difference between the sound of one being fired where it would do no harm, and one which would.

"We saw them!" Sally said in a wobbly voice. "One came haring down the main stairs out of nowhere and fired his musket up at you, then we heard the other gun go off in the room, and the one with you came pounding down past us, chasing the other one back up the main stairs." She sank down on the top step of the stairs. "In all the years I've worked here, I've never seen or heard them before. The one who came from your room almost went through Brenda!"

Rita had by now followed Gary out, and immediately went to the pale and shaken Brenda. "Are you okay, hen? Do you need to have a sit down?"

Brenda gave a small shake of her head. "No," she said, but rather weakly. "It's just a bit of a shock to actually see them after all this time, as Sal said." She looked hopefully at Rita. "Are you going to be able to get rid of them?"

Rita grimaced. "Get rid? Maybe not. Or at least not just yet. But calm them down? Yes, I think if we focus our efforts over the next few days, I certainly think we can take a bit of the sting out of things. If nothing else, we have names for them now, and if I have to resort to calling in the nearest priest to do his thing, it will be more targeted this time. But I'll only do that as a last resort, because that will be pretty awful for the two spirits concerned, and I'm already thinking that they're more grief-stricken than malevolent."

She went and opened the small windows in the housekeeper's room, saying over her shoulder to Sally, "Leave the sticky tape on your linen cupboards unless you need to open them, so that you don't get any incense or gun-smoke drifting in. The smell should clear in an hour or so, but I, at least, will have to come back and work with these spirits tomorrow and, I suspect, the day after."

"Not alone you're not!" Gary said instantly.

"Hugh's no dang…"

"No, Hugh's not! But after what he's told us about Gideon Corsan, until we know otherwise, I'm definitely treating him as suspect. I don't think he has the best of attitudes towards women, even if he's not as evil as Hugh seems to think. Careless at the very least, I'd say, and I'm not leaving *you* at the mercy of someone who doesn't think ahead properly."

His obvious protectiveness towards Rita made Anna turn away to hide her smile. If her aunt couldn't see how much Gary cared after this then there really wasn't any hope, but she'd spotted how Rita had been taken by surprise by his words, but hadn't bitten back at him about not being helpless, as Anna had half expected her to.

Retreating to Gary's cottage, the three of them first resorted to a good brew of coffee and Gary's special cheese on toast, which was both generously proportioned in terms of chunky bread and cheese, and with Worcestershire Sauce, making Anna's eyes water when she got a particularly well-sprinkled bite, plus a tot of whisky each.

"Good grief, Aunty," Anna spluttered around her first mouthful of hot cheese and toast. "That was a bit of an eye-opener, wasn't it?"

Rita nodded, being a bit more cautious over Gary's version of Welsh Rarebit, proving that she'd sampled it before – much to Anna's amusement. So they'd been close enough for that had they? Then what on earth had gone so wrong as to make Rita run for the hills metaphorically if not literally, and Gary feel that there was no hope? This, in Anna's mind, was just as important as the ghosts, because it involved the living, not the dead. However, right now it was the ghosts who were the hot topic of conversation.

"Anna, we need your skills on the computer," Rita said decisively. "Can you do a search for any women killed in the south-west of Scotland in the late seventeenth century? Specifically, the names Hugh gave us?"

"Yes," Anna agreed willingly. "But where does that get us?"

Rita had to pause to suck in cool air around a particularly hot bit of melted cheese which was threatening to burn her mouth. "Ooh! Aagh! …Gosh that was hot…women…south-west… Yes! I'm thinking that if we can tell Hugh that those two poor souls rest in peace in a proper grave, that that might assuage his grief. Especially if we can find similar locations for some of the other women he mentioned."

"Are you thinking of his mother?" Anna asked worriedly. "Only if you are, Aunty, I'm not sure that with my historical skills I can find much more than we had."

"In truth, I was thinking of having another 'chat' with his mum, and asking her if she knows where the other women are all buried. A kirk's name would be all we'd need. Only, if we can 'call them home', so to speak – get them back to where they lie – then they might truly leave this plane of existence. And if they go, then the pull to here on Hugh might not be as strong?"

"I'd say that's worth a try," Gary said cautiously. "Not enough to put all of our hopes on it, but if it works, by God, that would be a start and a half. But I think, Anna, that if you can find those women who died after his mum, that might do more than anything to help him. I just get the feeling that they really weigh heavily on his conscience. He's no fool. He knows he was but a lad when his mum died – or so I inferred, and it might be worth double-checking that with her, Rita, because if he has a guilty conscience there, then we're really in deep water."

Rita nodded in between slurps of coffee. "I got that feeling too. That Hugh *couldn't* save his mum, even though he wanted to. And the obvious reason for that would be that he was too young at the time. But I agree, it needs checking, just to be sure."

They were interrupted by a triumphant, "Ah-haah!" from Anna, who had already opened her laptop at the dining table and begun searching. "That wasn't as hard as I thought it would be. I've found our drowned ladies. Though I have to say that the sisters – who were Margaret and Agnes *Wilson*, and nothing to do with the Margaret and Agnes *Clark* who we knew about already, by the way – and an old lady called Margaret McLachlan, are the only ones named in these online references. No mention of Isobel or Grissell. …And by the way, has anyone else spotted what a wrench it must have been for Hugh to come across *another* pair of sisters called Margaret and Agnes being persecuted as witches in all but name, as the two who died alongside his mum Jannet?"

"Oh crap," Gary groaned. "That's another that's too close for comfort when you factor in the name Grissell as well."

"Isn't it!" Anna agreed. "But the two Margarets who Hugh referred to as Maggie and Meg, are buried in Wigtown, and with a later and rather grand memorial, too. It seems the cases became quite notorious. Enough that they got embellished down the years by certain elements who wanted to blacken Grierson of Lagg's name even further."

Then she stopped and read on a way, paused, and looked up with a grin. "I think we've found what we can use for Hugh."

"Do tell," Gary said with an approving smile which made Anna wish all over again that he'd been her dad, and not the wretched specimen she'd been saddled with.

"There are all sorts of legends surrounding the death of Robert Grierson – and he's the Grierson of Lagg Hugh talked about as the main instigator of the worst of the punishments in the 1680s, so this is someone Hugh really hates. Purely from the historical point of view, long after Hugh's time, Lagg and his oldest son were very involved in the Jacobite rebellions – though not the last and most famous one in 1745 to '46 – and he went from being a favoured man of James the Second, to being a wanted man by the early Georgian kings' governments.

"So although he got rewarded for his tough stance by James the Second when he came to the throne in… oh bloody hell, 1685 …the very same year that Isobel and young Grissell died!" She tapped more keys, leaving Gary and Rita in suspense for a moment. "…Wow! James the Second was crowned in late April 1685, so if Grierson got his reward as part of the coronation handouts, then that can't have been much beyond the end of April. But the women were also taken for trial in late April, and drowned in May 1685! Good Lord! So it's like Grierson gets his 'attaboys' off the King, and promptly gets the bit between his teeth and hands out one of the worst punishments of the time.

"That can't have sat well with Hugh, because if he was alive to see Isobel collapse and die, and Grissell being drowned, he had to know about Lagg's reward. The King's very public approval of a local laird would have gone around the district like wildfire. I've seen how fast rumours can spread through a large workplace to know that."

"Aye, but they didn't have wi-fi or phones back then, nor even like being stuck all together in married quarters like I knew," Rita objected. "It wouldn't have spread anything like as fast."

"Oh, I don't know," Gary cautioned. "You can't forget that weekly markets would have been attended by everyone, because that was the way you got food you couldn't grow yourself, or had run short of. And neighbouring towns, maybe ten to fifteen miles apart, wouldn't all have held their markets on the same day precisely so that local merchants could attend more than one. So you only need to have a local merchant going to two or three markets within a week on, say, a Tuesday, Thursday, and Friday, and then do the same in another district the next week, and within ten days news has ripped through the whole shire.

"No, I'm with Anna on this. And all the more so because remember what Hugh said? Isobel and Grissell would have been safe if they hadn't been taken into Lagg's own jurisdiction. They weren't half a shire away, they were on his doorstep. So as soon as

Lagg himself knew his good fortune, you can bet his servants had gossiped to everyone they knew about how their laird had been so honoured. And Hugh said he himself was stuck in the crowds, so you can bet your boots *somebody* gossiped to him about what had happened to the very man who'd ordered these punishments, *and* within the last week or three."

"Oh God!" Rita groaned, foreseeing all sorts of complications, as Anna carried on with,

"And we don't know yet how close to those events Hugh died, do we? Even if he died very shortly afterwards – maybe even as a consequence of those drownings in some way – yet before the news arrived, if what you've told me is right, Aunty, he'd have been more strongly attached to the physical world. But if he heard the news while he was alive, which I agree with Gary is much more likely, and they'd only just died, or even while he was *seeing* them die …jeepers! Seeing the man who – in his mind – as good as murdered two women he was trying to protect, then knowing that Lagg got rewarded by no less than the King for his actions, would have been salt in his wounds every bit as much as the salt-water on Grissell's.

"So that makes what I've found out about Grierson of Lagg all the more important to pass on to Hugh. You see when he finally died in…ooh. 1733 – he'd had a good innings, hadn't he for a man who was royally hated in every sense of the word. *Oooh…!*"

"When he died…?" Rita prompted a touch impatiently, and getting a scowl from Gary for it, because he knew that Anna was doing her best.

"Erm, yes. When Lagg died, there are all sorts of legends and rumours about his funeral. The most pervasive ones are about the horses pulling his hearse dying of exhaustion on the road between Lagg's townhouse in Dumfries, and the graveyard which was… Yikes! Just down the road from *here*."

"Exhaustion?" Gary echoed, looking bemused. "But there's hardly a hill worth mentioning between there and here. Certainly nothing that would be such a challenge for a pair of well-kept horses pulling nothing but one old man's coffin."

"But that's what it says here," Anna said with a shrug of confusion.

"The weight of the Devil," Rita said with more assurance. "That's what it's supposed to convey. His soul weighed heavier than it ought because he was the Devil's servant."

"Seriously?" Anna gasped. "They believed that back then? Heavy enough to kill two horses?"

"Most definitely," Rita assured her, and Anna wasn't entirely sure that Rita herself didn't believe such a thing.

"Wow! But here's the real crippler – a rook landed on Lagg's coffin, and didn't leave until it was in the grave and the first soil about to be thrown on it! Isn't that a witch sign, Aunty?"

Rita's face relaxed into a grin. "Oh yes! We can use *that* with Hugh! His mum and the women who died with her sent a sign that they'd make sure Lagg didn't lie easy. Yes, I can work that into something that will make him believe that Lagg didn't get off scot-free. And hopefully that will help him rest a little easier."

"This might help even more," Anna told her with a smile of her own. "It seems that Margaret McLachlan and Margaret Wilson got remembered even if Isobel and Grissell didn't. There's a monument been erected in Wigtown to commemorate them, along with others who were persecuted. Do you think you can work that into Isobel and Grissell being remembered, even if not by actual name?"

"I certainly can. And it might just work!"

Chapter 24

Anna was only going to get one full day off in the coming week because of the need to get set up for the wedding, and that would be on Thursday, but Rita was worried about leaving any further contact with any of the ghosts until then.

"It doesn't leave us much time if things don't go as well as we hope," she told Anna and Gary worriedly.

It meant that on the Monday morning they were back in the remains of the old kirk to talk to the female ghosts. And very swiftly they were able to ascertain where Grissell McCartney's and Geillis' remains lay. Grissell was in the burial ground at the parish church at Kirkcudbright, though she was able to tell them that she had gone into an unmarked grave, and not alongside her husband, William Corsan. He had been buried earlier in a regular grave, whereas she had been laid in a pauper's grave right by the graveyard wall. And as Gary explained later, those edges of consecrated ground were frequently disturbed.

"The Kirk charged to bury someone, and the main parish churches guarded their rights to that income verra jealously against the smaller chapels which gradually appeared. When archaeologists have been able to investigate the edges o' graveyards, they almost inevitably find the remains of babies and small children buried right up against the outer walls, because their parents couldn'a afford the burial fee. Sometimes you find an infant buried in wi' someone older, because the family had to wait until someone who the kirk knew about died, and then slip the wean in with them."

"That's awful!" Anna exclaimed. "Those poor parents."

"It was as close as they could get to them being on consecrated ground, you see. But the same goes for the inner edges. From the faith view, the edge is where the Devil would be more likely to get to you. So the wealthy made sure they were well inside, and the massed paupers' graves are right on the very edges – almost like a buffer for those more valued by the village or town, grim though that sounds to us now.

"So while William probably couldn'a afford a *good* grave site he, at least, got a decent one. And now that Grissell has told us that he died long before her, you can see that there wouldn'a have been the cloud hanging over him of her reputation when he passed, or at least nothing like as much. Whereas he wasn'a around to defend her when her time came."

The fact that the parish church at Kirkcudbright was called Greyfriars, and had been the former convent, wasn't lost on them either.

"Another connection to nuns," Anna told them from another online search. "And…good grief! A convent established in 1449 by…eh? James the Second? That can't be right!"

"Ach, you Sassenach, you!" Gary teased. "It means James the Second of *Scotland*, no' James the Second of England, who we've been talking about – he was James the *Seventh* here in Scotland."

Anna rolled her eyes in exasperation. "Okay. But up here in Scotland, we're still talking about a Catholic convent or nunnery, whichever James the Second we're talking about, aren't we?"

"Oh, aye. Definitely Catholic before it was reformed in the following century, just like here."

"And would our nuns and those nuns have known one another?"

Gary thought for a second. "Maybe no' personally, though it wouldn'a be beyond possible that the two prioresses, or whatever they were called, would ha' known one another. And the nuns at each place would surely have known *about* the other place."

"So is that why Grissell can connect to here more easily?" Anna asked, looking to Rita.

Her aunt was already nodding. "It could help the connection considerably, I would have thought, though never having dealt with connected burial places for a close family before, I can't be absolutely certain. But it's enough to think that I must go to this church in Kirkcudbright and do a bit of work there. Maybe, if the minister there is amenable, I might even be able to ask if he or she will say some prayers for Grissell."

Geillis, however, had predeceased her husband, Robert Clark, by many years, and he had ensured that she had been buried in the nearby parish church at Irongray.

"But, Irongray?" Anna said with a shiver. "The place where her sister-in-law was held and tortured – because let's stop pussyfooting around this 'questioning' business, and call it what it really was. It was nasty and psycho-sexual, what with all the stabbing their private parts with what any modern psychologist would identify as brutal phallic symbols."

That made Gary look at her a bit askance.

"Sorry, Gary, but it is. I may not have had the fanciest of educations, but I did do psychology up to A-level, and found it interesting enough to have read a bit since then. You're talking about men desperate to crush any woman with a jot of authority, but why did that have to involve what was pretty clearly genital mutilation, and stabbing their breasts? Hugh was right. The Covenanter women who actually got in front of a proper, legal trial, in places like Edinburgh, may have had the regular forms of bloody awful torture, like the thumbscrews, but they didn't get the worst of the creepy stuff. That was only witches, as he said."

"Then we need a trip to Irongray church, as well," Rita said grimly. "Because that has to be the reason why Geillis still links so tightly to her sister-in-law Jonet, as well as to her own daughters Margaret and Agnes."

"And don't forget Marione Corsan, Hugh's missing aunt," Anna reminded them. "She was tortured at Irongray Manse in 1650, eight years before Jonet. She's Grissell's daughter just like Hugh's mum Jannet is. Just because Grissell and Jannet don't know where she ended up, doesn't mean that they've forgotten that she was tortured in the place where Geillis is *buried*, and where Geillis' sister-in-law – that's also Agnes and Margaret's mum – Jonet was tortured, too. These women are so connected!"

"Then we've got to fit in a trip to Irongray," Rita groaned. "*Sheesh*, but we're getting tight on time!"

"Luckily I'm off tonight and tomorrow night," Gary said, "because like Anna, I'll be on all over the weekend. Tomorrow's Tuesday, and Anna's on in the morning again, so why don't you and I go to Kirkcudbright first thing, Rita? We can then come back and pick up Anna to do Irongray?"

Rita considered that and then agreed, saying, "Kirkcudbright sounds like it's nothing but a regular graveyard, so although I'd like three of us there, all we're doing there is calling Grissell back, and she was never actually tortured…was she? Please, Anna, tell me she's not on your list of women who died under questioning?"

"No. No, she wasn't. It's her connection to her daughters and sister-in-law, that's all."

"Thank the Goddess for that! Okay, Gary. Time for me to do a bit of coaching with you this afternoon while Anna goes to work. Anna, you're a bit more up to date, anyway, but I'll try and chat with you when you've finished the evening rush."

Come the following morning, Gary drove Rita down to Kirkcudbright, and they found the lovely little church of Greyfriar's, huddled in the lee of MacLellan's Castle in the centre of the quaint fishing port.

"What a lovely town." Rita said appreciatively, as they strolled in the spring sunshine to the church.

"Aye, it has quite the reputation as an artists' hang-out," Gary told her. "What you might find interesting is that time-wise this is definitely a late castle, and more of a tower-house like the one at our place would ha' been. This one would only ha' been around a hundred years old in 1685. …See? It's the same L-shape as the old tower-house at *Nuns' Kirk Haugh* would ha' been. And here's our kirk, just across the road."

Rita turned around taking in the full 360-degree view. "It really is lovely in both the physical sense and the psychic," she said with satisfaction, but then grimaced. "But *sheesh*, Gary! There's bugger-all of the original graveyard left."

She threw her hands in the air in exasperation. "I could go around here dowsing for days and never find

William, let alone where Grissell is – probably under God knows how many feet of hard core and tarmac!" For the old kirk was completely encircled by the roads around the quay area and parking places.

Gary gave a sigh. "Aye, we've struck out here, all right."

"All my preparations and we've been defeated by modern road builders, and whoever shovelled up the graves and took them to somewhere else," Rita grumbled. "That's if they even bothered with any bones they found that were that old! I can't imagine that there have been any burials here in the last century for anyone to bother about. In the name o' the Wee Man," she fumed, becoming very Glaswegian in her ire, "why could they no' have left consecrated ground well alone?" And she stomped off back towards Gary's truck in high dudgeon.

Nor did they do any better come the afternoon at Irongray, and with Anna in tow. The church as it stood was clearly from well after the time of the witches, having none of the welcoming atmosphere that Rita had experienced at Kirkcudbright, and Anna was able to tell them that the Irongray Manse of the present day was not the same building where the two witches had been imprisoned and tortured, either. Both buildings had been rebuilt in the following late-eighteenth-century, and yet for no obvious reason, Anna agreed with Rita that there was something about Irongray that made her uncomfortable.

"It's a pretty enough spot," Anna said to Gary, looking around her, "and the church is nice looking, so why do I feel like I'm being watched?"

Some elegant, old iron lampposts lined the walkway to the church, which was harled and painted white, except for the ashlars edging stones whose red sandstone was so dark from the recent rain as to almost be black.

"It's smart and very respectable," Anna observed, "and they obviously respect things like their war memorial, so why do I feel that this place is soulless? There's nothing warm here, and I don't just mean that today has turned chilly."

Rita smiled at her. "There's nothing wrong with your instincts, hen. You've tuned in to what I'm feeling too. It's as if somewhere along the historical line, people have felt the need to whitewash over what happened here. To forget women like Jonet and Marione, and what was done to them here."

"So who are we trying to find here?" Gary asked, bringing them back to the reason for their visit.

Rita gave a worried huff. "Ideally, we want to bring Geillis back here. She's buried somewhere here with her husband, but whether I'll get her back any easier than Grissell remains to be seen." And she looked around her with a frown.

"Does it help that the Manse is across the road and not immediately next to the church?" wondered Anna. "The torturing of Jonet and Marione was done there, not here."

Yet Rita was reluctant to commit on that. "The minister, or presbyter as we should properly call him, was the same man in both buildings. It might have made a difference for us if one was the original building and the other not, but when both have been rebuilt since, it's more to do with the pervading atmosphere than anything still standing today." And she began dowsing around the graveyard to try to locate Geillis' resting place.

"I still find this place creepy," Anna confessed softly to Gary, who drew her back out of Rita's hearing before saying comfortingly,

"Maybe it's a lot to do with the fact that once you know, you *know* – if that makes sense. You knew bad things had happened here even before you set foot in the place, and that's not something that your subconscious will allow you to let go of, even when you're not actively thinking of it. To the modern congregation, who know no different, it's probably just a nice old church."

He was glad when he saw Anna give a sigh of relief and nod to him gratefully, leading him to make a mental note to tell Rita to ease off a bit on Anna and the psychic stuff. It wasn't that he doubted Rita was right, nor that Anna had inherited talents in that direction. Indeed, he didn't question it for a moment. But Rita had long ago told him that she had grown up with a mum who had been very active in the alternative circles, and had encouraged her to do the same. That was very different to Anna having her parents, who never seemed to have thought her capable of anything. Shoving her too hard to assimilate the things Rita had known for a lifetime, might well make Anna run hard in the other direction.

For now, they went across the sodden grass to join Rita when called, but clearly Geillis was resisting her.

"It's as though she feels no connection to here at all," Rita growled in frustration after they'd given up and were getting back into Gary's truck. "You'd think the bloody woman had no kin here at all."

"Maybe she hasn't?" Anna suggested, making Rita swivel in the front seat to give her a sharp glance.

"What's that supposed to mean?"

"Easy, Rita," said Gary, firmly. "Don't snap her head off just because this didn'a go any better than

Kirkcudbright. Let Anna explain." That got him a glare of his own, but Rita turned back to face forwards yet addressed Anna via the vanity mirror in the front visor.

"Go on, then."

Anna shrugged. "Well, why assume she *does* have kin here? For all we know, she may have been born and brought up a long way from here. Just because she married Robert Clark, who *was* a local man, and settled here, it doesn't automatically mean that her parents and any siblings are here, does it?"

"Anna, it was before the bloody railways, let alone the motorways." Rita riposted in exasperation. "People didn't move about like nowadays!"

"Except they did," Gary contradicted her, and firmly. "Rita, in those days there was a lot of poverty in the Highlands, just as there is today. And just like now, Highlanders came south for work. It was nothing for the well-born men, whose equivalent they'd ha' called squires in England, to hire men seasonally. They couldn'a afford to take someone on as a bodyguard, for instance, and keep a grown man through the winter when they were no' travelling much. Whereas a Highland man could come south and make a goodly sum to take back to his family come the winter, and Highlanders were always known as bonny fighters. If you wanted a man to watch your back on the road between here and Edinburgh, for example, many would hire a Highlander bodyguard for the summer.

"And the same went for nursemaids. Wet nurses: now they were probably local women, because you couldn'a guarantee being able to get a woman to come south and still be able to nurse by the time milady's bairn came. But once weaned, you'd need a nursemaid for a few years, would you no'? So an unwed lass from up north quite often came down to work for those years in some middling-sized household, then went back home and got married wi' some money o' her own. So what's to say that Geillis wasn'a one o' those?"

It took a moment for Rita's expression to soften, but then she sighed and nodded. "Sorry for snapping at you, Anna. It's been a wearing day for me. Yes, it's the obvious reason when you think of it in that way, isn't it? If this wasn't Gellis' family's home, then the only thing here is her husband, and I've presumed a lot in thinking that it must have been a close marriage. People don't have to be endlessly at one another's throats, for a marriage to cool down to just peaceably sharing a house with one another, but compared to the love for a child, that marriage might not count for much in the end."

Anna was startled when Gary caught her eye and flicked a glance Rita's way. What was that supposed to mean? She'd always thought that Rita and Archie had been blissfully happy? This was something she was going to have to quiz Gary about, because if Rita hadn't been as contented as she'd assumed in her marriage, that could alter why she was reluctant to trust Gary.

And it was *trust*, Anna thought, as she settled back in the seat and watched the countryside go by. Rita clearly liked Gary a lot – was possibly in love with him – but the more Anna thought on it, the more she decided that Rita's ability to trust someone enough to marry them had taken a battering somewhere along the line. Whether that had been while Archie was alive was something else she felt she was going to have to ask Gary about, because she couldn't see Gary standing by and doing nothing if Archie had been too free with his fists, for instance – though the idea of Rita standing for that didn't feel right, either.

However, with Anna having another early start on Wednesday, once they got back to the hotel, all they could do was have something to eat, and then Anna get ready for bed. But as he hugged her goodnight, before she flitted around to her own cottage, Gary confirmed her suspicions by saying, "We'll chat when we're on late-night duty." He gave her a conspiratorial wink.

It was after that when Gary noticed that Rita soon went to bed, and in an obvious bad temper. It reminded him of years ago, when he used to call around to Rita and Archie's married quarters, and witnessed some spectacular rows. Both had been strong-willed and stubborn, and as able to give as good as they got, though back then the making up had been equally as passionate.

He'd known all along about Rita's temper, and if her fiery personality was one of the things which he admired, he also recognised that at times she could be an absolute pain the neck when things didn't go right. *Batten down the hatches, Gary, my lad,* he thought as he went to his own room. *Things are likely to get stormy if I'm not mistaken*! Although he did chuckle at the thought that life with Rita was never going to be dull.

Chapter 25

As soon as Sally and her two ladies had finished getting what they needed from the attic room in the morning, Rita went up there alone. For no logical reason, she felt the need to try to contact Gideon, because unlike Gary, she sensed that he was grieving for at least one of the women concerned. And Gary's protectiveness was all very well, but not if it was going to get in the way of quieting this second ghost. This afternoon they were going to drive over to Wigtown to look at the memorial there, and before they did that, she wanted to know if finding out about any of the women would help ease Gideon's misery.

"Gideon? …Gideon, if you're there, please come and speak to me. I want to hear your side of things. Gideon, are you there?"

It took a little longer than it had calling Hugh, and when Gideon appeared, he only came as far as the door. Or at least the ghostly door in his world.

"You can come in," Rita told him with a friendly smile, but he shook his bonneted head.

"Nay. I canna, mistress. If I do, *he'll* come," and Rita knew he meant Hugh.

"Okay." She picked up her chair and took it closer to the door, which in her time was firmly shut, but made sure she wasn't going to get bowled over if someone opened it unexpectedly. "Now then. Let's have a talk, just you and me. What's going on here? Why can't you rest?"

Gideon looked as gloomy as any man she'd ever

seen. "Why me?" he asked rhetorically. "Why did I have to have a faither who was hated far and wide? Hated so much that when I met a lass I loved, that she wouldn'a look at me twice except to spit?"

For a moment Rita was stumped. What on earth could she say to that? Finally she decided to ask, "What was her name? This lass you fell in love with?"

"Isobel. Isobel Milligan."

It took all of Rita's self-restraint not to give a whoop of triumph. Now she was getting somewhere. A love triangle!

"And did Isobel love Hugh Ferguson?"

"*Pfah*! Nay, she didn'a look twice at that witch's get."

Oh bugger! Rita thought. *Not a triangle, then.*

But luckily Gideon was carrying on with, "Edward bluidy McCartney, that's who she was all doe-eyed over! Why him? His faither was hand in glove wi' my miserable auld goat, and both o' them profited fra' getting those cursed witches burned. Mine was no' the only family whose pockets got filled! …Ha! She couldn'a look at me, but she was all over bluidy Edward. Edward who was as weak as water. Wouldn'a say boo to a goose, let alone stand up for her."

"So why do you hate Hugh Ferguson so much?"

Gideon's face became a fierce scowl. "He and that witch o' an aunt o' his left with her family and took another woman I longed for wi' them. They escaped justice, as my faither and John Corsan saw it. Went north wi' some Highlander, as I heard later. As a lad at the time, I didn'a realise that those bluidy families would tarnish my life, but I soon did. And then just when I thought life might get better. When ma faither put me in charge o' building this place, and

I'd ha' had somewhere good to bring a wife. Who turns up but bluidy Ferguson! Stirring the pot again."

"Oh dear, that must have been frustrating."

"It was a damn-sight more than that, ye' daft woman!" Rita bridled but managed to stay silent. "All o' a sudden I was back to being looked at like I was the cur that brought the plague to town. Folk who'd started to recall I'd just been a lad at the trials now looked at Ferguson and remembered he'd been one too, and became all sympathetic to him again."

He began pacing. "It was here – here outside this verra place – that he booted ma brother John. Hit him square i' the chest and sent him backwards. John hit his heid on the stones, and that was that! One day I was thinking that, at last, ma brother was old enough to help me with our faither in his infirmity. The next I had another dribbling idiot on ma hands. But at least it allowed me to get Isobel out o' old Presbyter Veitch's hands and into our house."

Rita couldn't stay silent at that. "Isobel was in the *Manse*? Did Veitch torture her?"

Gideon looked at her as if she'd gone mad. "Torture her? Why in God's name would he do that? Aye, she was a witch's daughter, and Thomas McBurney was quick to offer her to Veitch as housekeeper to save her soul. And aye, she was expected to warm Veitch's bed, too. But he was awful auld by then. He probably couldn'a have raised a stand for the Last Trump', let alone a woman. …Nay, when her husband died she was lucky McBurney found her that place, or else she'd ha' been out on the streets, since her ain faither wouldn'a have her under his roof again. He wanted no reminder of his witch o' a first wife, and certainly no' when he had his hands full wi' his second wife."

"And you didn't offer her a place in *your* house then?" Rita asked, having to practically grit her teeth over Gideon's blithe dismissal of what it would have cost Isobel to be forced even to sleep alongside a man, however old, who had been instrumental in murdering her mother, let alone have sex with him. At a grim best it would have been traumatic, at worst there was possibly repeated rape to factor in to the abuse. No wonder Hugh was furious if he knew about this.

"I couldn'a invite her in!" Gideon snapped, with a filthy look. "I was no' in charge back then. I was stuck wi' the auld man telling me to do this and do that, and get this bluidy place built that I never got to enjoy."

"Could you not have left home and got a croft of your own with her?" Rita asked innocently.

"Wi' what?" he sorted. "Crofts dinna grow on trees! I had nay money o' ma own, only what the auld miser would hand out. The only roof I had over ma heid was his, so I had to stick it out. Oh, I wished many a time that I'd left when our middle brother, Matthew, left and went to St Andrews, but then he – the bastard – was the cause of me nearly losing everything, so much good that would ha' done me."

God, you really are a self-centred sod, Rita thought in disgust. *Hugh seems to have managed without any money, so it wasn't impossible to do if you'd really wanted to leave. Oh, you're aggrieved, alright, but it's all about what's happened to you. How the heck am I supposed to get you to leave for the benefit of others if you never think of anyone else?*

However, trying to draw him back to the matter at hand, she asked, "So what about Isobel, then? You say you got her back. To here?"

Gideon gave a terse shake of his head. "Nay, this place wasn'a finished enough then. 'Twas the auld place. Isobel did the cooking and cleaning. Then she looked after John when he went soft i' the heid, while McKay did the heavy work for our faither, and then the lifting and shifting o' John as well when needed."

He gave an angry snort. "Ha! She did for the auld man for about two years. I didn'a know that McCartney had been sneaking around to see her. Thought she hated the McCartneys as much as she did us, especially as she and her man had been forced by her faither and him to work young McCartney's croft for him.

"God! If ma faither had handed me ma ain croft like his did for him, I'd ha' worked ma fingers to the bone to make it work. Instead, it all went to ruin once her man died. Auld John McCartney might ha' been a scheming auld devil, but he couldn'a leave a good croft to go to waste, so he threw bluidy Edward out to a smaller place, sold it to get something back on it, and sent Isobel to Veitch. Kept a roof over her heid, didn't it?"

By now Rita was thinking that Isobel had been dealt one of the roughest hands in life she'd ever come across. And clearly Gideon wasn't going to give her the details of how it had all gone wrong in the way that Hugh had, so all she felt she could ask was, "So how did Isobel die?"

"All bluidy Ferguson's fault!" Gideon immediately ranted. "Her and bluidy McCartney must ha' left wi' the army, though I doubt he had the balls or the backbone to join up." The last was said with a sneer of utter contempt. "But God-damn-him Ferguson was one o' the men who captured them on the road. Took them and made a run wi' them."

"Why would he do that?" Rita wondered aloud without thinking, because in her mind this version of events wasn't making much sense.

"To take his revenge on McCartney, o' course." Gideon told her in a voice that said she must be thick not to get that.

"But wasn't this Edward merely the son of the man who'd helped kill his mother?"

"Ach! And ye' think that made any difference? It didn'a stop him ruining ma life and ma brother's, did it? So why would it be different for McCartney's? I dinna ken what happened to McCartney until I heard he'd been brought home to bury, so Ferguson must ha' done him in on the road. Then I kent it. He was taking ma Isobel to his place to have as his ain. I wasn'a going to stand fer that!"

Rita could see Gideon's anger rising, but could only think that he had judged Hugh by his own standards. It had never entered his head that Hugh wouldn't have laid a finger on Isobel, let alone raped her in some perverse revenge, especially as…oh, God. That was it!

"Gideon, listen to me!" she said in what she hoped was her best stern aunty voice. "You got it wrong. Ferguson wouldn't have laid a hand on Isobel! She was the daughter of a woman who burned *alongside* his *mother*! Whatever he thought of Edward McCartney, there was *never* any question of him hurting a woman who he thought of as as much of a victim of the witch trials as himself."

That halted Gideon in his tracks, but only for a moment. "Then why did he chase us, eh? And who was that other lass he had wi' him? Her mither didn'a burn wi' his."

"No, she didn't, but the lass you saw had a mother who had since then been accused as a witch. The lass…she was called Grissell, the same as her own mother, and the same as Hu…the same as *Ferguson's* own grandmother. He didn't want to see another woman called Grissell get hurt, it was as simple as that. That's all he was doing."

"Ha! See? You ken naught. If she was a witch, she could ha' got away."

Losing patience with this ignorant ghost of a man, Rita retorted, "Oh? Like the nine women whose deaths you say blighted *your* life? Did they nip onto their besoms and fly away before the flames got them? Turn into their familiars and slink off like cats in the night, did they? No, they didn't! They stayed and they died. So were they really the threat you thought? Or just ordinary women who'd got in the way of powerful men?"

"They were the Devil's spawn! The Presbyter said so!"

"And how would he know? Did he have…?"

"…He's a man o' *God*!" Gideon roared at her. "Do ye' no' respect the word of *God*, woman?" And in that moment, Rita saw it.

"You were afraid of him, weren't you? Afraid of Veitch. What did he threaten you with? Eternal damnation if you didn't do as he said?"

Gideon look anxiously over his shoulder as if expecting to see the ghost of Presbyter Veitch appear and drag him to Hell, before he yelled back at her, "Never say those words!" And he began reciting, "I believe in the Covenant. I believe in God and the word o' God," in an almost panic-stricken way. "Be gone, foul woman! Away wi' ye' afore ye' bring hellfire and damnation down on me!"

And to Rita's horror, he swung the musket which was over his shoulder around and brought it to bear on her.

"Behave yourself, Gideon!" Rita managed to snap out, though she was more than a little shaken by his resorting to violence like this. "There's no need for that. Put that thing down!"

But Gideon wasn't listening, instead backing down a step or two and shouting, "Yer all trouble, you women. Ye' turn men soft i' the heid wi' all yer tempting ways. *I* saved Isobel when she fell and couldn'a take her punishment. *I* was the one who picked her up and carried her to where she could rest. But who did she call out to wi' her dying breath? Bastard Ferguson! …I'll no' let his bastard get their filthy hands on ma house, no' even now! …Treacherous whore!"

He was sobbing now and retreating further. "…Break ma heart, would ye'? …Ungrateful besom! I loved ye'! …Why did ye' never look at me? How dare ye' call upon him who seized ye' to rape ye'? …How could ye' betray me even in death?" And then he was gone.

Sitting back and gulping in breaths of relief, Rita was half glad that Gary hadn't been there, because he would certainly have had something to say about the way Gideon had spoken to her. But also half wishing he had been, because she wasn't sure just how lethal that musket might have been if Gideon had ever fired it, and she knew Gary would have known what to do if she'd been hurt. And what on earth was that all about at the end when he'd mentioned Ferguson's bastard? Had Hugh had a child he didn't know about? Heaven help them, that would really complicate matters if there was a third descendant in the mix alongside Anna and Gary, though who that could be, she couldn't imagine.

When she could stand up without her knees turning to jelly, she locked up the housekeeper's room again and went down to the main stairs where she handed the key to Sally, who was just finishing checking the rooms they'd had guests leave that morning.

"Is anyone in the Rosemary suite tonight?" she asked.

Sally shook her head. "No. Nobody's booked in there until the bride arrives on Friday evening."

"Bloody hell," Rita groaned. "That's only two days away."

"No luck with the ghosts, then?"

"The one, yes, in a way. But unfortunately, he's not the one who I think gives the trouble with amorous couples."

"Oh dear!"

"Very much so. Damn it, I'm going to have to go the full hog and expel him from the suite, at least, until we can resolve things properly. I'm still none the wiser as to why he's so active all of a sudden, but we can't take the chance that he'll wreck this young couple's wedding night. Have you enough Febreze to be able to get rid of the smell of incense if I do it tonight? Only I'm going to have to go in full-on, with candles and the lot."

Sally nodded grimly, understanding why Rita was so worried. "I tell you what. I'll get Gary to come and help me, and we'll get all of the soft furnishings out of there for a night or two. Strip the bed, take the curtains down, and take the little bedroom chairs up to the room Anna was using. That way, there'll be nothing for the scent to cling to, apart from the carpet, and a good spray around with the windows open ought to do it."

"Thank you, Sally," Rita said, genuinely grateful that Sally was being so proactive, because that hadn't always been the case when she'd gone to help folk.

Luckily, it didn't take Gary long to do the bits up stepladders to help Sally, lifting down the heavy brocade curtains, and so while she carried on stripping the bed, Gary was able to drive Rita and Anna over to Wigtown in the afternoon. He was far from pleased that Rita had contacted Gideon on her own, and said so, but Rita managed to deflect the conversation by telling them both of her fears.

"I can't think of any way to appeal to Gideon to *not* appear when the bride and groom are in that room," she said worriedly. "He's a complete mess of contradictions. One minute he's saying he was so in love with Isobel, the next he's cursing her for calling out Hugh's name with her dying breath."

"Do you think he's thrown that information at Hugh during this three-hundred-year battle?" Anna asked worriedly. "Because if he has, then that's only going to make Hugh feel worse for not getting to her in time."

Gary sighed. "Given the depth of hatred on Gideon's side, I canna imagine that he wouldn'a have. The 'it's all your fault' blame-throwing that yon Corsan man seems to indulge in, makes it all too likely. It would be too tempting for him not to."

"I agree," Anna said, and eager for Rita and Gary not to have a falling out, hurried on with, "So what is this plan, Aunty, that has you getting Sally to empty out the suite?"

"I think I'm going to have to banish Gideon from the whole of Rosemary suite."

"Don't snap my head off," Gary said dryly, "but you didn'a have much luck at getting shot of them the last time you tried just telling them to go."

Rita groaned. "I know. But…the big difference this time is that I'm not trying to get both of them to leave the building for good. I just want Gideon out of two of the rooms. That's a smaller ask in the first place. And secondly, I now know his name. That's a powerful thing to be able to use."

"And you're no' going to do the same to Hugh?"

"No, Gary, I'm not, and that's because I don't think it's Hugh who has such a lousy attitude towards people who are being loving towards one another. If he feels a person, and particularly a woman, is being threatened, then yes, I think he'd appear. That's what happened with Anna and Jensen. But I'm as sure as I can be now, that the ghost who frightened the life out of the young couple who were in the room before them was Gideon. He's the one who's a menace to young, happy couples, not Hugh. And I think if we beg Hugh to steer clear of those rooms just for the days while the wedding is on, I think he's a decent enough soul to agree."

"I hope you're right," Gary said, not very optimistically, but by now they had reached Wigtown.

With it being a tiny little town, it didn't take long to track down the memorial, which was uphill from the main road at a place called Windy Hill, and signposted. Anna had brought her tablet with her, and immediately began taking photos with both it and the camera on her phone.

"I'm taking some selective images with the tablet so that hopefully Hugh can see them," she explained, and showed Rita and Gary where she'd zoomed in on,

This Monument
has been erected

in memory of the noble army of Martyrs
in Galloway and other parts of Scotland
by whom during the age of persecution our
Religion and Liberties as now established
were secured

"That's general enough, isn't it? He doesn't need to know that neither Isobel nor Grissell is named on here in the way that the two Margarets are. And I thought this bit..."

were drowned by sentence of the Public
Authorities
in the water of the Bladnoch near this place
on the 15th May 1685
because they refused to forsake the principles
of the Scottish Reformation and to take the
government oath abjuring the right of the
people to resist the tyranny of their rulers

"And then this bit in particular..."

There lies a virgin Martyr here
Murdered for owning Christ supreme
Head of His Church and no more crime,
But not abjuring Presbitery
And her not owning Prelacy
They her condemned by unjust law
Of Heaven or Hell they stood no awe
Within the sea tied to a stake
She suffered for Christ Jesus sake
The actors of this cruel crime
Was Lagg, Strachan, Winram and Graham
Neither young years nor yet old age
Could stop the fury of their rage

"Surely that should lead Hugh to believe that these women are remembered, even if rather incorrectly as Covenanters? I can't easily remove the religious references and still be able to show him something of the inscriptions. If I tell him that there were men remembered on the monument too, he'll hopefully be convinced that eventually they were commemorated as religious victims and not witches, albeit not any time soon after he and they died.

"Somehow, I get the feeling that that might matter a lot more to him than it would us. We'd want them remembered, and any way better than none, but my feeling is that he regarded it as doubly deceitful to condemn them as Covenanters but kill them as witches. Well, there's not a hint of anything witchy on here, is there?"

Still feeling mentally bruised by her encounter with Gideon, Rita said nothing, but Gary was quick to say, "Aye, we can make this work. Job well done, Anna."

"Not tonight, though," Rita said rather more waspishly than she might have. "I can't go through another contact without a decent night's sleep."

As Rita was already heading back down to where Gary had parked, Anna realised that the chances of her getting to see the other memorials in the town were slight, not least because it had taken far longer than she'd expected to get here. The coast road, Gary had told her, was the faster route but longer, while the drive over the hills to Newton Stewart and then south was shorter but the road much more twisting and slower. So if Rita wanted to go straight back it was still going to take nearly two hours. Yet Anna looked out from the memorial over the estuary of the River

Bladnoch and wished that she could go and look at where Grissell died. There was something tugging at her deep inside, and she knew that she would have to come back here, even if it was alone.

It made for a quiet journey back, with Gary suggesting that maybe Anna should have Harris and Lewis with her that night because, as he said in an aside to Anna when they'd parked the truck and Rita was already heading for the door, "Your aunt and I have a few things to discuss."

That worried Anna a little, but she just smiled and said, "Bring them round whenever you like."

What she wasn't expecting was for Gary to appear just after eight with the dogs, and asking to come in.

"What's wrong?" Anna asked worriedly, praying that they hadn't had an almighty row.

Gary pulled a face. "I think Rita knows I want to have a serious talk wi' her, but got the wrong idea about what. So no sooner had we eaten, then she was off for a long bath, and then vanished into her room. Door shut in my face, so to speak."

"Oh, hell, Gary, please don't say she's packing her bags to go. I don't think I can handle this weekend and a distraught Aunty Rita."

"Nay, lass," he said comfortingly, with a gentle hug. "Come on, I've got the whisky wi' me. I've a secret to share wi' you instead."

Chapter 26

Harris and Lewis by now had been in Anna's cottage enough times to have their own blankets on an old sofa that Anna and Gary had dragged back over from storage, and promptly settled down to start dreaming about chasing rabbits, going by the twitching feet and excited yips in their sleep.

"Oh how I wish I could just drift straight off like that," Anna said enviously, watching them with fond amusement as Gary poured them each a Dalwhinnie – the light and delicate malt whisky that Anna had become rather fond of. "Come on, then, what's this secret you need to share? You've got me intrigued!"

Gary settled on the second armchair Anna had temporarily commandeered and asked, "How much do you know about Rita's marriage to Archie?"

Anna looked at him suspiciously. "Up until now, I'd have said that it was extremely happy and loving, but I've got a funny feeling that that wasn't the case?"

Gary grimaced and rocked a hand, signifying yes and no. "Did you ever meet Archie?"

"Sadly, no. He died, what, sixteen, seventeen years ago? I would have been in my teens then, and still very much under Mum and Dad's thumbs. Back then, I only knew of Aunty Rita as this half-sister of Dad's, who rang up every now and then and sent Dad into one of his massive temper tantrums. It was a birthday card on my twenty-first that came with the invitation to visit Rita, which really got us together. You see, she sent the rail ticket all paid for, with a fairly open date for using it – which I now realise must have cost her a bit, even if she bought it far in advance. Even then, it said to me that here was someone who wanted to know *me*, and that meant a lot.

"At the time I was going through a particularly rough patch with Mum, who kept trying to turn me into my older sister, Heather. So I thought, 'Sod it, what have I got to lose?' I booked time off from work, and told Mum I was going away with a friend from work for a week to Butlins. In Mum's eyes, that was so crass and vulgar, she couldn't even bring herself to ask me for any more details," and Anna laughed at the memory.

"I think when she finally realised that that had been the start of my relationship with Aunty Rita, she wished she'd stopped me going, though in truth there wasn't much she could have done aside from fully throwing me out. And she was never going to do that, because that would have meant relinquishing what little control she had left over me. I found that out with the massive row we had when I bought my own flat. Good Lord, Gary, you'd have thought I'd changed jobs and become a prostitute, the fuss she made, instead of working in the office at a supermarket," she said and laughed again.

"I'm glad you can laugh about it," Gary said fondly. "Many would let a childhood like yours warp them all out o' shape. So well done, you, for letting it go."

Anna gave a sardonic smile. "In truth, it wasn't so much letting it go, as thinking that it just wasn't worth the effort pushing back against them anymore. Not saintly as much as bloody exhausted! It's hard work being around narcissists like them, Gary. They suck the life out of you, and I will forever be grateful to

Mum's spinster aunt, who had sufficient by the end of her life to leave me a share of the money from her home and savings, which enabled me to use it as a deposit on my flat. Without that, because of the money Dad was demanding off me for 'keeping' me every month, I'd still be saving up now to get the deposit. The mortgage itself was a doddle after that."

"Christ!" Gary muttered in disgust, then took a deep breath and started again. "Fair enough, so you would ha' got to really know Rita by, what, about ten years ago?"

"Yes. Probably that."

"So did ye' never wonder why she was in a *rented* cottage? Her being a widow and all?"

That made Anna sit up and blink. "No. …I suppose if I thought about it at all, I thought that his army pension wasn't that great to allow a short-term, high-payment mortgage. I mean, by that time, the mortgage lenders had been caught out by the big banking crash in 2008 – something I'd had personal experience of, because they were really cagey about lending me money, even much later and with the size of deposit I could put down. So I supposed – and I guess you're going to tell me wrongly – that while Aunty Rita had more than enough to live on, that she just didn't satisfy the bank's criteria, not least because she wasn't going to be working for another twenty-odd years."

Gary looked at her surprised. "That's a slant on it I'd not thought of. Yes, I can see that from your point of view, and given Rita's age at the time, it would have seemed perfectly normal that she'd rent. …But did ye' never question where all o' Archie's wages for all o' those years had gone to? The man put in thirty years from when he enlisted at eighteen, for God's sake!

And he was a Colour Sergeant by the time he retired, no' still a bloody private. He wasn'a living on a pittance."

Now it was Anna's turned to rock her hand. "Yes, but living on a base and out in the civilian world are two different things, aren't they? I've worked with a couple of ladies whose hubbies have come out of the forces, and they both said that it was a lot more expensive once they were out in the 'normal' world. …And you, Gary. You aren't living in your own house, are you? You didn't come out and get a mortgage straightaway, did you?"

"Jeez, no! But I got married way too young, got royally fleeced by a wife who was canny enough to get a sharp lawyer on her side, and spent the next fifteen years paying alimony. And my ex was sharp enough to live wi' a guy but never marry him. So I had to carry on paying until she met someone richer than me, who made it worth her while to let me off the hook.

"*That's* why I haven'a any savings, Anna. I hadn'a anything but my monthly money coming in by the time she let me go, and in the few years I had left, it wasn'a sufficient to make a decent deposit – or at least no' on anywhere I'd ha' wanted to live, anyway. Maybe some scummy flat in an estate like those around Cumbernauld, where I'd ha' had to be prepared for it to be broken into several times a year. But I knew what I'd do to anyone I found doing that, and I had no desire to end my days in prison for wringing the neck o' some wee scrote."

That made Anna laugh. "No, I can't imagine you going easy on some delinquent you found ransacking your place."

"The term up here is a 'wee ned' – a non-educated delinquent."

That had Anna collapsing in laughter. "Oh, I shall have to remember that. A wee ned – suits the type perfectly!"

It made Gary smile to see Anna's genuine amusement, and relieving the tension made it easier to tell her the next bit.

"Rita's troubles have been altogether different," he began. "Archie loved her, no doubt about that, and there was never another woman. Not ever. But I think that's what blinded Rita. When he said everything was fine, it was. At least where their marriage was. But the thing is, Anna, Archie had an addiction." Anna's eyes went wide. "No' drugs or booze. The ponies. And the dogs. Basically, anything to take a chance on."

"Oh, God, no! He was a gambler?"

"Totally. He managed to keep it hidden while they were in married quarters, and o' course the postings overseas – often where he couldn'a put a bet on anything – helped. But back home he got bored. Craved a bit o' the old excitement, so he'd only been out a year or so when Rita found out that they were broke. And I mean spectacularly broke. Like, 'no' enough for the next month's rent' broke."

"Shit!"

"And she had no idea how much he was into some verra nasty people for until the silly sod got off his face to try and work up the courage to tell her. Instead, he never got to say a word, but having written it out in a rough draft o' a letter, went head first down the concrete steps from their flat pissed as a rat, and broke his neck. Literally. So Rita had the double shock o' finding him lying in the maisonette hallway when she came home from work; and then some verra nasty pieces o' work turning up the week after, demanding their money."

"Oh my God! Poor Aunty Rita."

Garry nodded. "Poor Rita, indeed. Archie was the love o' her life, no doubt about that, but in one week, all o' her trust was smashed to bits."

"Oh, Gary, that's terrible." Then light dawned for Anna. "Oh, my God, and poor you, too. That's why she thinks the world of you, but can't bring herself to trust you! Oh, that's too cruel. You've done nothing like that to her, I can see that. But I can also see, for the first time, why she finds it so hard to trust you enough to give you a chance to live together. She must eternally be worried that you will have some secret, as Archie did, that will leave her in a financial mess, or worse, for years to come. …It was years, wasn't it? Because I can't imagine some loan shark letting Rita off the hook because Archie had died?"

"Verra perceptive of you. No, the loan shark wasn'a happy. And all credit to Rita, because he was even less happy when she went to the polis and wore a wire which got the main man a prison sentence. That's why she was up in the Highlands under her maiden name. Mrs Archie Hamilton from Nairn was a verra different person to be looking for from Ms Rita Montrose in Grantown-upon-Spey, even if they're hardly half a country away from one another."

"Bloody hell!" Anna had to stop and take a few deep breaths to process that. "It never occurred to me that the reason why Aunty Rita lived up a farm track, miles from anywhere, was because she was being hunted by someone!"

"She's no' being hunted anymore," Gary said firmly, and Anna had the funny feeling that whoever the loan shark had passed his debt on to, to collect while he was inside, had come to regret that. There was that quiet steeliness about Gary that said woe betides anyone who crossed him, and even more, anyone who hurt somebody he cared about.

Anna found herself grinning at Gary, who at first looked surprised that she might have twigged what he really meant, and then a silent grin back which said that he knew that she knew, and that she wouldn't say anything, either.

"But you, Gary," Anna suddenly said, now appalled. "You are paying for Archie's faults that you had no part in. That's really unfair. You deserve to at least be judged by your own standards, not somebody else's."

"Aye, well, back at you, kiddo," he said with weary acceptance. "I look at you and wonder what the hell your parents were on that they couldn'a see what they had in front o' them. However good and bonny your sister was, it's no excuse for ignoring you. But worse, I'm cross wi' Rita for forgetting what you've been through already. I've seen you, Anna, having a wee sniffle into a tissue when you think nobody's noticing, and if none o' the others recognise it, I can see that it's because you look at what a grand thing this wedding at the weekend is going to be, and you wondering why the hell you couldn'a have had the same."

"Oh, Gary," Anna gulped. "Is it that obvious?"

"Do you mean, are the customers wondering who the weeping lass at the reception is? Then no, you've been verra discrete. Have Brenda and I noticed that it's a bit of a sore spot for you? Then yes, we have. Brenda's kicking herself for not having thought it through and taken on more of the wedding arrangements – particularly because this is the verra first wedding we've had since you've been here to do the arranging for. Because it dawned on both of us a wee bit late in the day, that it was no' exactly kind to expect you to be beaming wi' smiles at someone else's big day, when your own went down the pan less than six months ago."

Anna managed a watery smile. "I think 'down the pan' is a bit of an understatement. Completely trashed and out with the empties, would be better. But thank you, and please thank Brenda for me, too, if you talk to her before I do. It means the world to me to know that if I suddenly feel a bit overcome, I can ask one of you to man the fort for half an hour while I get myself back together again."

"No problem. And on the subject of you leaning a bit more on people who care about you. For the love of God, please stand up to Rita when she tries to steamroller you into this psychic stuff."

Anna blinked in surprised. "How do you mean?"

"Look, Rita's mum was a strong and forceful woman, who encouraged Rita all the way. The fact that Rita barely remembers her father, because he worked the rigs and was frequently away for months on end, means it was a verra women-only household. He was no' a bastard like your father's father who she mercifully missed out on having, but he wasn'a there for a lot o' her growing up, either. It means she has no idea of what it must ha' been like for you as a wee girl standing up to a father who threw his weight around in a bad sort o' way. I know you've said he didn'a hit you, but there's more than one way o' hurting folk, and your dad sounds like an expert in the emotional blackmail department."

"Oh, he was that all right."

"So please understand, I see how living wi' that all those years has given you scars, Anna. It doesn'a mean I think you weak. Quite the opposite. But Rita says jump, and you never stop to say 'wait a minute', you just ask how high. And in that she shares that strength o' mind wi' her half-brother, your dad – though she'd kill me for saying so!

"And in the case o' these two ghosts, I think that you're no' as detached as Rita is. You feel Hugh's hurt, do you no'? That caring for someone, and then finding that they dinna care for you as much as you'd hoped? For him it's Elspeth. For you, it's having nearly handed your life over to that fud Jensen," though he didn't enlighten Anna what a fud was, given that he didn't use more English terms like 'twat' in a woman's presence, "who didn'a value what he had in you. It's too close to being the different sides o' the same coin, Anna. So be careful."

Anna was momentarily stunned, never having thought of Rita in that way. But she very quickly realised that he was speaking out of kindness, especially when he added, "And young Cameron Wiseheart. He's a nice enough lad, but he's no' the only fish in the sea, Anna. You don't have to jump from yon' long streak o' pish Jensen straight to someone else. You're no' that short on time to have a family! Don't feel you have to grab the first one who shows an interest in you, because he's the only one who does, there and then."

"They weren't exactly queuing around the block for me before Jensen," Anna riposted bleakly. "That's why I was so easily sucked in."

She saw Gary visibly restraining himself from saying what he thought of Englishmen who could be so blind, instead pointing out, "But you were stuck down in the office, wi' just a few lassies. You said yourself, you didn'a go up onto the shop floor unless all hell was breaking out – and that's no' the time when some guy is going to stop and start chatting you up, 'cause the old wifeys behind him in the queue would as like lynch him for holding them up."

Anna laughed at the memories of furious old ladies in the till queues. "You're right about that. So many stressed shoppers at Christmas and Easter!"

"Aye. But now you're out in the hotel. And forgive me for saying this, but you're meeting a different kind o' person too. Most o' your old customers would ha' been women, or married couples, am I right?" Anna nodded. "But here we get a lot o' men on business. Some are workmen, but the kind we get here are craftsmen, whose bosses find it worth it to pay for their stay – they're no' filling in the potholes because they canna do anything but wield a shovel." Now Anna was giggling, and although Gary smiled with her, he added, "For the love o' God, please don't sell yourself short. Take your time and find someone who really sees *you.*"

Anna got up and stepped across to give him a hug. "Message received and understood. And thank you, Gary…for caring."

After he'd gone, his words still lingered with her, and she went to bed more determined than ever to be friendly with Cameron, but not let herself be carried away by daydreams that weren't how things would really turn out. And although her bedroom wasn't on the haunted side of her cottage, nonetheless Harris and Lewis snoozed on their blankets by the side of her, never twitching a whisker all night, which indicated that the nuns and other ladies were resting easy at the moment.

However, getting up on Thursday, she knew that they had to make the most of this only full day when she and Gary could help Rita, and braced herself for what might be as exhausting a day as the wedding to come. And Gary must have been thinking the same, because he was around bright and early to take the dogs out.

"Today's not the day to have them wi' us in the hotel," he said regretfully, "So if they're going to be cooped up in my place, I'd best give them a good run now."

"I'll come with you," Anna said, pulling on her newly acquired wellies. "A good blast of fresh air is probably just what I need before today."

It was therefore a very companionable walk around the fields surrounding the hotel, Gary throwing balls for Harris and Lewis, and Anna just enjoying seeing the spring flowers coming up in earnest now. Not a lot was said, and she thought that this was one of the things she wanted in life now – someone to go for a nice country walk with without feeling compelled to make small talk, or listen to them going on and on about themselves. So it was a bit of a surprise to see Rita's black look at her when they got back. What was that all about? And then Anna guessed.

"Aunty!" she said sharply. "How well have you been taking your own advice?"

Rita's head whipped back to her, looking affronted, but Anna wasn't put off.

"You've been like a bear with a sore bum with both Gary and me since yesterday, and the way you just looked at me when we got back is like I just cheated on you with your boyfriend – and that isn't you! That isn't you at all! So I know you told us that you warded the *room* when you went solo with Gideon yesterday, but how well did you ward *yourself*? Because this jealous anger at people is more him than you."

For a second there was a flash of fury on Rita's face and then she went pale.

"I'm guessing that that means not as well as you might have?" Anna asked innocently, and Rita had the good grace to blush. Gary, on the other hand had initially been shocked but now was looking smug.

"Excuse me," Rita said faintly, "I think I'd better go and have another bath. I raided Emilio's pantry for the right herbs for later on, so I have them, but have you got some salt, Gary?"

He couldn't refrain from grinning. "Good job I keep a big packet in store in case of needing to use it outside in the winter, then, isn't it?" he said, disappearing and coming back with a kilogram bag.

"I think I might be using quite a bit of this," Rita said with a wince, and retreated to the bathroom.

"Time for us to warm up wi' a mug o' coffee, then," Gary said cheerfully to Anna. "And well spotted! That stubborn woman will get herself into deep trouble one of these days if she canna learn to trust people to help her again."

Chapter 27

When Rita rejoined them, she looked much more like her old self, if a bit sheepish – not an expression seen from her very often.

"We need to go and raid the kitchens again, and the gardens," she told them. "We're going to make some heavy-duty smudge-sticks. I came with more than enough white sage, but I want some camomile for peace, protection, and purifying; and some basil leaves, because they'll bump up the protection, but also invite happiness. Would the bar have some of those rings of dried lemon for making fancy G&Ts with, Anna? Only lemon boosts energy and also does the purification and protection thing, but burning fresh lemon is going to smoke like mad." She stared off into space as she ran through her mental list. "Peppercorns would be helpful, and some peppermint, but I'd really like some pine fronds and some juniper ones, and some eucalyptus leaves."

"Sorry, Rita," Gary interrupted her, "but we haven'a any eucalyptus trees around here, and our grounds are no' an arboretum wi' lots o' difference species o' trees. I presume when you say pine, you mean a real pine tree, no' just a bit o' conifer?"

Rita groaned. "No, I'm afraid when the recipe calls for pine it means pine, not larch, or leylandii cut from a hedge."

"But we do have juniper in the cocktail bar!" Anna said triumphantly. "It comes in the same cocktail mixes that we get the dried lemon in. It's juniper seeds not the leaves, but will that do?"

"Actually, that might be even better," Rita approved, "because fresh leaves would be damp and likely to smoke in the wrong sort of way. We can't stink the bridal suite out and leave it smelling like we've had a bonfire in there, so yes, something that's actually dry will smoulder better. Right, come on, you two are going to make a smudge bundle each while I make mine. That way we've got three personalised ones, which should help protect you against bloody Gideon's presence. Damn the man, what a pest he's turning out to be!"

Having left a very perplexed Emilio in the kitchen, after they'd gone in and taken not only basil, but also bay leaves when Rita saw that he had them, they took themselves into the conference room.

"Let your intuition guide you as to how much of each you use," Rita told them. "We're doing it here, because this is part of the same building that connects through time, but we're not up in the danger zone yet."

For half an hour, they followed Rita's lead, carefully wrapping things like the juniper seeds into the leaves, and bundling them with the sprigs of white sage. Each of the smudge-sticks were tied carefully together with some of the clean white string which Emilio normally used to tie meat parcels together for cooking, until they had a tightly packed shape that looked like a rather large and fat sausage of herbs. They'd picked up some cinnamon sticks too, Rita only thinking that they would give Anna and Gary something to start working around, its meaning here for her being success, but it was interesting that both Anna and Gary chose to use three sticks of it when its other attributes were love and prosperity (and not just in the material sense). She knew Anna was subconsciously wishing for the kind of love that would lead to a wedding like this coming one, but the way Gary kept giving her odd glances said that he might not have given up hope that she'd relent, either.

That was for another day, though. Once they'd got their bundles, Rita led the way up to the Rosemary suite, and was glad to see that Sally had already been in and opened the windows, and that everything that could physically be taken out was gone.

"Right, let's do this," Rita said with grim determination.

She carefully lit each of the smudge-stick bundles so that they were just gently smouldering.

"We are of one mind that we are doing this to remove the presence of the person called Gideon Corsan from this room. Keep that to the fore of your intentions all the way through," she instructed. "We're not banishing him as some sort of punishment. We're protecting the young couple who will arrive tomorrow night. So we keep going until I can't feel him here anymore. If you feel something pulling you to a certain part of the room, follow that instinct, and waft the smoke around until you feel it's right to move on."

Rita went to Anna and, pulling a black crystal bracelet off her left wrist, slipped it over Anna's right – the one Anna was automatically holding the smudge in. "You wear this one. See? I've got the other one on my smudge hand? Gary, I'm not as worried about you, because I think Gideon has a particular antipathy towards women. The smudge should be enough protection for you, because you're far from weak-minded."

He quirked an eyebrow at her that said if Gideon tried any funny stuff with him, he might find he'd bitten off more than he could chew.

While Rita took up position as near to the middle of the room as the bed-frame would allow her, and began calling Gideon to her, Gary found himself doing what he thought of as 'patrolling the perimeter' with his smudge bundle, yet Anna felt a pressing need to go and smudge the bathroom. It was a space which might see quite a bit of fun if the bride and groom were really passionate, and all of Anna's instincts were saying that the last thing they needed was someone drowning in the big roll-edged bathtub. As she went into the little lobby of the suite, she felt something cold pass her, and guessed that Gideon had been tugged reluctantly to Rita.

She worked on wafting the herbal-scented smoke into every nook and cranny of the bathroom, also trying to be methodical, working from the door over to the window. She took a pause, then worked back the reverse way to the door, finally closing the door firmly and smudging all around it. The lobby would, she guessed, be the last place they would deal with, because they wanted to make sure Gideon had left, not become stuck, trapped by their smudging in the access to the room.

Back in the main bedroom, however, it was clear that Gideon was resisting.

"You have no right to blight the life of the people coming in here," Rita was saying in her sternest voice. "Leave these rooms, Gideon. Get out!"

"No!" the ghostly figure shouted back at her, and almost hysterical edge to his voice. "This is *my* room! *My* room, not theirs. How dare they come into my space and rut like animals?"

"You're *dead*, Gideon. What part of that do you not understand?" Gary interrupted. "Ye' blighted your own life with your jealousy and bitterness. Now bugger off and stop screwing over the living! Out! …Go on! …Shoo!" and he began wafting the smudge right in Gideon's face. "Out o' this room. Now! Go on."

Grasping what Gary was doing faster than Rita, Anna stepped up onto the bed base to form a kind of guard of honour to the doorway, wafting her smudge vigorously in a line to create a kind of funnel which led only one way. Then as Rita caught on too, she began smudging from where Anna's ended, leaving Gary to be the psychic sheepdog, herding Gideon to the door. At which point it was a good thing that Anna had followed her instinct to seal the bathroom, because Gideon instantly went to go that way the moment he had passed her at the doorway.

With a ghostly snarl, he battered his transparent fists on the door, yet couldn't get through. Turning towards Anna, he yelled.

"I curse y…!"

"…No!" Rita cut him off. "You curse *nobody*! Never again! *Enough*, Gideon! This stops now. If you cannot live in peace with the people who've come along after you, then we will force you to leave. And not just these rooms. I will expel you forever, if you force my hand, with the help of a priest. Do you want that?"

The ghostly face which was turned towards them was a mask of fury, and he screamed, "I'll no' let a Ferguson ha' ma place! Ye' ken? *Nay Fergusons*!"

But with the three of them now pushing him to retreat, alone he couldn't resist them. As he tried to make a final stand in the suite's door to the landing, Anna dodged under Rita's arm to stand by the bathroom door, wafting the smoke all around it again. When Rita stepped out of the bedroom, Gary followed Anna's lead in smudging the whole of the doorframe and the door itself. Meaning that finally, with his ghostly fingers scrabbling against the lobby's doorframe to no effect, Gideon was shoved out onto the landing, where he vanished as if he'd fallen off something high, and with a scream he was gone.

Gary shut the bedroom door and then he and Anna smudged the lobby while Rita did the landing side. As Gary and Anna stepped out onto the landing, Rita insisted, "Now smudge yourselves! Don't give that psychic vampire anything to cling to! Make sure you are absolutely clean before you move away."

They felt a bit daft wafting the remains of the smoke around them, and before they opened the fire-door onto the stairs, Anna ran along the landing and threw the window at the far end open wide. Only Sage and Thyme rooms had doors onto this section of the landing, the fire-door opposite the lift effectively sealing the corridor to the other five bedrooms on this floor, and nobody was coming in to any of them until Saturday morning, so the smoke had time to dissipate.

"Good job I moved all the remaining guests to the second floor or the four in the round tower," Anna said with a grin as she sprinted back to join Gary and Rita. Yet they all felt a chill as they opened the door to the stairs going down.

"Bloody hell, he isn't lurking around here, too, is he?" Anna asked worriedly, peering over the banister down onto the reception desk.

Rita paused and looked around, for all the world as if she was one of the hounds getting the scent of a rabbit. "I think *he*," – and she was very careful now not to say Gideon's name in case it pulled him back towards her – "had the strongest attachment to the rooms we've just done. Honestly? I didn't expect it to be so hard to get him to leave them.

"I think whatever Rosemary was in his time, it was a special space for him. All that bit about '*my* room' bothers me. And the fact that he wouldn't enter Sally's bit makes me think that Hugh has a particular link to that space which he can likewise successfully defend against his old adversary. Although if that's Hugh's space, and Sally hasn't ever had any problems, that makes me think that Hugh isn't going to be the problem *he* might be."

By now they had got down to the mezzanine seating area at the turn of the stairs, and Gary stopped.

"That's why there's a strange atmosphere here, too. Harris and Lewis picked up on it when I was sitting here talking to Cameron. And that's why I had the feeling that someone was listening in on us."

"Was it Hugh or G…?"

"No, Anna! Not his name! Not here, not today!" Rita cut her off with, startling Anna, who rephrased,

"Can we know which one is here, though. Or might it be both?"

Rita shrugged. "Could be both, but I think the fact that nobody has ever seen either here means that while they can come here, neither one has ascendancy over this space, and that's been its saving. Come on, let's give it a quick smudge and leave it at that. That should be enough to avoid any disasters for this weekend, at least."

They went down and outside to take the last smouldering smudges to where they could just burn out, though Rita carefully tucked one on each side of the main entrance out of sight, while Gary's went by the tackle room door as the only other access to the house on this side of the building.

"Now for the love o' God, can we go to my place and have some bacon and sausage baps?" Gary said. "I'm starving!"

Anna and Rita laughed, but Anna admitted that she was in need of some serious sustenance too.

"Okay, can I use his name now?" Anna asked when they were sharing their loaded baps with Harris and Lewis, whose large furry heads were resting hopefully on Gary's table, eyes swivelling from one person to another in eternal hope that a bit would come their way.

Rita nodded, mouth too full to answer.

"Then do you think we've seriously weakened Gideon's grip on the hotel?" Anna continued. "Because I've been thinking that maybe the reason why you couldn't shift them before is that each of them died somewhere in the old tower-house, and they set up their respective territories long ago. So long ago, and to resist attacks from one another, that they effectively fortified different parts of the place psychically if no longer physically?"

Rita looked at Anna, startled. "That's a very good analogy, and one I'd not thought of. Yes, that sense of building barricades against one another, and fighting in the territory in between fits too well to ignore. Well done, Anna. See? I told you you have the family talents!"

Yet Anna didn't seem as buoyed up by that as Gary thought she would, which was explained by her next words. "But we don't know *why*, do we? Why, all of a sudden, have they become more active? You can't tell me that this is the first happy couple we've had here, not even if our two ghosts can somehow see further into the future than we can, to be able to predict when they might need to manifest? In fact, they can't anticipate like that, can they, or Gideon would have been prepared for us today. So I keep coming back to, what's changed?"

"It can't be me," Rita said with some assurance, "not because I'm trying to duck out of being responsible, but because you had a period of peace after I came the last time, didn't you, Gary? And my odd visits stopping in the hotel never triggered anything, while this time I've arrived *after* things started kicking off."

"Fair point," Gary agreed. "And you're right, you being here doesn't match at any key point. But you do, Anna."

"Jeez!" Anna squeaked in horror. "*I* didn't invite them in."

Gary reached across the table and took her hand in his. "I'm no' blaming you, lass. But we have to acknowledge that something about you being here has been a catalyst. It might be something as simple as you being here all the time and being heartbroken. Do you see what I mean? Other people come and go. But you're over there a lot as the manager, and have been for months. And on top of that, that dunderhead Jensen coming and stirring the pot right in the worst possible room might mean that Hugh, at least, feels a need to watch over you to defend you. And if he's quietly watching over you against yon' fanny-baws…"

"Gary!" Rita remonstrated. "Language!"

Anna laughed. "After working where I did, I've heard a lot worse, Aunty, and you have to admit, it does rather fit Jensen."

Rita rolled her eyes. "Please! Don't encourage him," making Anna giggle, having seen Gary's covert wink at her, both of them relieved that this was the Rita they knew and loved, not the angry woman of yesterday.

However, Gary had got Rita thinking. "I'm really sorry, Anna, but I think that Gary's right. It does all rather point to you being the catalyst. So we really need to get you well protected with some crystals, and psychically tooled up with your protection. That should help enormously if neither of them can feel you quite as intensely."

However, when Anna nipped out to the loo, Rita immediately whispered to Gary, "It's got to be more than that. I don't want to frighten Anna, but there's something about her that's doing this, and it's not just what went on with her and that nugget Jensen."

"I agree," Gary said, then he grinned at her. "Language, Rita! You can take the woman outta Glasgow, but ye' canna take Glasgow outta the woman!"

Rita sat back and folded her arms underneath her breasts as she'd seen the older women doing when she was a girl, and with fake indignation said, "Well he *is* a nugget! A full-blown eejit, too."

"I'm no' arguing!" Gary laughed rising his hands in mock surrender, making Anna smile when she came back in at the end of the banter.

It pleased her no end to see her two favourite people relaxed enough in each other's company to be talking like that. But now she had to throw something into the mix that wasn't going to be much fun.

"Aunty, your mum and my miserable old grandfather were the parents of my dad, right? But then your mum married somebody else entirely, who was your dad. So, any 'gift' that's come to me from *your* mum *had* to come to me through my dad. Doesn't it have to come fully through the female line to be potent? I don't know that much, but I thought that had to be the case? I'm flattered that you think that I've got so much potential, but can that really be from your mum? And in that case, am I from that *particular* long line of wise-women?"

Rita was lost for words, because Anna was right, the talent normally went from mother to daughter. She could have inherited something, but coming via her father, it would surely be diluted.

"Your mum's heritage?" Gary wondered. "What do you know of that?"

"Not a lot, if I'm honest. Though now I come to think of it, Great-Aunty Morag, who gave me the deposit for my flat, was Scottish. As a kid I didn't identify the accent, but having come up here, I think that there was definitely a trace of Scottish in there even though she'd lived in England for decades. …And by the way, Aunty, what was Gideon blathering on about no Fergusons having his house? Hugh could no more possess the current building than he can."

"Ach, jings," Rita groaned. "When I spoke to him he seemed to have some barmy idea about a Ferguson owning *his* house," and in an instant Ana and Gary caught on.

"Holy shit!" Gary sighed with a roll of his eyes. "I knew Cameron and I were being listened to when we talked on the mezzanine level, back when he told me who he really is. You wouldn'a have any reason to know this Rita, but his brother – or should I say *half*-brother – is Austin Ferguson."

Rita's eyebrows shot up in shock.

"Aye," Gary agreed with a nod. "Bit of a facer that one, eh? The thing is, though, it didn'a register wi' me at the time because we didn'a know Hugh's name back then then – or at least no' as one o' the ghosts. And since then, if I gave it any thought, it was that Ferguson is no' exactly a rare name anywhere in Scotland."

He gave a huff of frustration. "In fact, I seriously doubt whether there's any biological link at all, because when Cameron talked about his mum – who used to be Helen Ferguson back when she had Austin, but is now Mrs Wiseheart like Cameron and his dad – he said she had long connections wi' Fife and the southern parts o' Angus. Well that's the other side o' the country to here, isn't it? Hardly on the doorstep for making connections. And in truth, I'm no' convinced that there is an actual connection. It's just that Gideon's nasty habit o' listening at ghostly keyholes has given him wholly the wrong impression."

"But how did he hear the name Ferguson connected to the hotel?" Rita wondered.

"Oh, that's easy," Anna sighed. "There was a lot of talk down at the reception desk about who the heck *Ferguson Investments* are, especially when we had no idea if they were ever going to start behaving like businessmen and give us things like contracts."

Rita gave a groan. "And Gideon has taken two totally separate things and put them together and come up with five. Bugger! We really need to know if there are any true genetic links to here, don't we? People living who actually *do* link back to this place's past. …Right, folks, back to the old kirk. We've some questions for those ladies again."

With the pillar candles and the tapers burning again in their now familiar places, Rita tried not to sound as weary as she felt calling the nuns and the other women to her.

"I'm afraid I have to ask for your help. All of your help, actually." The remaining women swam more or less into view depending on the strength of their attachment. "You see, we've worked out that it's possibly something to do with our Anna here that's made the two male ghosts more active. Strange though it seems to us, she's the one factor which fits all the circumstances connected to them suddenly becoming more active. So can you tell us, do any of you feel any particular attachment to her? Is there something we're missing?"

As she expected, the nuns were as mystified as they were, and the women who had always been hazy and in the background remained that way, but Jonet Clark came forward with a slightly surprised expression.

"I thought that's why you came, lass?" she said to Anna, who could only mutely shake her head in shock. "I feel you. You're one o' mine."

Chapter 28

While Anna stared at the ghost of Jonet in astonishment, Rita managed to recover and ask, "What do you mean, 'one o' mine?' How yours?"

Jonet also seemed to struggle to explain what she felt. "It's as if you are far, far away, and yet I ken you. You are my kin. Maybe more than just kin. Of my line."

Gary leaned in and asked, "Are you trying to tell us that Anna is a direct descendent of yours?"

Jonet was clearly bemused by the concept but managed a vague sort of nod.

"Do you understand that we are far, far in your future?" Rita asked, now proceeding very carefully. "You died in…"

She had to look to Anna, who supplied, "…1659. The witch trials when these ladies died was in 1659."

"…Aye. That's over three hundred and fifty… no, three hundred and *sixty* years in our past. That's a lot of generations between you and her. At the very least nine, and maybe as many as twelve, depending on how quickly they had children. The blood lines are bound to be very diluted over that length of time."

Jonet's niece Agnes drifted closer. "I think what my aunt is trying to tell you is that we – herself, Margaret, and I – can feel something, or should I say some*one*, familiar in her." She came a little closer again, looking at Anna more closely, then a ghostly hand went to her mouth and she gave a small gasp. "Elspeth! I can feel Elspeth in you."

"Okay…freaked out now." Anna said shakily. "Really freaked out… Are you saying that there's someone else living inside of me? Because I can't cope with that."

Gary instantly leaned over and took her nearest hand in his and held on tightly to her, Anna returning his grip so hard that Rita could see her knuckles turning white with the intensity of her hold, but though it must hurt, Gary wasn't letting go or pulling away.

"I don't think she means a whole other person hiding in your psyche, hen," Rita said soothingly. "It's more the sense of who Elspeth was, and who they knew, has come down the line very strongly in you." She turned to the three Clark women, who now were grouped around them and staring unnervingly at Anna as though she was the ghost and not them. "You aren't saying you can actually feel Elspeth in her entirety in Anna, are you?" and she hoped that Anna couldn't see that she had her fingers crossed on her side farthest from her.

"N…no…" Agnes managed to say cagily, before repeating more firmly, "No, not Elspeth as we knew her. Hmmm… Yes, it's the *essence* of Elspeth that we can feel."

"And did Elspeth have a daughter?" Rita asked, almost hoping that the answer would be 'no', because that would mean that this was just a coincidence. Then she had the horrible thought that if not these ladies, then Anna's nightmare of a mother might connect her to Gideon and the Corsan women, which would undoubtedly be worse.

"Erm, we're not really sure," Agnes admitted, with Jonet giving a sad shrug.

Gary cleared his throat, making all the women look to him as he dared to say, "Did Hugh no' say that he took Elspeth wi' his cousin and his parents up north into the Highlands? And then something about them leaving there?"

However, the women here could only look bemused.

"We have no knowledge of that," Agnes confessed. "All we ever knew was that not that long after we died, we stopped being able to feel Elspeth close by in the land of the living."

Then Jannet Corsan shimmered closer into their view. "There was a man. A Highlander. He'd come to work for Grierson at Lagg as a bodyguard – as many Highlanders do…did. My lad Hugh worked alongside him, and said in my last months on earth that Sorley McAllister had taught him how to slip through the heather like a ghost. It was McAllister who made it possible for Hugh and Alex to take food to Jonet, so that she wasn'a the starved shreds o' a woman that God-curse-him Veitch hoped she would be when she was questioned.

"I'm as sure as I can be that it was that same McAllister who helped Hugh get my dear husband away to safety, and my sister Marione and her family too, along wi' Johnny Allen and Elspeth after Jonet here was struck down by the sight o' us being burned. The sisters here said there was a Catholic man who paid his respects to them at the time, which we think must ha' been him, though having never seen him, their description meant nothing to us."

The prioress came to join them at her words, agreeing, "There was indeed a Catholic Highlander. A man we felt had high morals and principles, and the last we saw of him was in the company of the young woman called Elspeth."

Yet Anna was shocked to hear Gary say in a voice filled with shock, "McAllister? You're sure it as that name?"

"Oh yes," Jannet assured him. "Sorley McAllister. He came from Argyll, or so he said."

"Jings!" Anna heard Rita breathe in awe, and saw her looking at Gary as if seeing him in a whole new light.

"Aunty? What is it?"

Rita turned to her asking, "Don't you remember Gary's surname?"

Anna only had to think for an instant before gulping. "Bloody hell. Gary! You're a McAllister too."

"And the west of Glasgow where Gary was born is right next to the county border with Argyll," Rita said with a wry grimace. "Good grief. It's not just you, Anna. It's Gary being here and then you arriving *too*!"

"You are kin to that man?" the prioress asked Gary, but he was the one who now could only shrug.

"It's my family name, but I've never chased my ancestors back to know if we had anyone called Sorley in the past, let alone if that could be the same man."

"I think we need to ask Hugh if he feels anything familiar about you," Rita said, "but not today. Summoning Hugh when we've just thrown Gideon out of his lair might only aggravate the situation between them."

However, Anna had an idea. "Could you nip into the housekeeper's room first thing tomorrow and start by just asking Hugh nicely not to manifest for a couple of days until the wedding is over? Only, if Gideon feels you making the same 'demand' of Hugh – as he will no doubt view it – that might mollify him a tad. And then at the end, if Gary goes with you, you can ask Hugh almost as an aside. Gideon's always going to be tetchy, but this might get around his crankiness. What a pity Cameron isn't here so that we could ask the ladies and Hugh if they feel anything of them in him, too."

Thanking the women and the nuns, Rita closed the circle and they went back downstairs, but with her conceding that Anna's might be the way to go, especially since Hugh was the caring one of the two ghosts.

And so come the Friday morning, Anna helped Sally set the bridal suite straight again, and liberally sprayed the entrances with Holy Water as an extra precaution, to which Rita had added essential oils of rose, lavender, and geranium to promote love – vaguely thinking that a bit of love in his soul might do Gideon the world of good too if he got a whiff from the other side of the doors. Meanwhile, Rita and Gary had a short session up in the attic room, but reported back that Hugh had been most understanding, especially once he knew that Gideon's claws had been cut.

Rather more disconcerting for Gary was that Hugh felt a familiarity to him. It wasn't that immediate passing down of a family line that Jonet and Agnes had felt towards Anna, but more of a general family connection. Moreover, while he admitted that he felt a connection to Gary, albeit very vague, he was quick to say that he'd felt nothing towards anyone else who'd come through the hotel of late. It made them think that in Cameron's case – or rather his half-brother Austin's – it was nothing more than a coincidence of name which Gideon had jumped to an erroneous conclusion over.

"It certainly explains why things have got rowdy of late, though," Rita said, as they sneaked into the service kitchen to grab a much-needed mug of coffee and some biscuits. They had got up at the crack of dawn to do this, in order to make sure that they didn't interfere with the hotel's preparations, and had had little time to do more than grab a croissant. "What a headache!"

"What's a headache?" Anna asked, coming in to grab a mug for herself.

Rita grimaced. "Well, neither of you want to leave here, do you? You're very much at home in your jobs. But your being here has unwittingly created this situation. It's neither of your faults, and in a way it's a good thing that it wasn't a frequent guest who has the family links – heaven knows how we'd have sorted the ghost situation then, because you could hardly ask someone who's paying not to come. But it does mean that *we* have to sort this, for everyone's sakes."

However, with the bridal party starting to arrive after lunch, Anna and Gary's focus had to be on them. Part of Anna had been hoping that the reason why she had so far dealt with the bride's parents, rather than her, was because the bride was being an utter nightmare. Some spoiled brat throwing her weight around would give Anna something to vent her pent-up emotions over in a controlled way, and would be very different to her own situation. What she was dreading was seeing another woman being dragged with utter disregard through daddy's corporate event wedding. Yet when the bride came it was something very different.

Arriving in a wheelchair, it turned out that the reason why the bride's parents wanted this to be extra perfect was because their much-loved Sophie had almost not made it. A long run of chemotherapy for an aggressive bowel cancer had been nearly as debilitating as the illness, and the reason they had come to Brenda in the autumn asking them to squeeze in a wedding early in the season, was that that had been when the specialists has said that Sophie was in remission, and likely to recover. It meant that they wanted her to have her special day while she felt well enough to enjoy it, and though the specialist had said that Sophie's prospects were now good, nobody wanted to delay in case she had to have more long stays in hospital.

"Harry's been a diamond," Sophie's mum told Anna and Brenda, with affectionate glances to the groom. "Every day at the hospital without fail, even though he's had to carry on working. And because we have a bungalow, he moved in with us so that it was easier to care for Sophie – and that was when it was touch and go whether she'd even live to marry him. We want this day to be the one they've dreamed of and nearly didn't have."

The fact that Brenda was having to have a little sniffle into a tissue after that, as did several of the other staff, meant that Anna didn't feel so out of step when she had to as well. Yes, there was a real sense of celebration here, but it was so far removed both from what she'd had and even what she'd anticipated, that she actually found herself throwing genuine enthusiasm into the event. Guests, the photographers, and the cake all arrived as planned, and even the fact that it wasn't a traditional fruit cake but a sponge didn't tweak Anna's sore spot, because Sophie couldn't cope with a heavy fruit cake, and so it had been made with her in mind. And a beautiful, tastefully decorated single, large cake it was too, not like Anna's dreadful unicorn cupcakes.

It meant that they got to Sunday lunchtime, and most of the guests departing – including the happy couple, who were off to a romantic lodge in the Highlands for their honeymoon – with everyone worn out but chipper that everything had gone like clockwork.

"Great job done, everyone." Anna congratulated her team, as they gathered in the dining room with the door shut to celebrate. A couple of bottles of bubbly shared amongst them all was something that Anna though they'd all deserved. "Our first wedding of the season ticked off, and an absolute triumph! You've all been wonderful."

And they had, including the youngsters who had come from the college and for whom this was their first experience of dealing with both a big event, and one where it really mattered if things went wrong. A conference you could always reschedule, but a wedding you couldn't go back and redo. And so Anna, who was just handing over to Polly for the evening and looking forward to collapsing into an early night in bed, was exhausted but happy when the reception doors banged open and in walked disaster.

"Ah, the two gentlemen booked in for tonight," Polly said, immediately going to the computer to book them in. "Mr McBurney and Mr Corsan, yes?"

The room swam for Anna, and she had to grab the frame of the back-office door to stop herself swaying and falling.

"They're not Mr McBurney and Mr Corsan," she almost sobbed. "That's my father and father-in-law!"

Polly took one look at how white Anna had gone, and the nasty smirks on the two older men's faces, and sent the emergency code to Gary's mobile. It had been Gary himself who had thought to set it up, and in the years he'd been here, they'd only used it twice before – both times when fights had broken out between drunken guests over the Christmas/Hogmanay season. As Anna stood transfixed, it was only moments before the mobile for whoever was on duty rang.

"What's wrong?" Gary's voice came slightly breathlessly, as Polly heard the rustling of him shrugging on his jacket even as he was clearly starting to run towards them.

Turning away into the back-office so that the two men wouldn't hear, Polly told him, "Anna's father and father-in-law have just shown up."

"Fuck!" And she heard him move the phone away so that he wouldn't deafen her as he bellowed back to the cottage, "Rita! Your bastard brother's arrived!"

In reception, Jensen's father had stepped up to the desk. "Well, young lady? Have you nothing to say for yourself after the appalling way you've behaved? Do you have any idea what you've done to my son?"

Yet the fact that John Coleborn spoke to her as if she was a naughty teenager, rather than a grown woman who had made a serious decision, actually worked against him. It brought Anna around, her own sense of outrage at being spoken to so derisively kicking in.

"I've spoken to Jensen," she said firmly. "He knows how I feel, and I've told him that I won't contest a divorce on the grounds of abandonment. We hadn't even bought anything together because of the way you and your wife steamrollered over our lives. So there's nothing I have any claim to or would want. He knows I won't come back, and as far as I was concerned, he was fully aware of that, albeit not very happy about it because of what he'd have to face from *you*."

"You ruined him! He's walked out on his job, and he's not likely to get that back, you selfish bitch." John Coleborn ranted at her. "He's left. Gone who knows where! His mother's beside herself with worry. He said he had to recover. He's never done that before. Not ever."

"Then thank God he's finally acting like a man in his thirties who knows his own mind," Anna riposted.

"What's that supposed to mean?" Gordon Gracie demanded, coming to stand shoulder to shoulder with John Coleborn, and glaring just as furiously at his daughter. "What did you do? How could you be so evil, Anna? So ungrateful, after everything we did for you! What have you *done* to Jensen? And why?"

"I didn't *do* anything to him, Dad. I just made him wake up and see the reality of what went on. Jensen *and* I never got a word in about what *we* wanted. If you'd left us alone to be a normal courting couple, who knows, we'd probably still be together and planning a wedding in a couple of years' time – with a marriage that might actually have survived.

"But you – you and Mr Coleborn – you had to push, push, push. To make everything fit to *your* agenda. Forcing the promotions *you* thought Jensen should have onto him, and the life *you* thought we should have together. Not the jobs he wanted or thought he could cope with. Have you no concept of how out of his depth he felt with that latest fast-track promotion? How he didn't really want to move down to London, but was happy where he was? Did you ever actually *listen* to him?"

Coleborn sneered. "And what would a mere *shop-girl* like you know about what Jensen did? Much less what he wanted out of life." He couldn't have sounded any more dismissive. "You? All you know is passing cans of beans past a bar-coder! Jensen wouldn't have told you what he did because you're too thick to understand."

"Now jus…!" Anna began, but the double doors to reception flew open like a western movie's bar, and Gary pounded in like the wrath of God.

"Who the hell are…?!" John Coleborn was shouting over the top of Anna's words, before Gary was nose to nose with him, overriding him with a parade-ground bellow of,

"*Back off! NOW!*"

Forced by the sheer presence of Gary, John Coleborn had to make a few steps back away from the desk and Anna, Gary turned to Gordon Gracie snarling, "And that means you, too, fanny baws!"

"Who the fuck is this mad man?" Gordon demanded, but backing up to the conference room door nonetheless.

Meanwhile Anna was quietly amused that for all of John Coleborn's posturing and long-term bullying of her father and many others, he hadn't managed to wring a single word out while Gary had him locked eyeball to eyeball, with a look that would have frozen a penguin's tail to ice. So much for Coleborn being the big man and her dad following, because right now Coleborn looked one small move away from needing a change of undies.

One of the doors banged open again, and a flushed-faced, slightly breathless Rita strode in and slapped her half-brother smartly around the ear, demanding, "Are you being an arsehole again Gordon

Gracie? Jeez, man, you're like a broken record stuck i' the same spot! Find another tune, for God's sake."

"Ouch! Rita. For fuck's sake! What was that for?" her half-brother protested.

"What are you doing here?" Rita demanded.

"Trying to get this stupid daughter of mine to behave and come home, and stop playing silly sods." Gordon snapped back. "Stay out of this, Rita. You've no idea of the trouble she's caused."

"Trouble? To whom?"

Gordon looked at her as though she'd lost her mind. "What do you mean, 'to whom'? To *us*, of course! Her mother and me!" Then he caught a glimpse of John Coleborn finally dredging up some shred of courage to face this strange man who was still glacially eyeballing him, and added, "And to the Coleborns too! I bet she's told you nothing of the misery she's caused them."

Rita's eyes narrowed. "Oh, I've heard *all* about it, brother. All! About how you never gave her, or that dobber of a son o' theirs, a moment's peace. Oh, aye. Don't you look at Anna like that! Gary, here, told me about yon Jensen coming here and making a spectacle o' himself. No' exactly catch o' the century, was he? Mebbe for you and your social climbing wi' yon dunderhead over there, but not for Anna."

Using Jensen's name was enough to stir his father into fury again, and he tore his gaze from Gary's icy glare to snap at her, "Don't you dare take my son's name in vain, you old witch."

"Witch, am I?" Rita threw back at him. "Man, if I'm a witch, you should be real careful about what you say about my niece, because I tell you, I'm no' in a forgiving frame o' mind!"

"You villainous old shrew!" Coleborn hurled back at her. "It's time they brought back burning at the stake for women like you. The world would be better off without you!"

Yet even as Rita bridled and her full Glaswegian upbringing kicked in as she growled, "Now you listen to me, you fud-faced walloper…!" the temperature in reception plummeted.

The word 'witch' yelled as a threat was the final straw on top of the toxic atmosphere.

Even as Anna yelped, "Stop it! Everyone, stop it!" it was already too late.

Swarming down the main stairs came the ghost of Gideon Corsan, but through from what must once have been a doorway from the family part of the tower-house came Hugh Ferguson's. Yet John Coleborn had his back to both, while Gordon Gracie was too busy glaring at Rita to notice.

Rita spotted them, and so did Gary, who now backed away, saying, "Steady on! There's no need for vengeance." He addressed the ghosts, but Coleborn totally misread his backing off as a sign of cowardice.

"Ha! Not such the big man after all!" he crowed. "I'll teach you to cross swords with *me*, you thug!" now lurching forward into Gary's personal space, and adopting the kind of domineering, finger-jabbing posture which had no doubt served him well with those unfortunate enough to depend on keeping their jobs with him.

"Behind you, you nugget." Gary snarled back, waving his hand in the direction of the ghosts. But even as he was starting to add, "Look out! Be…" Coleborn mistook his hand for a blow coming, even though it would have been an open-handed slap, not a punch with the way Gary's hand was.

Coleborn's eyes went wide with temper and he raised a fist of his own, yelling, "I'll bloody kill you!" But even as he went on with, "Don't you touch me, or I'll sue…!"

Gideon Corsan's ghost cried triumphantly, "I'm wi' ye', McBurney! They'll no' escape us this time!" and his spirit-form streaked straight into Coleborn's body, screaming, "We'll do fer Ferguson together this time!"

Gordon Gracie gave a girl-like shriek of alarm as he saw the ghosts for the first time, and practically welded himself the wood panelling behind him in his attempt to retreat, while Rita was already moving towards them calling, "No! You *must not* do that!"

At the moment of collision between ghostly Gideon and John Coleborn, Coleborn's whole posture changed, stiffening, and then his expression shifting from temper to something colder and more deadly. The fact that Coleborn was unused to throwing actual punches, rather than merely threatening with his fist, was born out by the way they all heard his thumb dislocate as he hit out at Gary with the thumb curled under his fingers in a fist instead over them. And if Coleborn had weight, it was from too many business lunches and with next to no muscle, meaning that it barely clipped Gary, who'd anticipated it and was moving before it landed.

The spasm of pain from the dislocation that flashed across Coleborn's face was disregarded by the ghost now in the driving seat of Coleborn's body, and he spun it around to face Hugh, who was there with a ghostly flintlock pistol in his hand pointed at Coleborn-Corsan. There was a puff of smoke and a loud bang, but whatever it did to Corsan's ghost, for John Coleborn his killer was those business lunches.

Clasping his hands to his chest, he gave a terrible cry of pain and folded onto the floor, dead before he even hit it.

"Fuck! Get the defibrillator." Gary yelled, instantly recovering and taking charge, and as Anna sprinted into the back-office and brought the case out, she had to jump over her father, who had fainted onto the floor and who Rita was trying to tug out of the way. Polly had recovered enough to be straight on the phone to call 999 for an ambulance, though it was clear within a couple of attempts by Gary to revive Coleborn that he was past any medical intervention. And sitting back on his heels, Gary looked up at the others and simply shook his head.

That was just the point when the reception doors opened and the familiar voice of Cameron Wiseheart asked, "What's going on here?"

Chapter 29

As arrivals went, Cameron's reappearance couldn't have come at a worse time. He'd barely been told that a guest had had a heart attack, when Gordon Gracie came around and began throwing accusations at Gary as having killed Coleborn, and despite Anna's pleas of, "Dad! Please, shut up! That wasn't what happened at all," Gordon wouldn't.

Cora came in for reasons which they didn't discover until later, given that she wasn't due on shift, saw the body on the floor and had hysterics, storming out saying that she quit and would never set foot in the place again. And then the place was taken over by a paramedic and then the ambulance staff, soon followed by the police, who got summoned by the paramedic on account of Gordon's accusations. And in all of that, Rita, Gary, and Anna only managed to have the briefest of words together to agree that the word 'ghost' should never come up in their statements. The situation was bad enough without the police thinking they had a trio of flaky hippies involved who'd all been at the wacky-baccy and seeing things, and luckily, Polly had only seen an overweight businessman getting aggressive with Gary and then having a massive coronary.

"You won't find a mark on him," Gary told the policeman who was questioning him. "*He* made a swing at me, but I've enough experience to avoid that, and then he grabbed his chest and went down like a sack o' tatties."

And mercifully, once the police had taken Gordon to one side and finally got it out of him that he'd been flaked out on the floor because he'd seen a ghost – something nobody else had mentioned – his accusations were considered utterly unfounded and unsubstantiated. In fact, he was cautioned that he was in grave danger of being considered to be wasting police time if he kept on with the claims, and so although Gordon continued to witter on about Anna and Rita, there was no longer any danger of him being taken seriously.

More worrying from Anna's point of view was what Cameron thought about it. He certainly hadn't come back gushing with concern for her, even to the extent of keeping his friendship notably cooler during the remainder of the evening. So she was understandably worried when he called her into the conference room the next day, which was the Monday morning, and asked, "Is this thing with your father likely to be an ongoing problem?"

He left it hanging at that, but Anna was shrewd enough to know that the next words might well be, 'because I can't have that, and if he won't stay away, I'll have to let you go.' And she could well understand why he might. Any member of staff causing these kinds of issues wasn't good for a hotel's image, let alone when it was the manager's doing.

Yet he reacted with surprise when she told him, "I think I can safely say that my father will never want to see me again after this," and saw something which looked very like sympathy in his eyes. It certainly made her wonder what had gone on with his family in the time he'd been away, but he didn't share that with her, and she'd have been more surprised if he had right now.

When his next question was, "Why didn't you know that they were coming?" it was even easier to answer.

"They only booked the rooms Saturday evening," she explained, "and not under their own names, either." And then the penny dropped as she continued, "Cora made the reservations because the rest of us were up to our ears with the wedding that was still going on. We weren't expecting any further guests to be arriving, so she was literally just manning the phones, getting the odd drinks from the bar, and answering any guest's enquiries if they couldn't find anyone else."

She was also telling the truth when she said, "The names Corsan and McBurney wouldn't have meant anything to her," though she was sure that a malevolent influence in the form of Gideon had whispered those names in her ear, and that Cora had almost certainly known who both of them really were, writing those names into the bookings in the full knowledge of *what* she was doing even if not the significance of those particular pseudonyms. Even Gideon was unlikely to have a ghostly reach as far as the Midlands to sway what names the fathers were booking in under from their end – they'd surely only asked for false names, and Cora had fallen for their lies.

Only later, and in the sanctity of Gary's lounge, did she tell Rita and Gary, "The little bitch obviously thought to have the last laugh on me for Jensen dumping her when he left. Stupid, stupid girl! Well, it's bounced back on her in a way she never expected, hasn't it?"

"You think she knew who they really were?" wondered Rita.

But it was Gary who answered, "Oh yes. Verra taken wi' Jensen and his fancy leather man-bags was Cora. It was terrible luck that it was her at the desk taking the reservations. If it had been Brenda, for instance, she'd have immediately told them there was no room for them here, and then told Anna and me."

"Luck?" Rita wasn't convinced.

"Oh yes, Aunty. Bad luck, nothing more. Because my father, for one, would never have so much as considered that there might be people here on my side. He'll have assumed that I told everyone a pack of lies, and therefore so as long as he didn't get me on the phone, that he'd be able to bullshit his way into getting a reservation. And he left it to the last minute so that I wouldn't see his name on the booking entry."

Rita rolled her eyes in exasperation. "That sounds like Gordon, all right. And it makes more sense of them using the names Corsan and McCartney if it was Gideon Corsan whispering his ghostly poison into Cora's ear, and he could hear Gordon's end of the conversation even if he couldn't converse with him himself. God knows, she's not the brightest with real people, let alone with a ghost."

"It was actually John Coleborn who made the reservations," Gary corrected her. "Anna's dad told me that when I drove him down to the train station first thing."

Gordon Gracie was far from a welcome guest, but even Cameron had had to admit that by the time the police left, they could hardly boot him out at that late hour, especially as the pair had arrived by taxi not a car. But Gordon had been under no illusion that he was being thrown out as soon as possible after that. So it had been at the crack of dawn, before Anna had her conversation with Cameron, that Gary had shoved her father and his overnight bag into his truck, and left him to sort his own way home at Dumfries station.

"But I did get something interesting out o' him. It turns out that he's well aware that not only did his wife's family originally came from around here, but also his."

"Really?" Rita was shocked. "Here?"

"No' your *mum's* side, Rita. His *father's* – so no blood connection to you at all."

"Oh, my God!" Rita was already working through the possibilities. "So when I traced our mum's family back up to the Highlands, albeit a few generations back from when they arrived in Glasgow, that was correct. But of course, I never even bothered with dreadful Dennis Gracie's family tree, because he might have been Gordon's father, but he wasn't mine.

"Good grief, Anna, that means that you've got connections via both of your parents to this part of the world. No wonder you were such a catalyst. And now I'm kicking myself for not having spotted this earlier, but Gracie is a surname that we've seen on gravestones around here, yet I didn't see so much of up in the north-east, though given that it wasn't *my* maiden name, I wasn't taking that much notice. Do you know what your mum's maiden name was?"

Anna went rather pale. "Clarke, but with an 'e'. But I suppose that down the years that's one of the simpler changes that get made to names, and it's a common name, isn't it? At one point, where I worked there were four of us with that name, and none of us remotely related, so knowing that, it's why I didn't think of a connection between me and Jonet – especially as Jonet's daughter would have been Elspeth *Allen*, not Elspeth Clark. And if this connection goes down from mother to daughter, who knows how many changes of surname would have happened down the generations?"

Rita breathed a sigh of relief. "Of course! Thank goodness for that – it gave me quite a turn for a moment there. But you're right, Jonet's niece Margaret Clark said that apart from her unfortunate Isobel whom both Hugh and Gideon loved, she had two sons. And their surnames would have been Milligan, the same as Isobel's, not hers. So even if they had descendants straight down the male line, they wouldn't have been Clarks. Gosh, that's going to be a genealogical puzzle to unravel!"

Gary was listening intently, but then pondered, "Why did Gideon push Cora into using the names Corsan and McBurney, then? Was it just his fixation on those descendents he thought would be on his side to get his revenge on this unknown Ferguson he thinks owns the place? I mean, one of the things we've no' even started on yet is what was the connection to the evil John Corsan, and consequently Gideon, of the woman who married yon Captain who bought the house. He was a Ferguson, was he no'?"

Anna groaned and grabbed her now rather battered copy of the pamphlet from her fleece pocket. "*Aagh!*" she groaned. "We've forgotten about her, haven't we. Who the heck was the *Jean* Corsan who had inherited by 1689? That's only four years after the 1685 disasters, isn't it? Is the pamphlet even correct? Because our lady ghosts have never mentioned a Jean, have they? And was Captain Hector Ferguson anything at all to do with Hugh, or just unfortunate enough to share the same name?"

"Aye, that's another tangle we have to unravel," Gary agreed with a wince. "Was that family's misfortune down to a recently departed Gideon haunting the place even then? Or heaven help us, is that another reason why Hugh lingers here? We're no' done by a long chalk."

Then he had another thought. "And why did he assign the names to each man – because it was only when he said the name McBurney and shot into Coleborn that we had any idea which man had which fake name. Did he seize on John Coleborn as simply being *like* the McBurney man we know of, because o' his lust for revenge? Or did he maybe sense the McBurney line in Jensen when he was here? Or did he feel something o' the Corsan line in your father, Anna? Because whichever way it was, Gideon was the one to attach the fake names to the specific men. Do you know anything about that family tree?"

"Not really. If Dad ever mentioned it, it was to say that his own dad had said that the best thing he ever did was leave Scotland. So there was no family tree on the wall or anything. I think Dad saw himself as a self-made man rather than building on the generations before."

"Typical Gordon," Rita tutted.

"Aye," Gary sympathised with Rita's disgust in her half-brother. "But all my instincts are telling me that we need to sort out this web of connections between the past and now. We're all agreed that there's something in Anna's DNA, for want o' a better way of expressing it, that keeps calling to these ghosts. Granted, I seem to have a link, but it was only when Anna got here that things started hotting up. Do you see, Rita? We canna have both sides o' this ancient feud warring for different halves of Anna!"

He reached out and held Anna's hand again as she went pale. "I'm no' trying to frighten the life out o' you, lass. We know that there's probably a connection to Jonet through Elspeth, but before we draw a line under that, we must know that there's no link between you and Corsan as well. And that's partly because I think that that 'feeling' of Elspeth makes Hugh verra protective o' you on the other side. But if we lay him to rest, and there's even a sniff o' a Corsan link in you, we might be laying you open to attack by Gideon."

He turned to Rita. "Because you canna absolutely guarantee that Gideon will go if we persuade Hugh to leave, can you?" She shook her head. "So even in a considerably weakened state, and with no anchor to a specific part o' the hotel anymore, he could still be a pest for Anna. A nasty wee ghost who jostles her elbow to send a drink over a guest, kind o' thing."

"Jeez, Gary! Stop it!" Anna pleaded. "You're scaring the living daylights out of me."

"No, he's right," Rita sighed. "I wish he wasn't, but he is. We have to know *if* Gideon felt any link to you in particular. With luck he didn't, but we mustn't take any chances. And damn the crachit soul, he's hardly likely to be honest with us if we ask him directly, is he?"

"I'll go and brief young Cameron," Gary volunteered. "He's more likely to take talk o' ghosts off a man o' my background, and God knows it's no' your average troublesome guest problem."

Cameron watched Gary approaching him in the main hall, which today was very quiet, no new guests being expected until tonight. Sally and her ladies were working flat out, and all but Hannah of the kitchen staff were having a well-earned day off, and so there was only Brenda in on the day shift at the desk.

"I've got a lot to tell you," Gary began, having been through to the service kitchen and brought through a cafetière of fresh coffee for them.

"So I gather," Cameron said dryly, but as Gary worked his way through what had happened in the last weeks, in spite of his own intention to dismiss this stuff about ghosts, Cameron found himself getting more and more drawn in. It had been easy dismiss his dogs being spooked once he was back in Edinburgh, and anyway, he'd been rather up to his ears in sorting out his own finances and going through with the transfer of ownership of the hotel. Coming back to walk in on a dead guest had been a shock, but also had him wondering what on earth he'd been thinking of buying the place off his brother.

And in spite of him promising himself that he'd be more cautious about getting involved with Anna, he found himself asking, "And is she alright? Anna?" with more concern than he'd meant to let show.

"Considering what's been going on, aye, she's doing remarkably well. She's a brave one. …A bit spooked right now, as you can imagine. But I think her father turning up was almost worse than this connection wi' the past."

"That I can appreciate," Cameron said with feeling. "I had one encounter with my mother while I was in Edinburgh, and that was enough."

"All sorted?"

"Not even close! But then it's not going to be over with for a long time, I'm afraid. The difference for me is that I've handed over my brother's financial affairs to his bank, and I'm able to walk away from it all on a day-to-day basis. My problems are back in Edinburgh, not on our doorstep. From what you're saying, these ghosts are going to be an ongoing problem if we don't fix things?"

"Aye. And having been woken up good and proper now, I don't think Anna leaving would necessarily calm things down – or at least no' enough, anyhow." Gary felt obliged to stick that in, just to make sure that Cameron wasn't thinking of anything like moving Anna on. "In fact, her connection to Hugh and the lady ghosts might make it easier, not harder, to settle things down." He carefully avoided telling Cameron that there might be a link to him, too – the last thing he wanted right now was for Cameron to panic, slap the hotel on the market, and sell up before this situation got resolved.

It was the following late afternoon when Anna felt up to another encounter with the lady ghosts in the old kirk, and this time they had Cameron with them. When the nuns and others first appeared, Rita and Gary – who he was sitting between – each put a hand out to grab him in case he fully fainted, because he went as white as a sheet. But unlike Jensen, he managed to pull himself together.

"Can you still feel Gideon Corsan as strongly?" was Rita's first question. "I know we haven't got rid of him, but have we weakened him?"

It was Jannet, Hugh's mother, who answered.

"He's my kin, my second cousin, so I suppose that why I feel him more than some o' the others here, and so I can tell ye' that ye' have broken one o' his strong attachments to this place. We weren't over there at the time he died, ye' understand, but I believe the room ye' cleansed was where he retreated to, and died o' his wounds from his fight wi' Hugh."

"Did you know that before?" Anna asked, thinking it would have been very useful to have known this in advance.

However, Jannet replied, "Could we ha' sent you to that room afore ye' broke his hold? No. We didn'a ken the exact place in the auld house, just that he died in one part o' it and that it wasn'a the ground floor. It wasn'a until we felt ye' working over there that we kent that that was the spot, but only because we could feel him fighting back so hard against what ye' were doing."

"There's something strange, though," Agnes came forward to say. "Did another just die over there? Only we felt a very strange shift, and someone who we thought was Corsan cry out as if he died all over again."

"Of course!" Rita gasped. "He went into a man who'd come here to cause trouble, but the man died moments after he entered him. Was there a blood connection between them, too?"

"No' that we could sense, but they are strangely entangled now," Agnes said, "though the other spirit wants to leave, not stay here."

"Can I get that one to the Light?" Rita wondered, and got a definite affirmative from the ghosts and the nuns. "And will that have weakened Corsan's abilities to manifest here?"

The prioress spoke. "Certainly in the short term. We feel he's fragmented. Broken up into scattered parts of himself. If you do not contrive to send him to the other side, he will gradually reform as he connects the parts of himself. But that will not be a fast process, and if you succeed in sending the other to the Light, he may well take parts of Corsan with him, leaving him permanently weakened. But I have to tell you, I have no experience of what's happened to Corsan and the other man. I may be hopelessly wrong in thinking that only part of Corsan can pass over."

"Well for Anna's sake," Gary said firmly, "we need to get bloody John Coleborn shifted out o' the way! He was a malicious bastard in life, and I canna think he'll be any better as a ghost."

"And better it was done fast, before he has chance to anchor himself to the reception area!" Rita said with conviction.

And so to Cameron's continued disconcertion, he found himself on guard duty outside of the reception doors in the entrance hall at midnight that night, while Anna, Rita, and Gary set up to rid themselves of Coleborn's spirit. With no hesitation, this time Rita went in forcefully with candles, smudge-sticks, and Holy Water, but focused very tightly on the reception area and the stairs to the side of and just above the desk. That Cameron saw the ghost of John Coleborn appear at Rita's summoning was proven by seeing him staring open-mouthed through the glass doors, but Anna – who was the one facing his way – felt a sneaking pleasure at his shock, if only because she felt it vindicated her and her inability to simply halt all of this chaos.

As for John Coleborn, he proved remarkably easy to send off to the other side. Rita put it down to him having no attachments to the place, but Anna thought that much might have to do with his personality, and that deep down he'd been a coward, only bullying those he knew he could get away with it with.

"Are we done?" Cameron asked, coming in through the doors when he saw the others packing up their stuff.

"As much as can be done for now," Rita confirmed, then saw how he was looking at Anna and gave Gary's sleeve a light tug. "Come on, give me a hand with all this stuff." And from her nod to Anna and Cameron, Gary took the hint and followed her out, teasing,

"You just like bossing me about, don't you? You canna con me into thinking you're too weak to carry your own candles, Rita Montrose!" and they heard her laughter retreating towards the cottages.

"I suppose I'd better come and fetch Harris and Lewis," Cameron said, thinking that that would be a simple opener for a conversation, so was shocked when she turned on him angrily, saying,

"Oh no you don't! Not tonight! Those poor dogs pined for you! You never even brought them across to Gary's for an overnight before the day you left them. How do you think they felt? They thought you'd abandoned them! …No! We'll get you set up in the small cottage, and *then* you can have them back.

"They're not coming back to be cooped up in one room again for days on end, and *you* are going to learn to look after them *properly*! That room fair stank of damp dog after you left, but Gary towels them down after wet walks and there's no smell at all. I won't stand by and let you keep picking them up and then pushing them away!" Anna hating the way that a huge bubble of emotions came up as she was talking, until that last sentence was filled with tears.

Startled, Cameron stood speechless for a second, but unlike Jensen, he was far more tuned in to Anna, and suddenly realised that part of this was that she thought he was toying with *her* as well as the dogs.

"I'm…I'm sorry. Truly I am. I…"

"You didn't even *call*! Not once, to see how they were!" Anna said, having to resort to a tissue and barely holding back from a full sobbing fit.

"*Err*, no, I didn't, did I? I'm so sorry. It's just…I've never had anyone miss me when I've gone away, so it never occurred to me that you would…*err*, that the dogs would…I, *err*…" and he prayed he wasn't just digging the hole deeper.

But his words hit home to Anna, and she remembered their conversation about how awful his mother had been. It meant it rang true to her that this might well be the first time he'd ever left somewhere where anyone gave a damn about whether he came back or not, with the possible exception of places where he'd worked, and that wouldn't have been any kind of emotional attachment.

"Well you were missed," she said around sniffling into her tissue. "Very much!"

"And you've had a really tough week or two, haven't you?" Cameron sympathised, similarly realising that someone who'd taken such an emotional battering as Anna had, might run for the hills before he had the chance to make things right between them if he presumed the 'missing' was too much on her part. So he was trying to give her a get-out for being tearful at him being around, and was rewarded with a weak smile and,

"You can say that again! Honestly, what a rollercoaster! Dealing with ghosts at all has been a whole new world for me, but then finding out that I might be related to some of them…*phew*! Head-exploding or what! And to be frank, it's freaking me out a bit to find that I've come to a place where both my mum's family and part of my dad's come from, when I arrived here and suddenly felt so at home. I mean a real, 'I feel I belong here' sensation, after I'd only been here a few days. But I just thought it was being stress free after nearly a year of living on my nerves, not that I'd literally come to my ancestral home!"

"That would freak me out too," Cameron admitted, and risked pulling her into a hug. "I'm so sorry, Anna. I should have been here to help," just about managing to stop before he added 'you', because it was *her* he felt he'd let down, rather than just the staff. But this was all part of a delicate dance he knew he was going to have to do if he wasn't going to lose this incredibly brave lady. "And speaking of help, after all this time, are you not due a holiday week?"

"I suppose so. …But we've got another wedding in a fortnight's time! I can't leave Brenda to sort that on her own."

"And don't you think that having your abusive father arriving here with your soon to be ex- father-in-law, and then the father-in-law dying on arrival, constitutes enough trauma for you to need some time off?" Cameron asked with a kind smile. "Heavens, Anna! If it's been a bit of a shock to the others it's been ten times that for you. You don't have to prove anything, you know. We all know you're the best thing to happen to this hotel in a long time, with the possible exception of Gary's arrival, and I can't imagine you'd argue with that?"

The way she suddenly looked so relieved made him realise that she must have been far more worried about how he'd take having a dead guest than he'd appreciated. But then he mentally kicked himself for not bearing in mind that while he had a lot of choices about where he lived, the roof over Anna's head was tied to this job. *What an idiot you've been*, he thought, adding,

"Take next week off. I'm sure you can juggle a couple of shifts with people, and if not the full week, then at least a few consecutive days."

Anna nodded, and he was pleased to see her brightening up, if still looking incredibly tired.

"Come on, I'll walk you up to the cottage," he said, holding the reception door open for her as she grabbed her coat.

Outside the elements were conspiring to make it a very romantic walk, with a near-full moon shining down to light their way as they walked arm in arm up the path. Pausing to look back at the hotel, Anna said,

"I wish I could find out my links to those poor lost women, though, because I feel we're far from done with sorting out the past. And it's not been lost on me that nine women died at the same time in 1659, which Aunty Rita will tell you is a potent number, and with seven of them dying in a particularly horrific way. Yet for some reason only some of them seem to connect to me, and that can't be random. And then there's Isobel. Why do I feel I have to go back to where she and the other Grissell died? What possible connection do I have to them?"

"Then why don't you start with one of those family DNA tests?" Cameron suggested. "I tell you what. I'll buy it for you as a personal thank you from me for holding this all together while I've been so negligently absent in the crisis. …And you don't have to remind me that if I'd bothered to call, you could have told me about this, and I shouldn't have presumed you would ring me when – as I now know – you were up to your ears just trying to cope. I really owe you some help, Anna. You never know, someone like a distant third cousin twice removed might already have done a lot of the research for you, and there'll be some family trees that might make sense of some of this."

"Oh wow! Yes! I would love that," Anna told him, eyes shining. "Yes. To find ancestors better than my father's dreadful father would be quite a relief," but then didn't get chance to say anymore as Cameron leaned in and kissed her.

And from the shadows of the rhododendrons, a very knowing fox watched them and approved, but although the ghost of Hugh also watched them from his perch up in his tower and was happy for her, Gideon had taken refuge in the attic above his former room, and was swearing vengeance.

Anna's story continues in

FAR FROM OVER

where you'll discover more about Gideon and Hugh, as well as Rita and Gary.

Author's Notes

First of all, I hope you were able to keep up with my attempts to differentiate between Highlanders, when they spoke, and Lowlanders. Once you have your ear in to the accents, there's a big difference between even the dialects of Dumfries and Galloway – which are closer to, but not the same as, the very north of England's dialects in Cumbria and Northumbria – and even those of Glasgow and Edinburgh, which are less than a hundred miles apart. A true Highland accent is hard to reproduce on the page without turning into a stage Scotsman, but I hope I've managed to give you a hint of the difference between them when my characters are speaking. Apologies to any Scots reading this who feel I've fallen short of the mark.

The hotel in this novel, *Nuns' Kirk Haugh*, is fictitious, and while there are hotels in the immediate vicinity of where I have set it, none of them were the inspiration for this place. That honour goes to the wonderful *Friar's Carse Country House Hotel*, which is a touch further north on the banks of the River Nith, and which is one of my favourite places to visit. *Friar's Carse* itself has no known links with the Covenanters, and as far as I'm aware, no ghosts either! Please don't go there and ask where the ghosts are, but it does have a link with the famous Robert Burns.

However, the other inspiration, which is *Caitloch House* at Moniaive (privately owned and not visitable), really was used as a refuge by Covenanters while they were being persecuted. Both real houses were built or substantially expanded around the same time in the late eighteenth century, and on the sites of older houses dating to the turn of the sixteenth-seventeenth century, so the 'history' of my *Nuns' Kirk Haugh* is not abnormal for the Lowlands of the times I've written about, and they are far from being the only examples. I chose the name because there is a Nunwood right on the outskirts of modern-day Dumfries and close to the Cluden Water, but with no grand house to confuse it with. However, the nearest Benedictine nunnery was the lovely Lincluden Collegieate college, the ruins of which lie just on the outskirts of Dumfries itself.

A *haugh* is a Scottish term for a flat piece of alluvial land beside a river, which certainly fits my fictional location as well as echoing the setting of the real hotel.

The Apostles' Stones, on the other hand, are a real and substantial stone circle near the Cluden Water. It is the largest diameter stone circle on mainland Scotland, with only the magnificent Ring of Brodgar up on Orkney being larger. When built in the Neolithic era it probably had eighteen upright stones, but sadly only eleven now remain, a twelfth survivor into the modern age was destroyed by a farmer in the nineteenth century. The stone circle is part of a much larger stone age complex which extends around the modern village of Holywood, again, almost a suburb of Dumfries nowadays – and the chance to make Holywood the same place as the otherwise unidentified 'Hollowyairds of Hills' where the real Jonet Clark and Johnne Allen lived was too good to pass by.
https://witches.hca.ed.ac.uk/index.cfm/accused/A/EGD/1171)

The current Irongray Manse was built in 1797, and so dates from long after the women in this story were held prisoner in its cellars. It is now a private house and is no longer the manse for the church, with the current owners having no relationship to whomever it was who lived there and tortured the women. Irongray church as it stands now was built in 1872-3, and on the plan of a previous church built in 1803, so again, you can't take what the church looks like now as any indicator of what it would have looked like in the seventeenth-century. But as a name Irongray was just too good not to use, especially when it has such a threatening history. Please don't hold it against the modern parishioners of Irongray that this happened in the past.

As for what a normal house would have been like inside, I have had to rely on a couple of living museums for that – the Highland Folk Museum at Newtonmore, where some of *Outlander* was filmed, but also Auchindrain Township in Argyll. So Elspeth's home is based on that concept of a large single room, with wooden box beds on either side. They wouldn't have had chairs but stools, and the fire would have been in the centre of the room, with its smoke filtering out through the thatch or turf roof – no smoke hole, please note, because archaeological experiments have found that that was the fastest way for sparks to set the thatch/turf alight! Instead, the smoke circulating up around the eaves kept insects out of the roof, and allowed things like a leg of meat to be hung high over the fire and smoked in order to preserve it. By this time, away from the true Highlands with their turf walls, most small croft houses would have been of a solid construction, and probably lime-washed to both help preserve them and to keep pests at bay. Slightly larger houses would have had more than one room, and maybe bedroom space up under the eaves reached by a simple ladder, but it's rare to find normal people's houses of that era which are still lived in (and there are plenty of them about) whose interiors *haven't* been altered, so please bear in mind that if you visit one, it's probably seen a lot of changes since Elspeth and Hugh's time.

With regard to the witches, I have taken the liberty of using the names of the real women who suffered in these trials, because so little is known of them that I doubt anyone could trace their ancestry back to them with any degree of certainty. (If you *are* a descendent, I hope you feel I've treated them sympathetically.) Sadly, women are very poorly represented in any form of legal documents, some even in the witch trials being known as nothing more than 'the wife of X' – which is pretty appalling given that they were on trial for their lives in many cases. When it comes to the Covenanter men, it's rather a different story, and to avoid anyone being horribly offended by my portrayal of their ancient relative, I have introduced new characters amongst the 'martyrs'.

There is a grim fascination in going through the Edinburgh University online database of witches (https://witches.is.ed.ac.uk/), not least because you swiftly realise how often you are looking at very localised clusters of what are nothing less than very worldly persecutions. As in the very real case of Agnes Clark, you find yourself looking at widows who were at the mercy of a male relative, who had their eye on getting what property the widow had inherited. To us in modern times, a croft with a tiny flock of sheep and a horse (which was probably more like what we would call a rugged pony than any thoroughbred) might not sound like much, but in the seventeenth century, a man who could get his hands on a second croft was a substantial step above his neighbours. Not necessarily of the standing of an actual farmer who could employ workers, but certainly above those who lived in simple cotts, and whose existence was precarious to say the least.

And this was where being used to working with medieval records and their limited survival came in very handy. Having been trained to look at what was *not* there as well as what was, you start to see patterns, such as with the real Corsan family. Now much of rural lowland Scotland was considerably more inhabited in terms of scattered family dwellings than nowadays, but when you take into account the fact that during the seventeenth century the entire Scottish population only managed to tip over one million by around 1700, and a hefty percentage of those would have been in Edinburgh (fifty thousand) and Glasgow (twelve thousand), there wouldn't have been *that* many families of that name in Dumfriesshire.

With a general round-up of local women – as happened in the Fife village of Crail in the records – you get twenty different surnames for twenty different women. Whereas when you look at the Dumfries investigations and trials, it's very noticeable that you get two surnames cropping up within a comparatively small number of cases. So it's not stretching credibility to think that someone had it in for these women and their families.

As far as the records go, only two women were ever held at Irongray Manse, and these were indeed Marione Corsan in 1650 and Jonet Clark in 1658, who

I've made my fictional Elspeth's mother. However, it seems unlikely that a Presbyter willing to incarcerate witches would only do it twice in virtually a decade if he had such a strong place to hold them. There is a recorded case where two Covenanter men were taken at the village of Crocketford in 1685, and then marched the eight miles to Irongray to be executed, when in fact it would have been easier, if not much closer, to take them to Dumfries, with its tolbooth which was the local prison.

So someone at Irongray was known to have shady morals! And it is what has made me create a character like Veitch, who is really more concerned with what he can get in this world than what he might be saving up for the hereafter, and willing to go with both sides if it suited him. Therefore I've made my fictitious Presbyter Veitch something of a witch-hater, which was sadly not uncommon amongst Covenanting clergy at the time. The real Presbyter of Irongray was a famous man called John Welsh, descended from John Knox who helped bring Protestantism to Scotland. But Welsh is someone I felt I couldn't twist to the plot, and so I used the family name of another real minister, who suffered for his Covenanting beliefs some decades later in Dumfries itself.

What is true is that there was never a massed witch burning in Dumfries after the death of those nine women on the one day – eight burned, but Bigis Cairns probably didn't die on the same day, so I've had Jonet die then as well for the purpose of making hers the arcanely potent ninth death. The date and circumstances of those deaths are directly taken from the records. Others in the century and a half of witch trials were accused singly, but they are rare cases. So it wasn't too much of a stretch to think that the ordinary people were indeed horrified at what happened at the Tolbooth on the day that these women died. Witnessing such a thing might well have turned a lot of stomachs and made previous zealots think twice.

Similarly, a notorious event during the Killing Times was when two women, Margaret McLachlan and Margaret Wilson, were reputedly tied to posts in the estuary near Wigtown, and drowned by the incoming tide for being Covenanters. As far as historical documentation goes, this is questionable, and it's possible that the writ from Edinburgh demanding their release, obtained by Margaret and Agnes Wilson's father, was indeed obeyed and the final punishment never carried out. Even in the nineteenth century the case was controversial, and many thought that the drowning did not take place while others believed it had – hence the still-standing memorials in Wigtown erected by them.

Drowning was a death which was only handed out to women, whereas Covenanter men caught in Dumfries & Galloway were hanged or shot by the troops who caught them. To me it sounds very much as though, in this case, they were falling back on the punishments they had used for witches for nearly a century already, albeit in not that many actual cases – and it's worth noting that, as I've had Hugh say in the book, there were women hanged in Edinburgh at fully legal Covenanter trials there, making these drownings very much a local, radical, and divisive solution. However, given that there were contemporaries who later swore on record that they'd seen it happen, it's a personal choice whether you believe it happened or not. Young Agnes Wilson's reprieve is certainly recorded, and there is reference to another woman being 'scourged' through the town with the two Margarets, though she isn't one of those who died in the Solway.

This made her ripe for being made into my fictional Isobel and also Grissell, and Grissell into a fictional third woman to die by drowning – sometimes as an author you can't pass up the chance to tell a good story, even if you do stretch the real incidents a little! There is something very dark about ordering women to be whipped with scourges, and then plunged into saltwater, which their persecutors had to have known would take the pain to a whole other level. What the case of these Wigtown martyrs does show is how desperately the local magistrates wanted to be rid of the Covenanters, because both women were locally accused of being at the battle at Bothwell Bridge, which was patently not true even then. But such an accusation would have carried considerable weight at the time, and gave the magistrates a legal reason to act decisively – indeed possibly the *only* reason to carry out a corporal punishment without reference to a higher court!

Grierson of Lagg was indeed connected via his wife to the Douglas earls of Queensberry, making him in seventeenth-century terms pretty untouchable. He actually was rewarded by James II upon his accession for his hard-line stance, and that would have been in not only in the same year that the two Margarets died, but within the month, so again, you can see why local feelings undoubtedly ran pretty high. (And I really can't understand why other historians haven't made the connection between when Lagg was rewarded and him taking the law into his own hands, because I've not come across that highly significant connection being made elsewhere!) An unwanted Catholic king almost immediately rewarding a local laird for what the Presbyterian locals would have viewed as little short of murdering local people, because the two women were by no means the only ones to die in 1685-6, makes it little wonder that Lagg's name is still mud in the two counties.

When Lagg finally died in 1733 in the family house in Dumfries, having by then been in and out of trouble with the Hanoverian kings for supporting the Jacobite rebellions, he was buried in the old Dunscore burial ground, which is not at Dunscore itself, but near where I have set my fictional hotel, and also the real one I used as inspiration. Local legend really does have it that the horses pulling his hearse died of exhaustion on the way – which sounds a bit odd given that, having driven that road myself many times, I can vouch for the fact that none of the hills on the road from Dumfries are *that* steep! A black raven is also supposed to have settled on his coffin, and only flown away when it had been lowered into the grave. With ravens famously having associations with witchcraft, this was too good an incident to leave out!

I hope that you are now as invested in finding out more of these women's fates as I am, and will forgive me for not being able to resolve everything within the confines of one book. In *Far from Over*, we will rejoin Anna, Rita and Gary as our modern-day sleuths, and find out more of what happened in south-west Scotland in the seventeenth century.

Printed in Dunstable, United Kingdom

66251190R00343